Unicorn Crossing

Another Phoebe and Her Unicorn Adventure

Complete Your Phoebe and Her Unicorn Collection

Phoebe and Her Unicorn
Dana Simpson

Unicorn on a Roll
Another Phoebe and Her Unicorn Adventure
Dana Simpson

Unicorn vs. Goblins
Another Phoebe and Her Unicorn Adventure
Dana Simpson

Razzle Dazzle Unicorn
Another Phoebe and Her Unicorn Adventure
Dana Simpson

Phoebe and Her Unicorn in
The Magic Storm
Dana Simpson

Unicorn of Many Hats
Another Phoebe and Her Unicorn Adventure
Dana Simpson

Phoebe and Her Unicorn in
Unicorn Theater
Dana Simpson

Unicorn Bowling
Another Phoebe and Her Unicorn Adventure
Dana Simpson

The Unicorn Whisperer
Another Phoebe and Her Unicorn Adventure
Dana Simpson

Camping with Unicorns
Another Phoebe and Her Unicorn Adventure
Dana Simpson

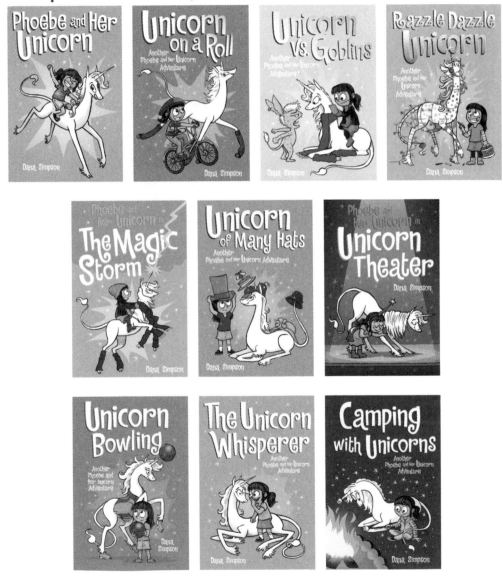

Unicorn Crossing

Another Phoebe and Her Unicorn Adventure

Dana Simpson

Andrews McMeel
PUBLISHING®

Andrews McMeel Publishing
a division of Andrews McMeel Universal
1130 Walnut Street, Kansas City, Missouri 64106

www.andrewsmcmeel.com

20 21 22 23 24 RR2 11 10 9 8 7 6

ISBN: 978-1-4494-8357-9

Library of Congress Control Number: 2016950036

Made by:
LSC Communications US, LLC
Address and location of manufacturer:
1009 Sloan Street
Crawfordsville, IN 47933
6th Printing—5/22/20

ATTENTION: SCHOOLS AND BUSINESSES

Andrews McMeel books are available at quantity discounts with bulk purchase for educational, business, or sales promotional use. For information, please e-mail the Andrews McMeel Publishing Special Sales Department: specialsales@amuniversal.com.

Hey, kids!

Check out the glossary starting on page 173
if you come across words you don't know.

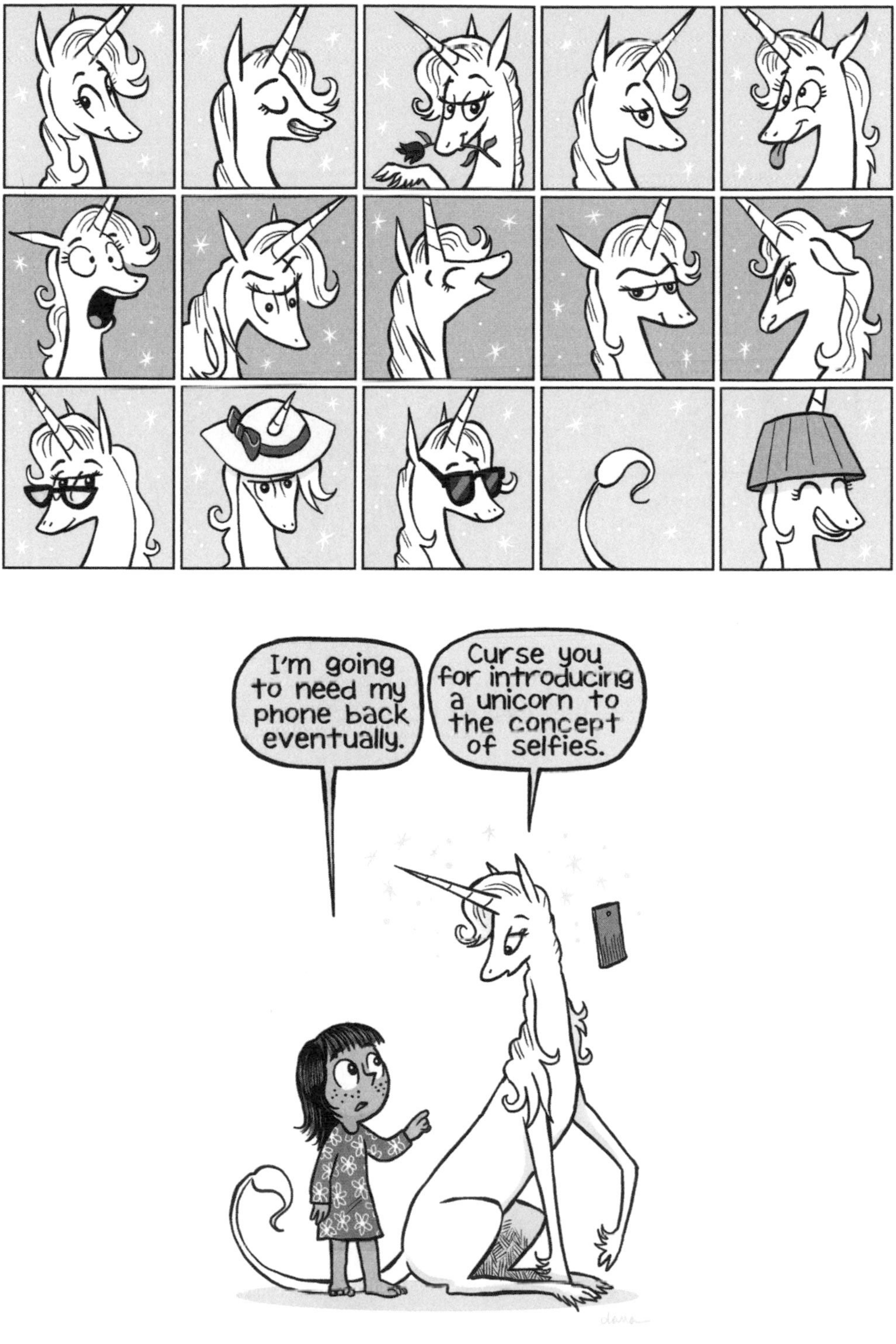
I'm going to need my phone back eventually.
Curse you for introducing a unicorn to the concept of selfies.

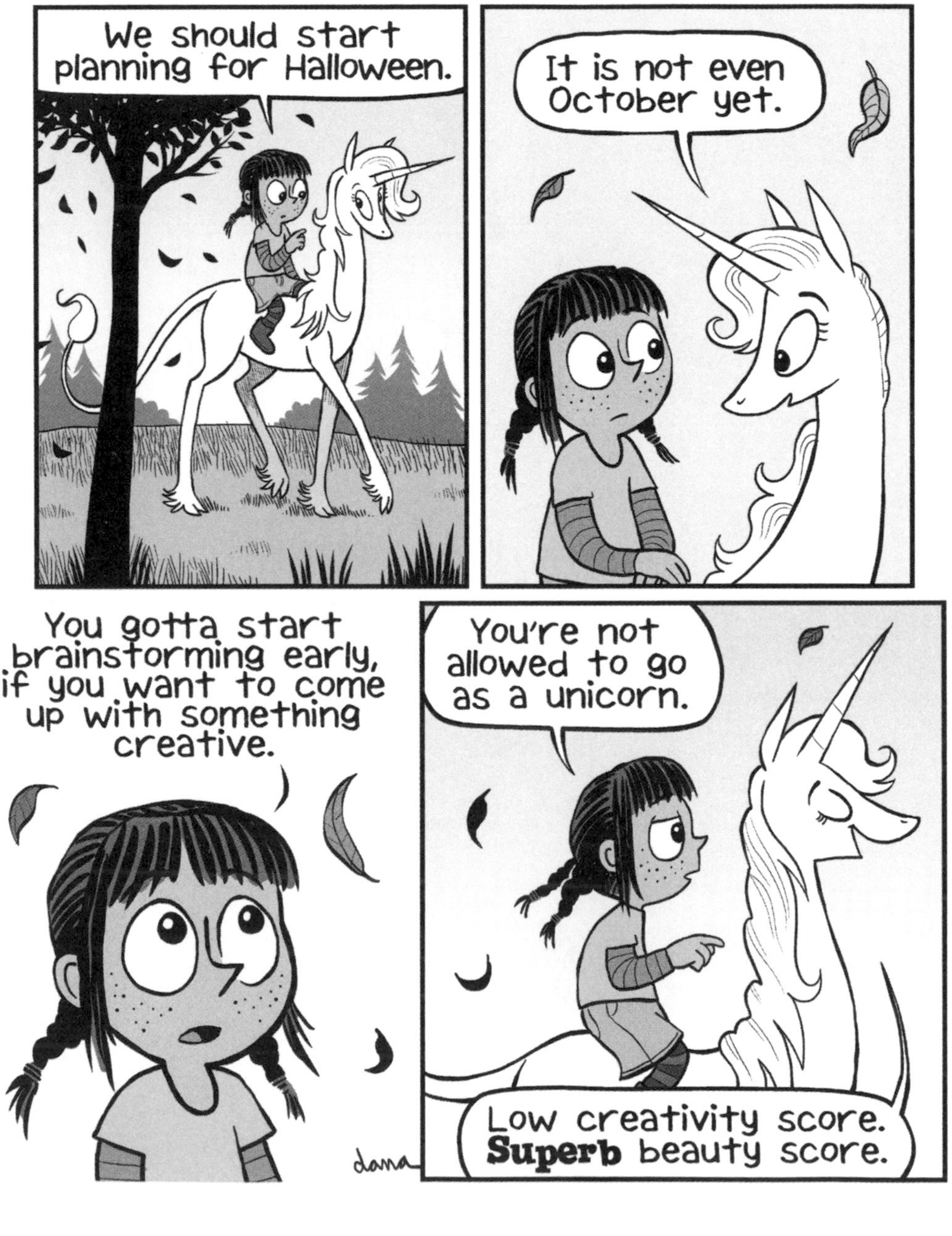
We should start planning for Halloween.
It is not even October yet.
You gotta start brainstorming early, if you want to come up with something creative.
You're not allowed to go as a unicorn.
Low creativity score. **Superb** beauty score.
dana

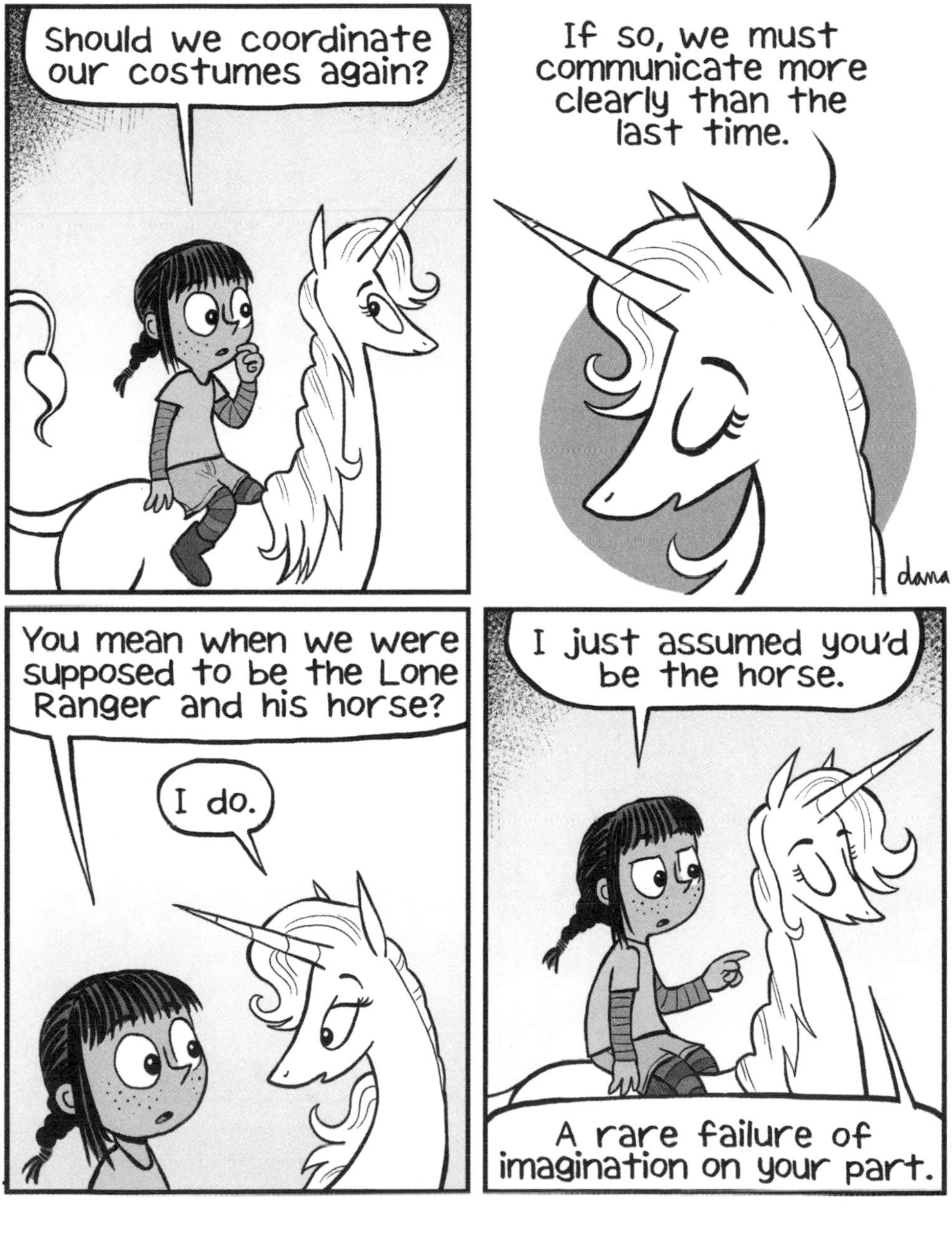
Should we coordinate our costumes again?
If so, we must communicate more clearly than the last time.
dana
You mean when we were supposed to be the Lone Ranger and his horse?
I do.
I just assumed you'd be the horse.
A rare failure of imagination on your part.

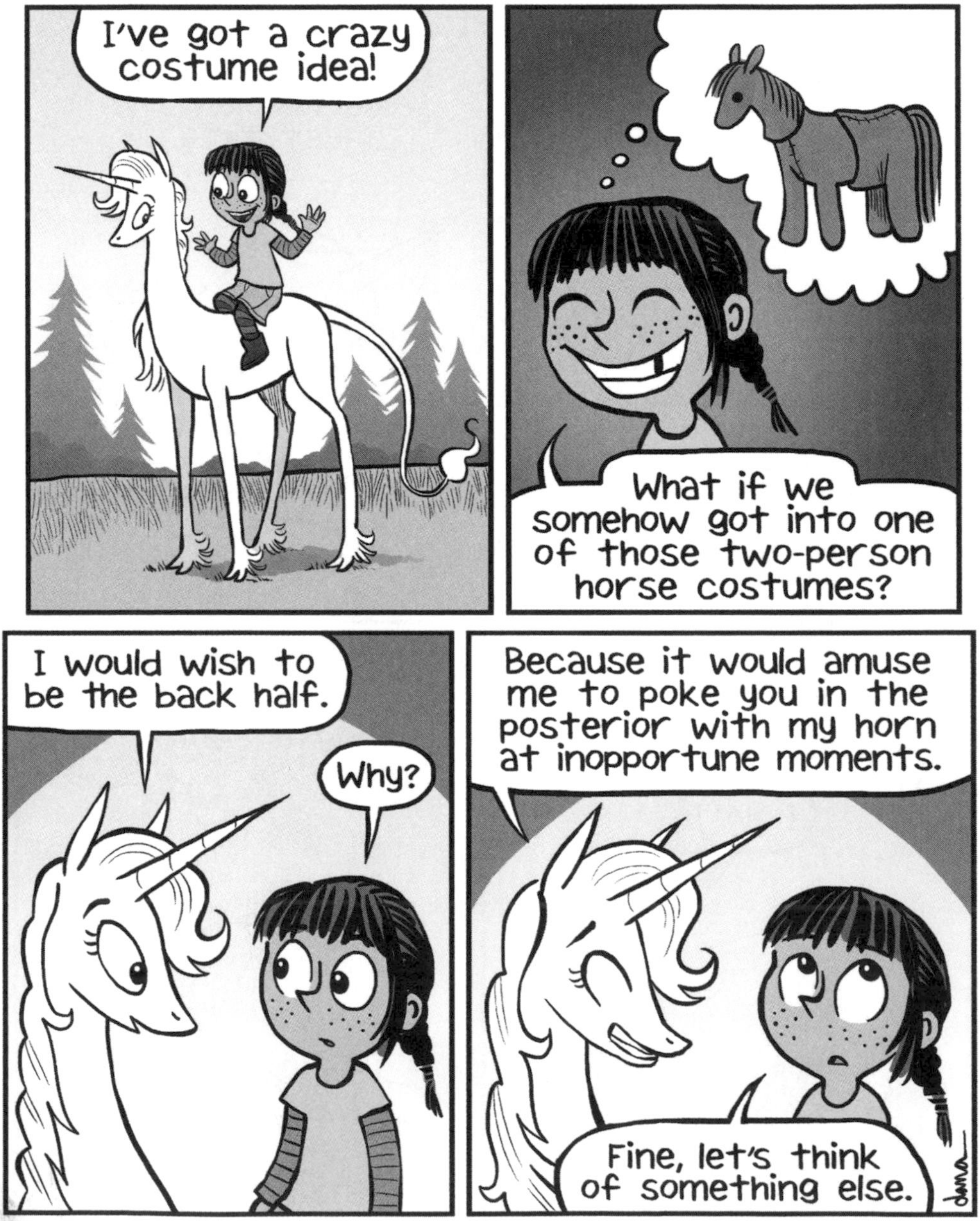
I've got a crazy costume idea!
What if we somehow got into one of those two-person horse costumes?
I would wish to be the back half.
Why?
Because it would amuse me to poke you in the posterior with my horn at inopportune moments.
Fine, let's think of something else.
dana

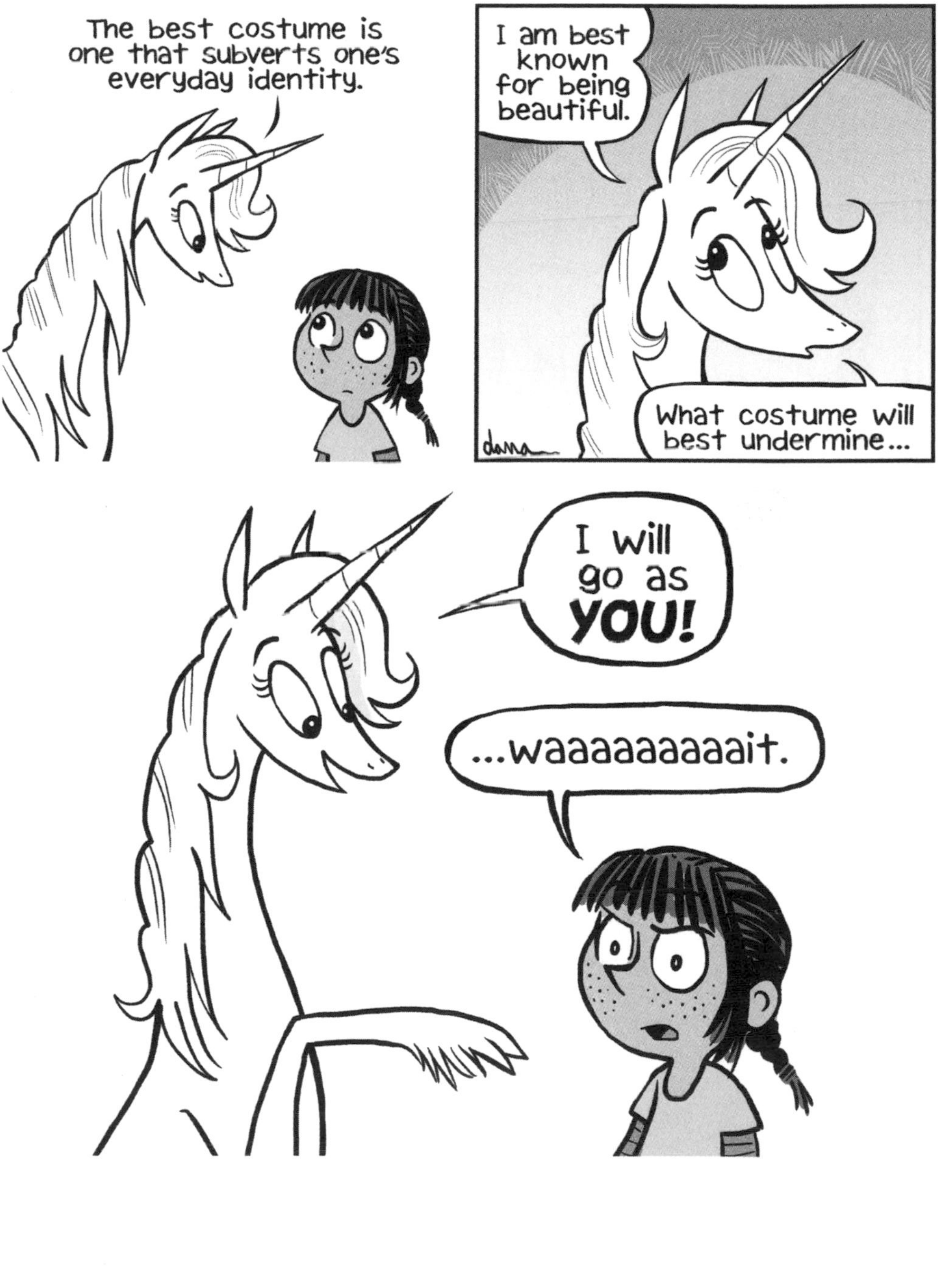
The best costume is one that subverts one's everyday identity.
I am best known for being beautiful.
What costume will best undermine...
dana
I will go as YOU!
...waaaaaaaaait.

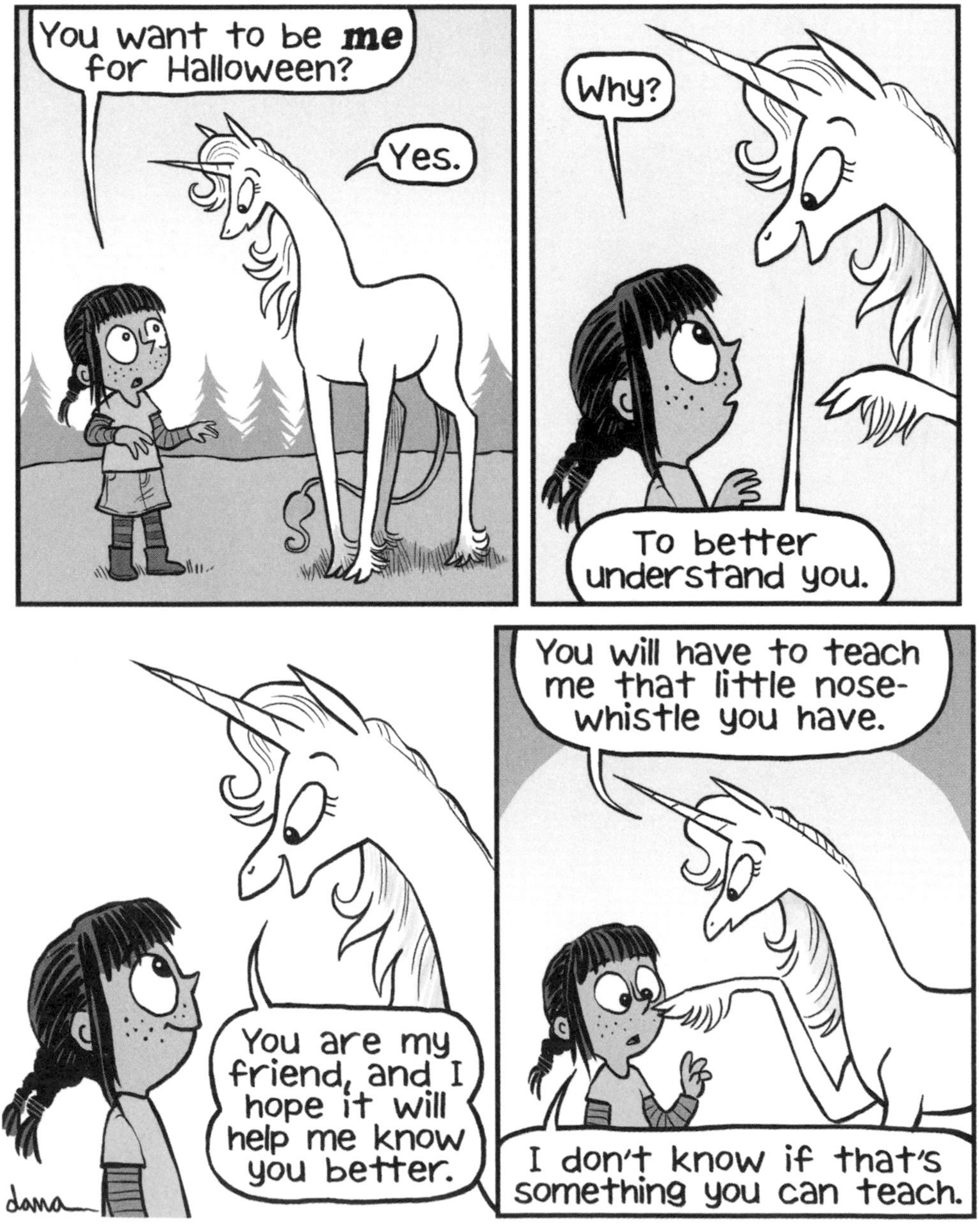
You want to be **me** for Halloween?
Yes.
Why?
To better understand you.
You are my friend, and I hope it will help me know you better.
You will have to teach me that little nose-whistle you have.
I don't know if that's something you can teach.
dana

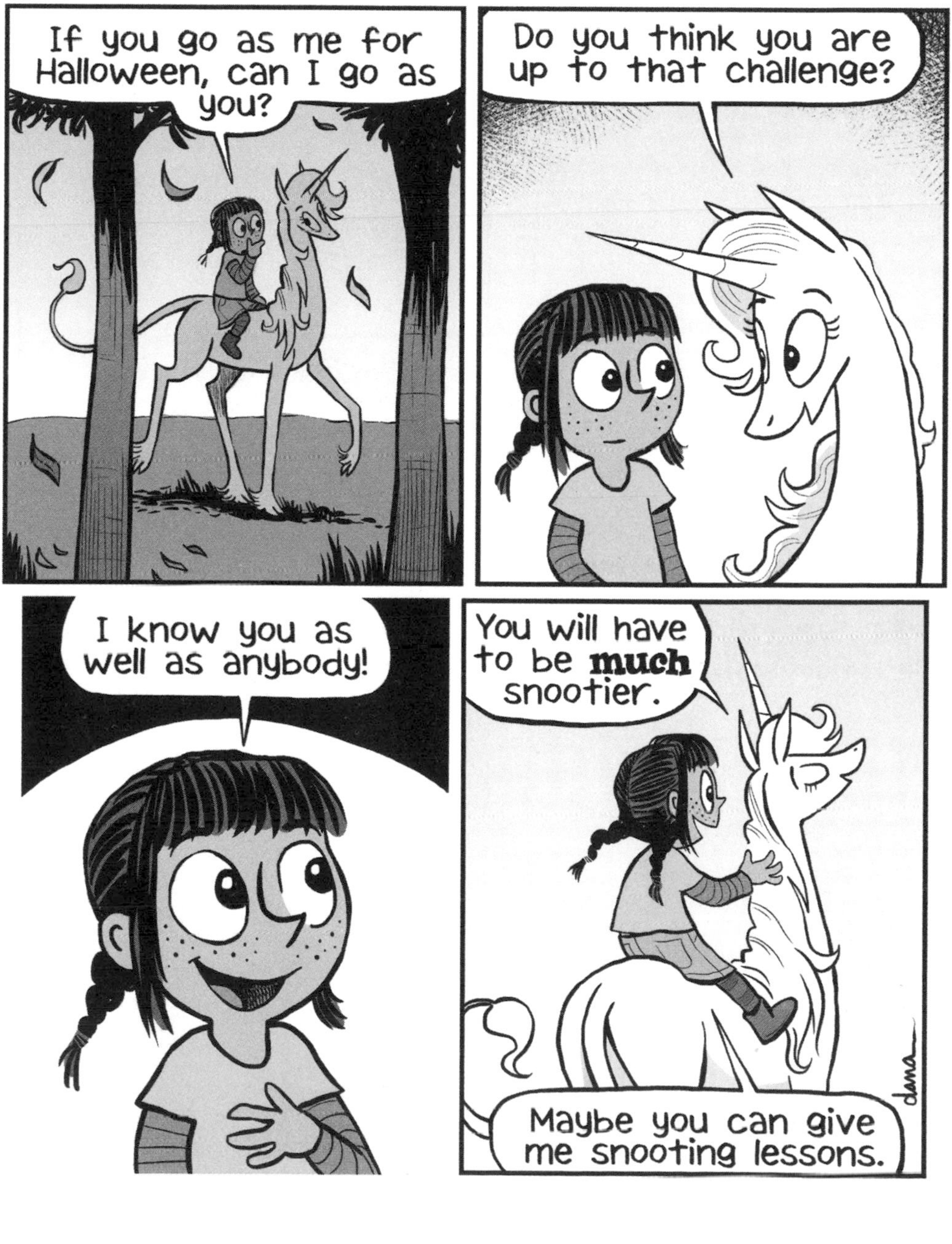
If you go as me for Halloween, can I go as you?
Do you think you are up to that challenge?
I know you as well as anybody!
You will have to be **much** snootier.
Maybe you can give me snooting lessons.
dana

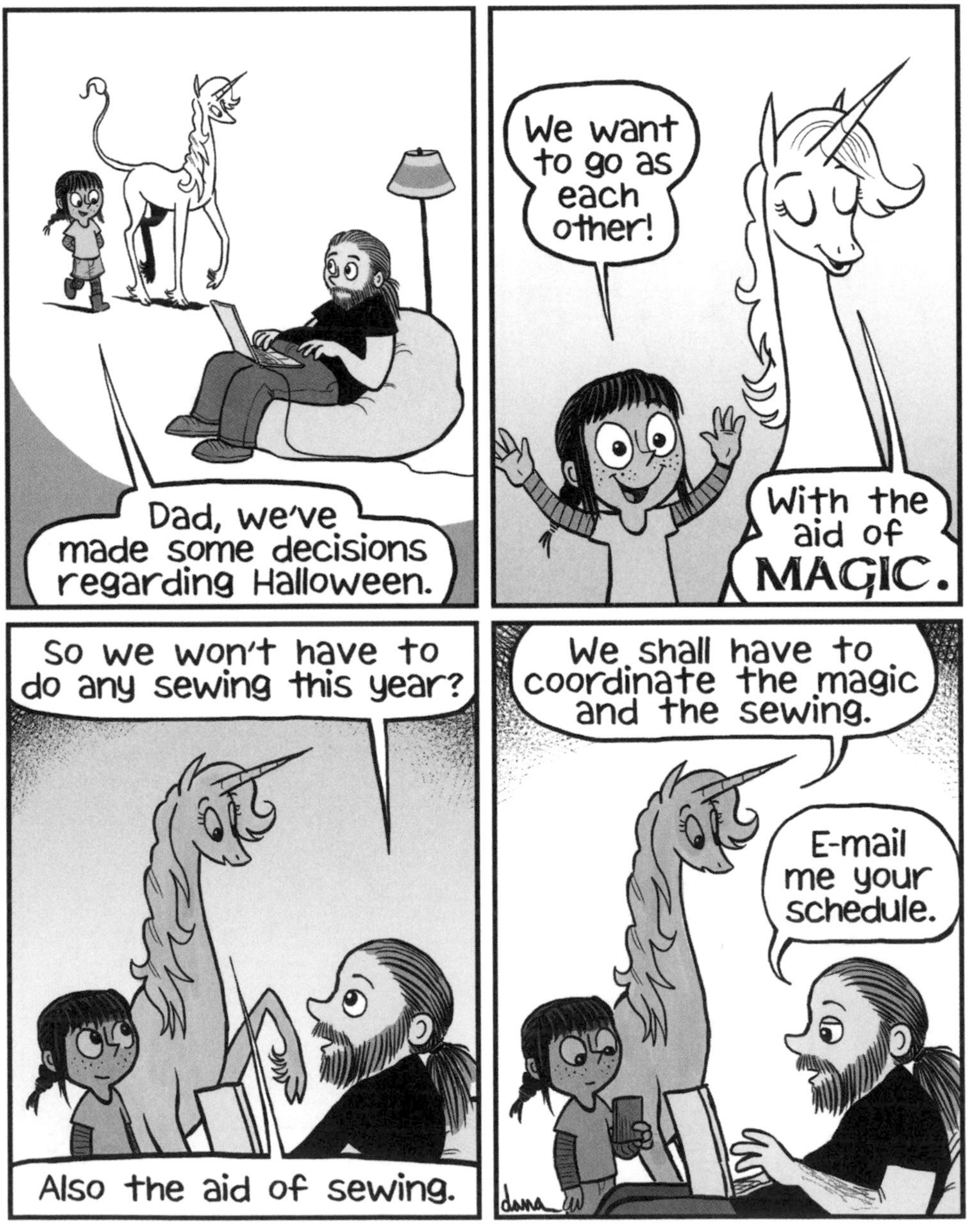
Dad, we've made some decisions regarding Halloween.
We want to go as each other!
With the aid of MAGIC.
So we won't have to do any sewing this year?
Also the aid of sewing.
We shall have to coordinate the magic and the sewing.
E-mail me your schedule.
dana

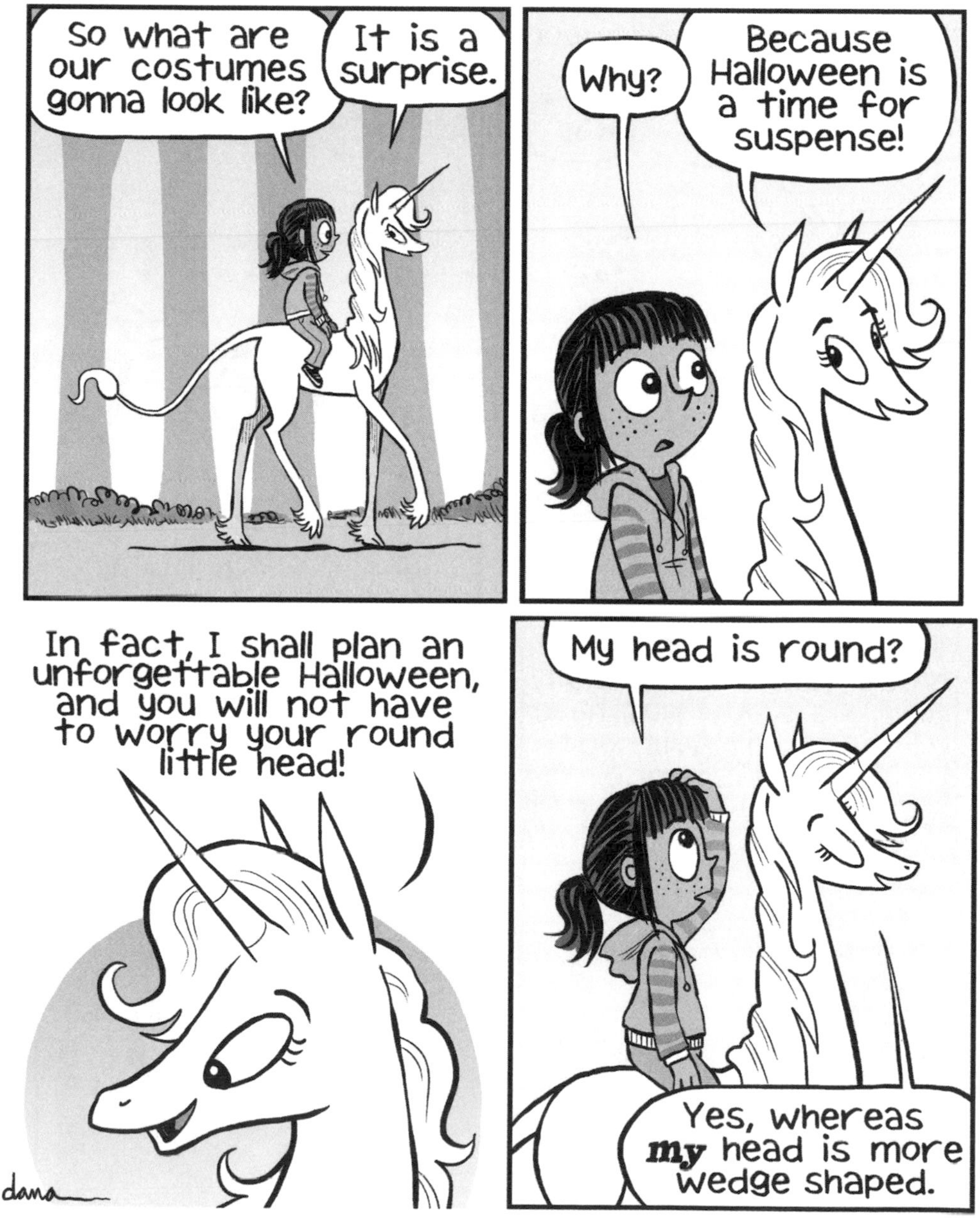
So what are our costumes gonna look like?
It is a surprise.
Why?
Because Halloween is a time for suspense!
In fact, I shall plan an unforgettable Halloween, and you will not have to worry your round little head!
dana
My head is round?
Yes, whereas **my** head is more wedge shaped.

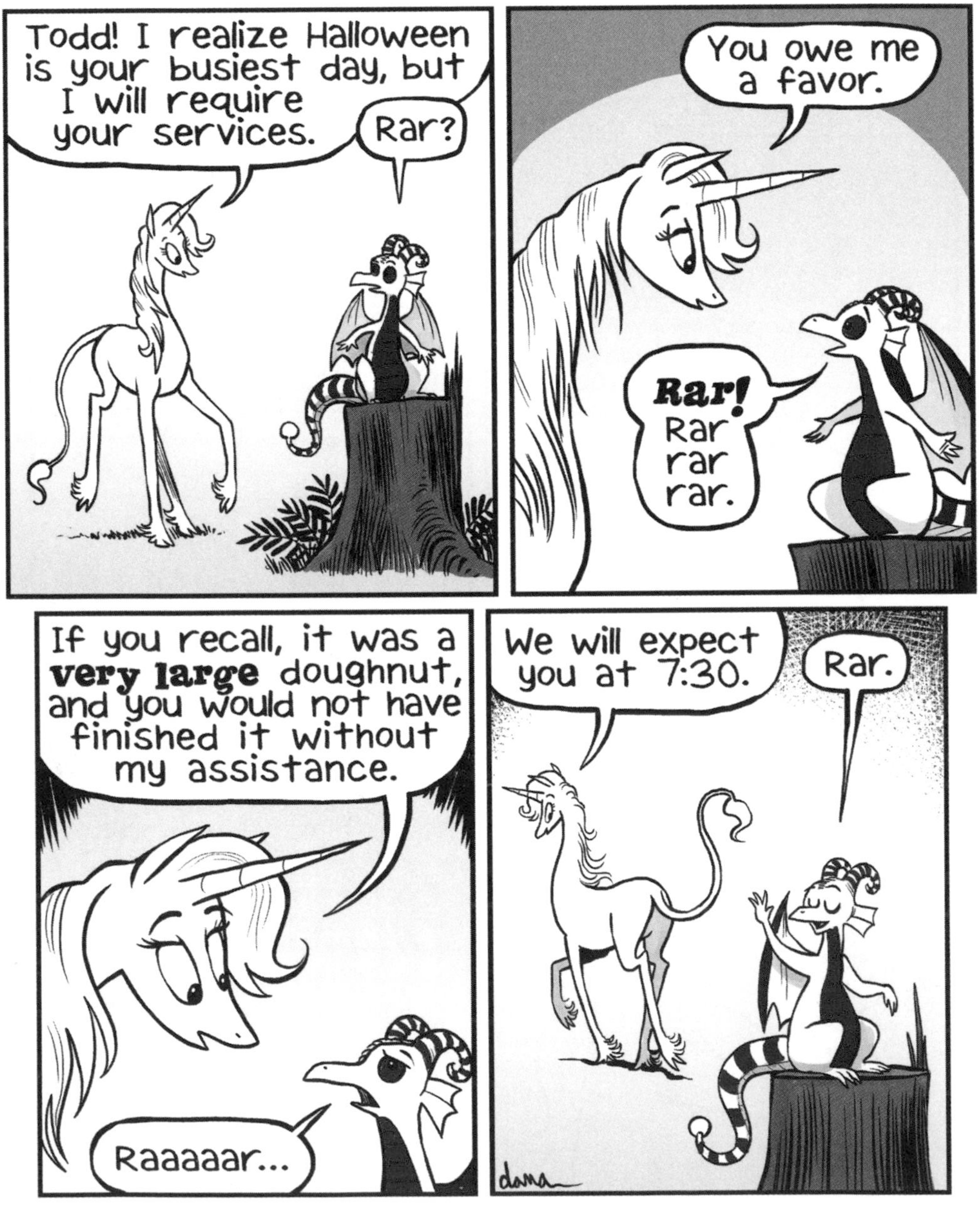
Todd! I realize Halloween is your busiest day, but I will require your services.
Rar?
You owe me a favor.
Rar! Rar rar rar.
If you recall, it was a **very large** doughnut, and you would not have finished it without my assistance.
Raaaaar...
We will expect you at 7:30.
Rar.
dana

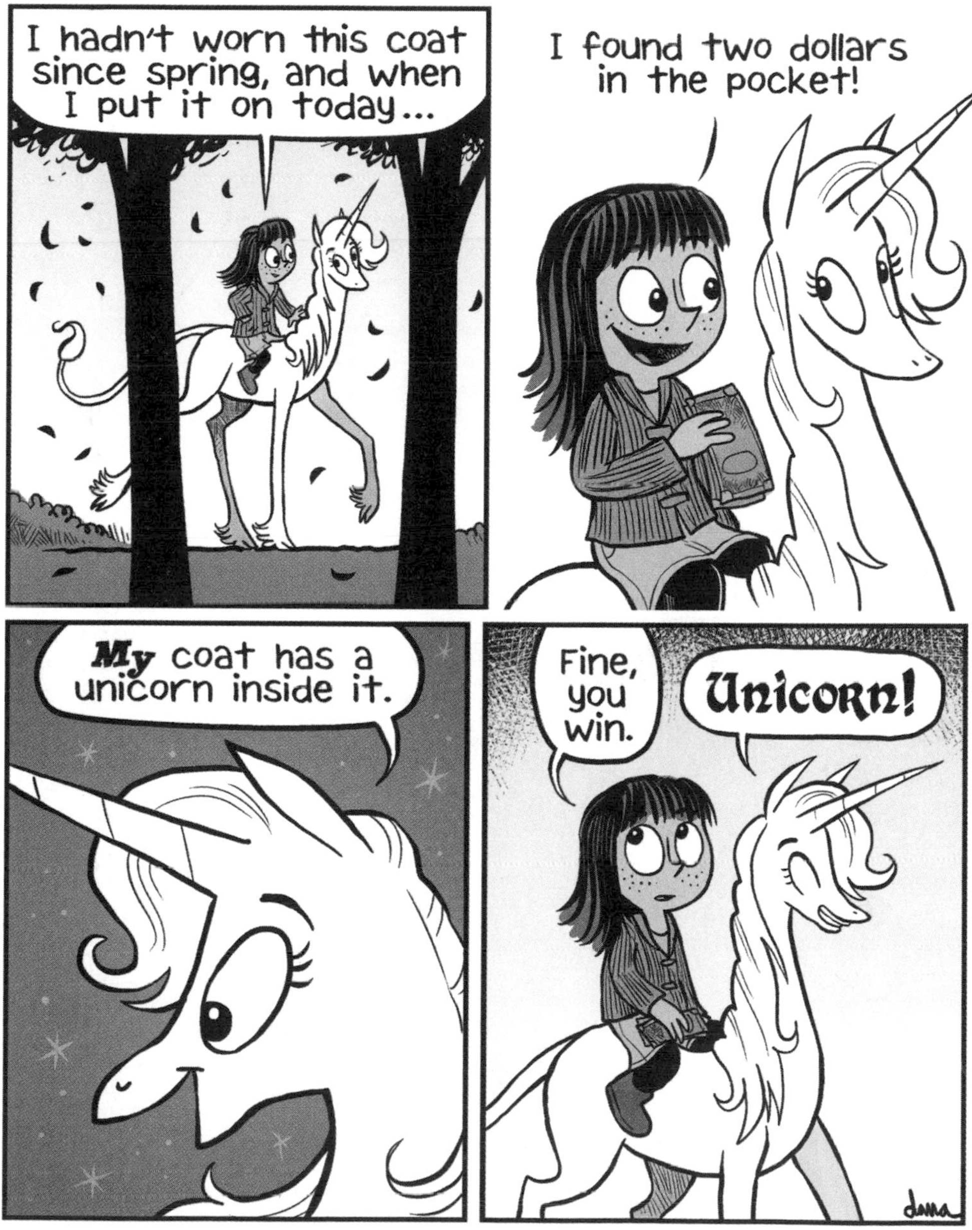
I hadn't worn this coat since spring, and when I put it on today...
I found two dollars in the pocket!
My coat has a unicorn inside it.
Fine, you win.
Unicorn!
dana

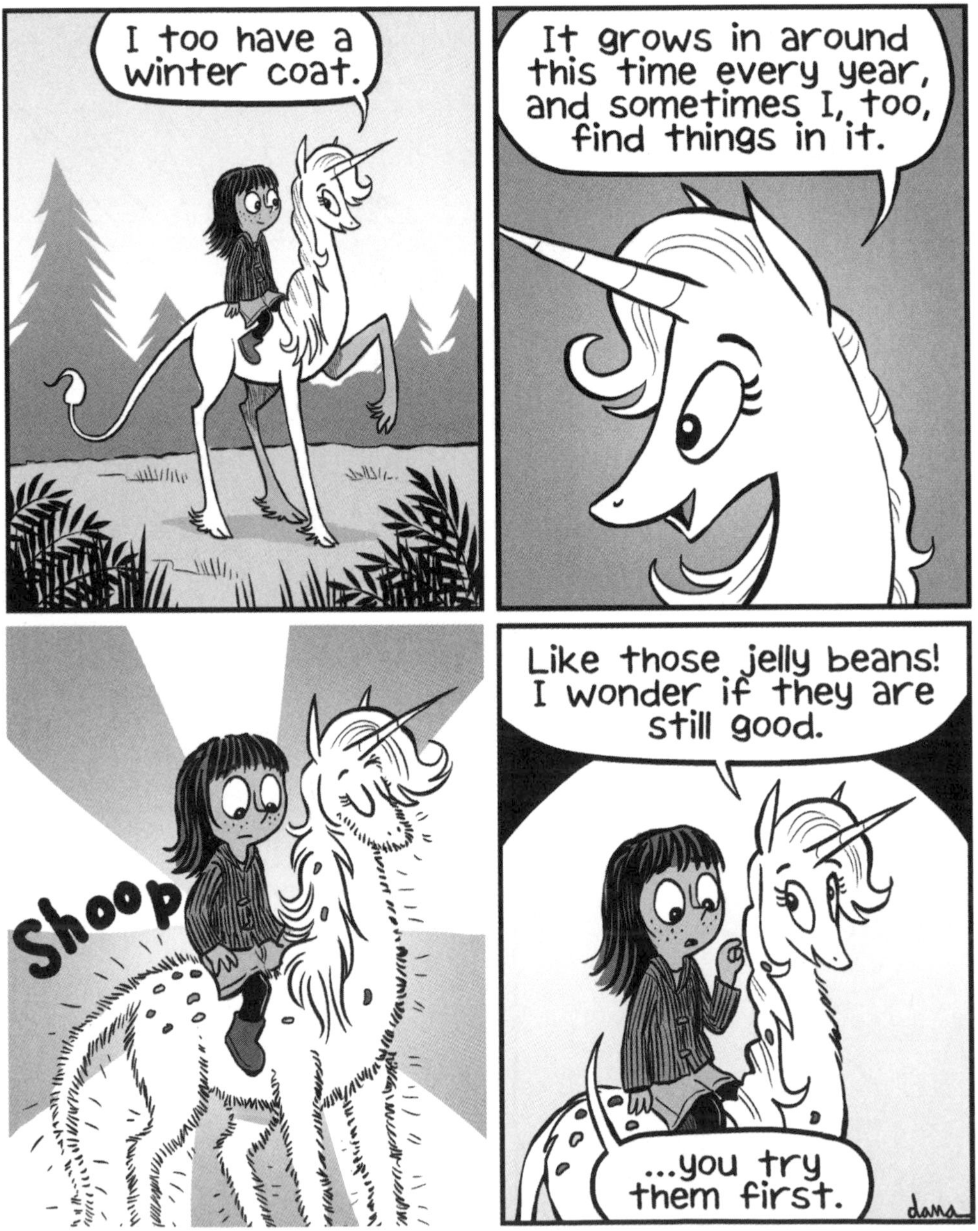
I too have a winter coat.
It grows in around this time every year, and sometimes I, too, find things in it.
Shoop
Like those jelly beans! I wonder if they are still good.
...you try them first.
dana

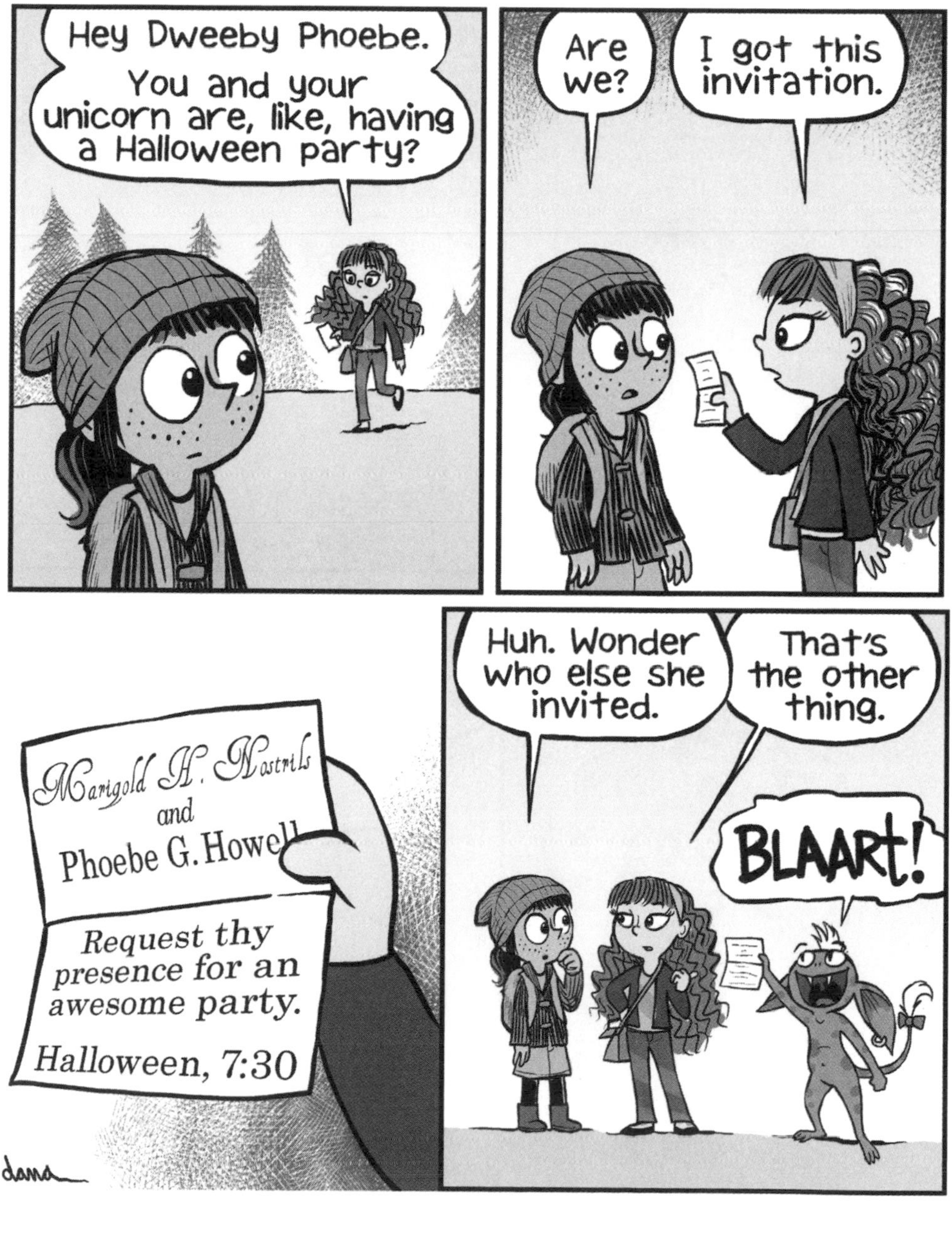
Hey Dweeby Phoebe.
You and your unicorn are, like, having a Halloween party?
Are we?
I got this invitation.
Marigold H. Nostrils
and
Phoebe G. Howell
Request thy presence for an awesome party.
Halloween, 7:30
Huh. Wonder who else she invited.
That's the other thing.
BLAART!
dana

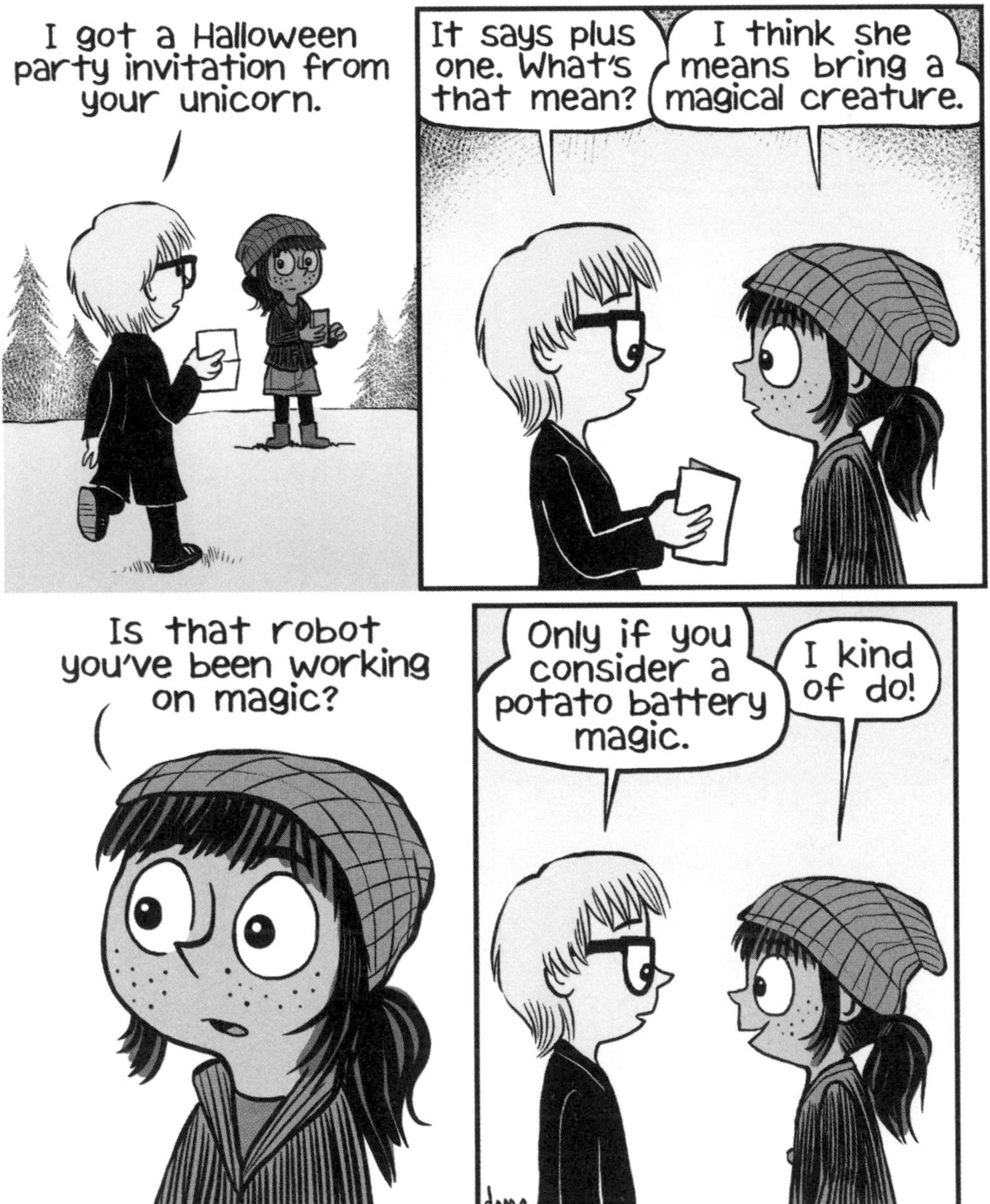
I got a Halloween party invitation from your unicorn.
It says plus one. What's that mean?
I think she means bring a magical creature.
Is that robot you've been working on magic?
Only if you consider a potato battery magic.
I kind of do!
dana

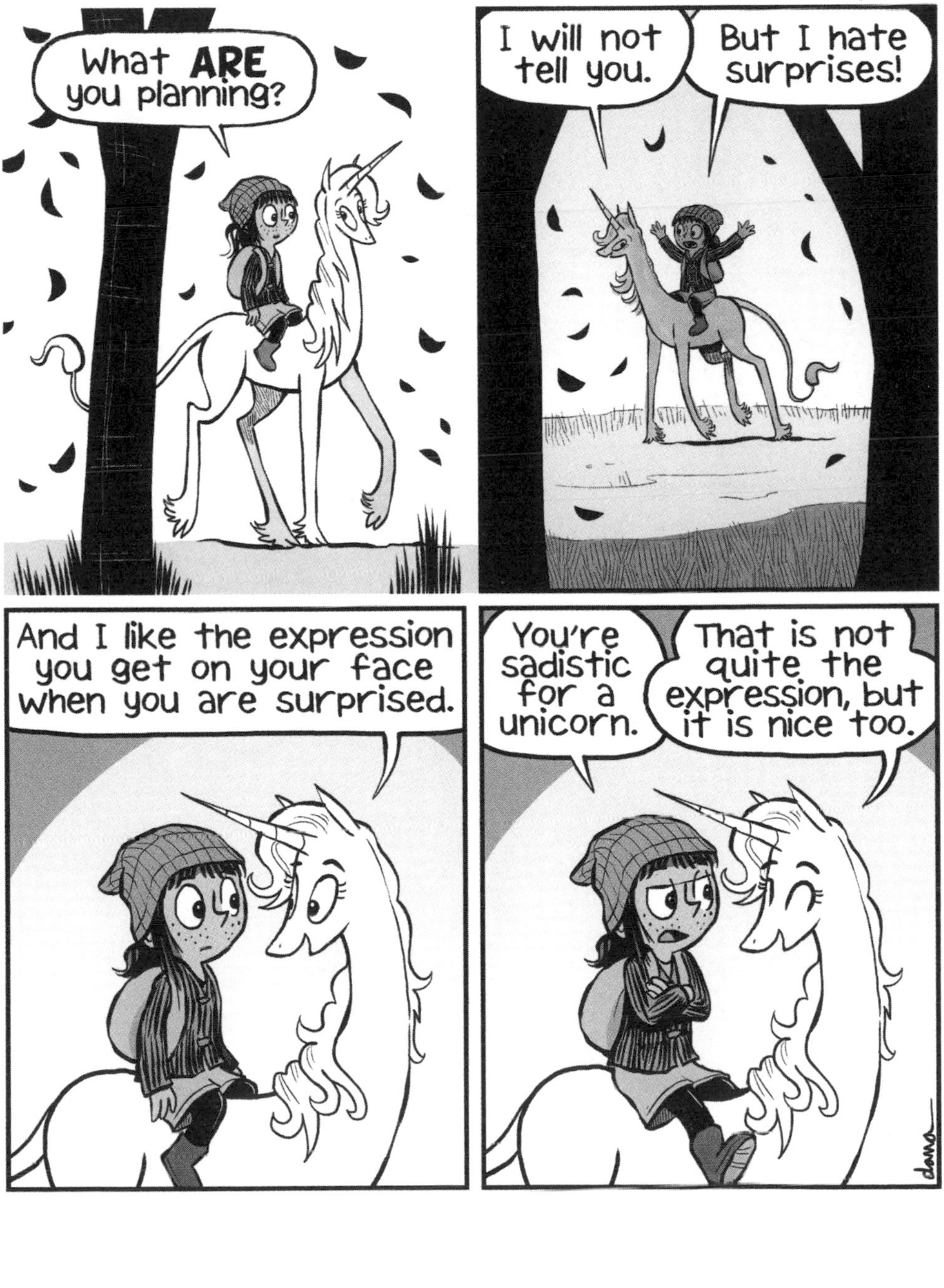
What ARE you planning?
I will not tell you.
But I hate surprises!
And I like the expression you get on your face when you are surprised.
You're sadistic for a unicorn.
That is not quite the expression, but it is nice too.
dana

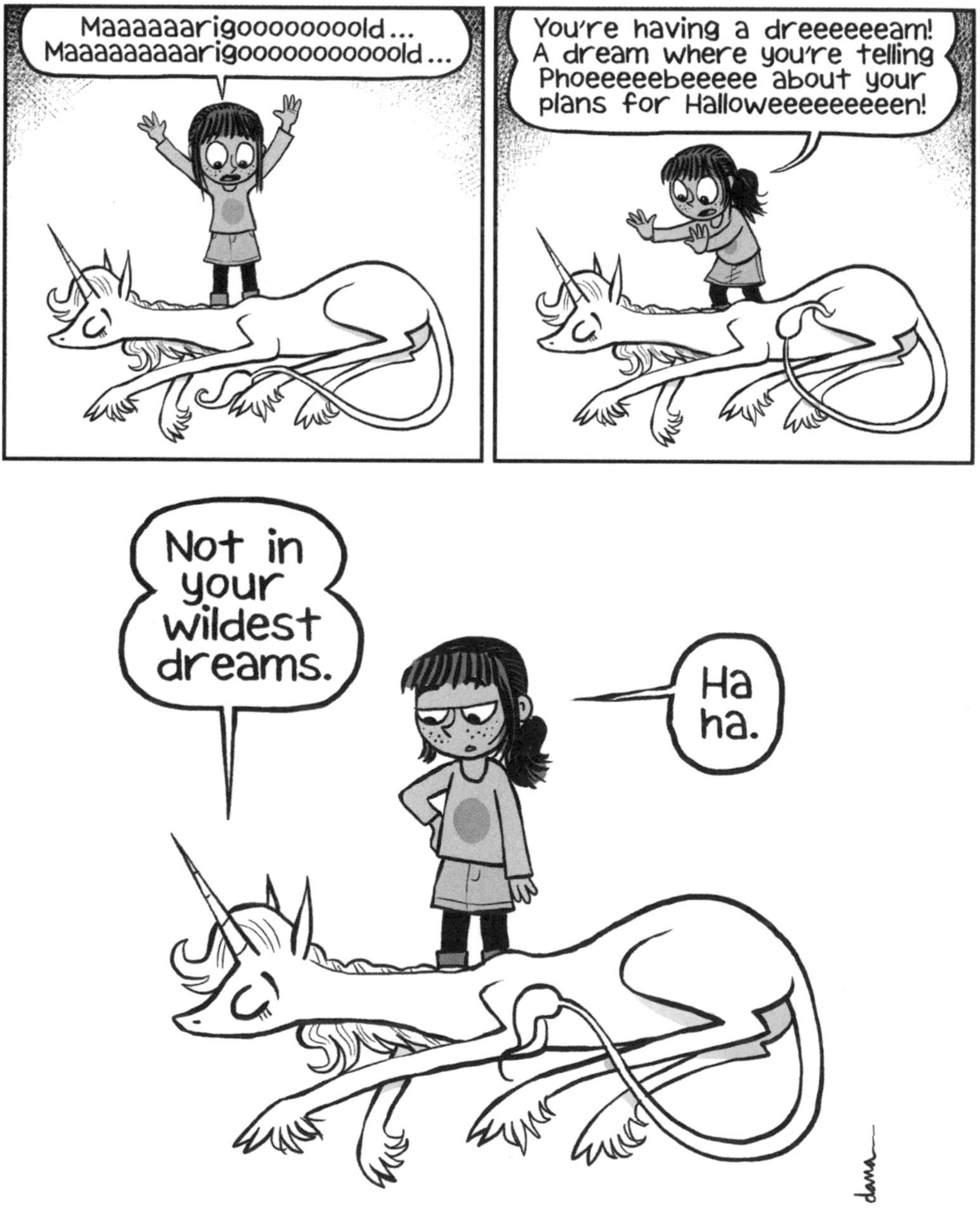
Maaaaaarigoooooooold...
Maaaaaaaaarigooooooooooold...
You're having a dreeeeeeam! A dream where you're telling Phoeeeeebeeeee about your plans for Halloweeeeeeeeen!
Not in your wildest dreams.
Ha ha.

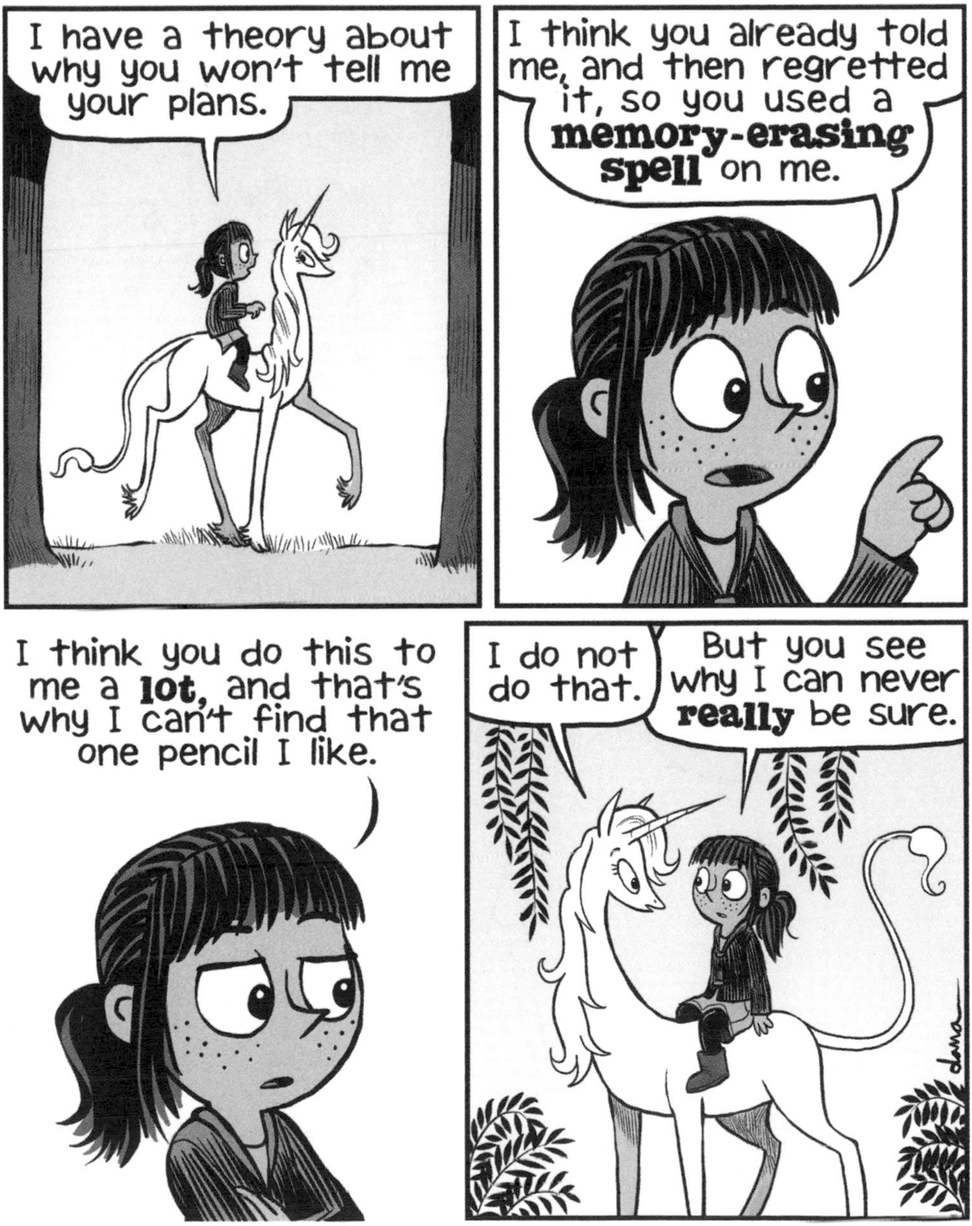
I have a theory about why you won't tell me your plans.
I think you already told me, and then regretted it, so you used a **memory-erasing spell** on me.
I think you do this to me a **lot,** and that's why I can't find that one pencil I like.
I do not do that.
But you see why I can never **really** be sure.
dana

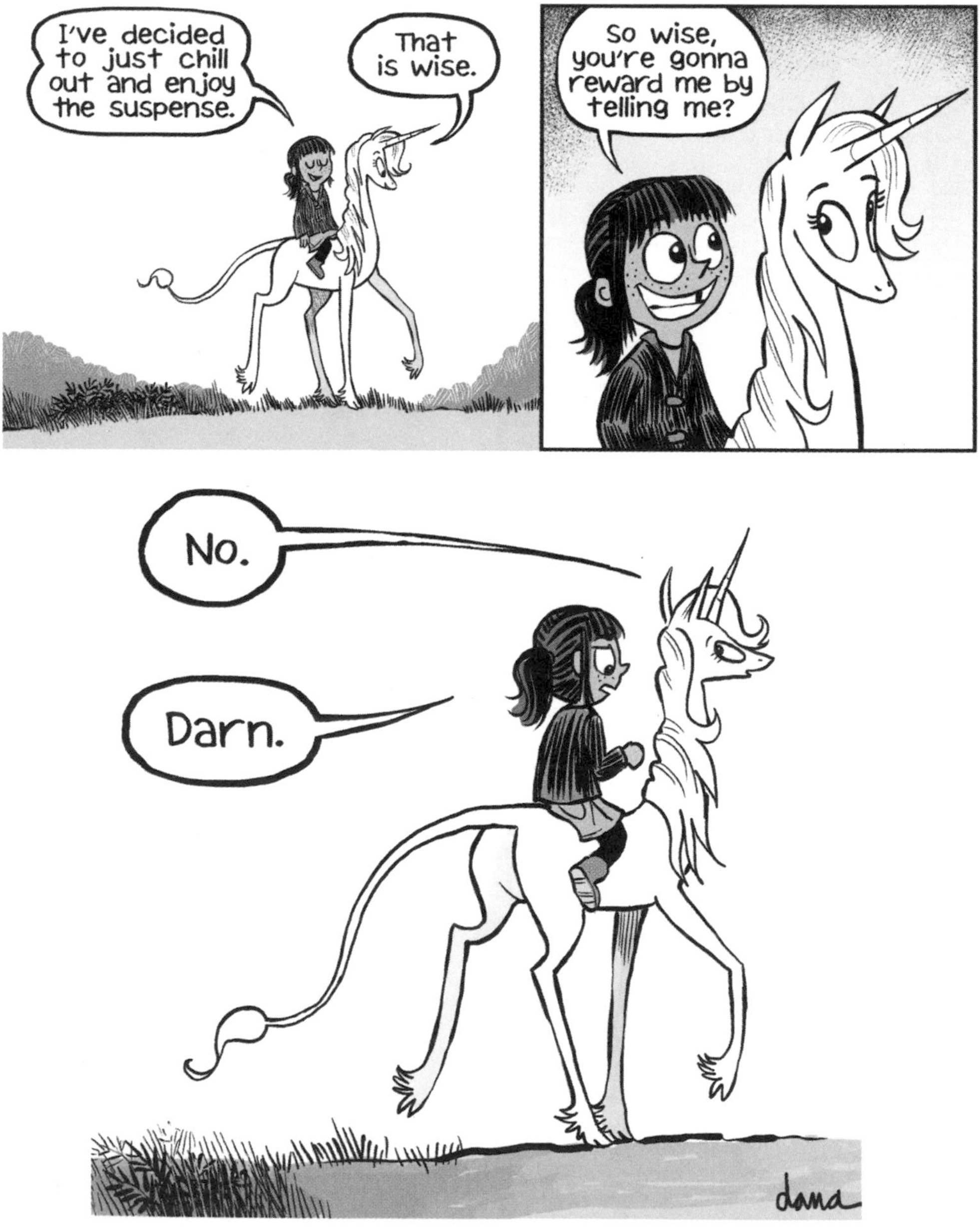
I've decided to just chill out and enjoy the suspense.
That is wise.
So wise, you're gonna reward me by telling me?
No.
Darn.
dana

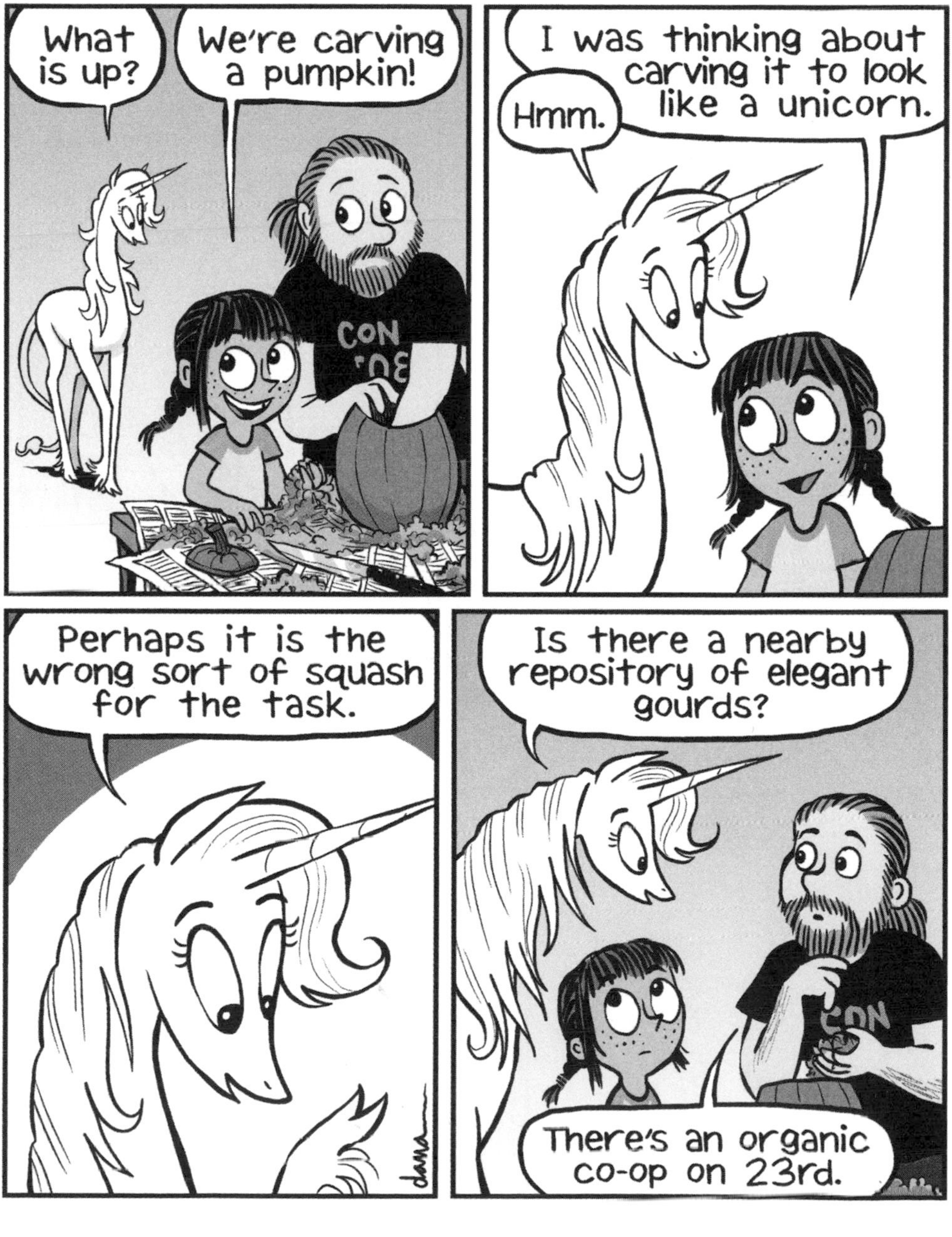
What is up?
We're carving a pumpkin!
CON
I was thinking about carving it to look like a unicorn.
Hmm.
Perhaps it is the wrong sort of squash for the task.
Is there a nearby repository of elegant gourds?
There's an organic co-op on 23rd.
CON
dana

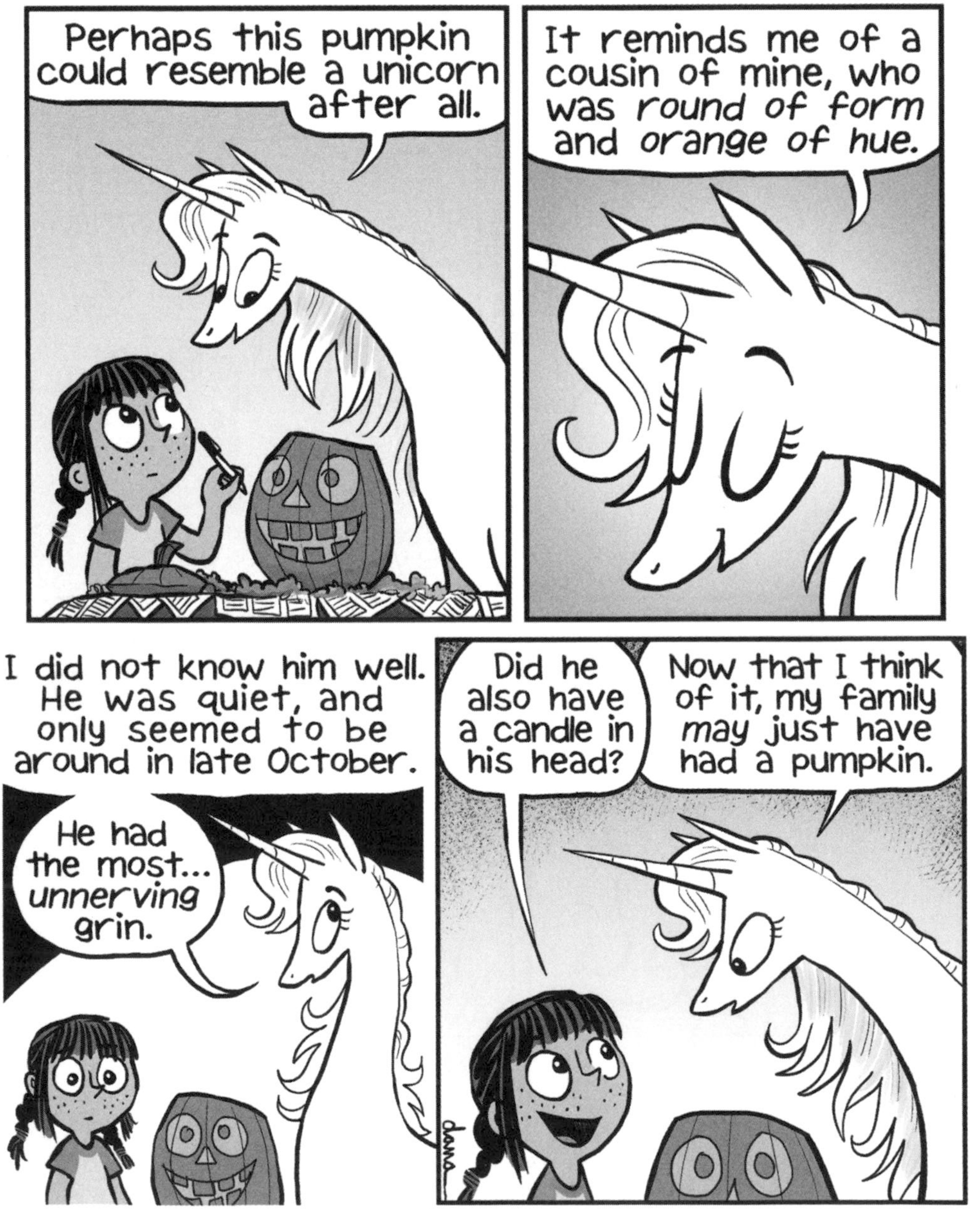
Perhaps this pumpkin could resemble a unicorn after all.
It reminds me of a cousin of mine, who was *round of form* and *orange of hue.*
I did not know him well. He was quiet, and only seemed to be around in late October.
He had the most... *unnerving* grin.
Did he also have a candle in his head?
Now that I think of it, my family *may* just have had a pumpkin.
dana

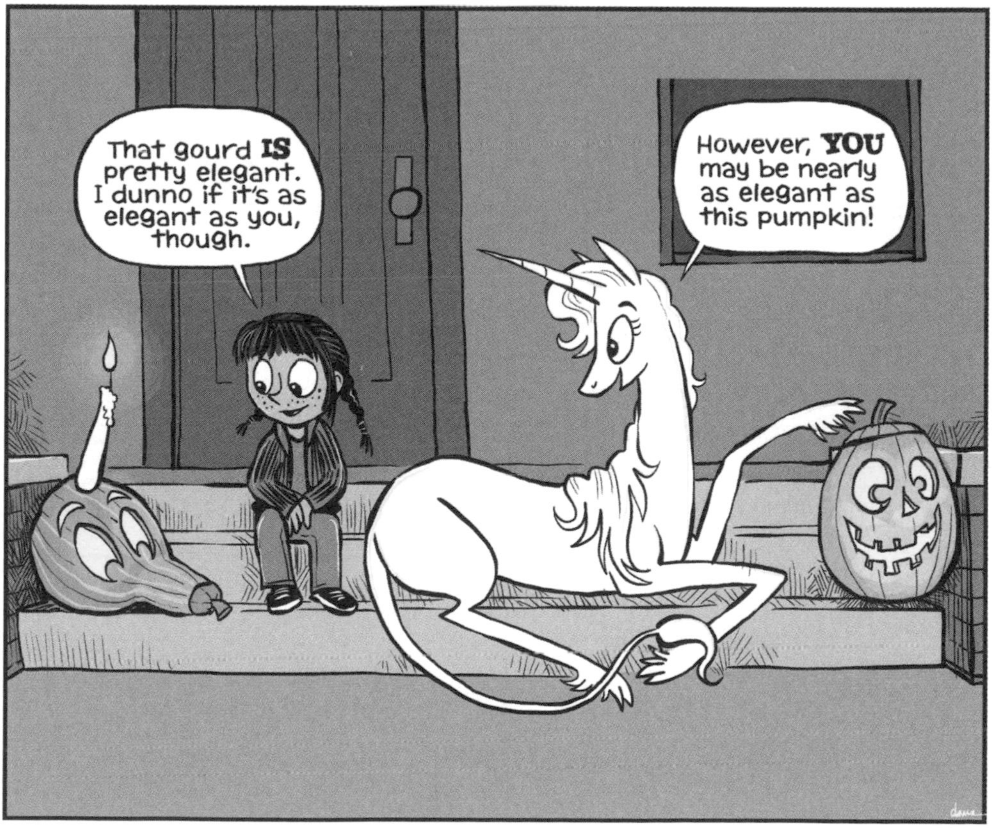
That gourd **IS** pretty elegant. I dunno if it's as elegant as you, though.
However, **YOU** may be nearly as elegant as this pumpkin!

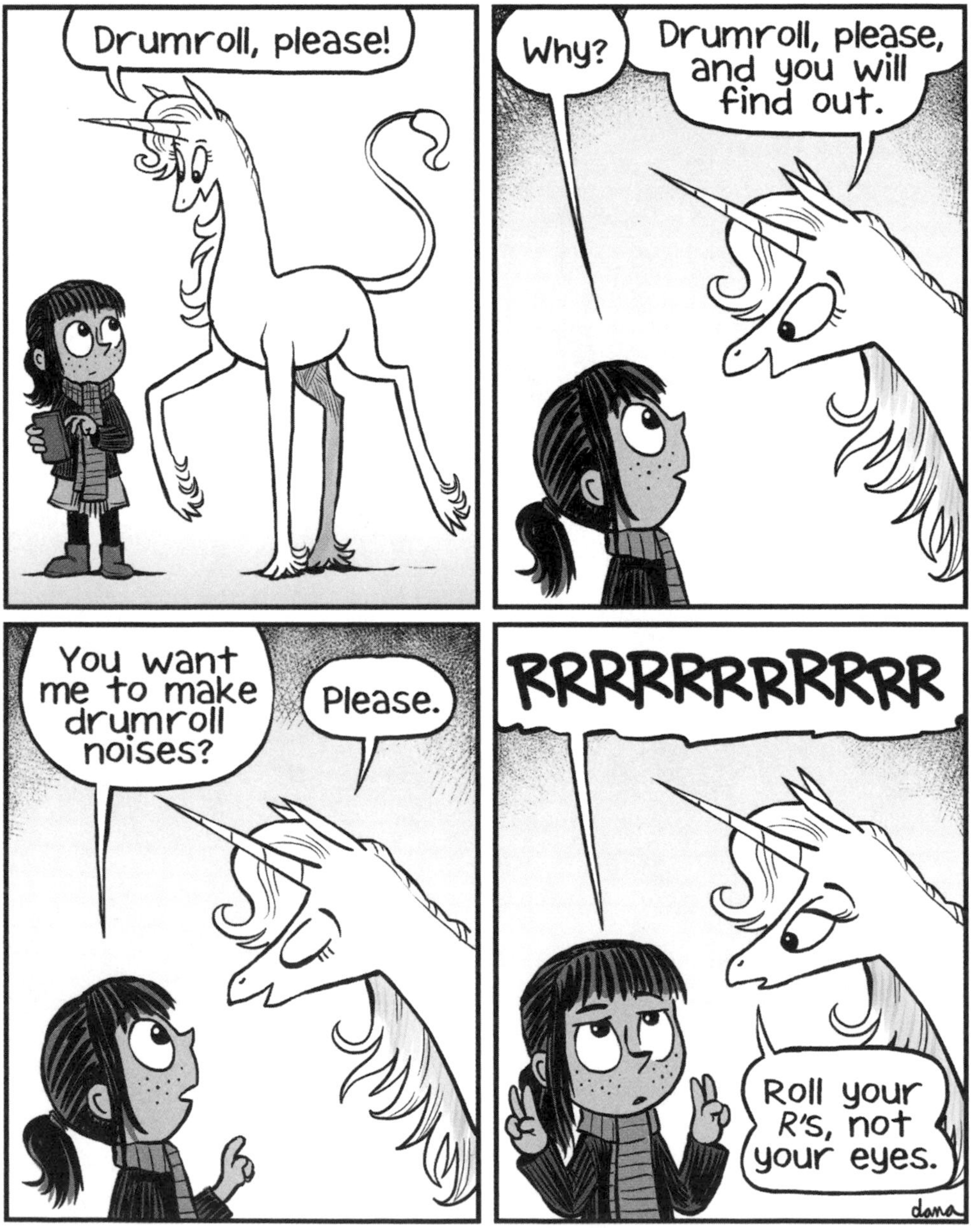
Drumroll, please!
Why?
Drumroll, please, and you will find out.
You want me to make drumroll noises?
Please.
RRRRRRRRRRR
Roll your R's, not your eyes.
dana

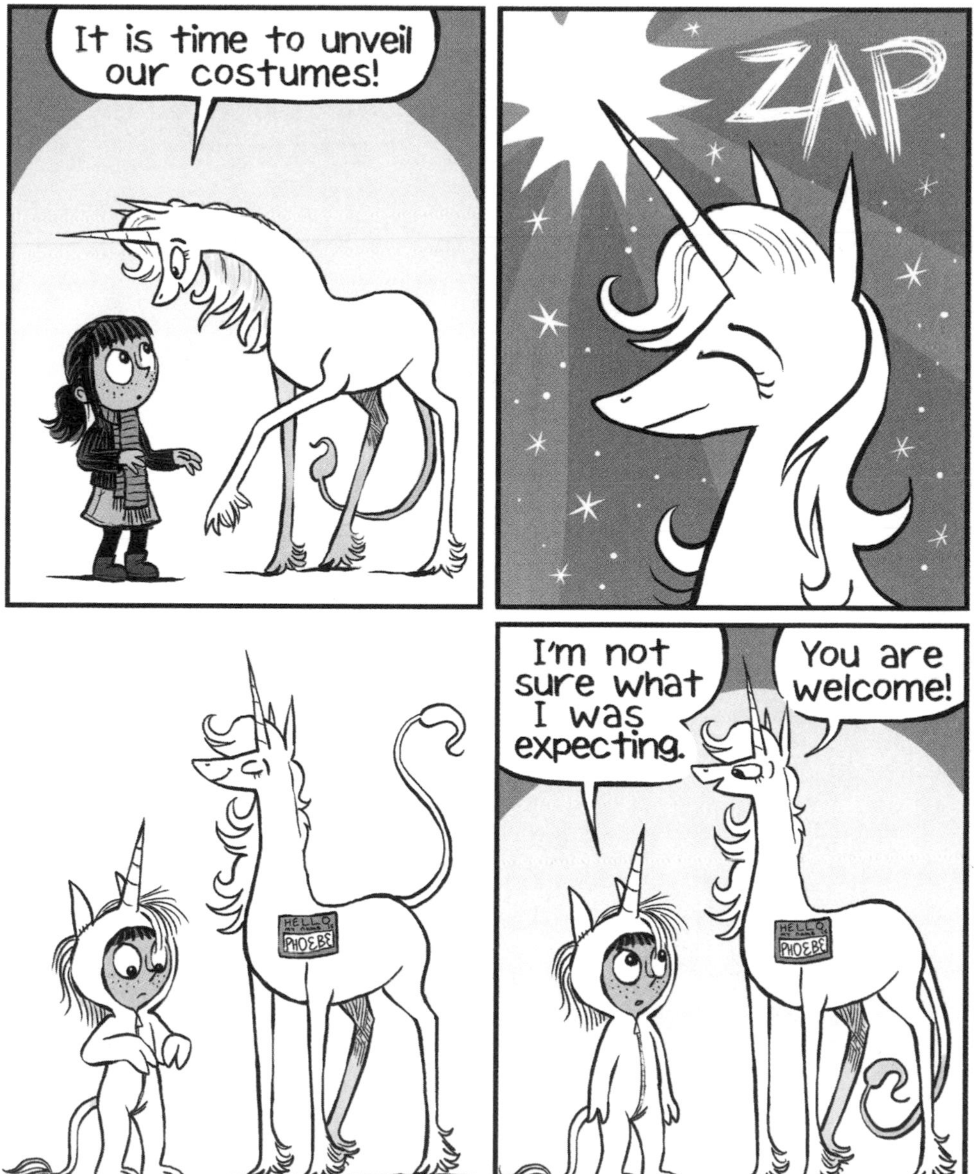
It is time to unveil our costumes!
ZAP
HELLO my name is PHOEBE
I'm not sure what I was expecting.
You are welcome!
HELLO my name is PHOEBE

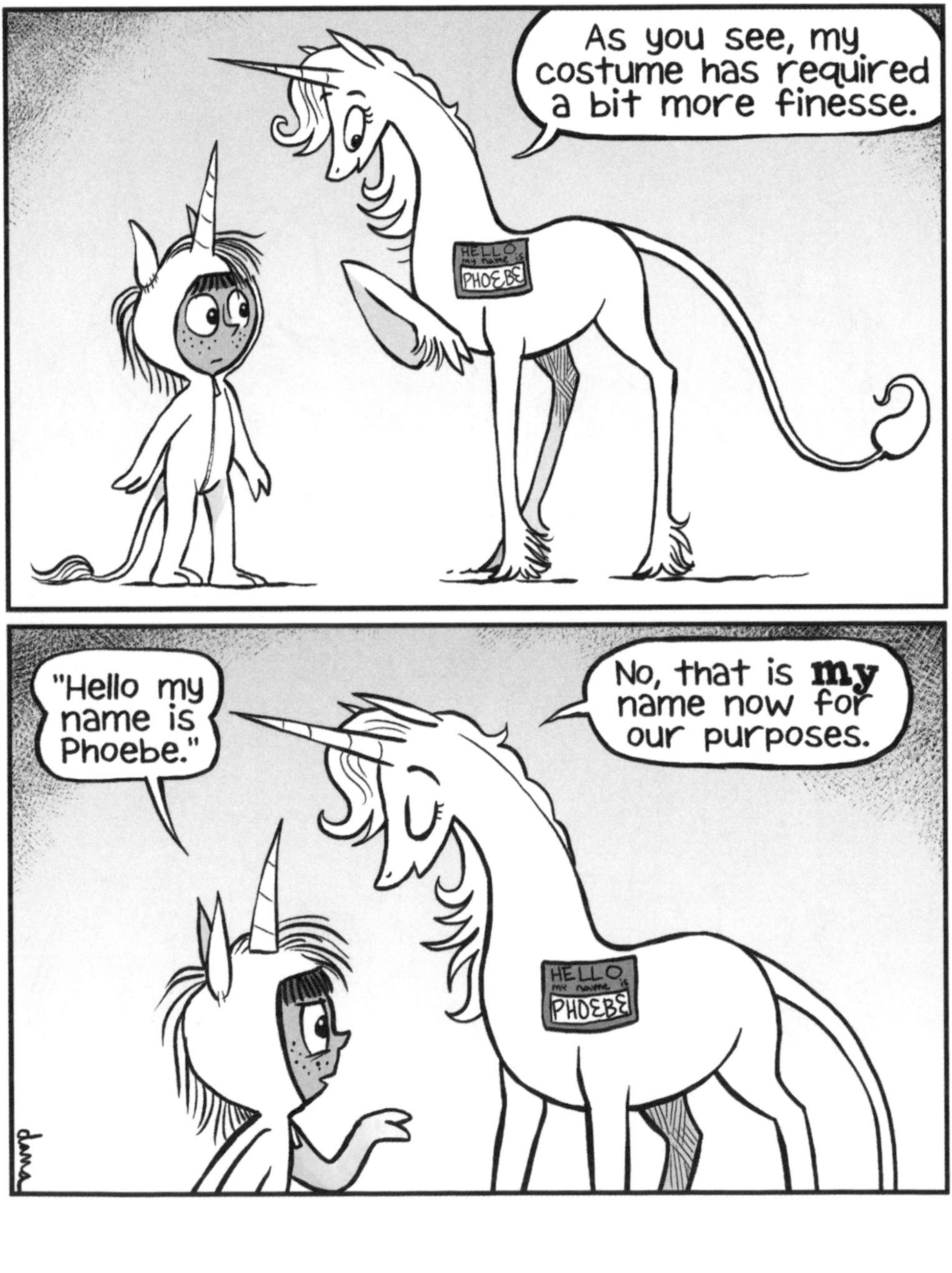
As you see, my costume has required a bit more finesse.
HELLO my name is PHOEBE
"Hello my name is Phoebe."
No, that is **my** name now for our purposes.
HELLO my name is PHOEBE
dana

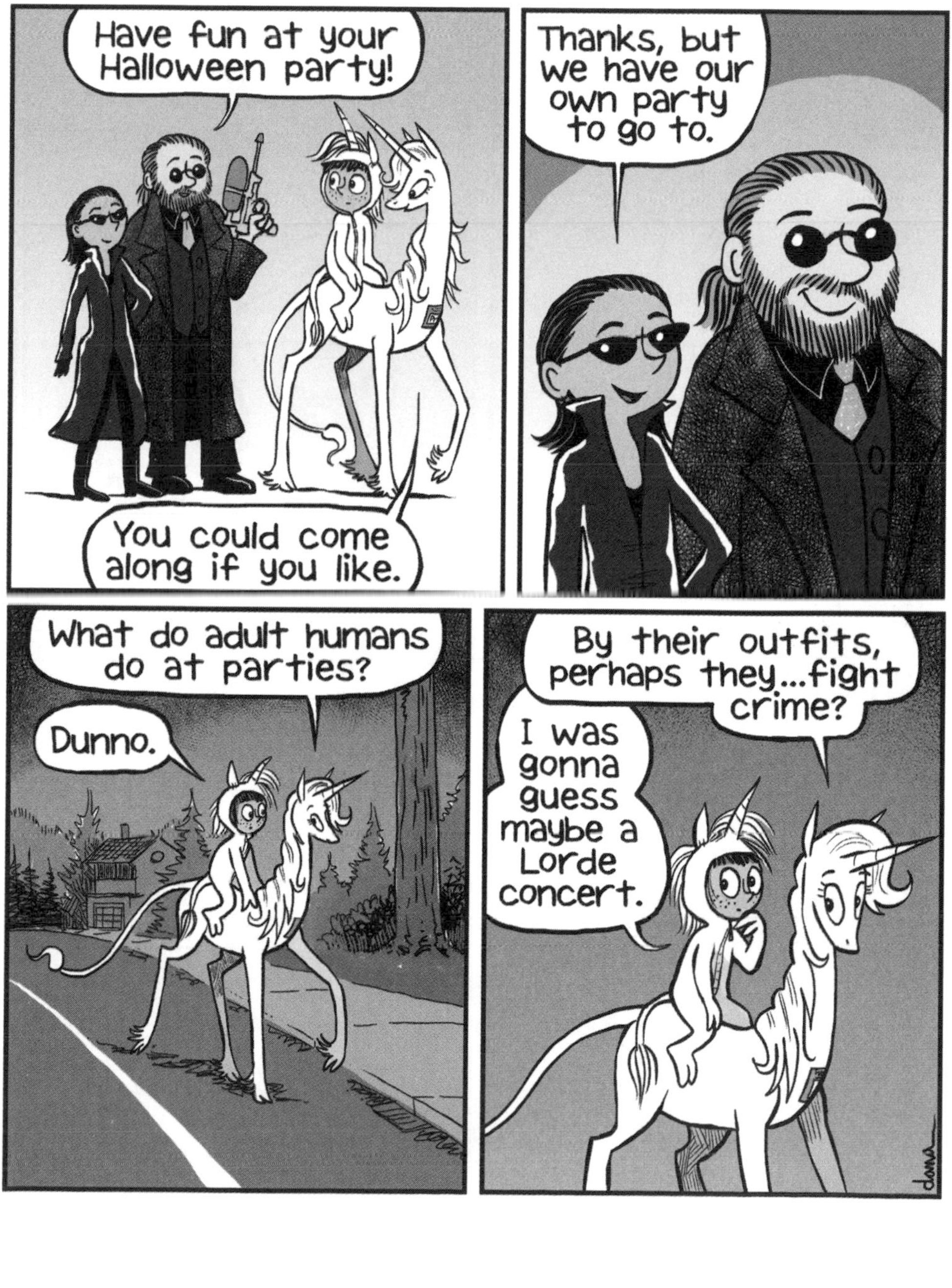
Have fun at your Halloween party!
You could come along if you like.
Thanks, but we have our own party to go to.
What do adult humans do at parties?
Dunno.
By their outfits, perhaps they...fight crime?
I was gonna guess maybe a Lorde concert.

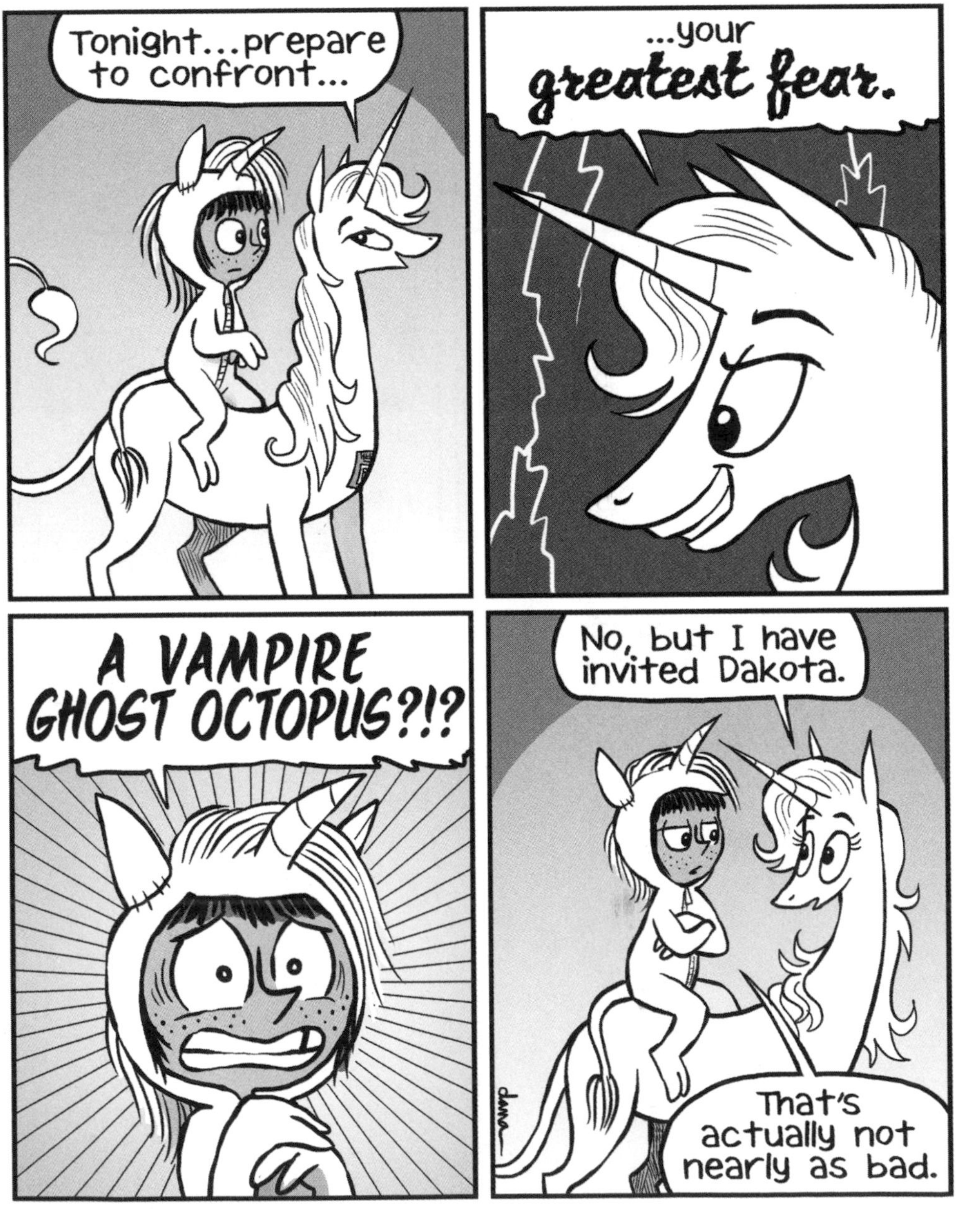
Tonight...prepare to confront...
...your greatest fear.
A VAMPIRE GHOST OCTOPUS?!?
No, but I have invited Dakota.
That's actually not nearly as bad.

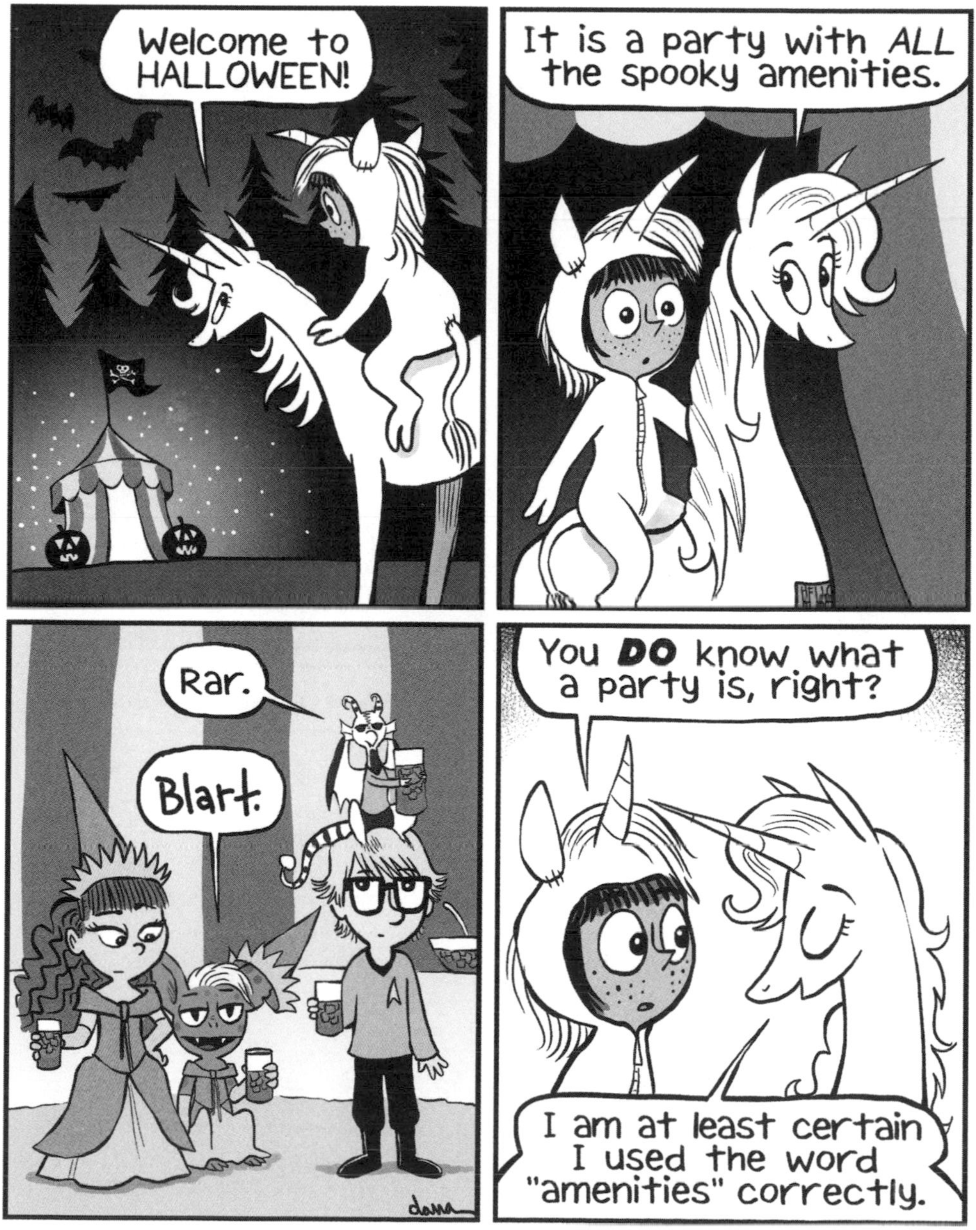
Welcome to HALLOWEEN!
It is a party with ALL the spooky amenities.
Rar.
Blart.
You DO know what a party is, right?
I am at least certain I used the word "amenities" correctly.
dana

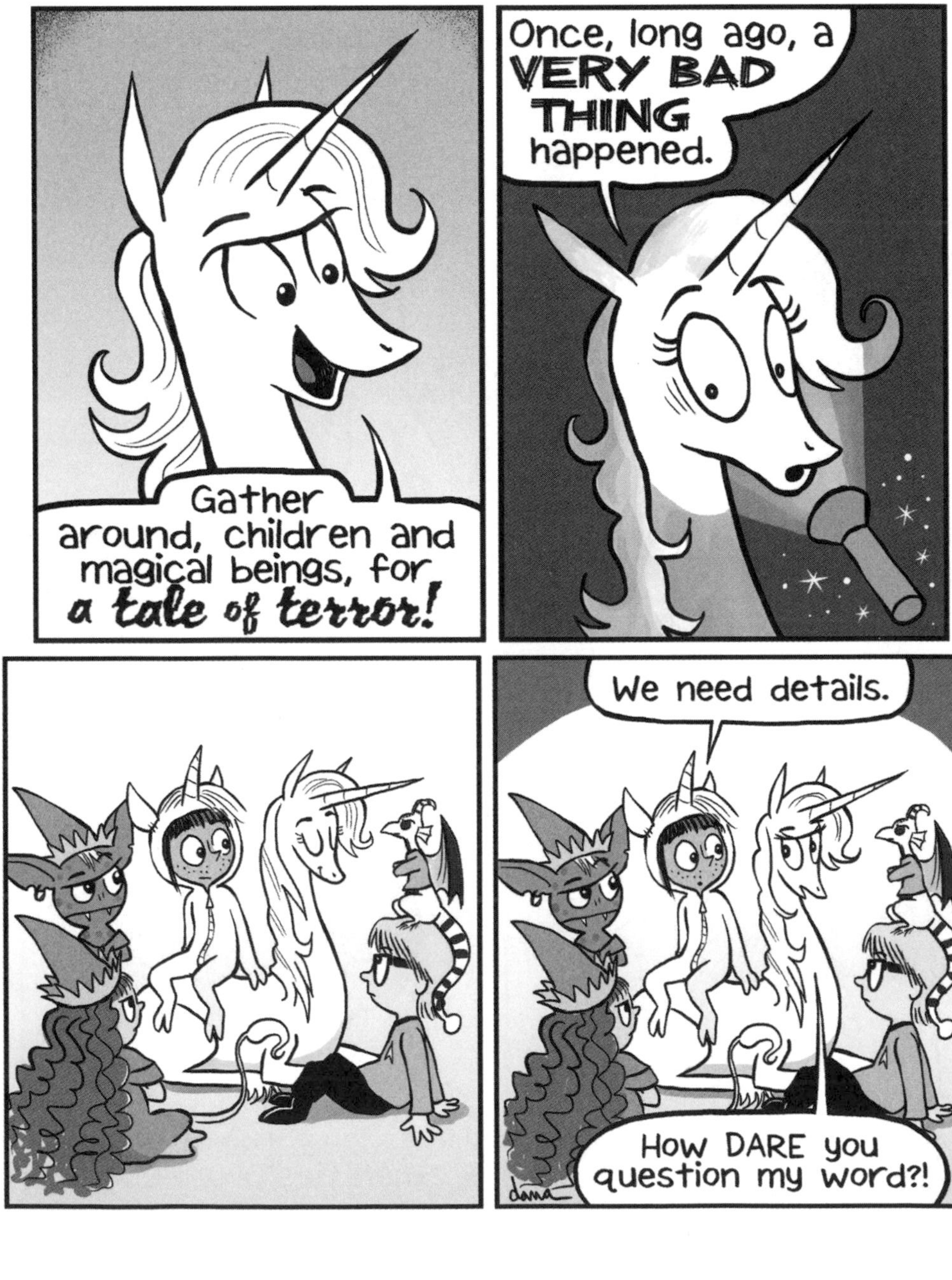
Gather around, children and magical beings, for *a tale of terror!*
Once, long ago, a **VERY BAD THING** happened.
We need details.
How DARE you question my word?!
dana

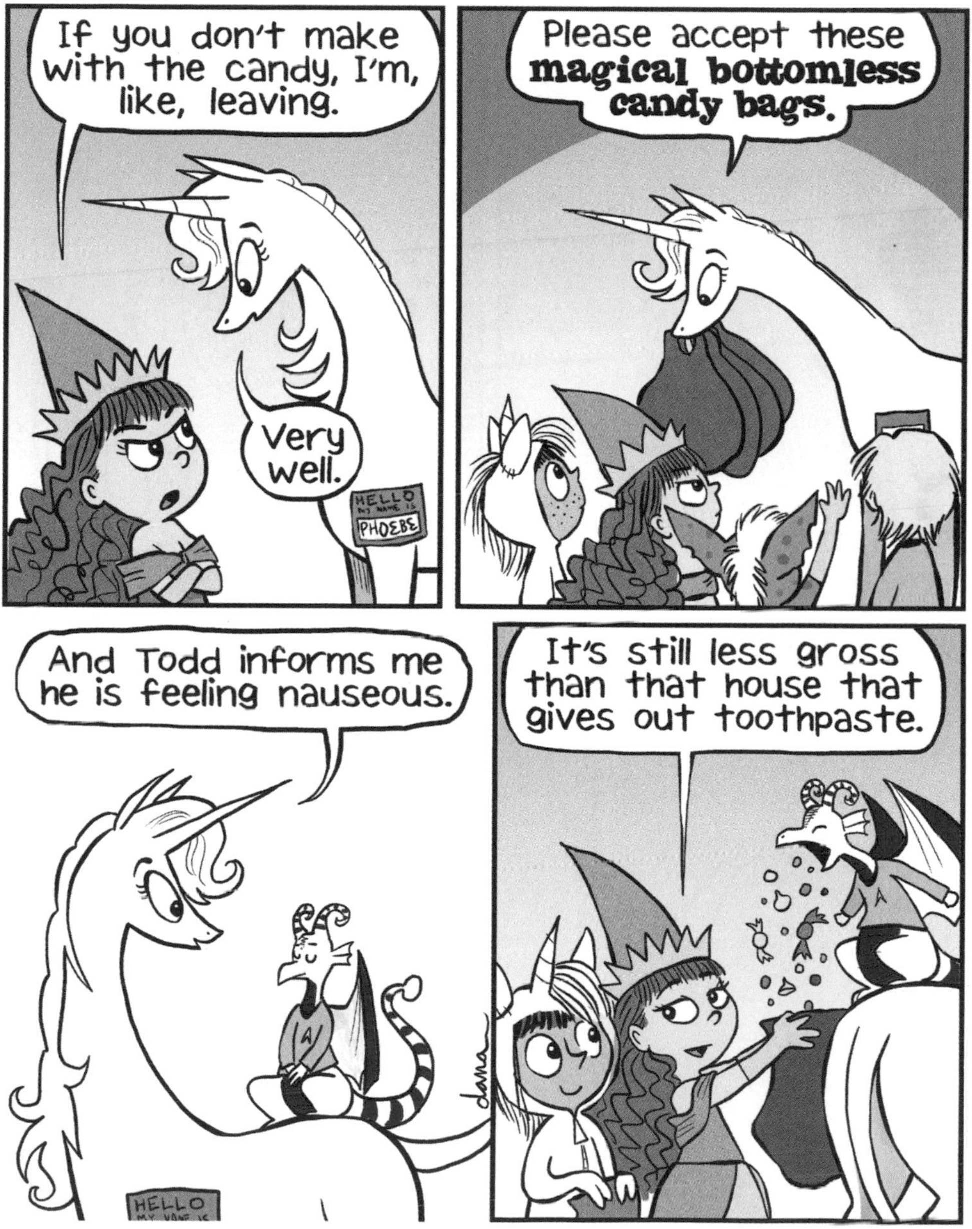
If you don't make with the candy, I'm, like, leaving.
Very well.
HELLO MY NAME IS PHOEBE
Please accept these **magical bottomless candy bags.**
And Todd informs me he is feeling nauseous.
HELLO
It's still less gross than that house that gives out toothpaste.
dana

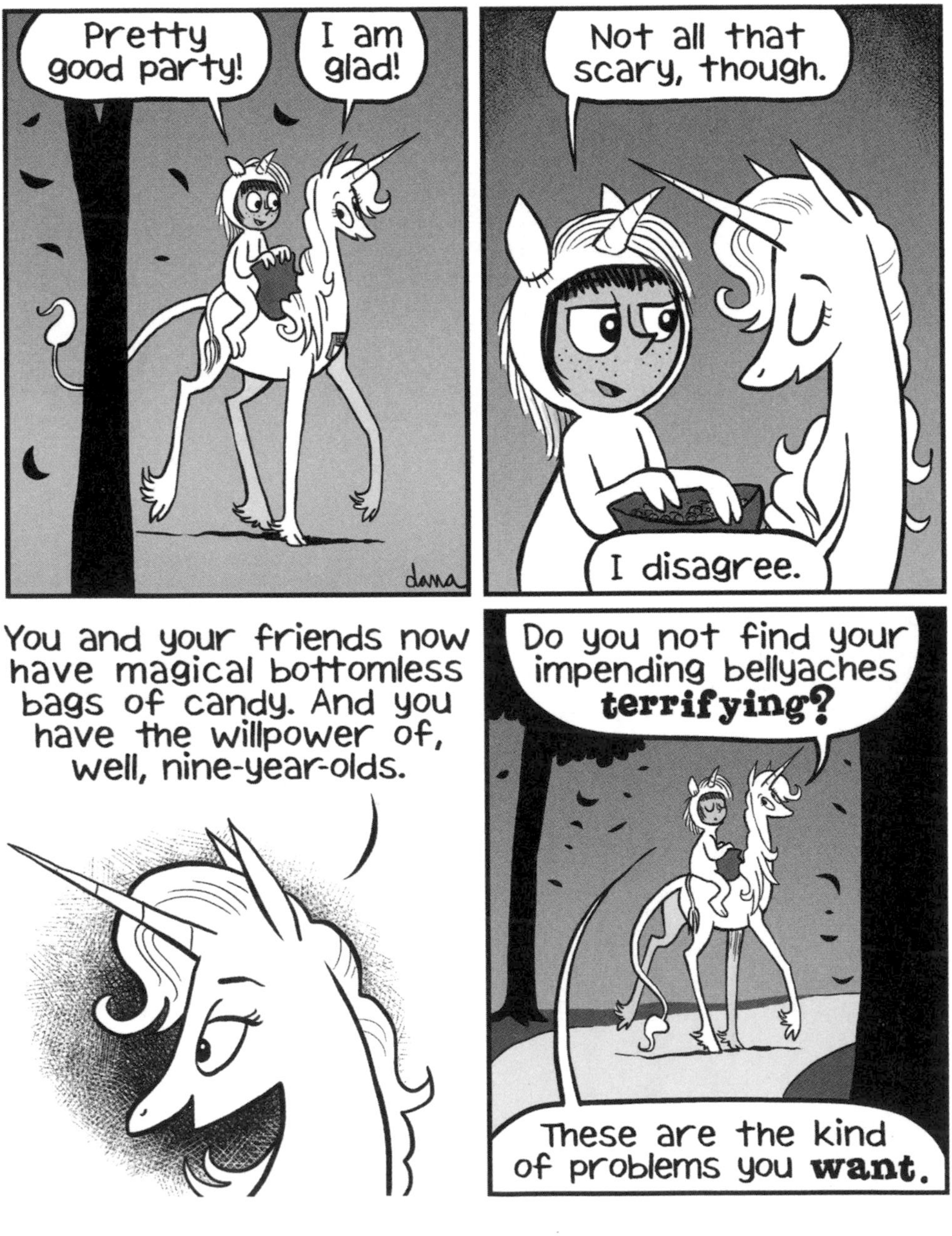
Pretty good party!
I am glad!
Not all that scary, though.
I disagree.
You and your friends now have magical bottomless bags of candy. And you have the willpower of, well, nine-year-olds.
Do you not find your impending bellyaches **terrifying?**
These are the kind of problems you **want.**

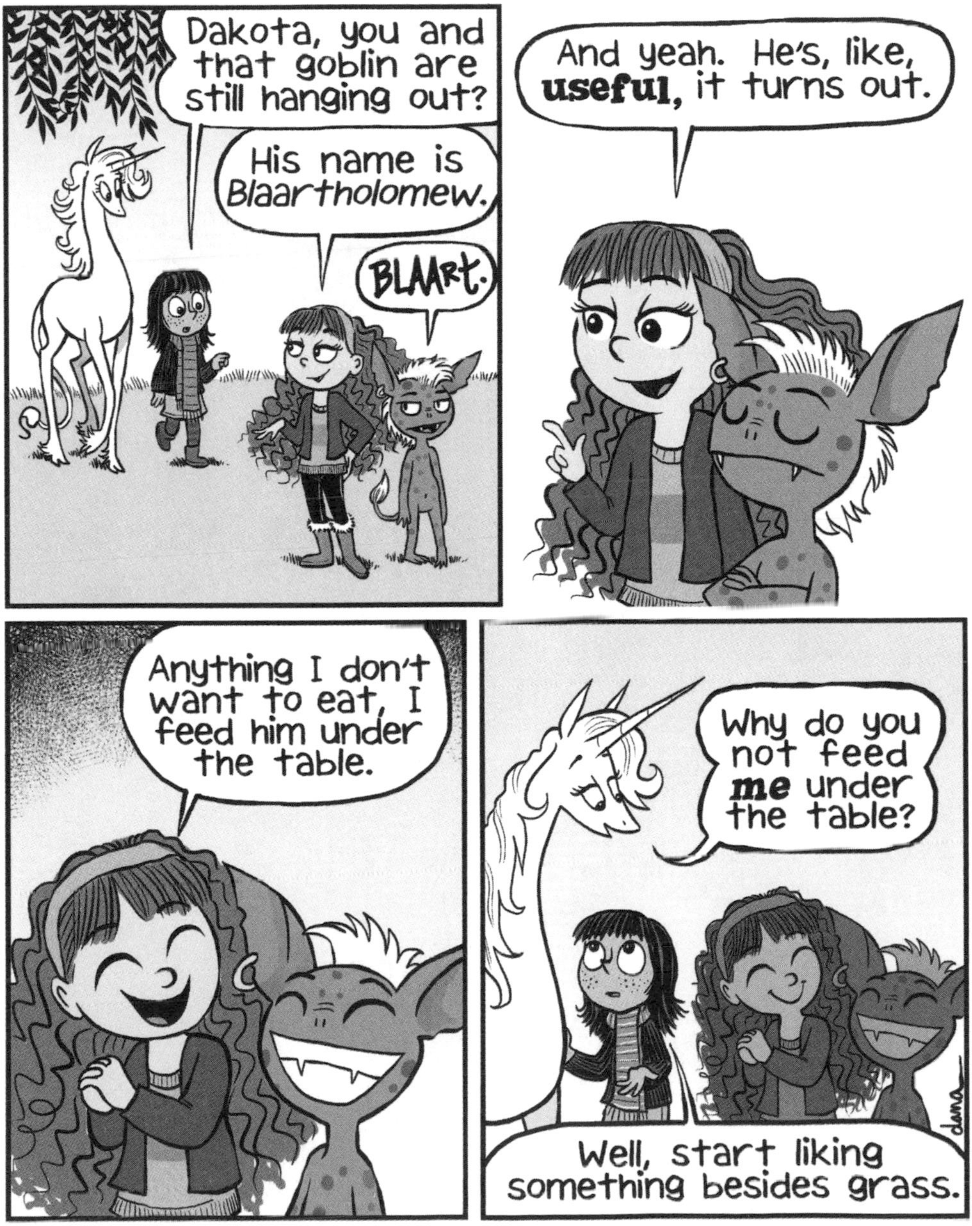
Dakota, you and that goblin are still hanging out?
His name is *Blaartholomew.*
BLAARt.
And yeah. He's, like, **useful**, it turns out.
Anything I don't want to eat, I feed him under the table.
Why do you not feed **me** under the table?
Well, start liking something besides grass.
dana

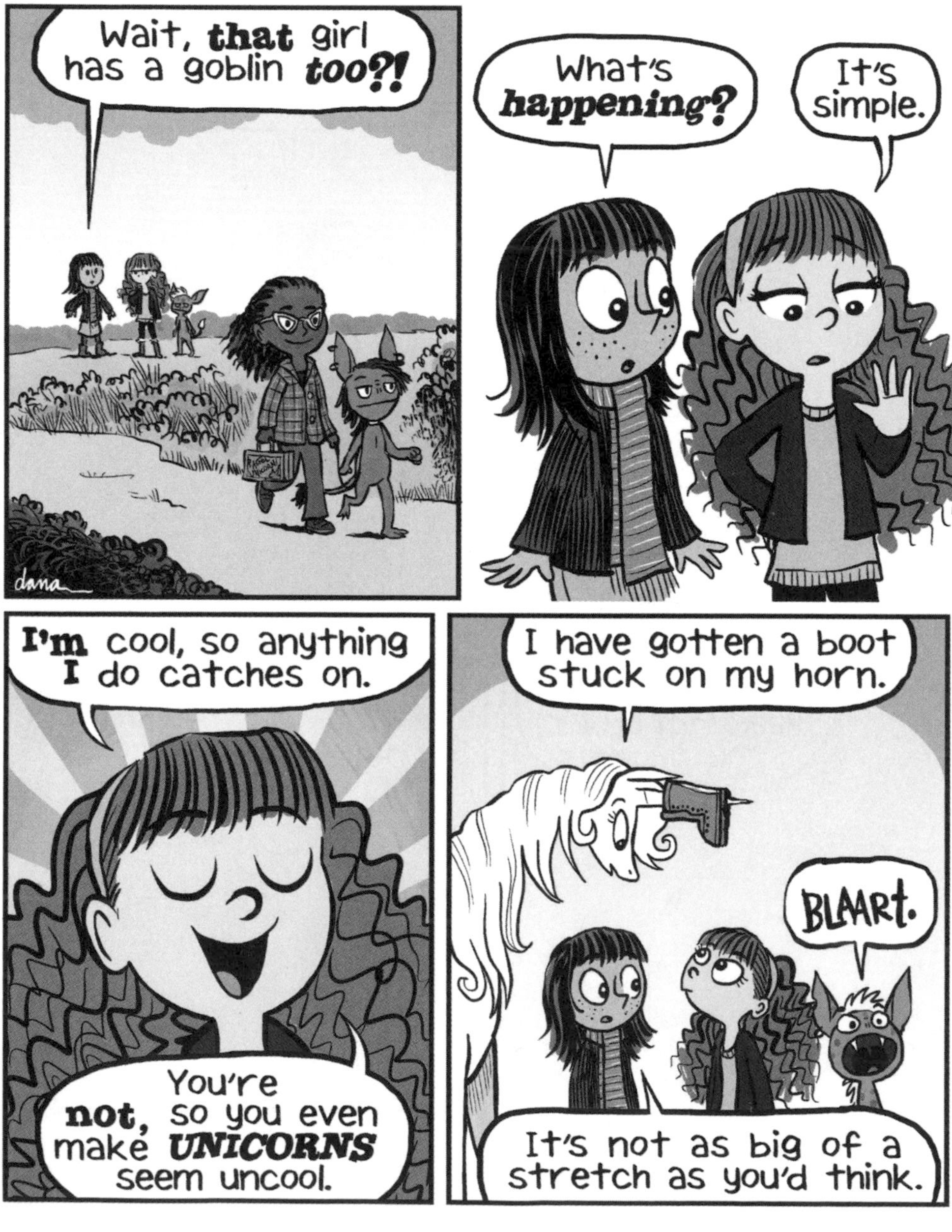
Wait, **that** girl has a goblin ***too?!***
What's **happening?**
It's simple.
I'm cool, so anything **I** do catches on.
You're **not,** so you even make ***UNICORNS*** seem uncool.
I have gotten a boot stuck on my horn.
BLAART.
It's not as big of a stretch as you'd think.
dana

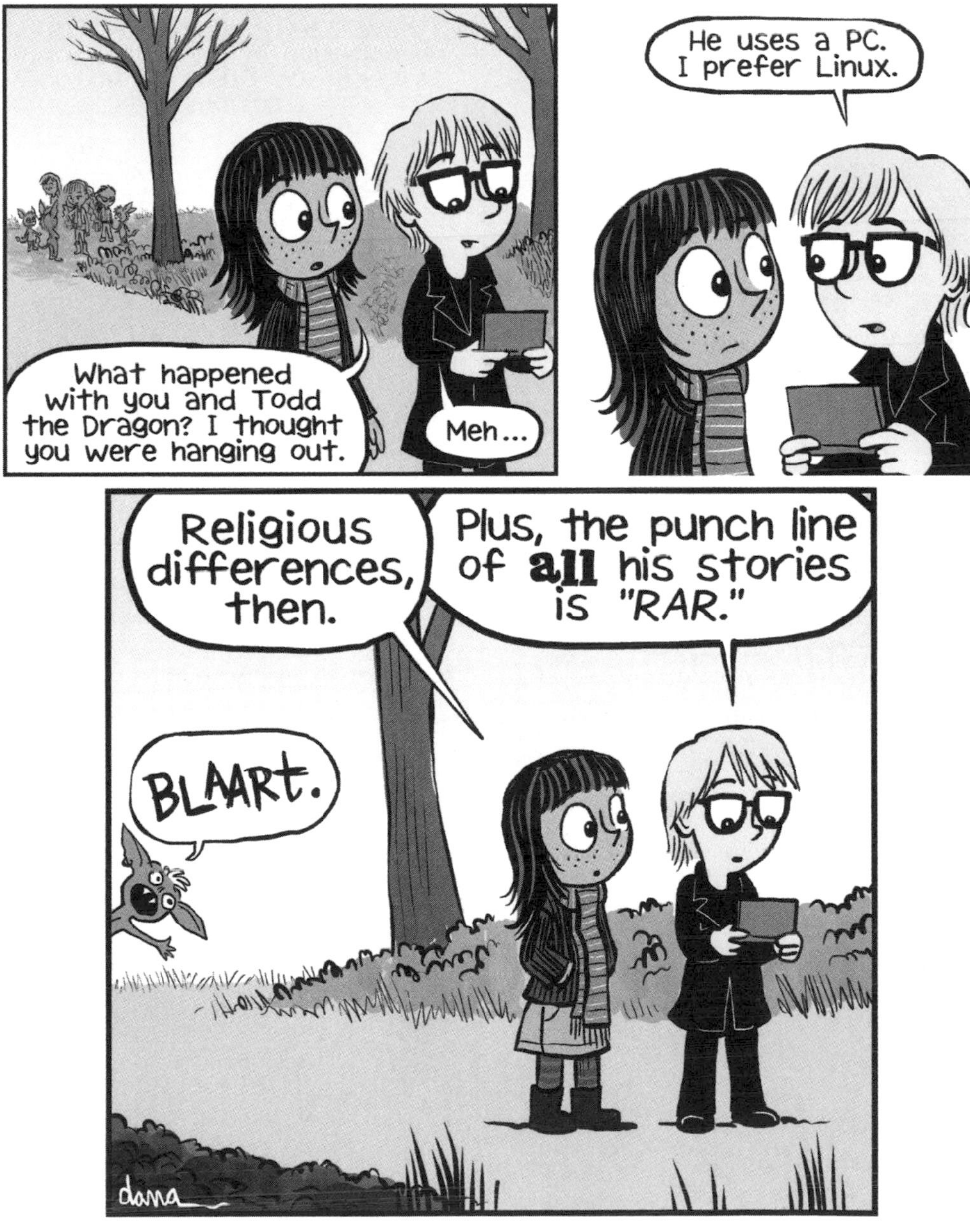
What happened with you and Todd the Dragon? I thought you were hanging out.
Meh...
He uses a PC. I prefer Linux.
Religious differences, then.
Plus, the punch line of **all** his stories is "RAR."
BLAART.
dana

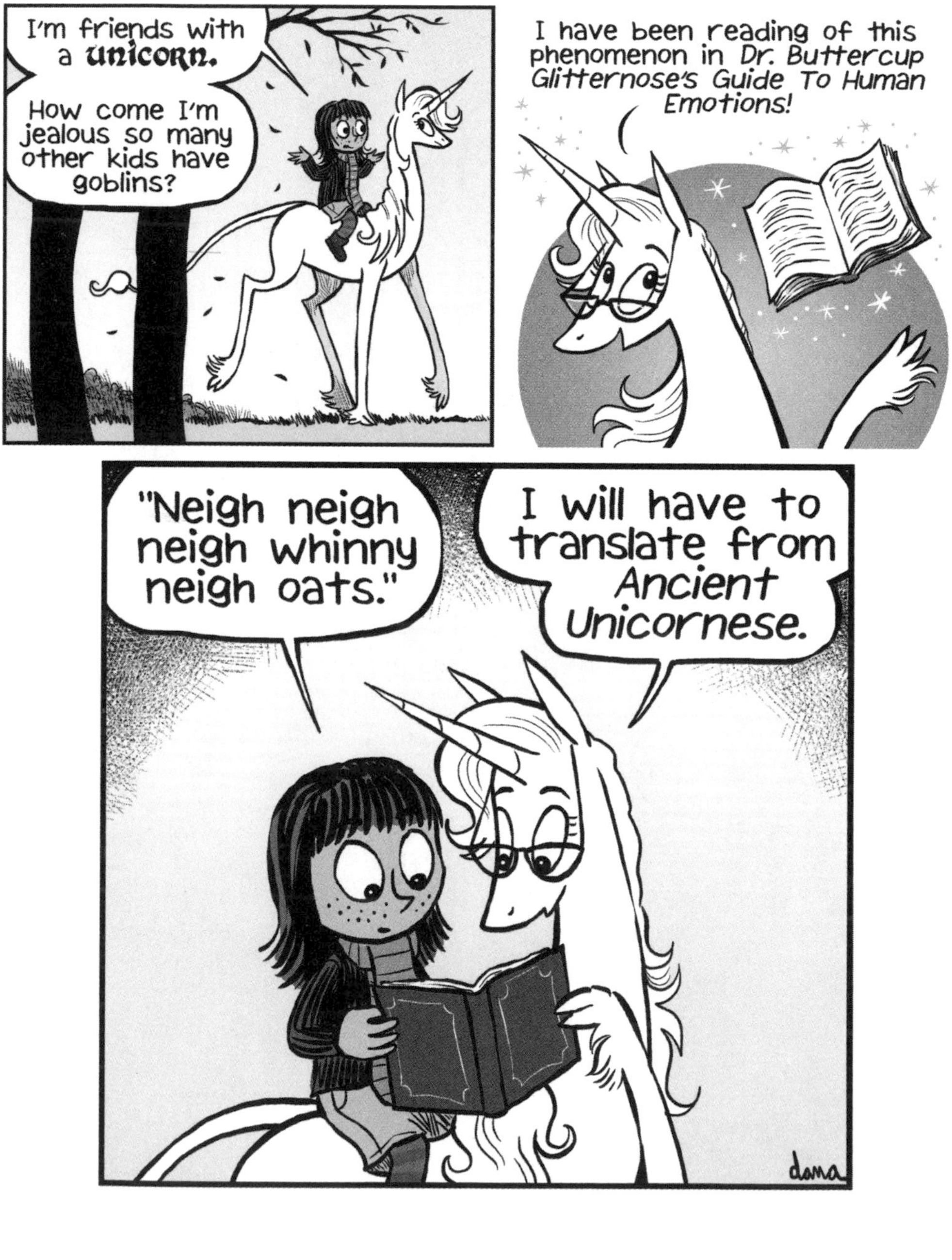
I'm friends with a **unicorn.**
How come I'm jealous so many other kids have goblins?
I have been reading of this phenomenon in *Dr. Buttercup Glitternose's Guide To Human Emotions!*
"Neigh neigh neigh whinny neigh oats."
I will have to translate from *Ancient Unicornese.*
dana

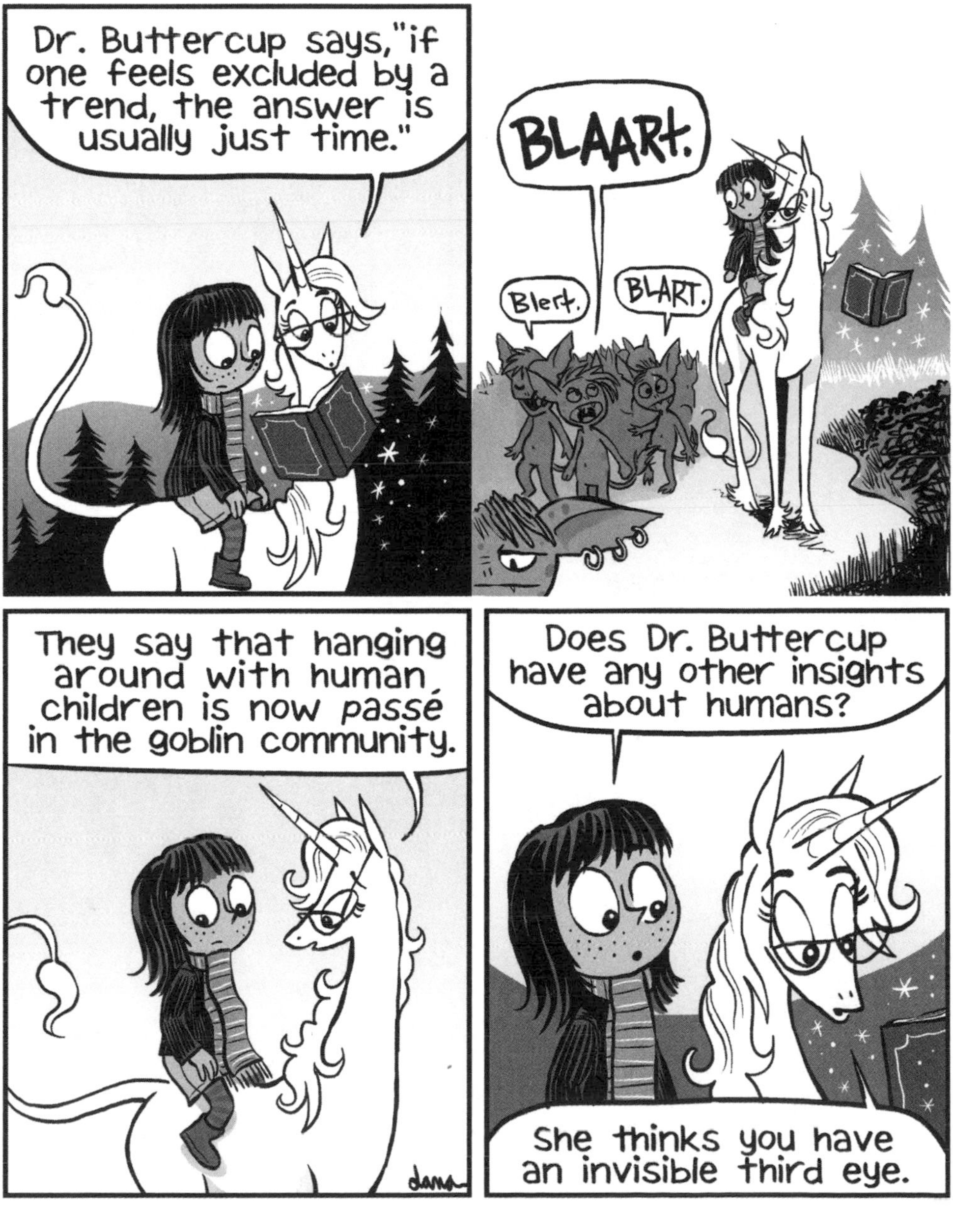

Dr. Buttercup says, "if one feels excluded by a trend, the answer is usually just time."
BLAART.
Blert.
BLART.
They say that hanging around with human children is now *passé* in the goblin community.
Does Dr. Buttercup have any other insights about humans?
She thinks you have an invisible third eye.
dana

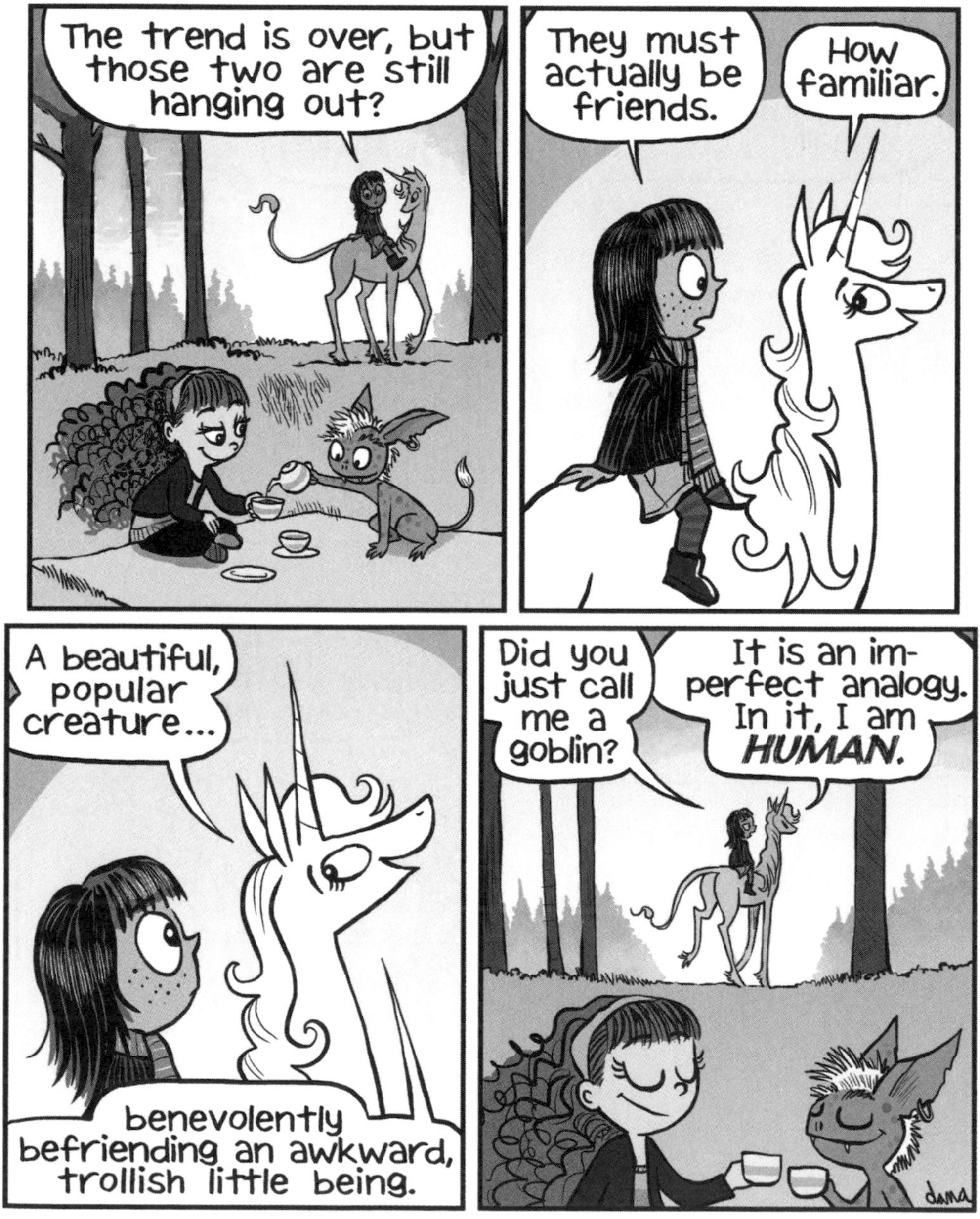
The trend is over, but those two are still hanging out?
They must actually be friends.
How familiar.
A beautiful, popular creature...
benevolently befriending an awkward, trollish little being.
Did you just call me a goblin?
It is an im-perfect analogy. In it, I am ***HUMAN.***
dana

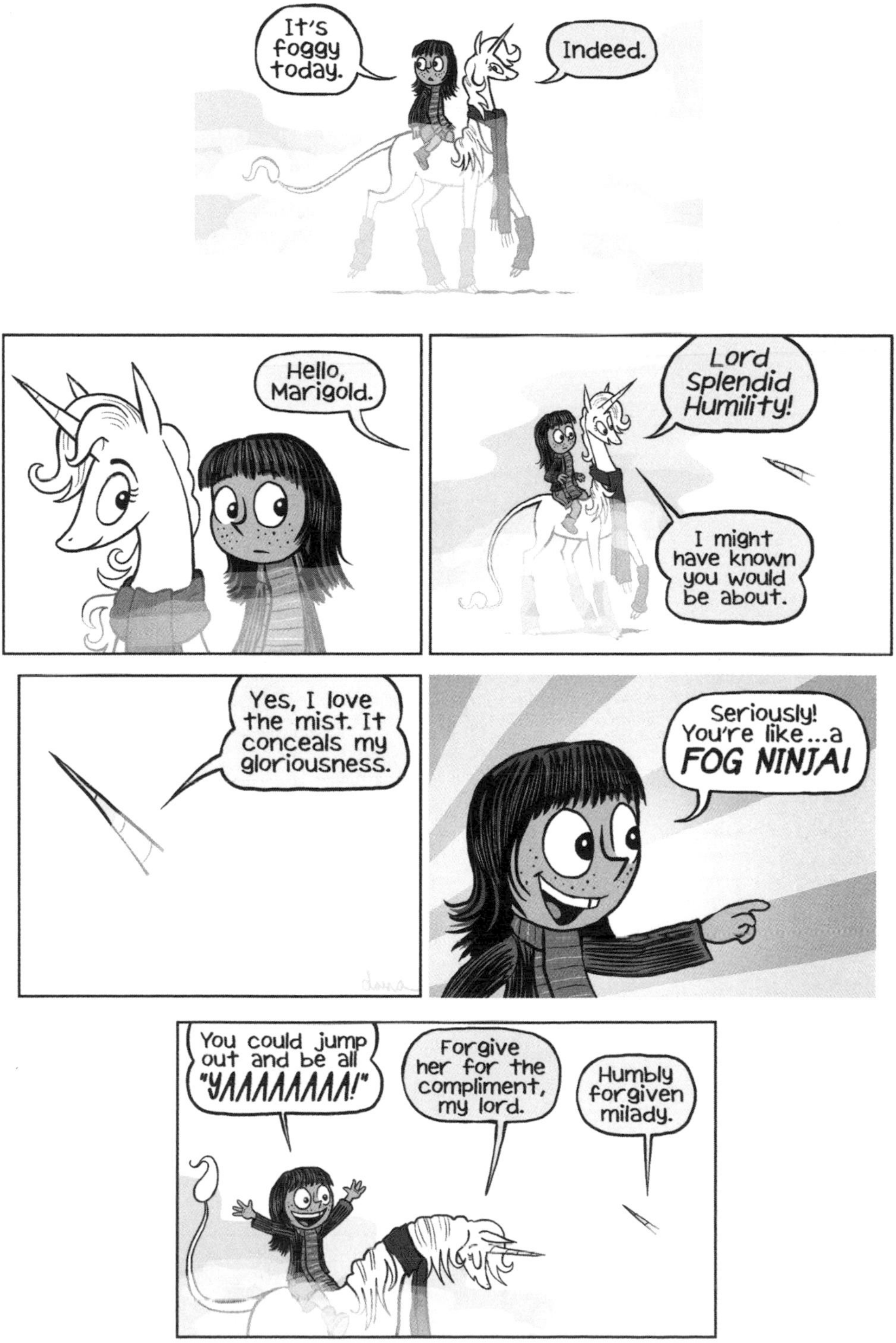

It's foggy today.
Indeed.
Hello, Marigold.
Lord Splendid Humility!
I might have known you would be about.
Yes, I love the mist. It conceals my gloriousness.
Seriously! You're like...a FOG NINJA!
You could jump out and be all "YAAAAAAAA!"
Forgive her for the compliment, my lord.
Humbly forgiven milady.

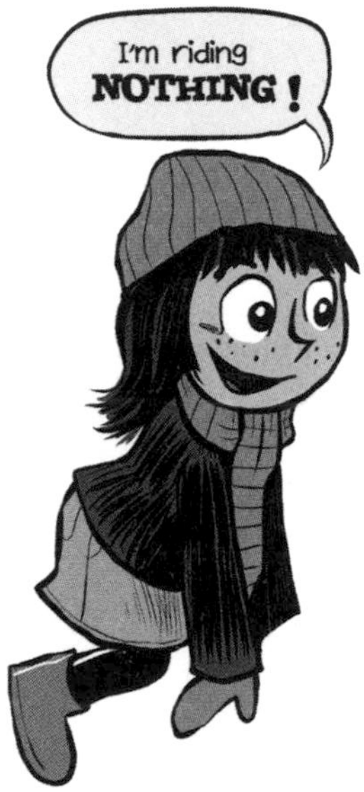
I'm riding
NOTHING!

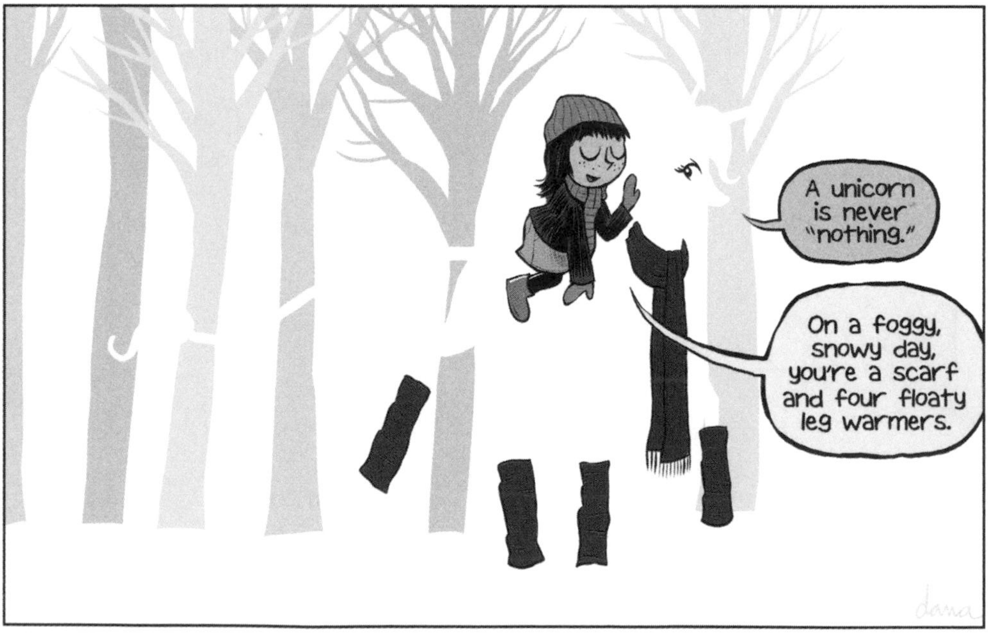
A unicorn is never "nothing."
On a foggy, snowy day, you're a scarf and four floaty leg warmers.

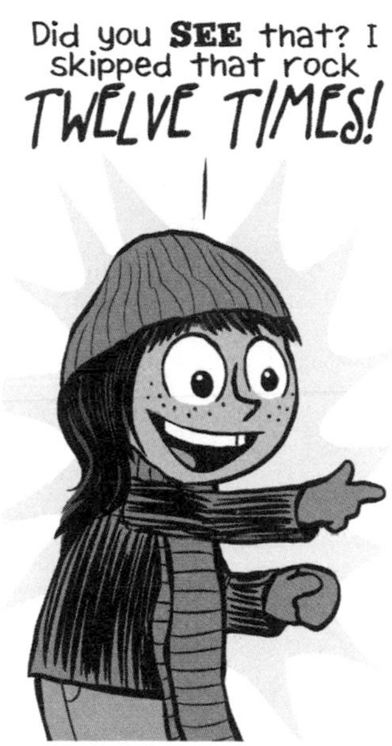
Did you **SEE** that? I skipped that rock TWELVE TIMES!

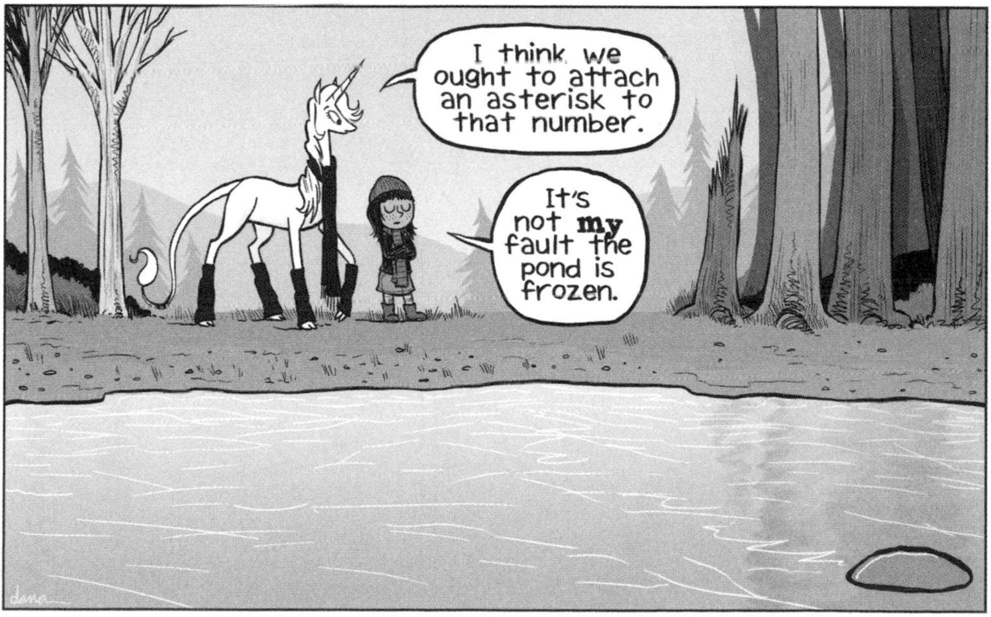
I think we ought to attach an asterisk to that number.
It's not **my** fault the pond is frozen.
dana

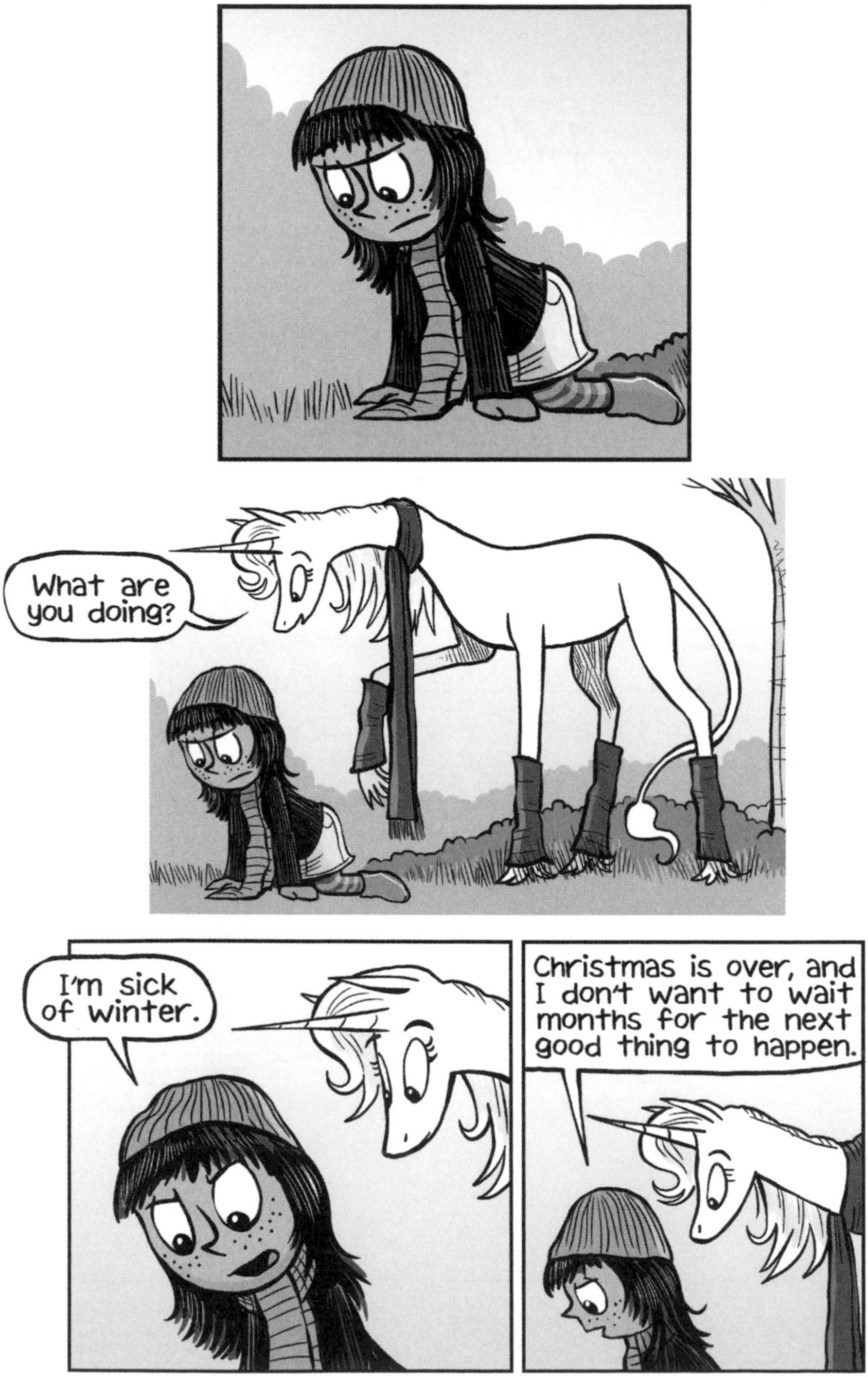
What are you doing?
I'm sick of winter.
Christmas is over, and I don't want to wait months for the next good thing to happen.

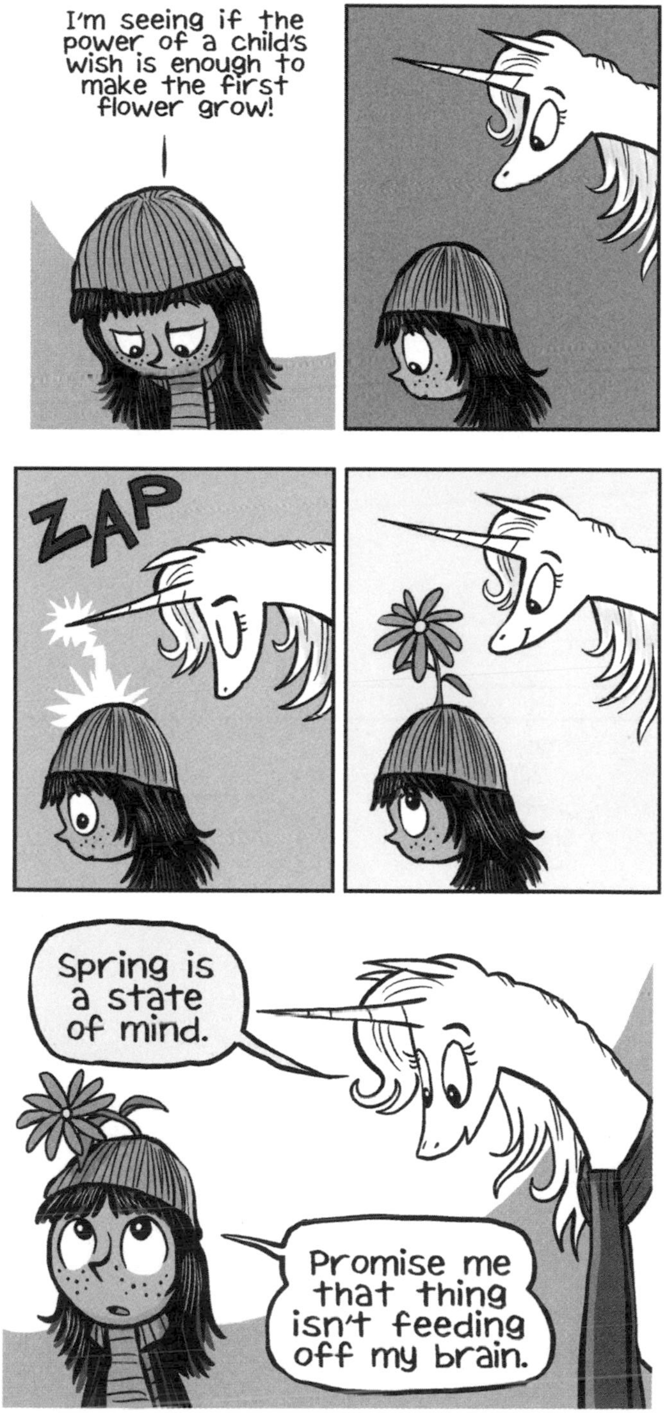
I'm seeing if the power of a child's wish is enough to make the first flower grow!
ZAP
Spring is a state of mind.
Promise me that thing isn't feeding off my brain.

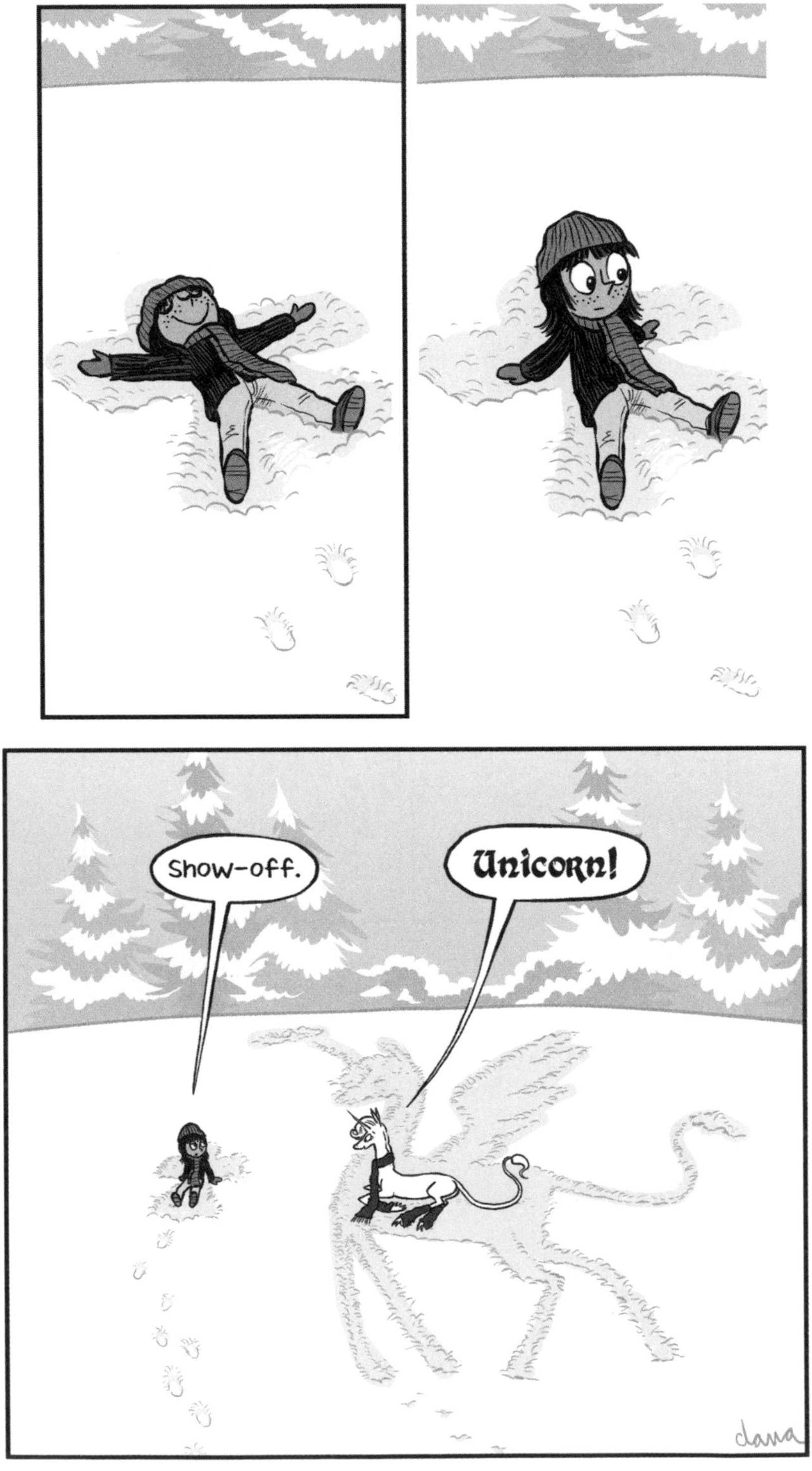
Show-off.
Unicorn!
dana

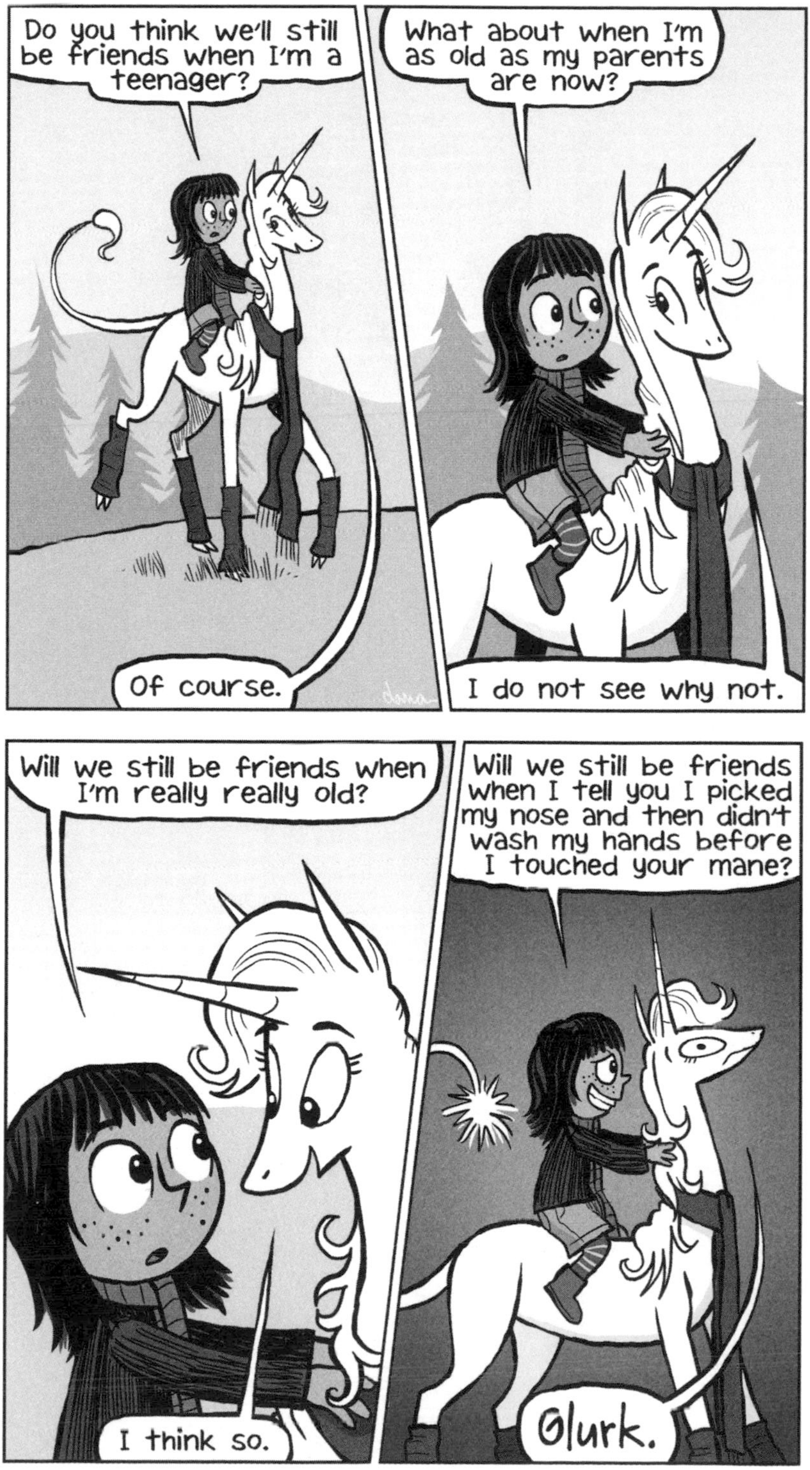
Do you think we'll still be friends when I'm a teenager?
Of course.
What about when I'm as old as my parents are now?
I do not see why not.
Will we still be friends when I'm really really old?
I think so.
Will we still be friends when I tell you I picked my nose and then didn't wash my hands before I touched your mane?
Glurk.

Phoebe?
What?
You should get up.
Why?
Out here there are unicorns!

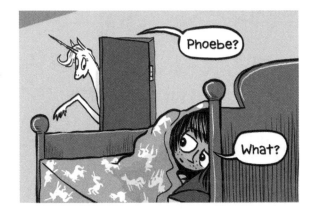

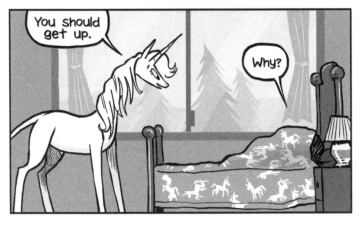

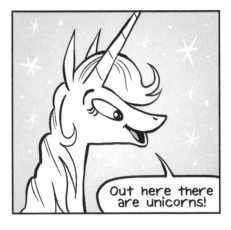

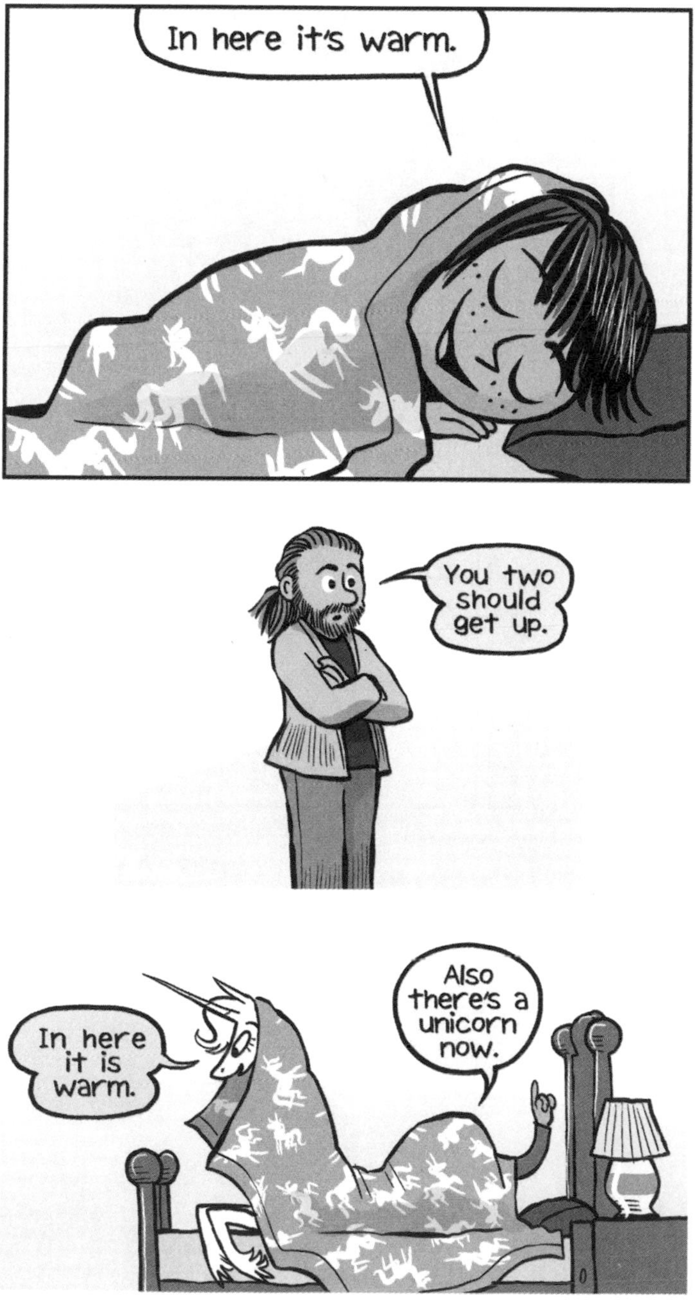
In here it's warm.
You two should get up.
In here it is warm.
Also there's a unicorn now.

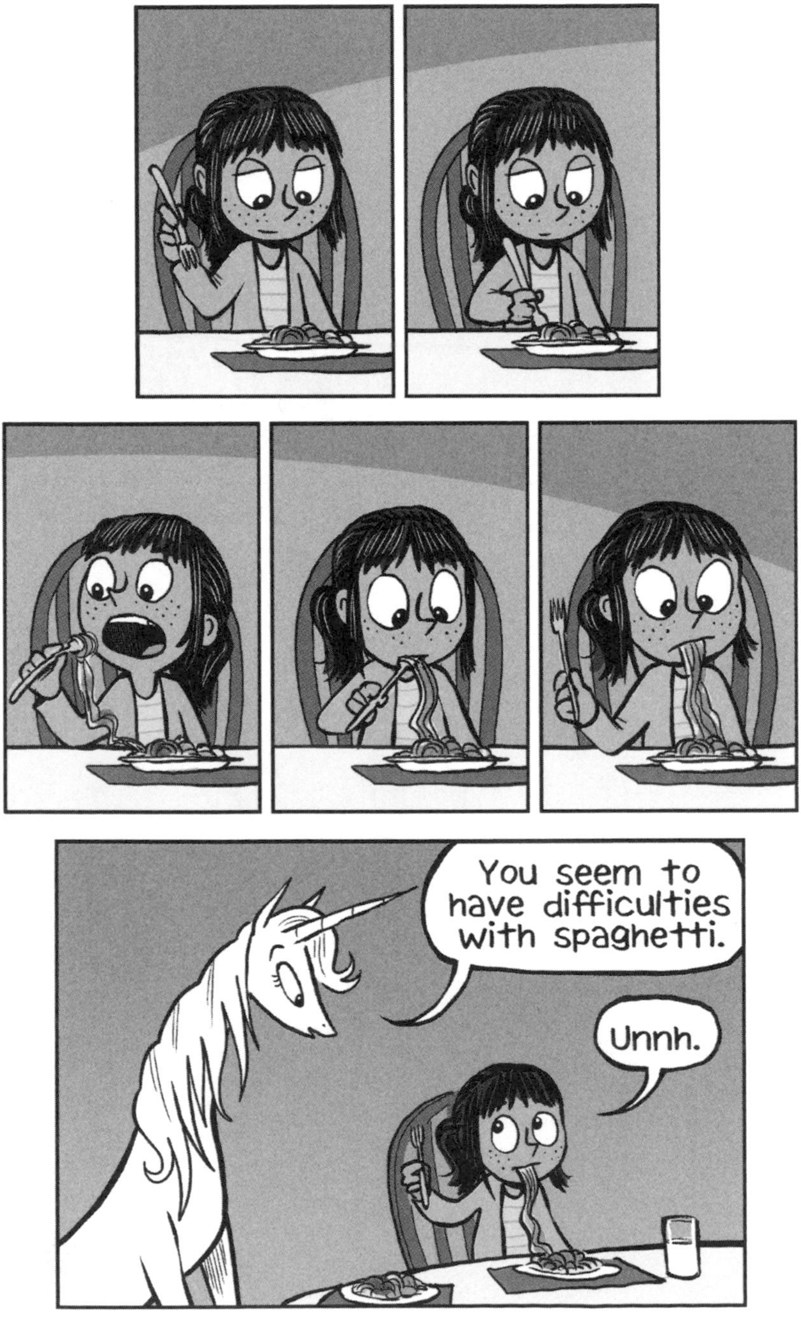
You seem to have difficulties with spaghetti.
Unnh.

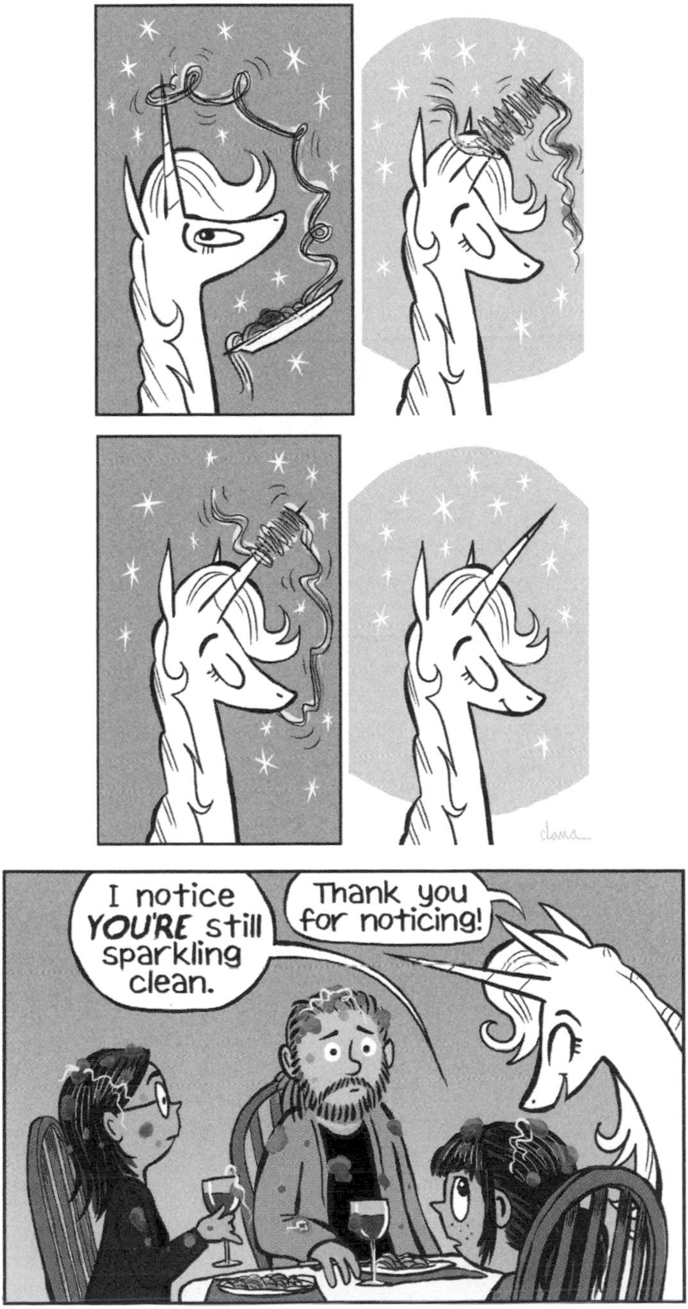
I notice YOU'RE still sparkling clean.
Thank you for noticing!

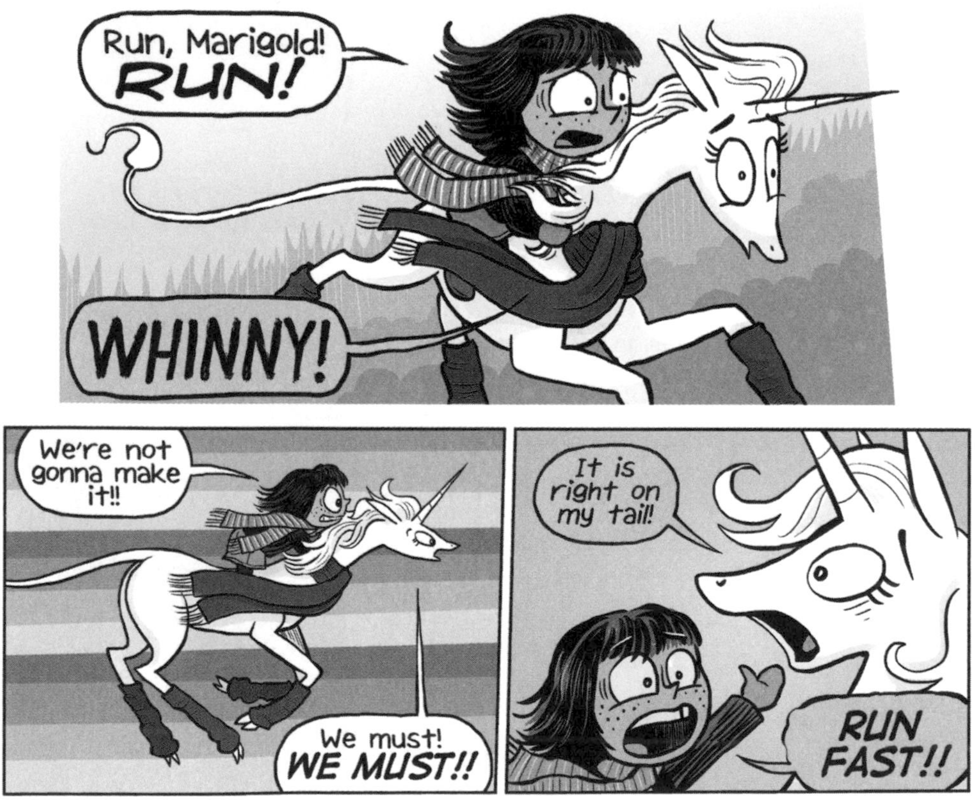
Run, Marigold! RUN!
WHINNY!
We're not gonna make it!!
We must! WE MUST!!
It is right on my tail!
RUN FAST!!

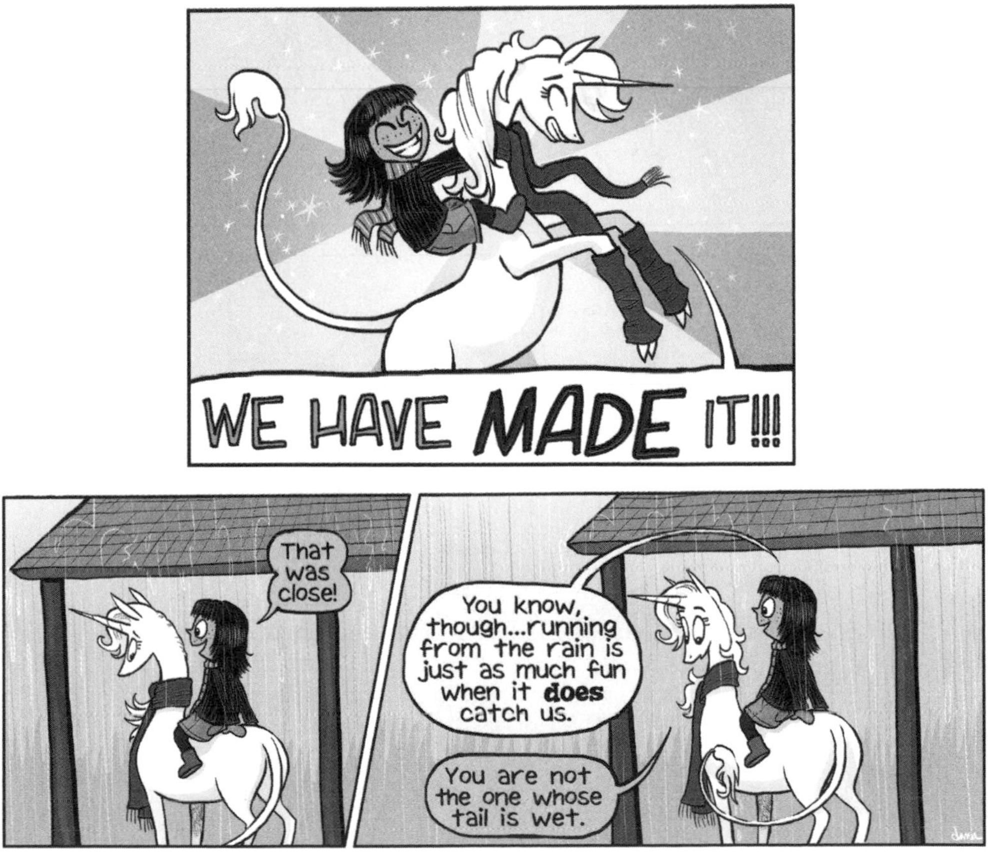
WE HAVE MADE IT!!!
That was close!
You know, though...running from the rain is just as much fun when it **does** catch us.
You are not the one whose tail is wet.

Your book is just ONE book.
Our e-reader thingies have LOTS of books.
I still like how books smell, and I like turning pages.
"Books" indeed. You humans and your newfangled devices.

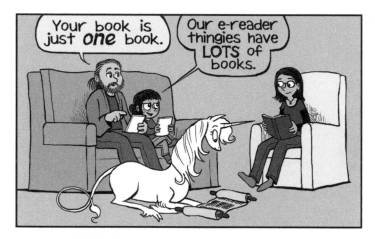

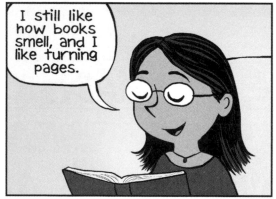

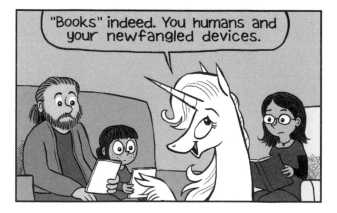

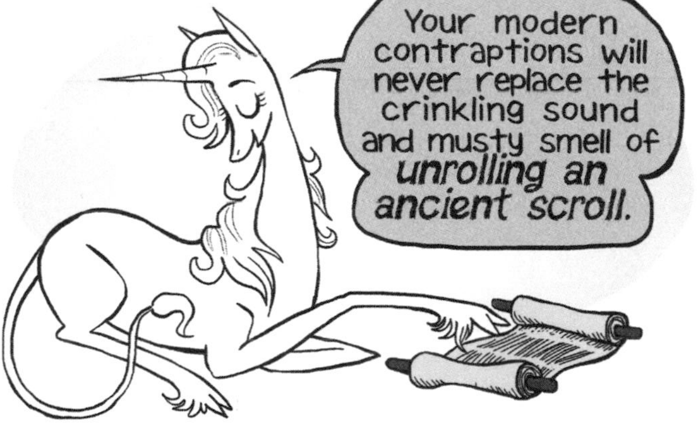
Your modern contraptions will never replace the crinkling sound and musty smell of ***unrolling an ancient scroll.***

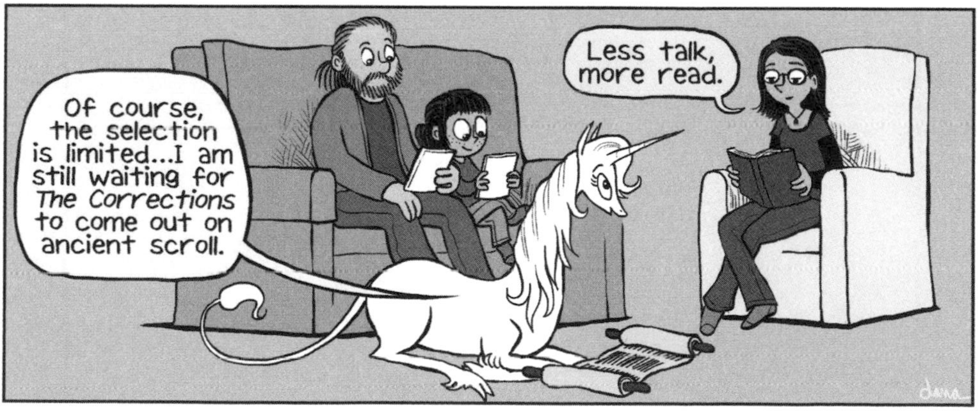
Of course, the selection is limited...I am still waiting for *The Corrections* to come out on ancient scroll.
Less talk, more read.
dana

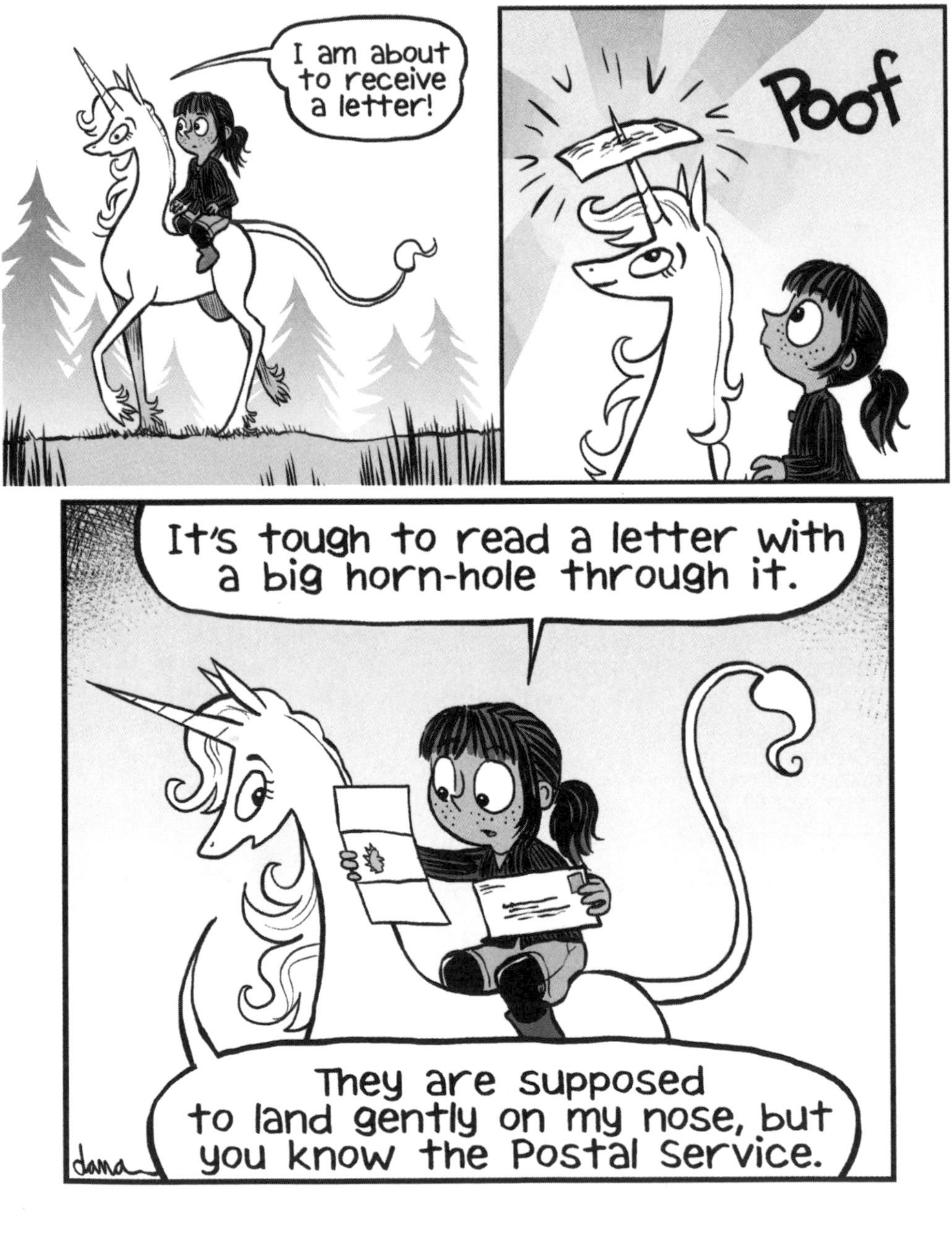
I am about to receive a letter!
Poof
It's tough to read a letter with a big horn-hole through it.
They are supposed to land gently on my nose, but you know the Postal Service.
dana

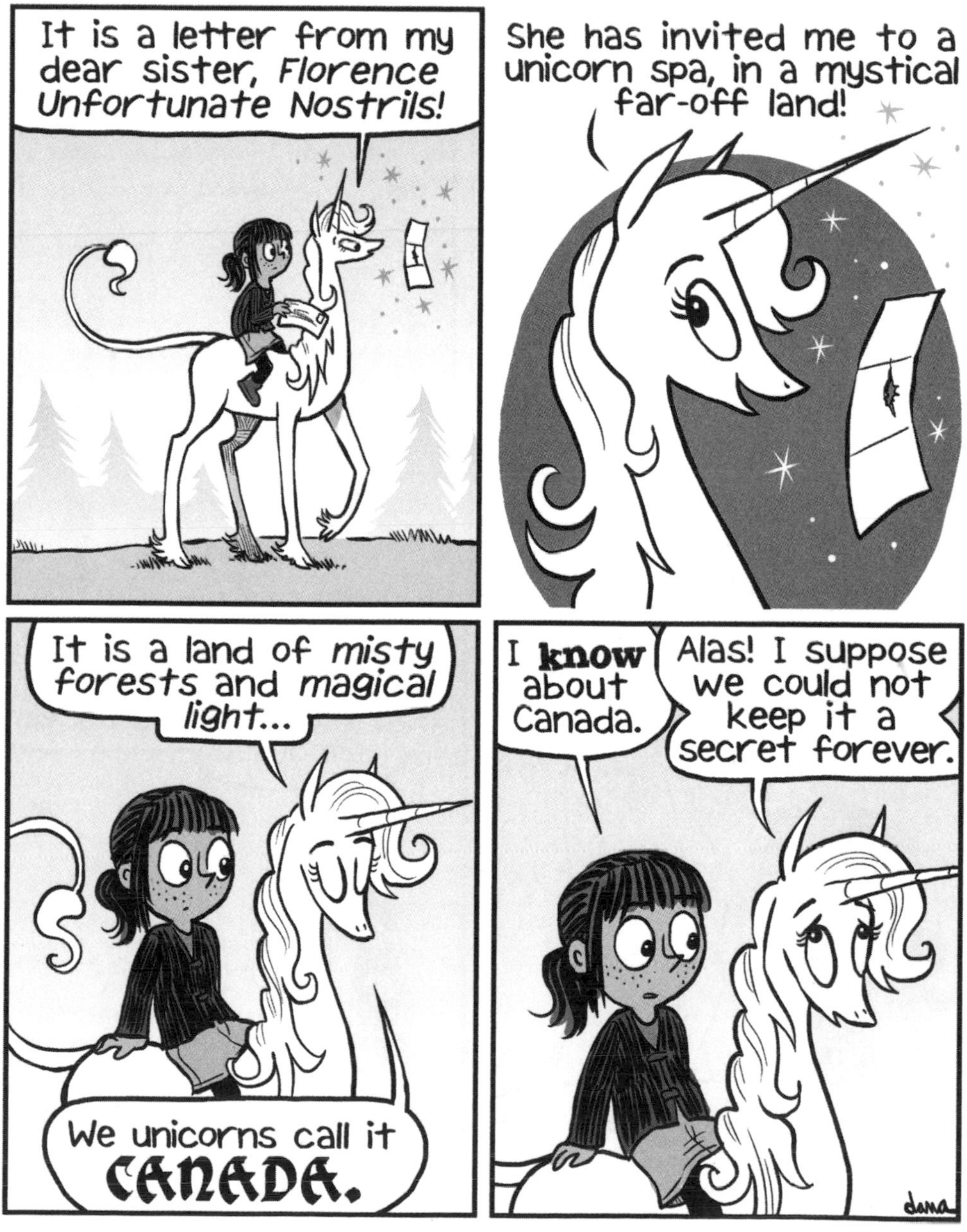

It is a letter from my dear sister, *Florence Unfortunate Nostrils!*
She has invited me to a unicorn spa, in a mystical far-off land!
It is a land of *misty forests* and *magical light...*
We unicorns call it
CANADA.
I **know** about Canada.
Alas! I suppose we could not keep it a secret forever.
dana

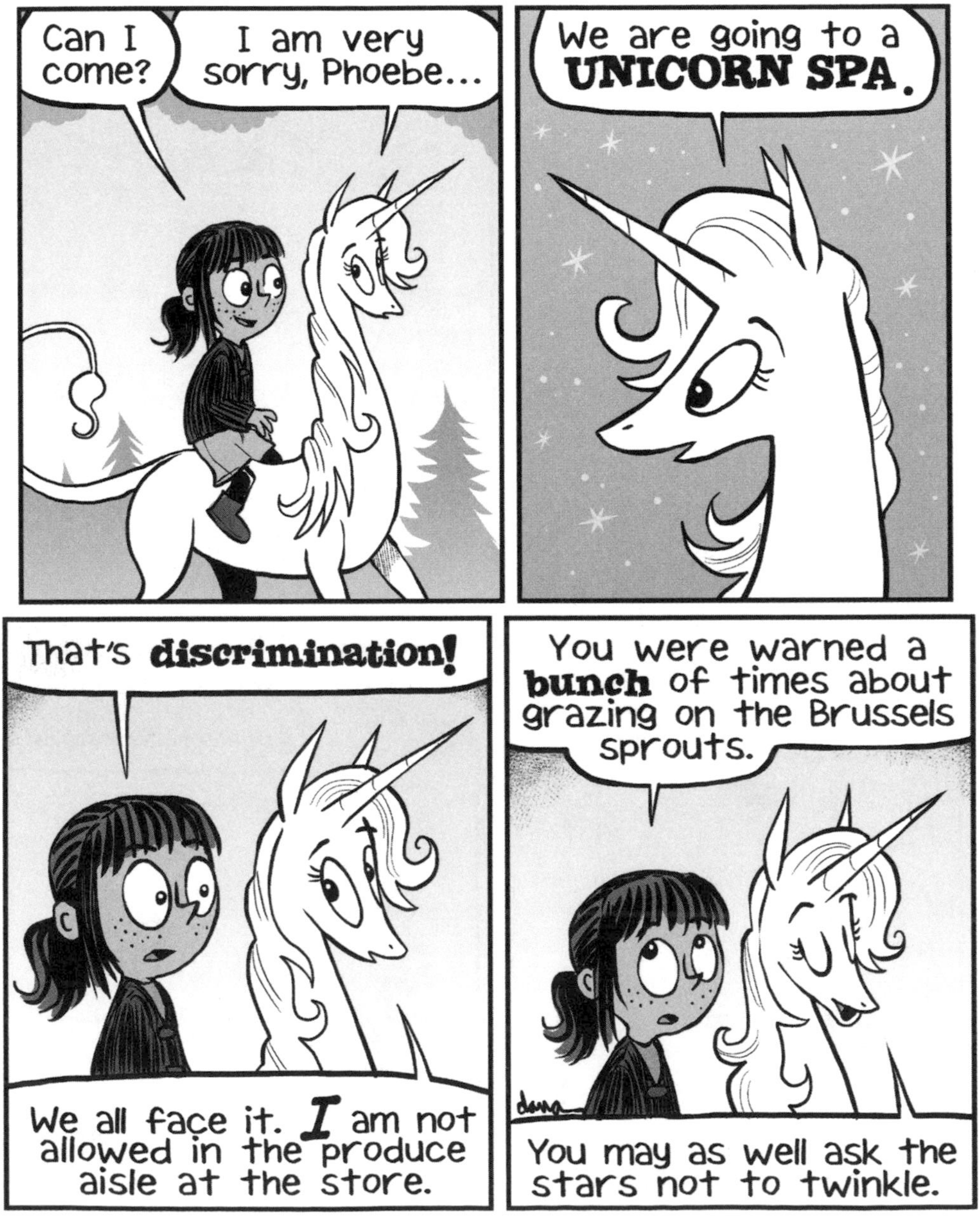
Can I come?
I am very sorry, Phoebe...
We are going to a UNICORN SPA.
That's **discrimination!**
We all face it. *I* am not allowed in the produce aisle at the store.
You were warned a **bunch** of times about grazing on the Brussels sprouts.
You may as well ask the stars not to twinkle.
dana

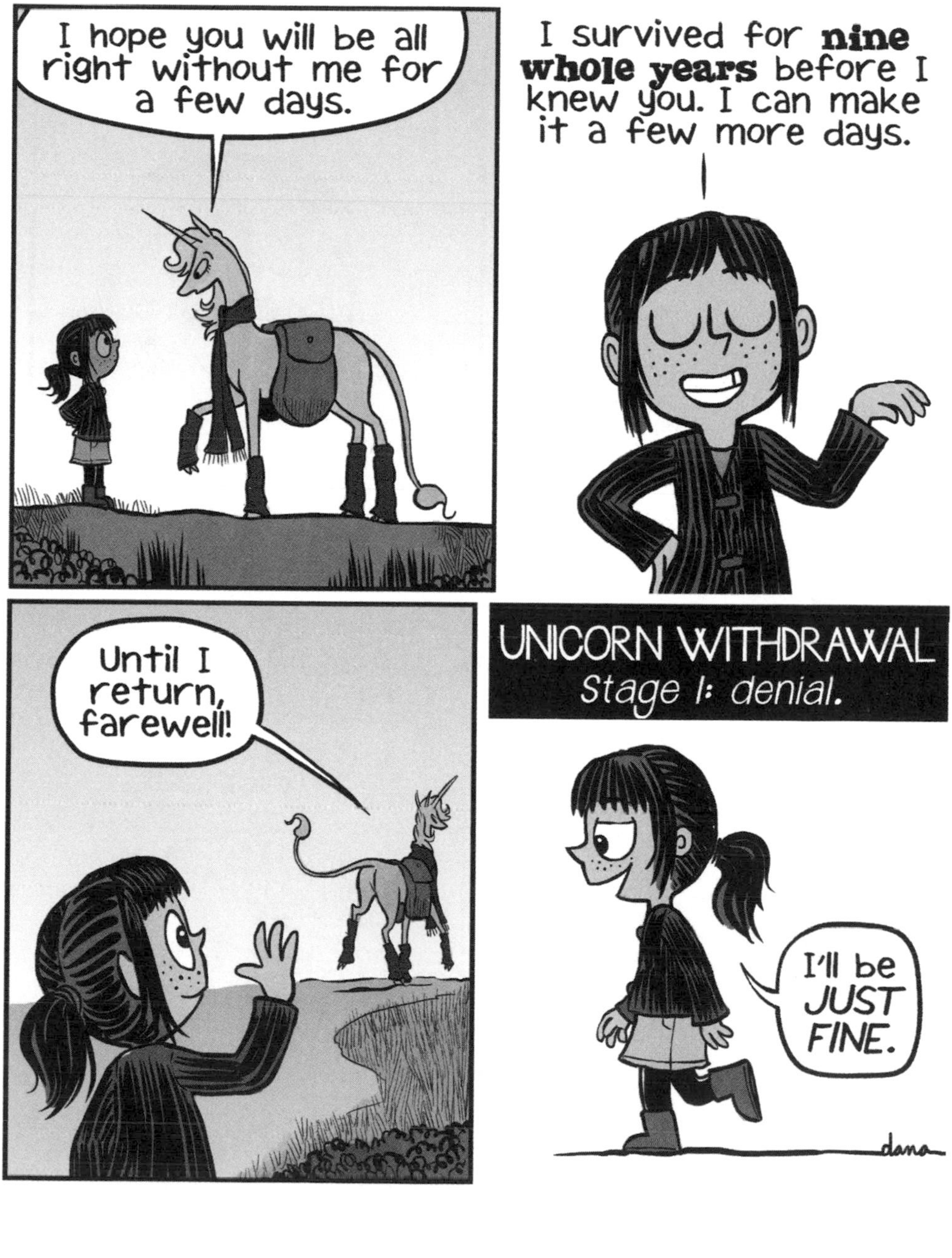
I hope you will be all right without me for a few days.
I survived for **nine whole years** before I knew you. I can make it a few more days.
Until I return, farewell!
UNICORN WITHDRAWAL
Stage 1: denial.
I'll be JUST FINE.
dana

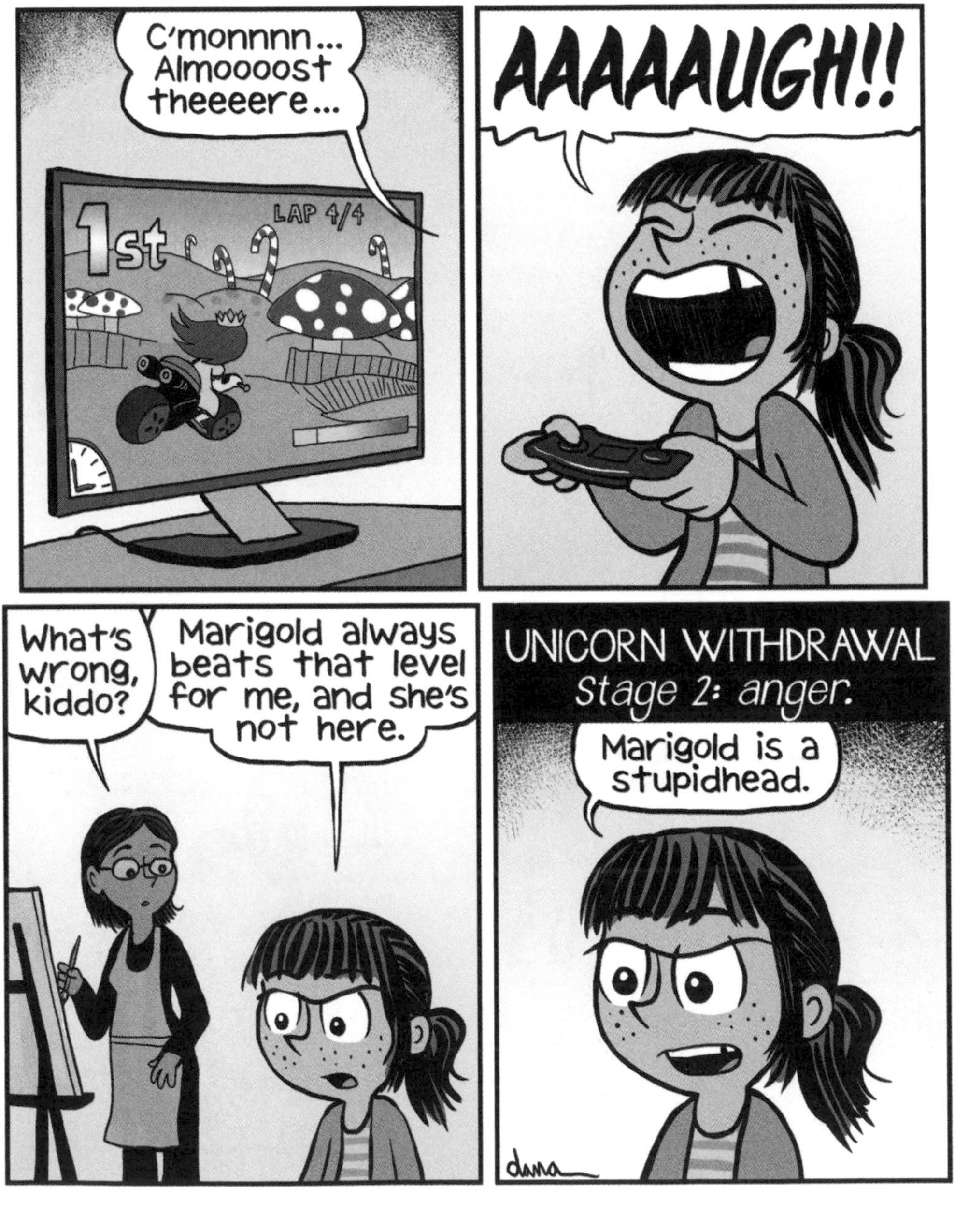

C'monnnn... Almoooost theeeere...
1st
LAP 4/4
AAAAAUGH!!
What's wrong, kiddo?
Marigold always beats that level for me, and she's not here.
UNICORN WITHDRAWAL
Stage 2: anger.
Marigold is a stupidhead.
dana

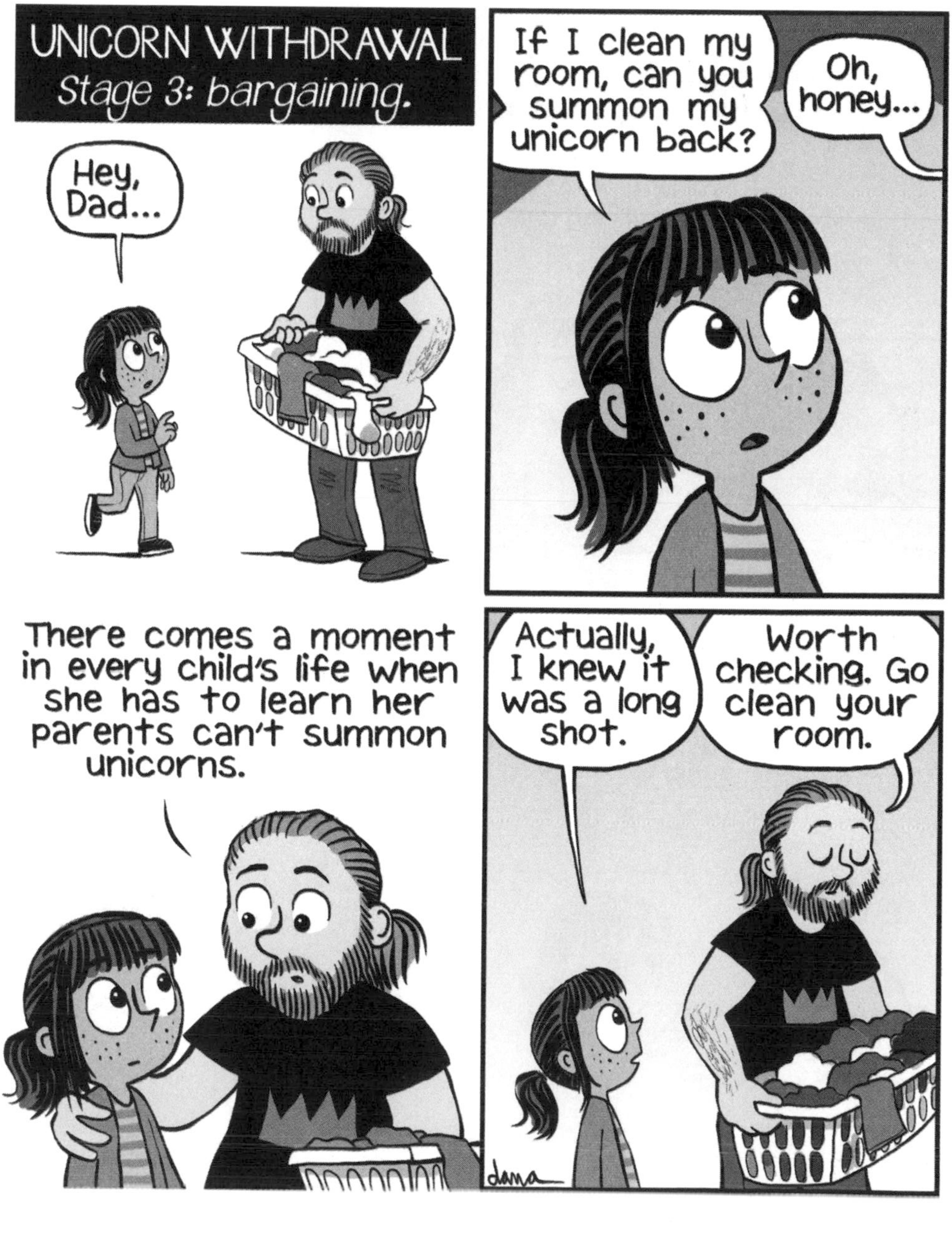
UNICORN WITHDRAWAL
Stage 3: bargaining.
Hey, Dad...
If I clean my room, can you summon my unicorn back?
Oh, honey...
There comes a moment in every child's life when she has to learn her parents can't summon unicorns.
Actually, I knew it was a long shot.
Worth checking. Go clean your room.
dana

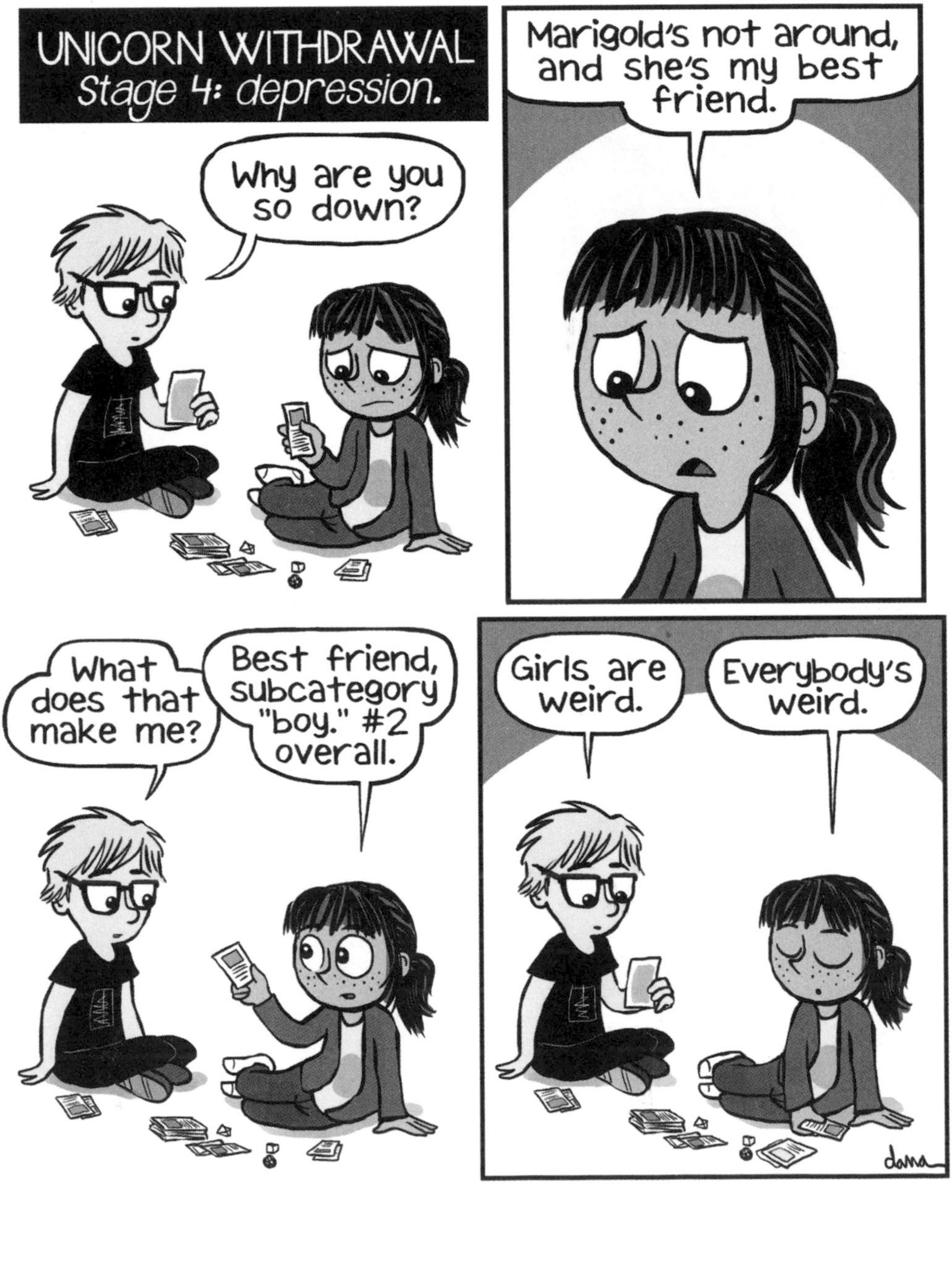
UNICORN WITHDRAWAL
Stage 4: depression.
Why are you so down?
Marigold's not around, and she's my best friend.
What does that make me?
Best friend, subcategory "boy." #2 overall.
Girls are weird.
Everybody's weird.
dana

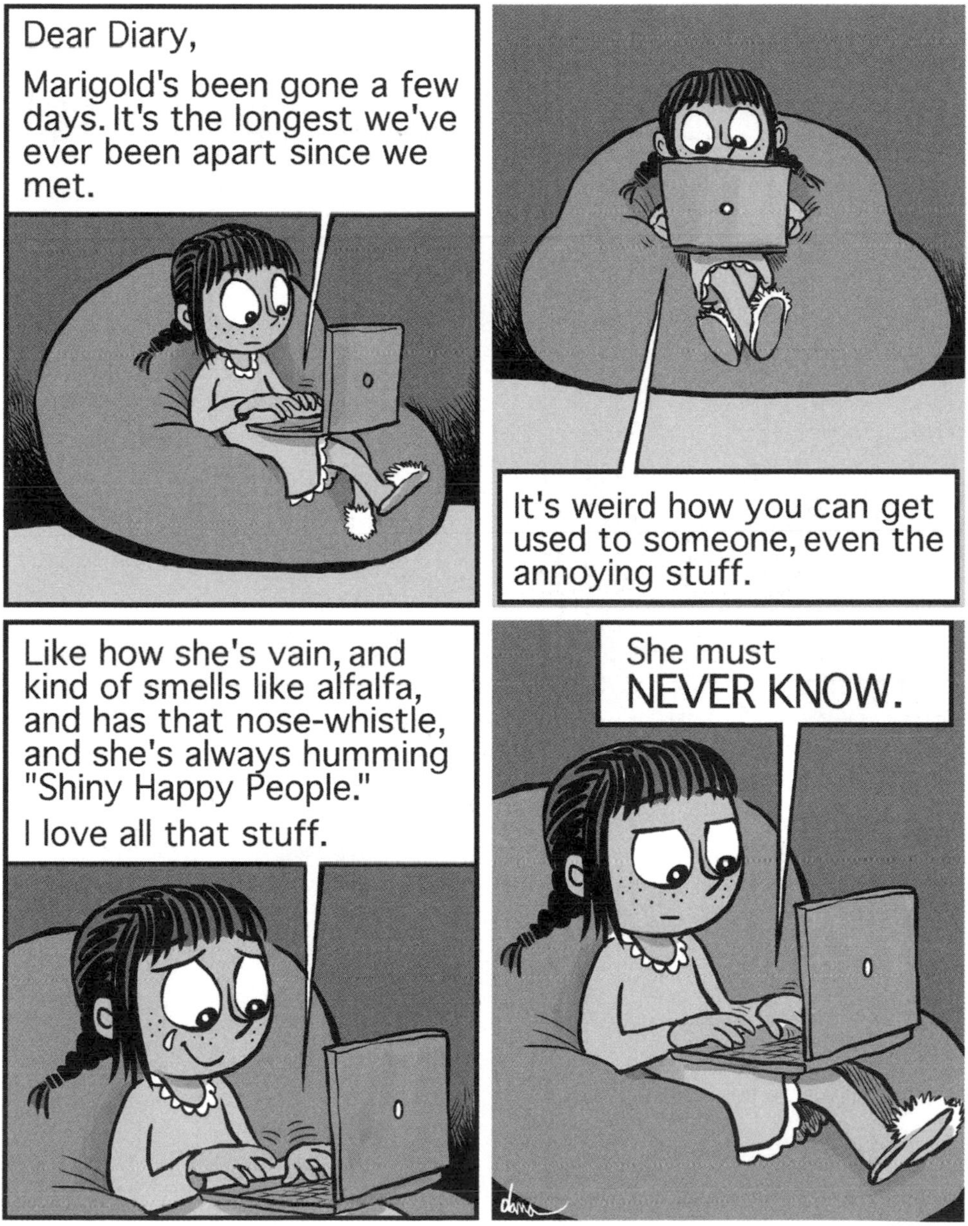
Dear Diary,
Marigold's been gone a few days. It's the longest we've ever been apart since we met.
It's weird how you can get used to someone, even the annoying stuff.
Like how she's vain, and kind of smells like alfalfa, and has that nose-whistle, and she's always humming "Shiny Happy People."
I love all that stuff.
She must
NEVER KNOW.

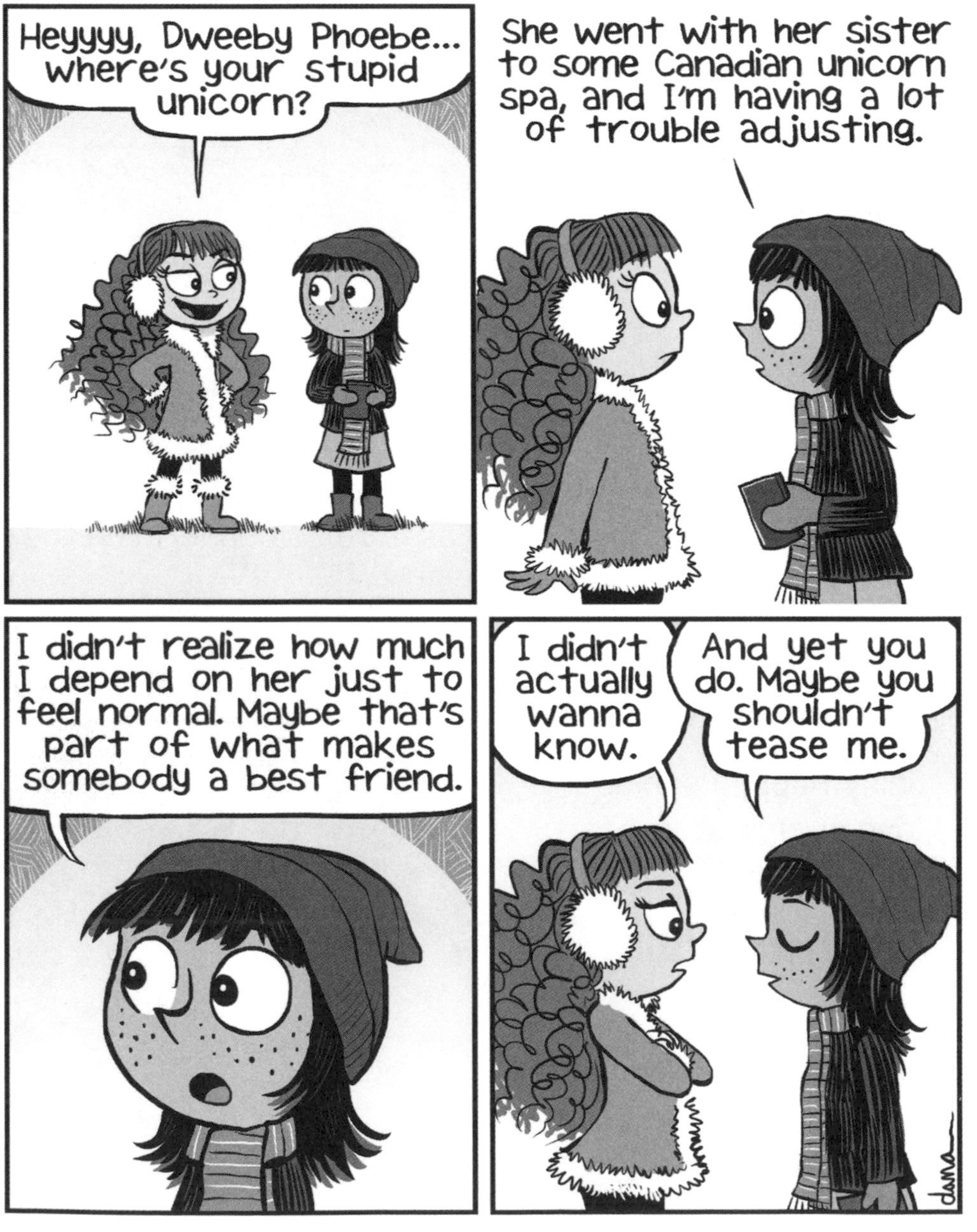
Heyyyy, Dweeby Phoebe... where's your stupid unicorn?
She went with her sister to some Canadian unicorn spa, and I'm having a lot of trouble adjusting.
I didn't realize how much I depend on her just to feel normal. Maybe that's part of what makes somebody a best friend.
I didn't actually wanna know.
And yet you do. Maybe you shouldn't tease me.
dana

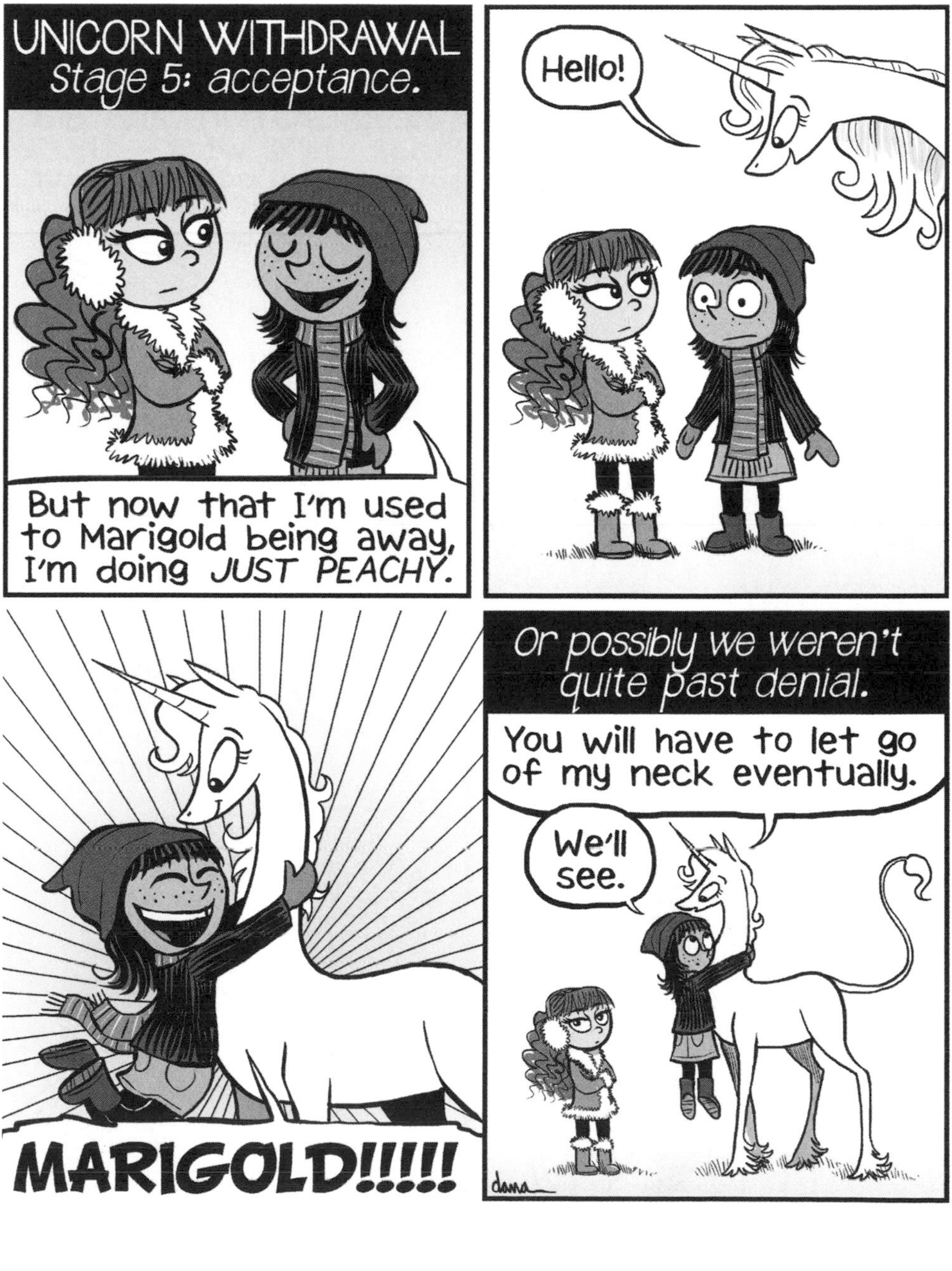
UNICORN WITHDRAWAL
Stage 5: acceptance.
But now that I'm used to Marigold being away, I'm doing JUST PEACHY.
Hello!
MARIGOLD!!!!!
Or possibly we weren't quite past denial.
You will have to let go of my neck eventually.
We'll see.
dana

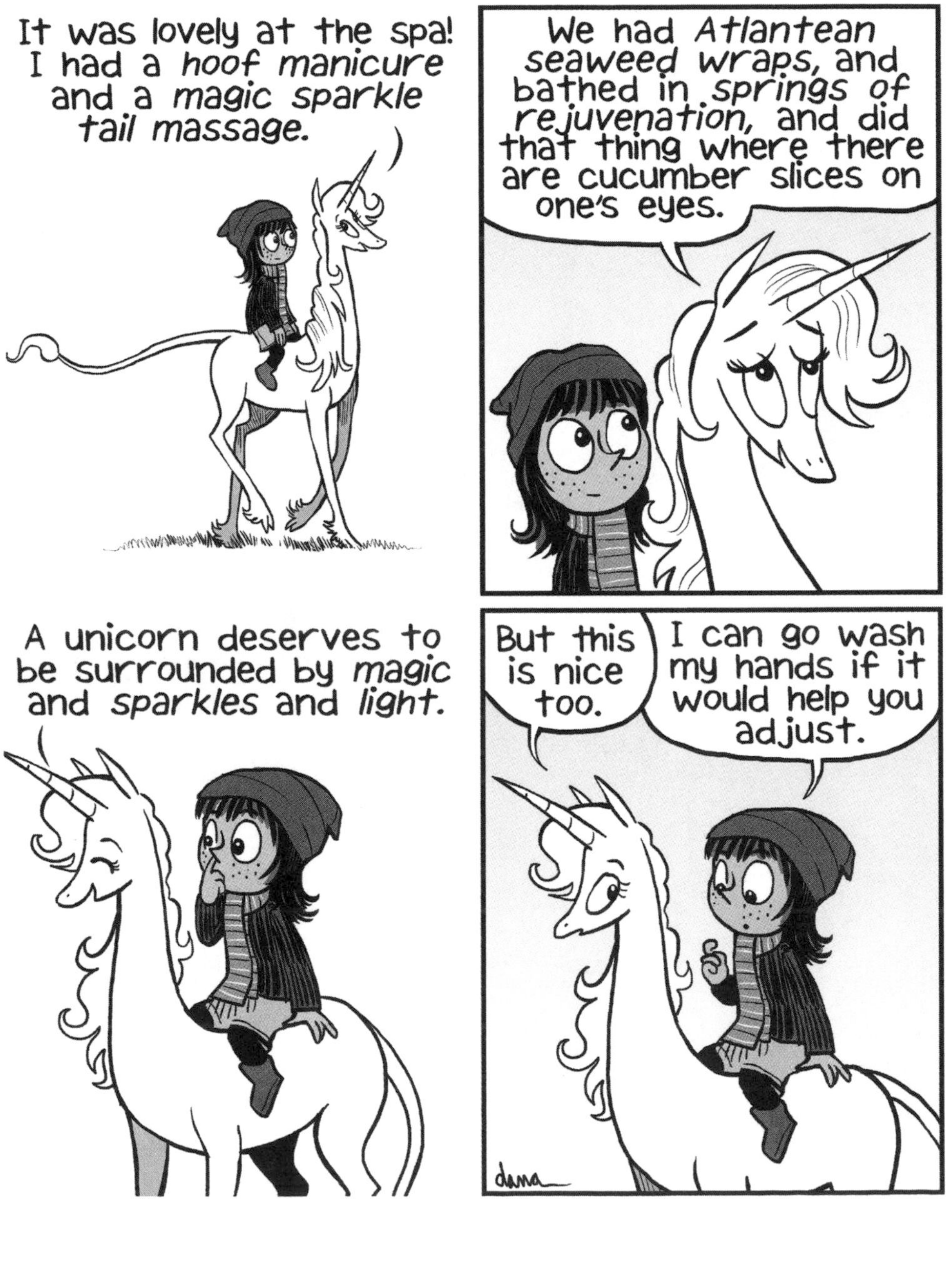
It was lovely at the spa! I had a *hoof manicure* and a *magic sparkle tail massage.*
We had *Atlantean seaweed wraps,* and bathed in *springs of rejuvenation,* and did that thing where there are cucumber slices on one's eyes.
A unicorn deserves to be surrounded by *magic* and *sparkles* and *light.*
But this is nice too.
I can go wash my hands if it would help you adjust.
dana

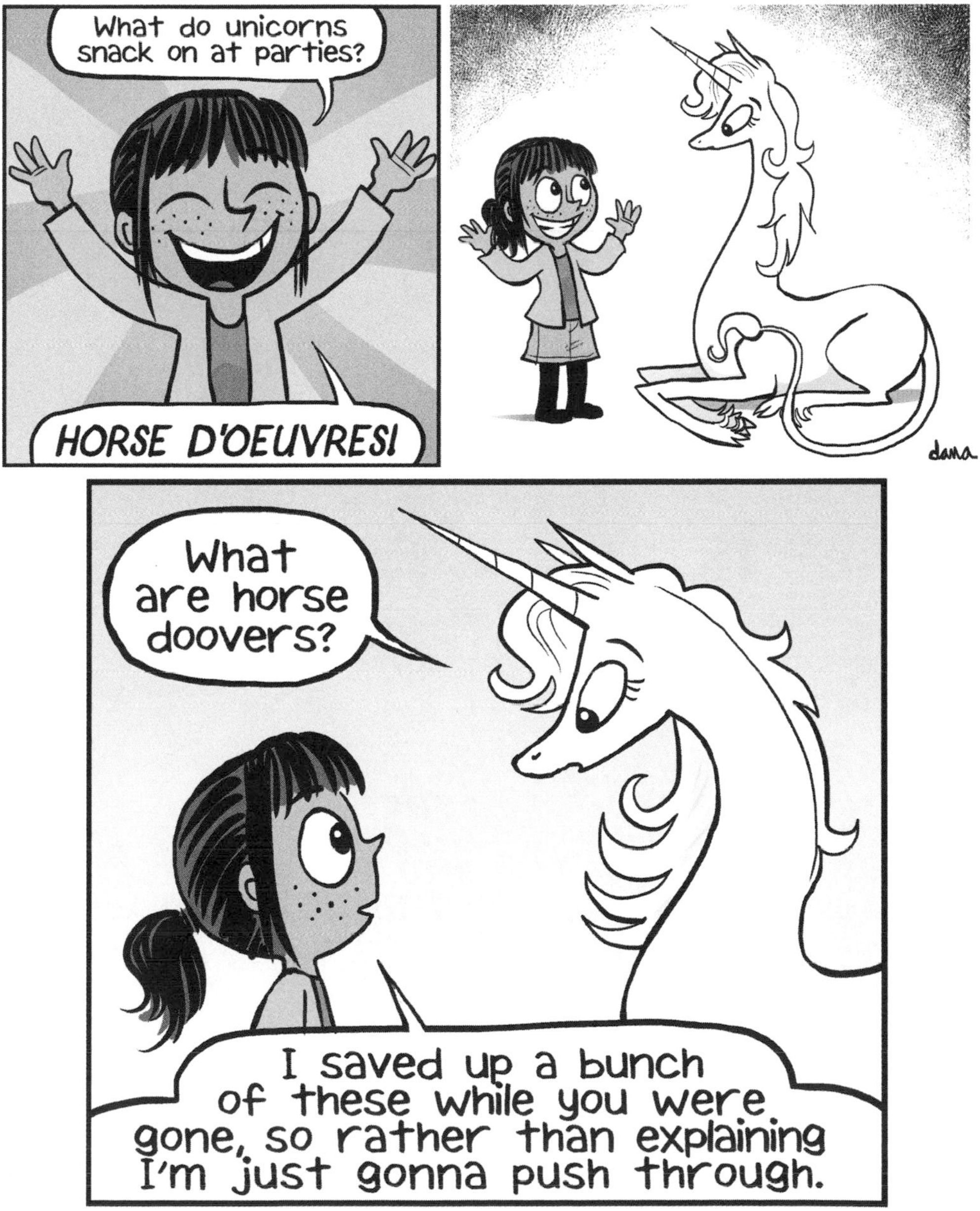
What do unicorns snack on at parties?
HORSE D'OEUVRES!
dana
What are horse doovers?
I saved up a bunch of these while you were gone, so rather than explaining I'm just gonna push through.

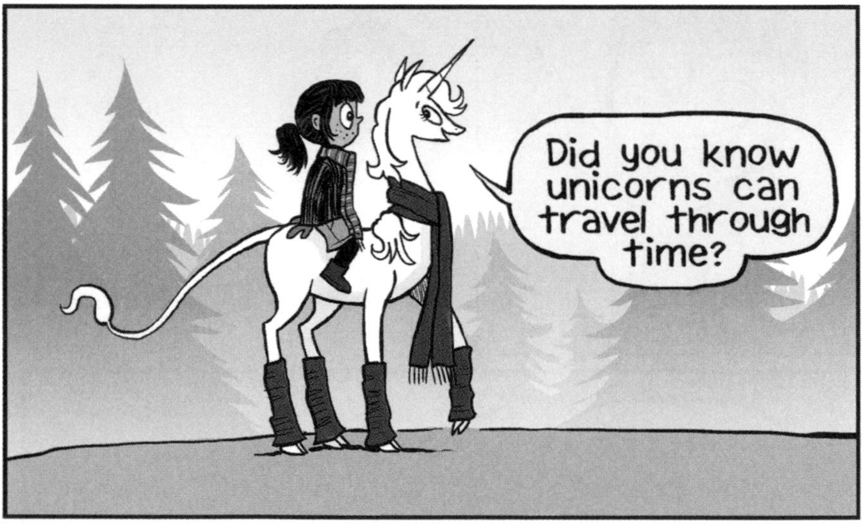
Did you know unicorns can travel through time?

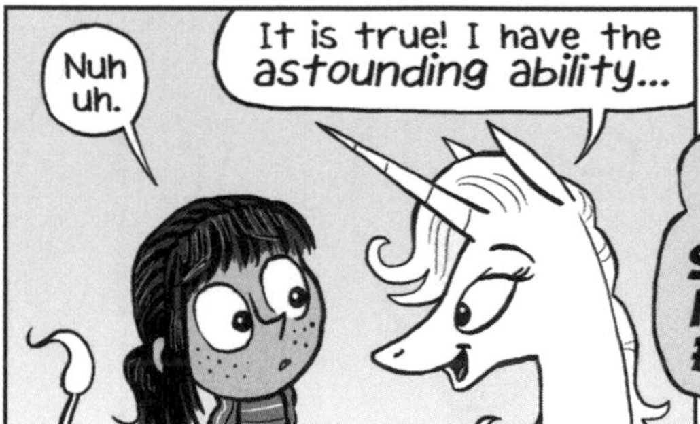
Nuh uh.
It is true! I have the astounding ability...

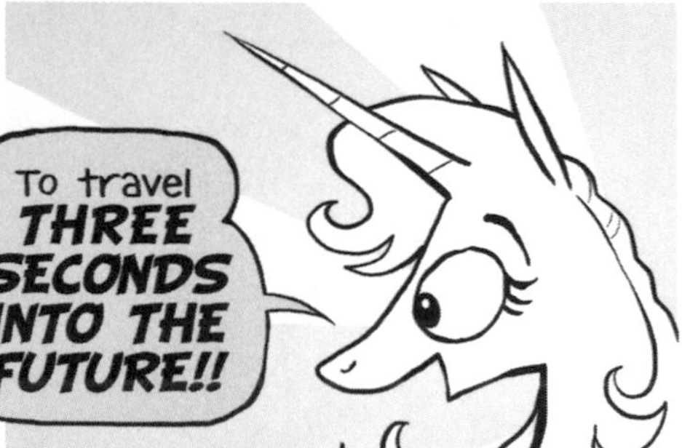
To travel THREE SECONDS INTO THE FUTURE!!

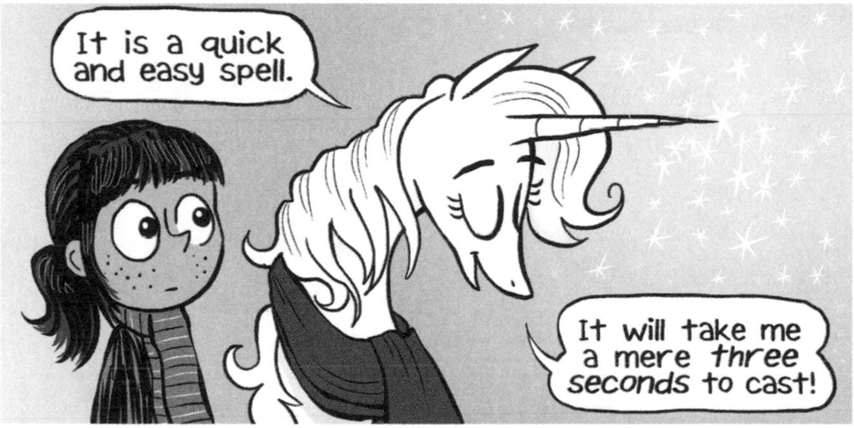
It is a quick and easy spell.
It will take me a mere *three seconds* to cast!

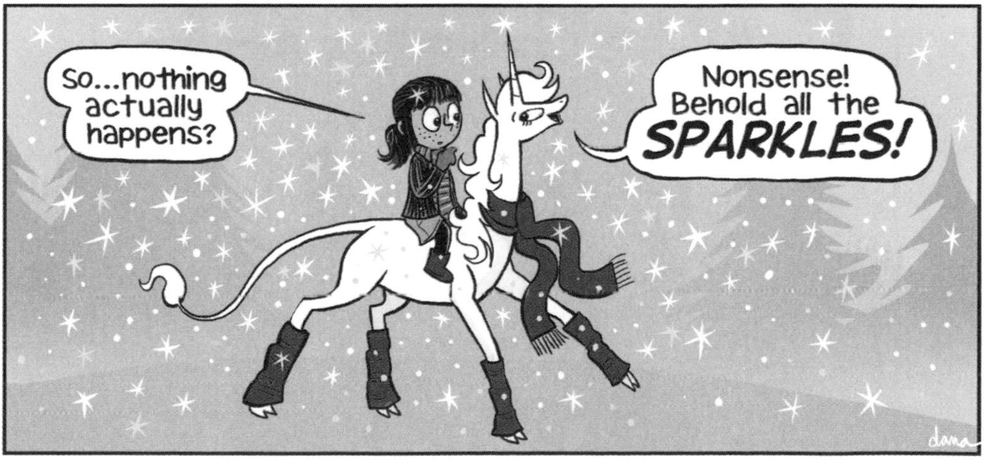
So...nothing actually happens?
Nonsense! Behold all the **SPARKLES!**
dana

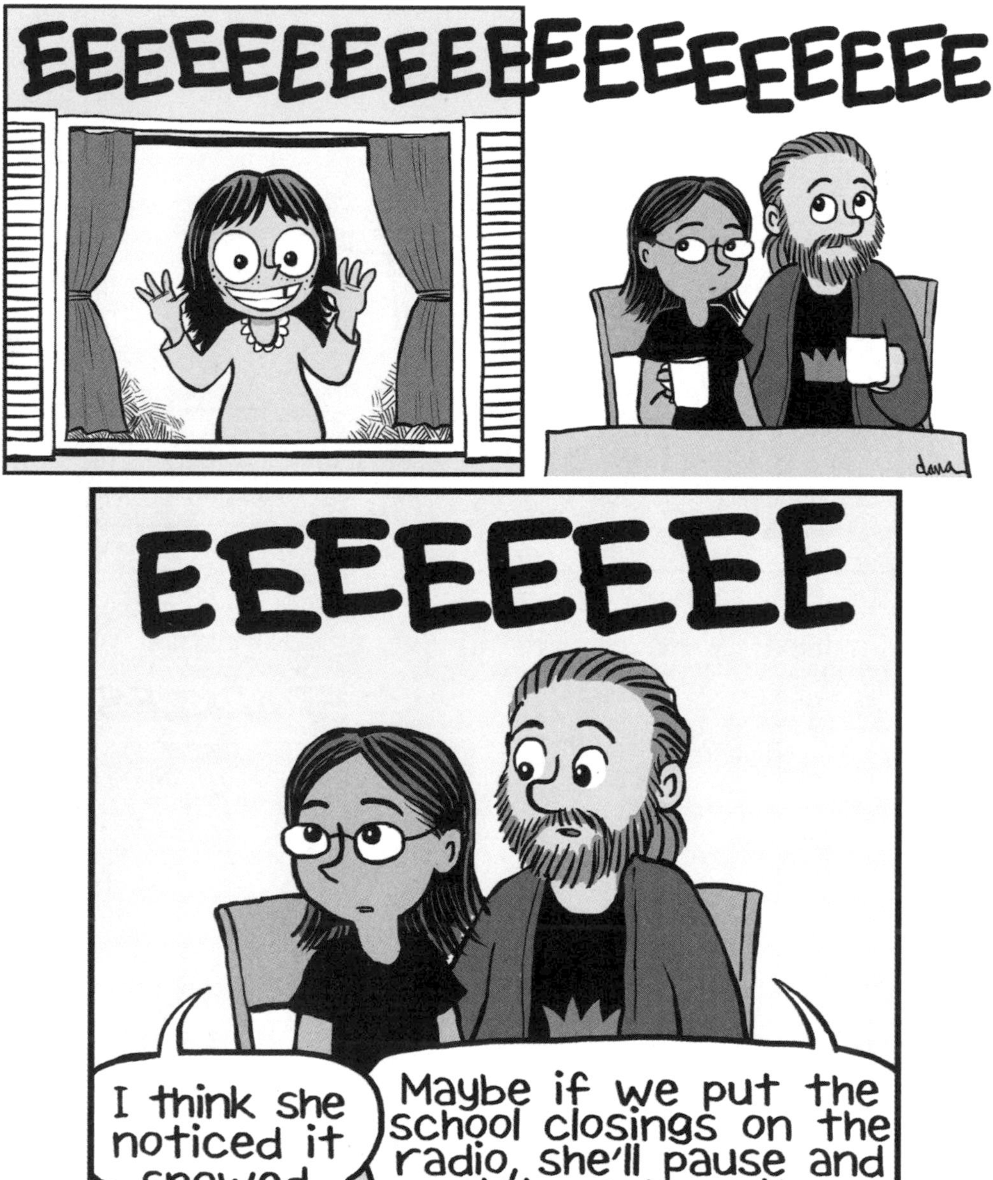
EEEEEEEEEEEEEEEEEEEE
dana
EEEEEEEEE
I think she noticed it snowed.
Maybe if we put the school closings on the radio, she'll pause and take a breath.

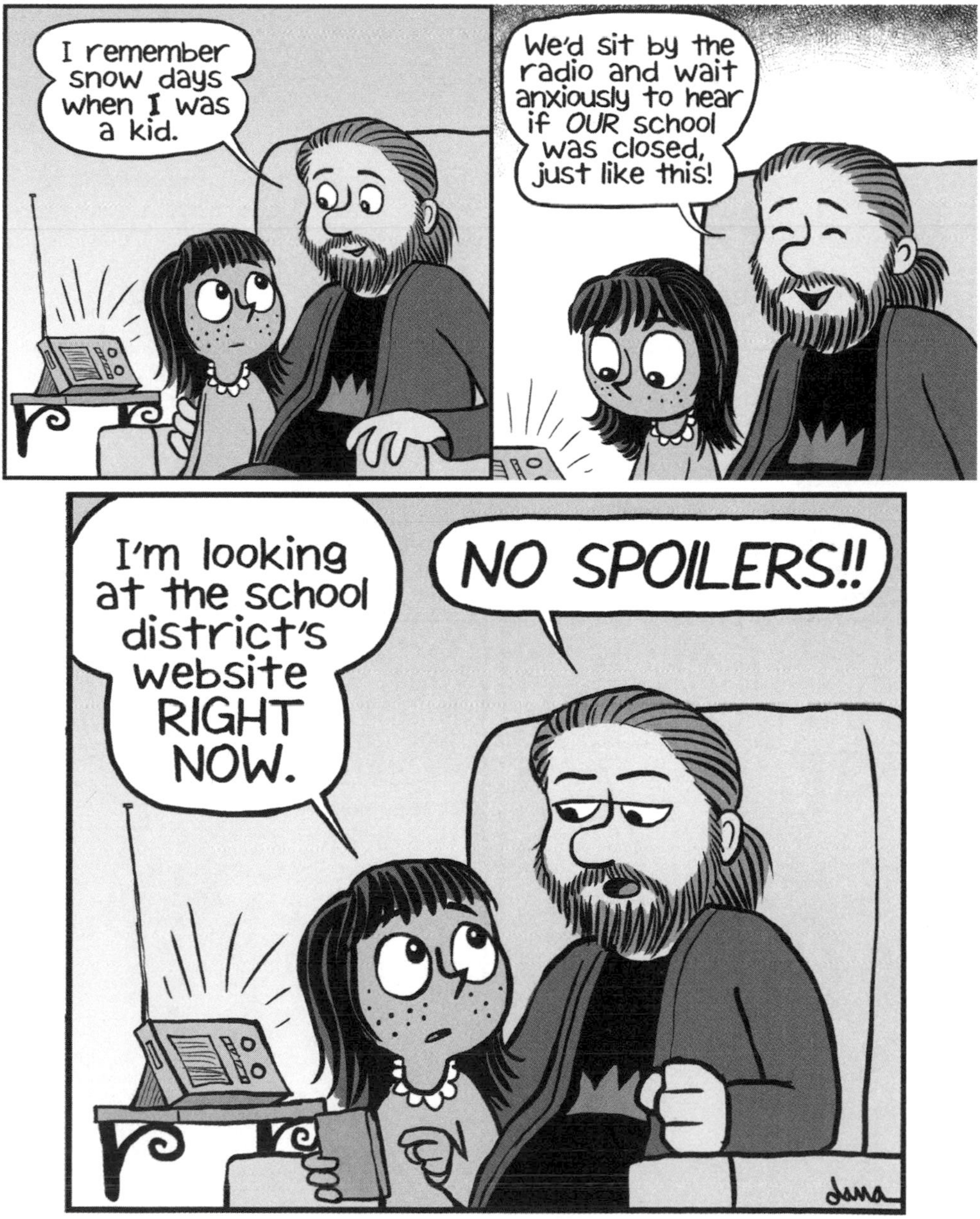

I remember snow days when I was a kid.
We'd sit by the radio and wait anxiously to hear if OUR school was closed, just like this!
I'm looking at the school district's website RIGHT NOW.
NO SPOILERS!!
dana

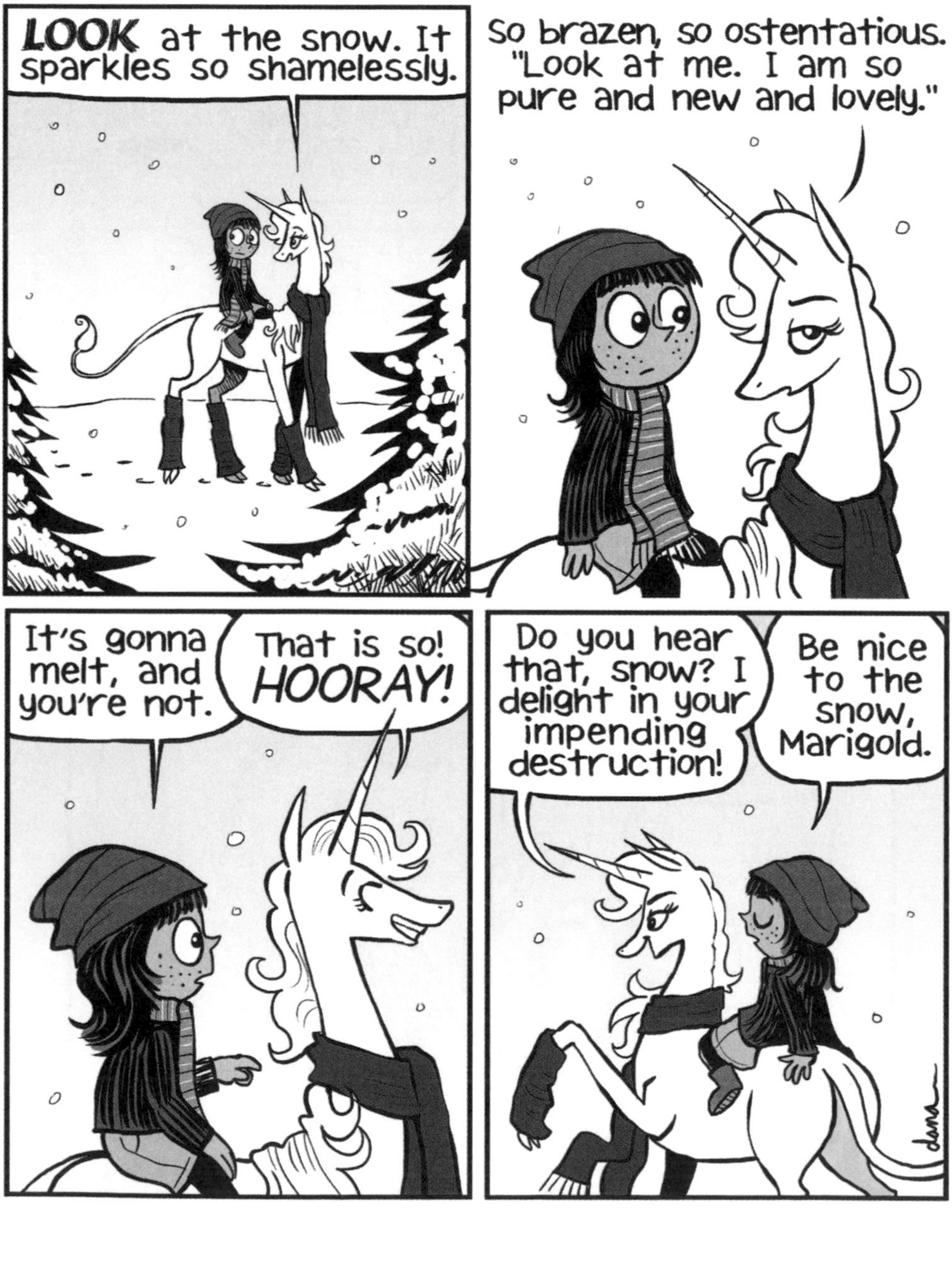
LOOK at the snow. It sparkles so shamelessly.
So brazen, so ostentatious. "Look at me. I am so pure and new and lovely."
It's gonna melt, and you're not.
That is so! HOORAY!
Do you hear that, snow? I delight in your impending destruction!
Be nice to the snow, Marigold.
dana

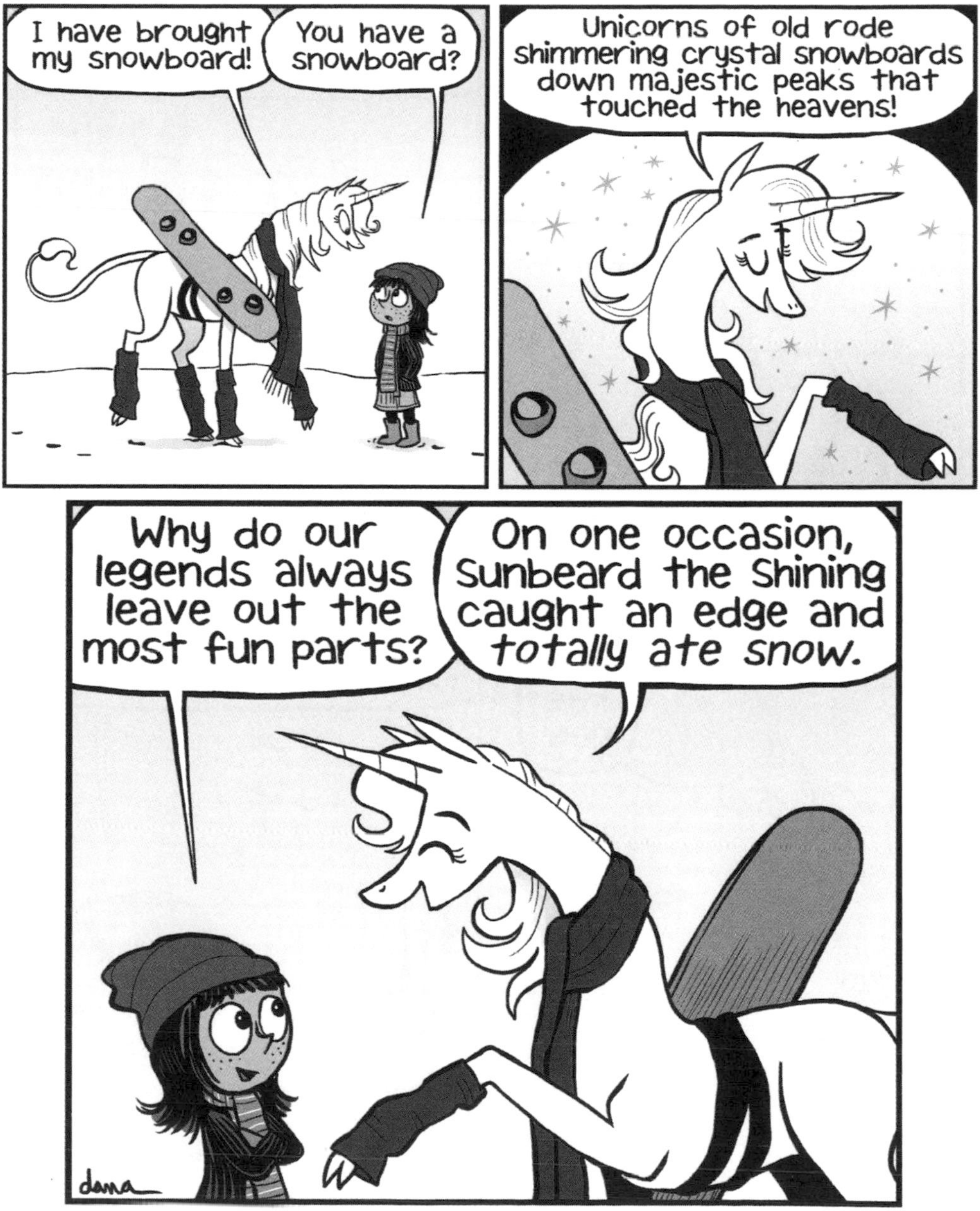
I have brought my snowboard!
You have a snowboard?
Unicorns of old rode shimmering crystal snowboards down majestic peaks that touched the heavens!
Why do our legends always leave out the most fun parts?
On one occasion, Sunbeard the Shining caught an edge and *totally* ate snow.
dana

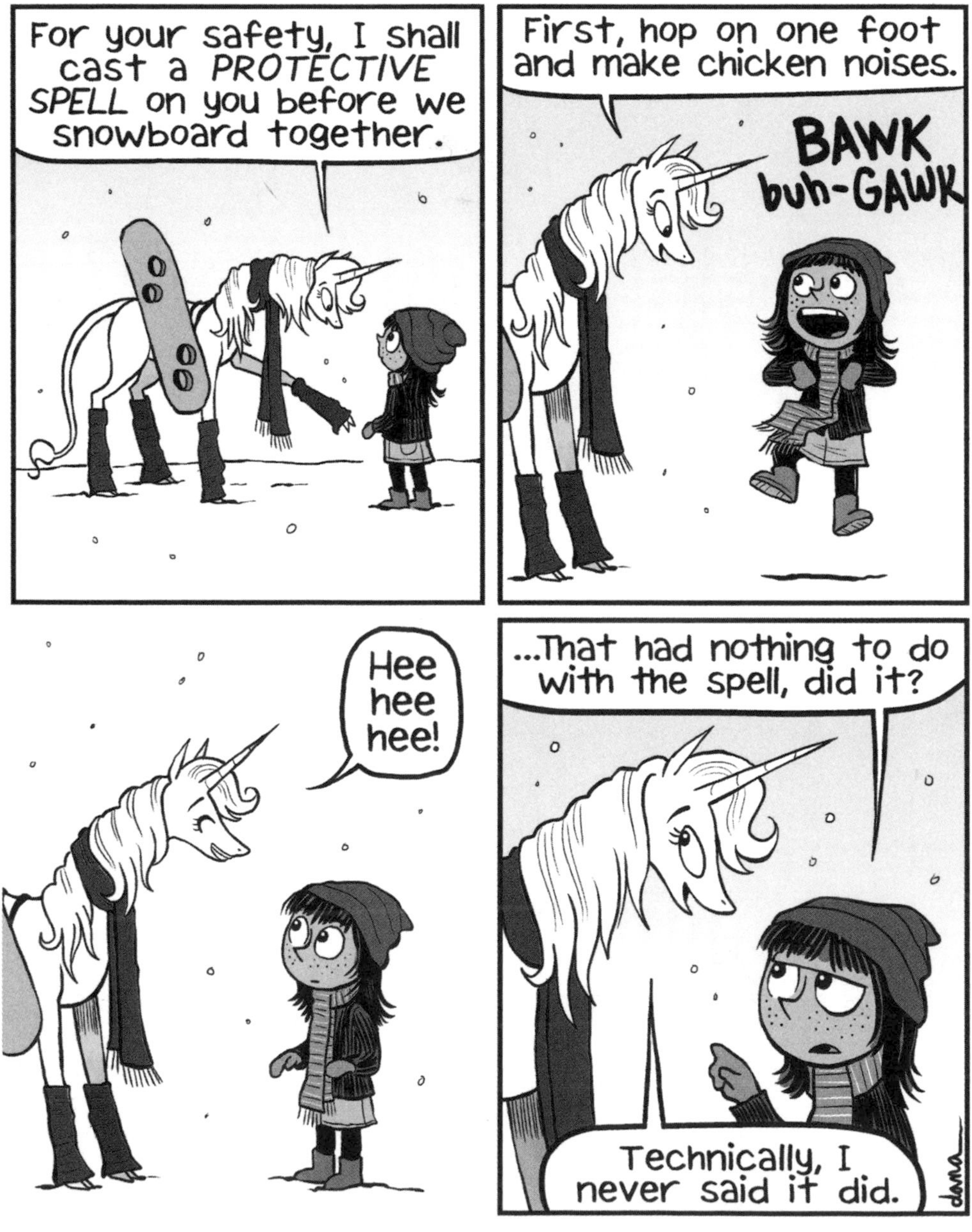
For your safety, I shall cast a *PROTECTIVE SPELL* on you before we snowboard together.
First, hop on one foot and make chicken noises.
BAWK buh-GAWK
Hee hee hee!
...That had nothing to do with the spell, did it?
Technically, I never said it did.
dana

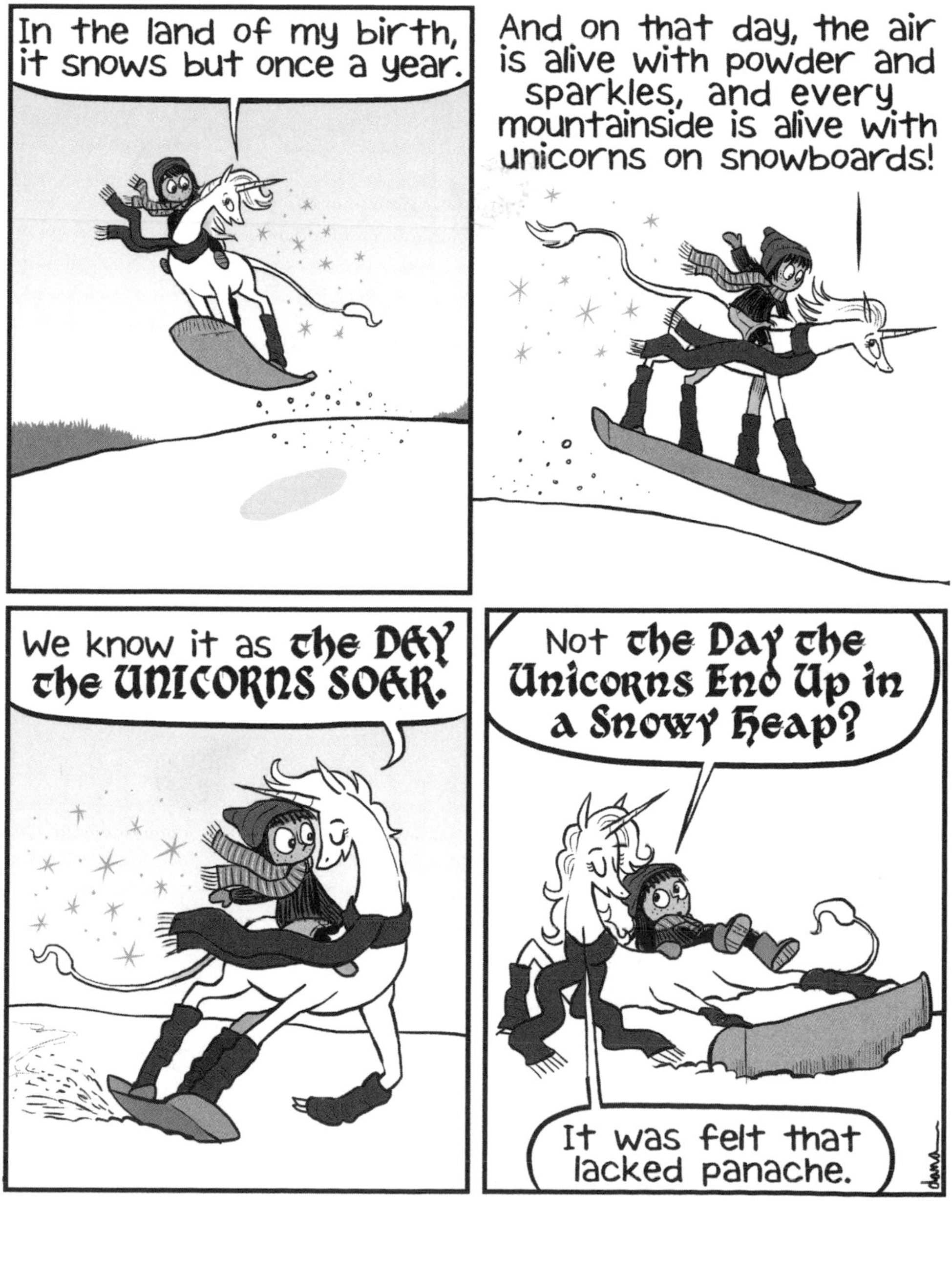
In the land of my birth, it snows but once a year.
And on that day, the air is alive with powder and sparkles, and every mountainside is alive with unicorns on snowboards!
We know it as the DAY the UNICORNS SOAR.
Not the Day the Unicorns End Up in a Snowy Heap?
It was felt that lacked panache.

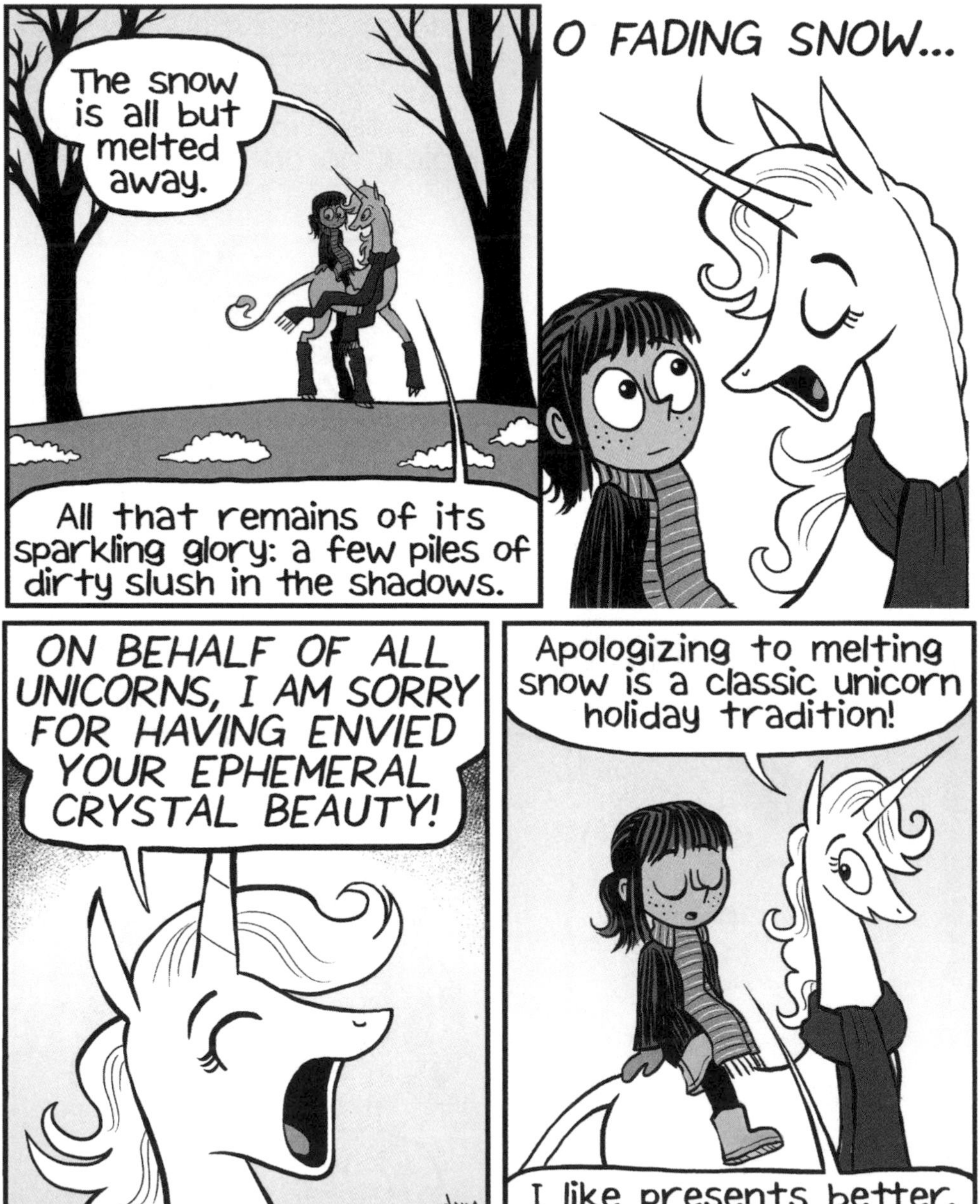

The snow is all but melted away.
All that remains of its sparkling glory: a few piles of dirty slush in the shadows.
O FADING SNOW...
ON BEHALF OF ALL UNICORNS, I AM SORRY FOR HAVING ENVIED YOUR EPHEMERAL CRYSTAL BEAUTY!
Apologizing to melting snow is a classic unicorn holiday tradition!
I like presents better.

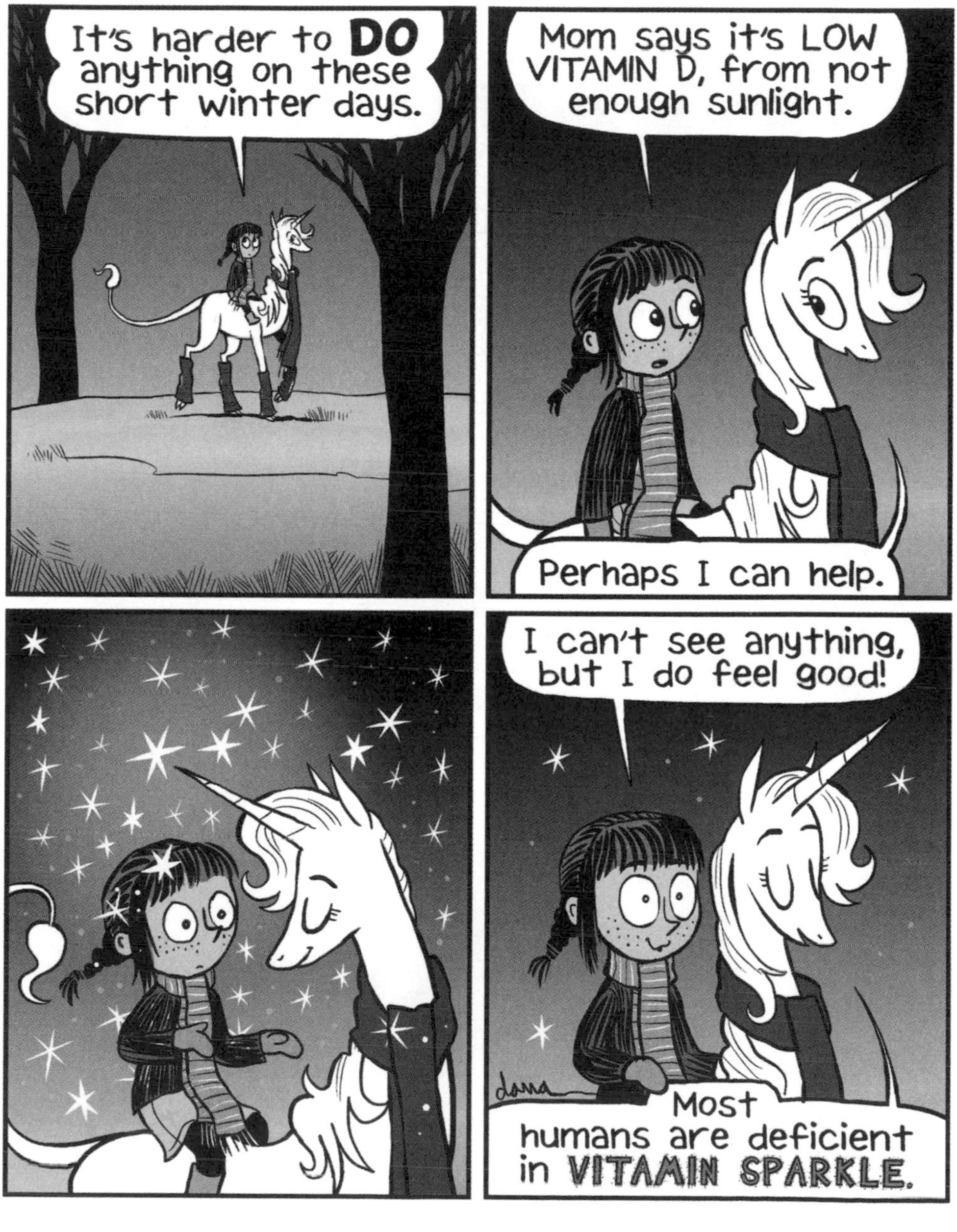
It's harder to DO anything on these short winter days.
Mom says it's LOW VITAMIN D, from not enough sunlight.
Perhaps I can help.
I can't see anything, but I do feel good!
Most humans are deficient in VITAMIN SPARKLE.
dana

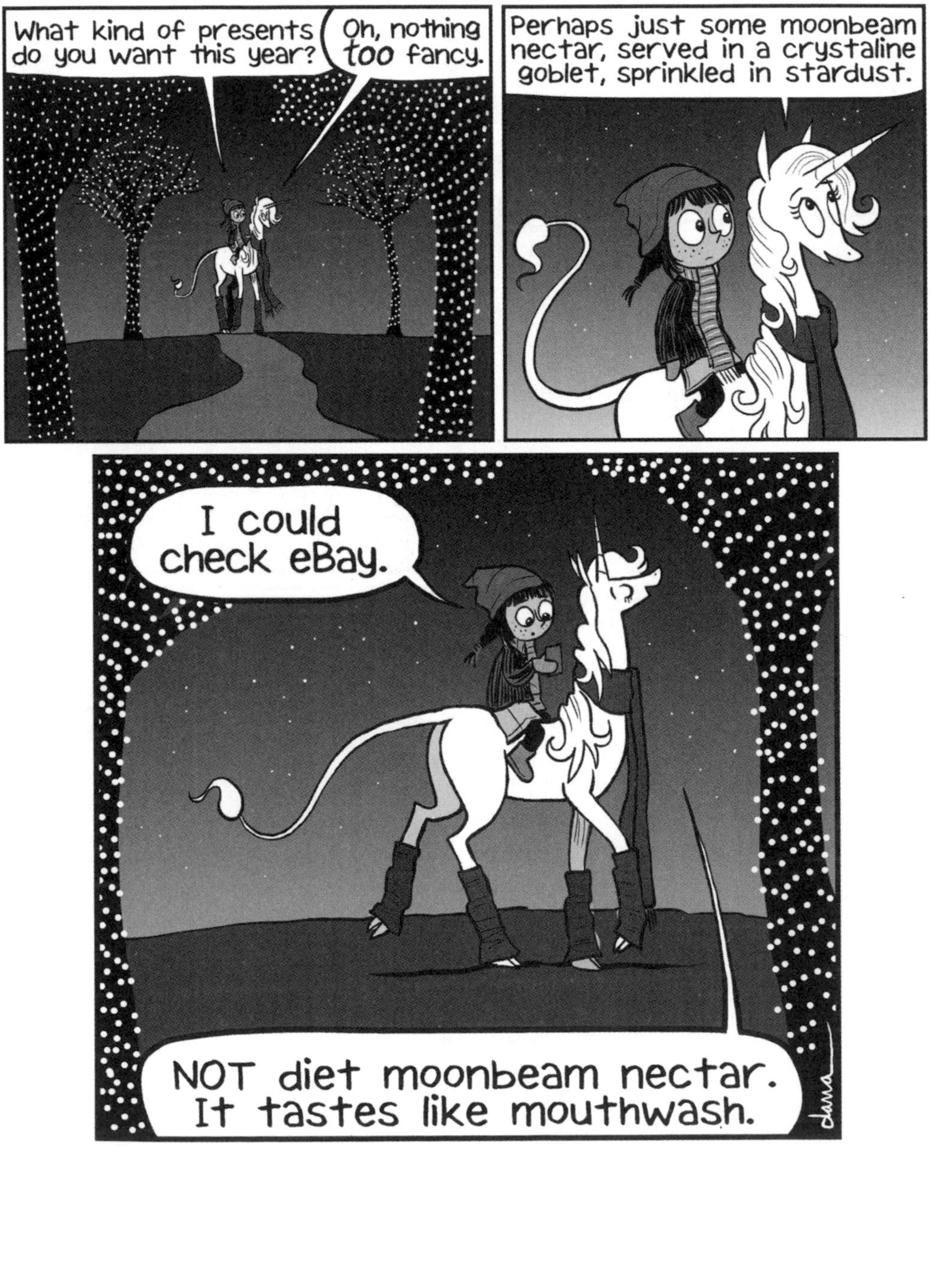
What kind of presents do you want this year?
Oh, nothing *too* fancy.
Perhaps just some moonbeam nectar, served in a crystaline goblet, sprinkled in stardust.
I could check eBay.
NOT diet moonbeam nectar. It tastes like mouthwash.
dana

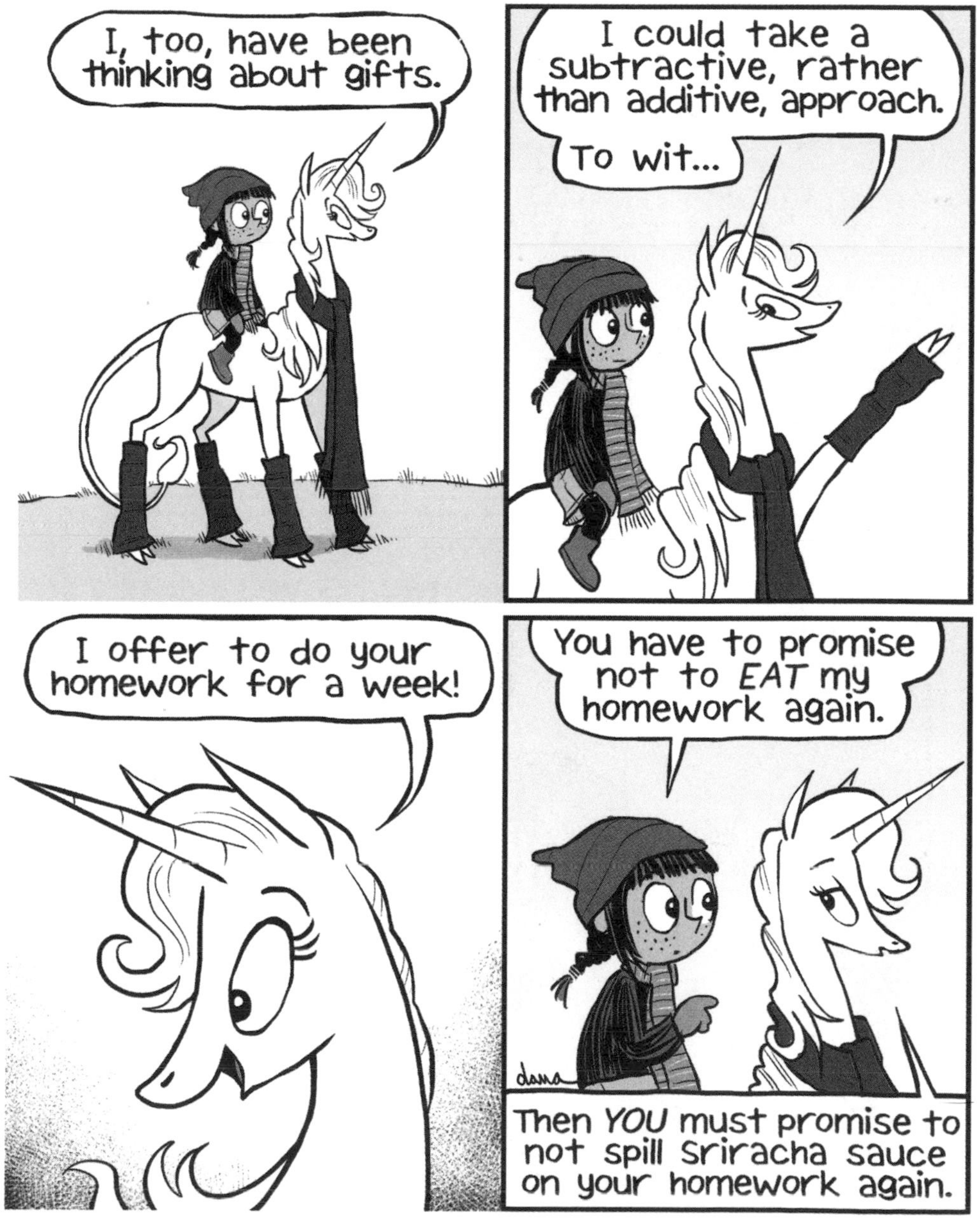
I, too, have been thinking about gifts.
I could take a subtractive, rather than additive, approach.
To wit...
I offer to do your homework for a week!
You have to promise not to *EAT* my homework again.
dana
Then *YOU* must promise to not spill Sriracha sauce on your homework again.

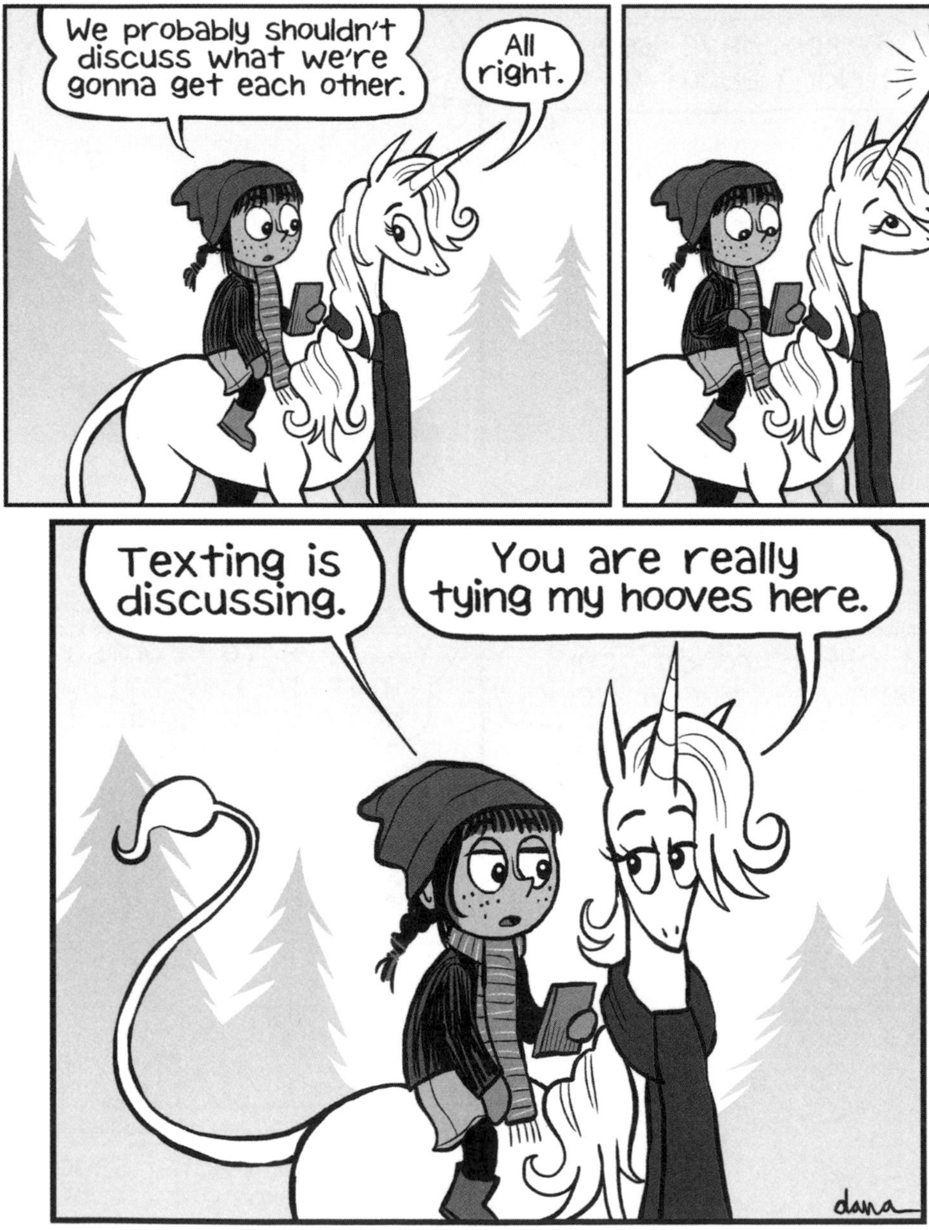
We probably shouldn't discuss what we're gonna get each other.
All right.
Texting is discussing.
You are really tying my hooves here.
dana

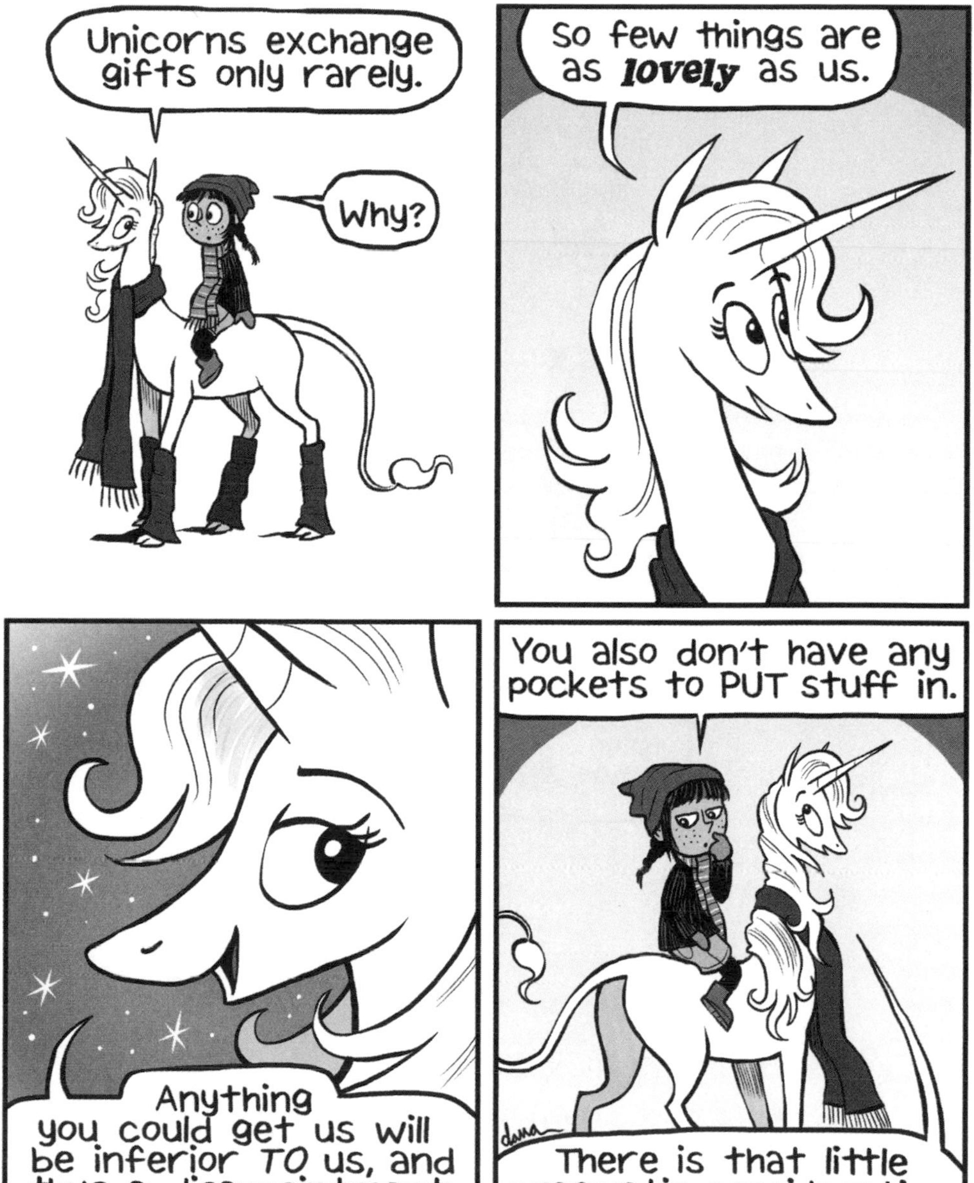
Unicorns exchange gifts only rarely.
Why?
So few things are as **lovely** as us.
Anything you could get us will be inferior *TO* us, and thus a disappointment.
You also don't have any pockets to PUT stuff in.
There is that little pragmatic consideration.
dana

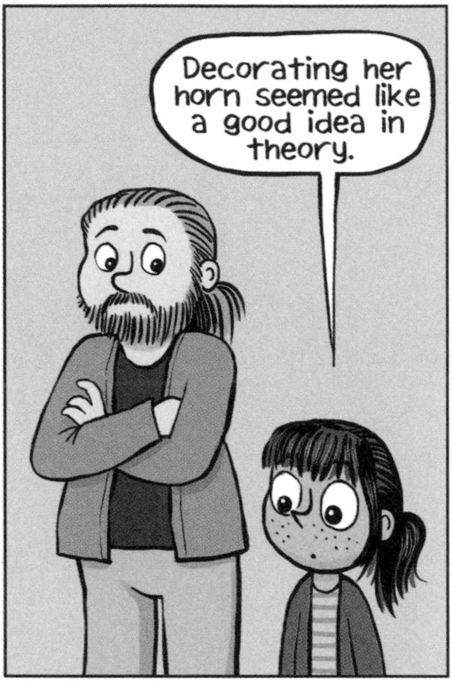
Decorating her horn seemed like a good idea in theory.

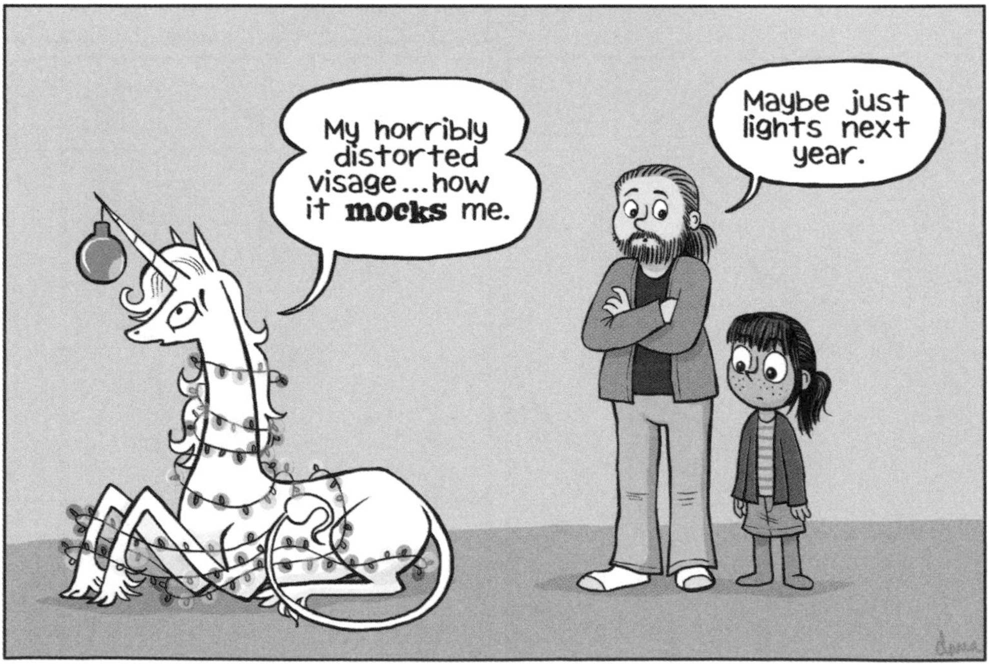
My horribly distorted visage...how it **mocks** me.
Maybe just lights next year.

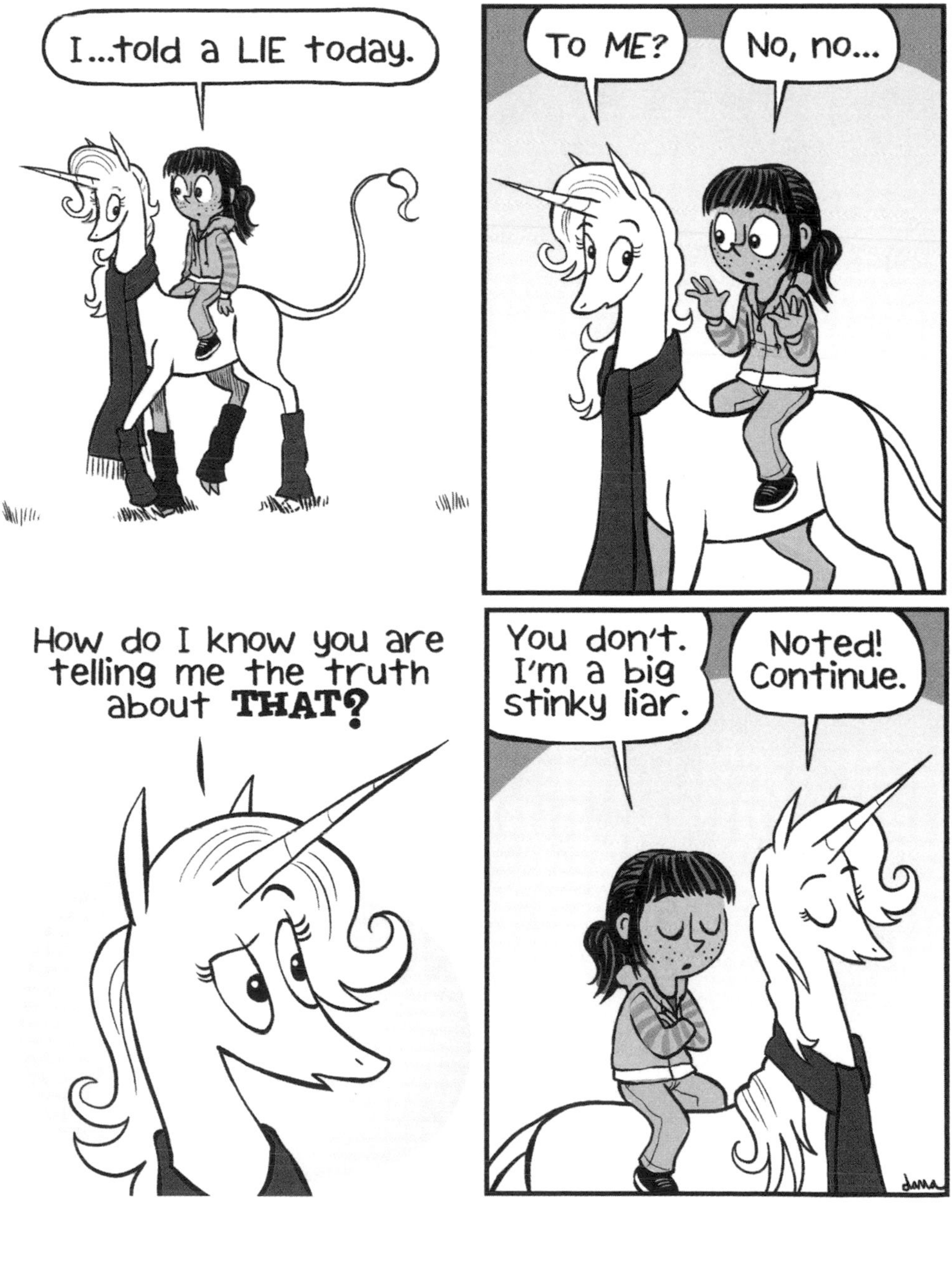
I...told a LIE today.
To ME?
No, no...
How do I know you are telling me the truth about THAT?
You don't. I'm a big stinky liar.
Noted! Continue.

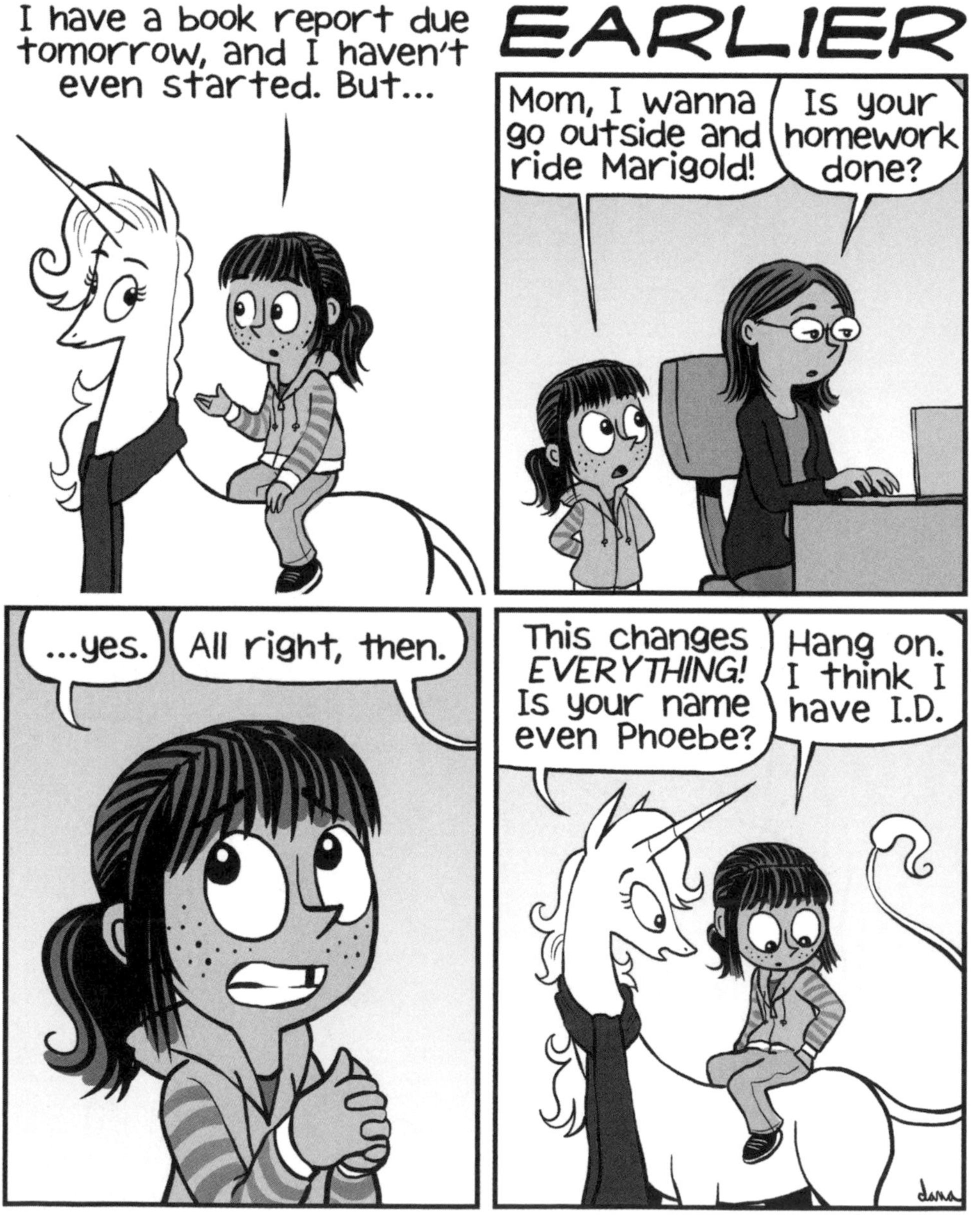

I have a book report due tomorrow, and I haven't even started. But...
EARLIER
Mom, I wanna go outside and ride Marigold!
Is your homework done?
...yes.
All right, then.
This changes *EVERYTHING!* Is your name even Phoebe?
Hang on. I think I have I.D.
dana

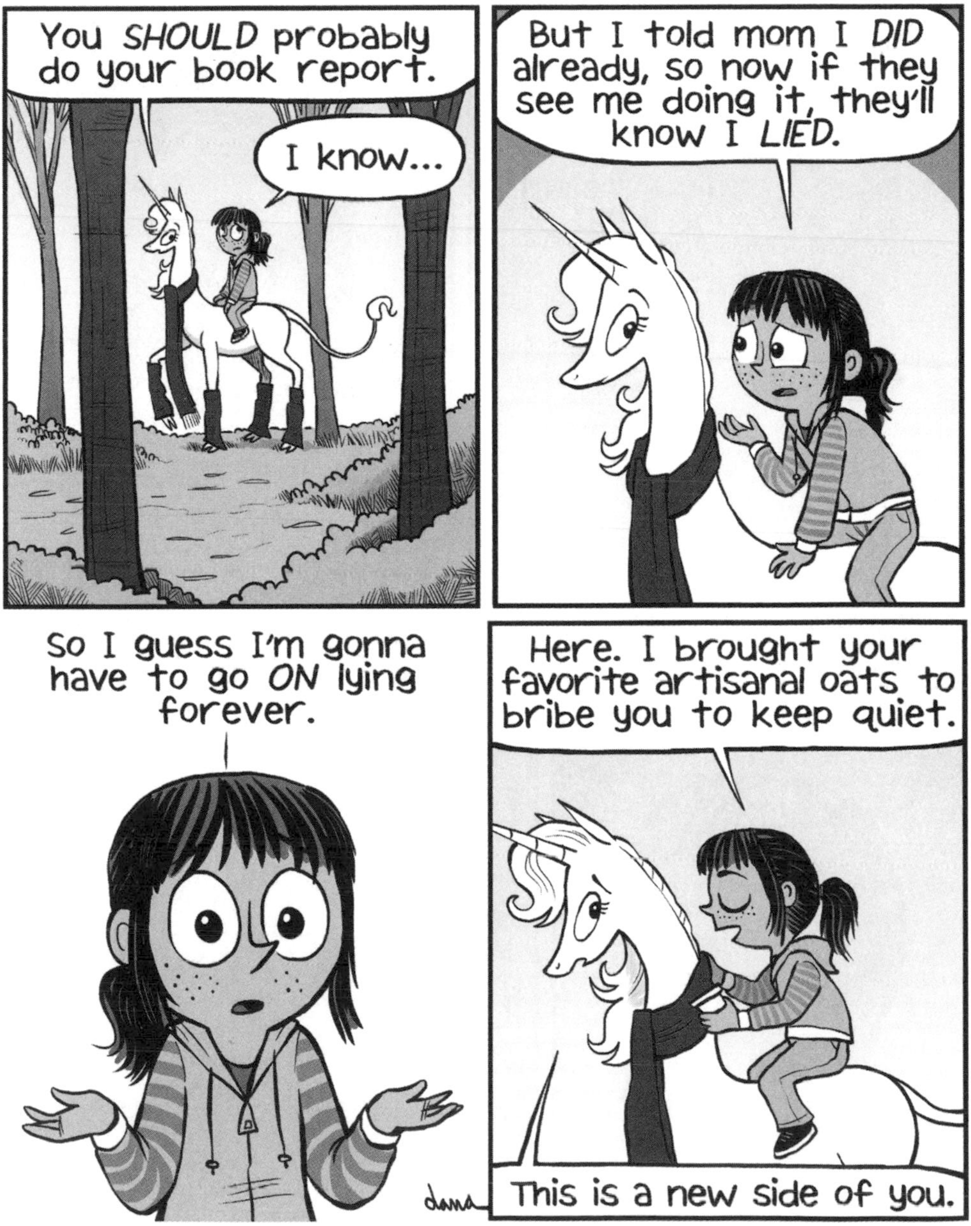
You *SHOULD* probably do your book report.
I know...
But I told mom I *DID* already, so now if they see me doing it, they'll know I *LIED*.
So I guess I'm gonna have to go *ON* lying forever.
Here. I brought your favorite artisanal oats to bribe you to keep quiet.
This is a new side of you.
dana

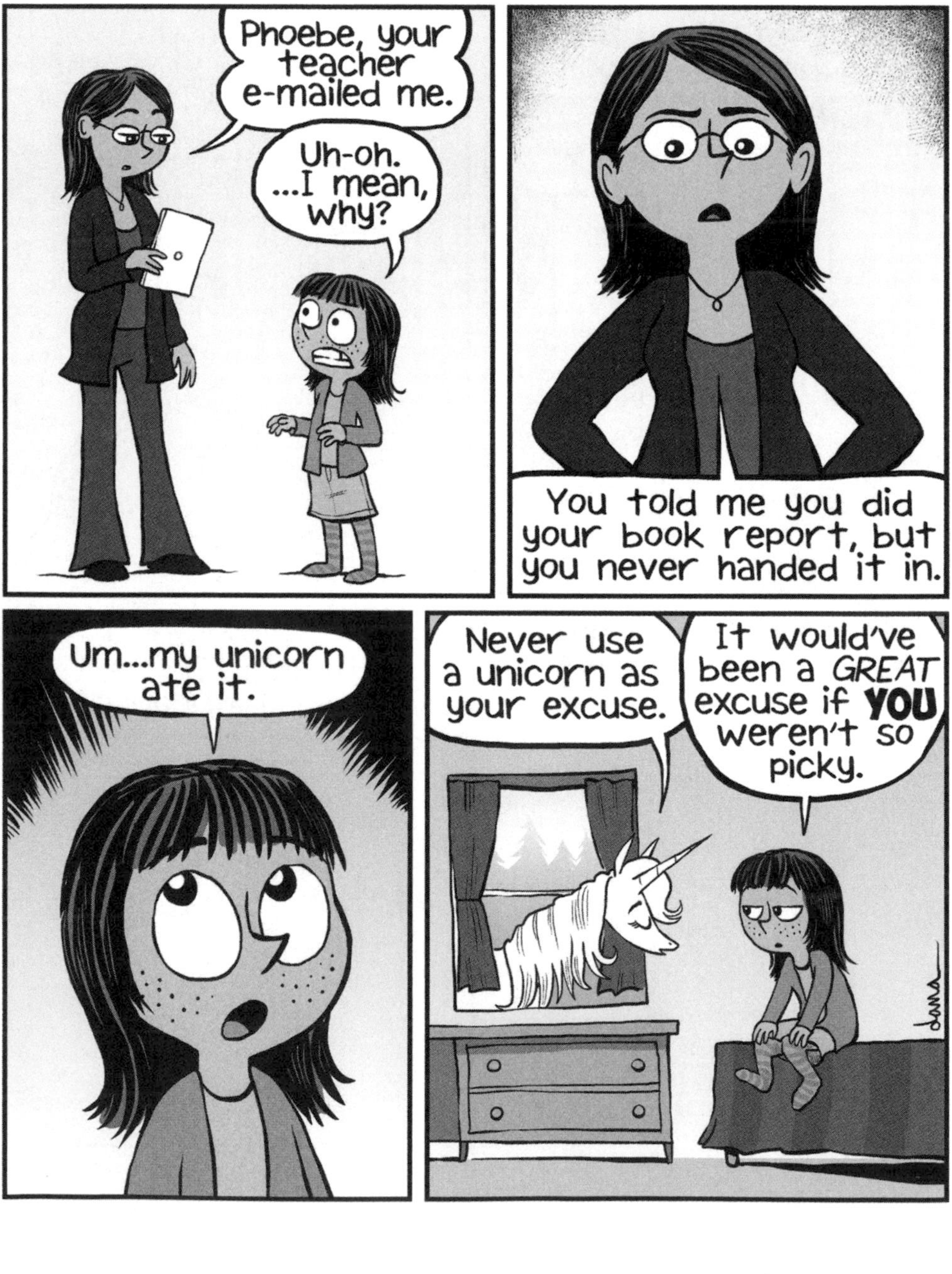
Phoebe, your teacher e-mailed me.
Uh-oh. ...I mean, why?
You told me you did your book report, but you never handed it in.
Um...my unicorn ate it.
Never use a unicorn as your excuse.
It would've been a *GREAT* excuse if **YOU** weren't so picky.

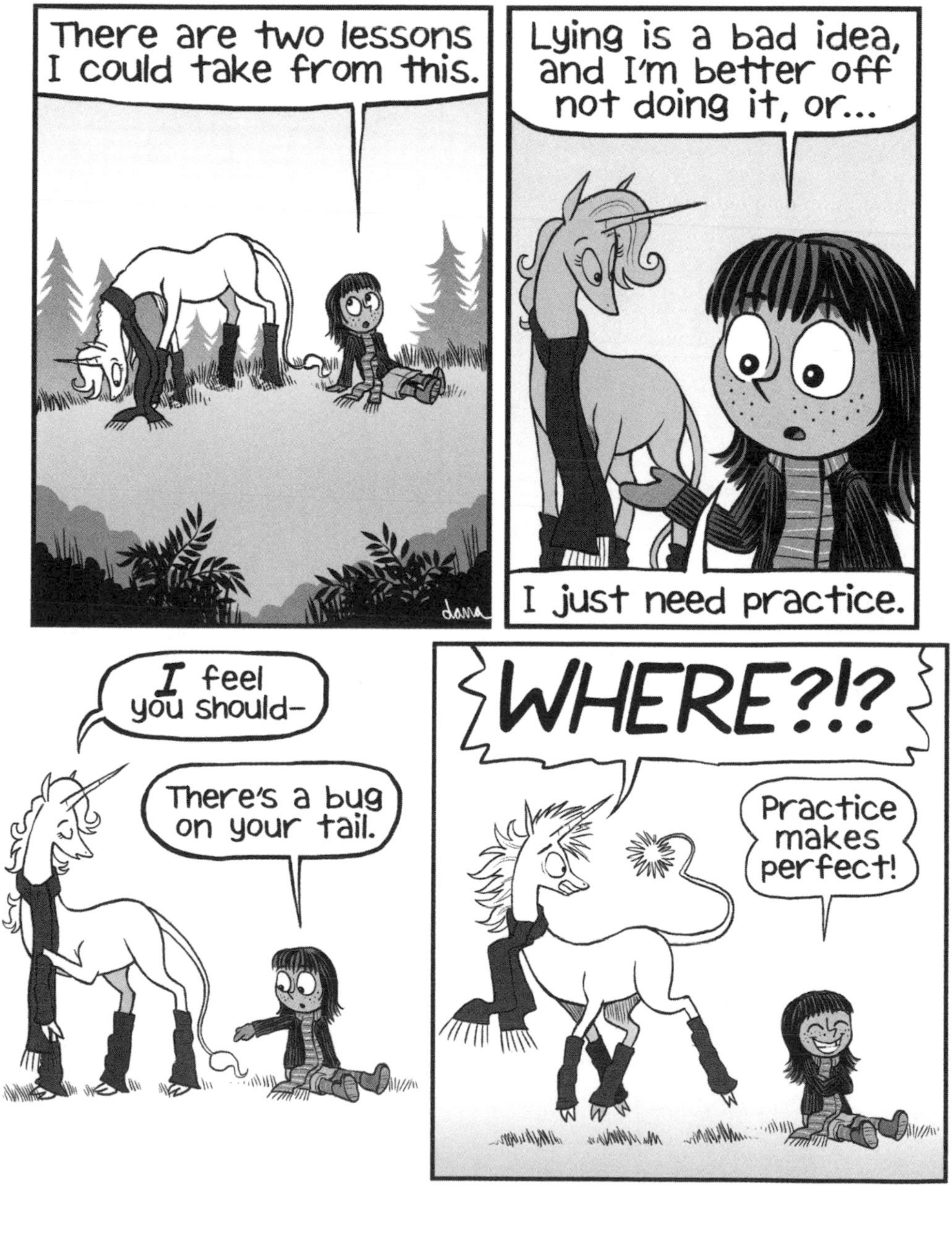

There are two lessons I could take from this.
dana
Lying is a bad idea, and I'm better off not doing it, or...
I just need practice.
I feel you should-
There's a bug on your tail.
WHERE?!?
Practice makes perfect!

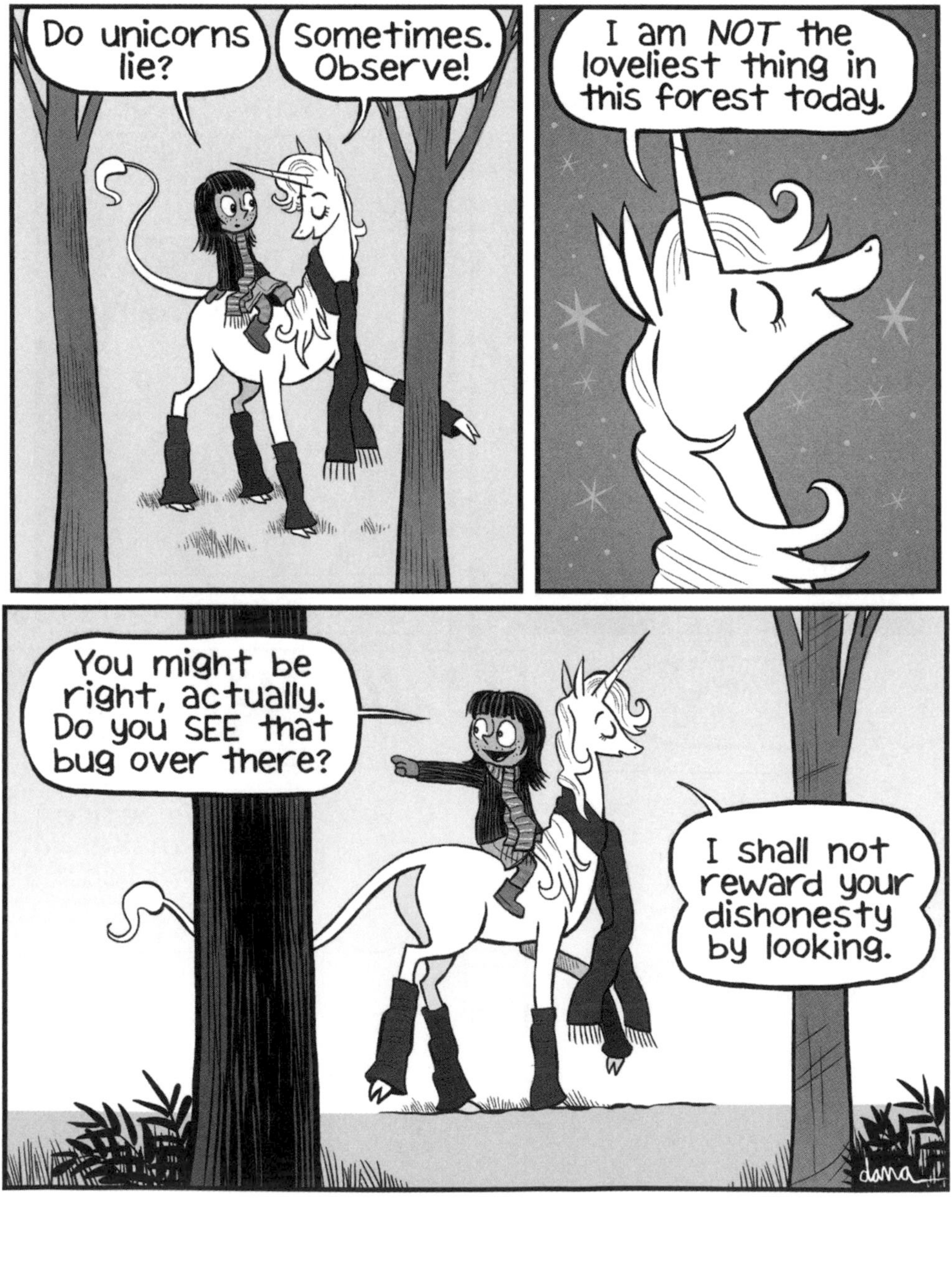
Do unicorns lie?
Sometimes. Observe!
I am *NOT* the loveliest thing in this forest today.
You might be right, actually. Do you SEE that bug over there?
I shall not reward your dishonesty by looking.
dana

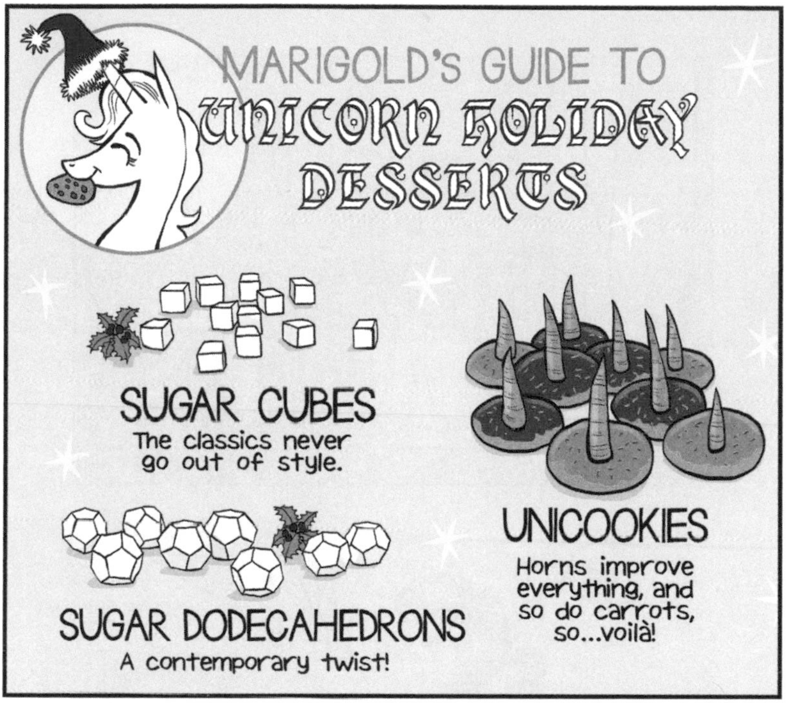
MARIGOLD'S GUIDE TO
UNICORN HOLIDAY DESSERTS
SUGAR CUBES
The classics never go out of style.
UNICOOKIES
Horns improve everything, and so do carrots, so...voilà!
SUGAR DODECAHEDRONS
A contemporary twist!

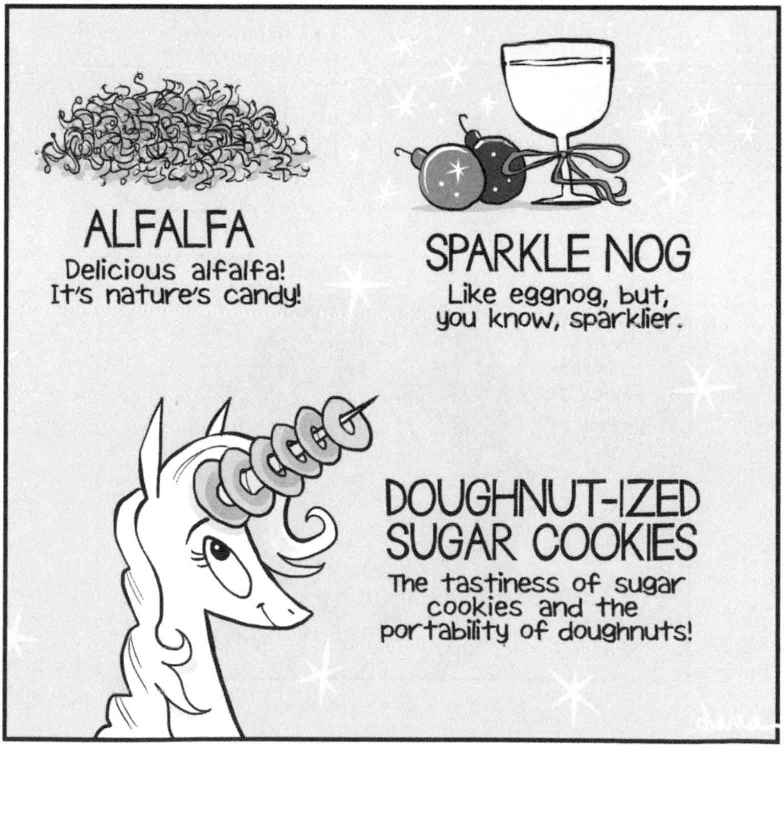
ALFALFA
Delicious alfalfa! It's nature's candy!
SPARKLE NOG
Like eggnog, but, you know, sparklier.
DOUGHNUT-IZED SUGAR COOKIES
The tastiness of sugar cookies and the portability of doughnuts!

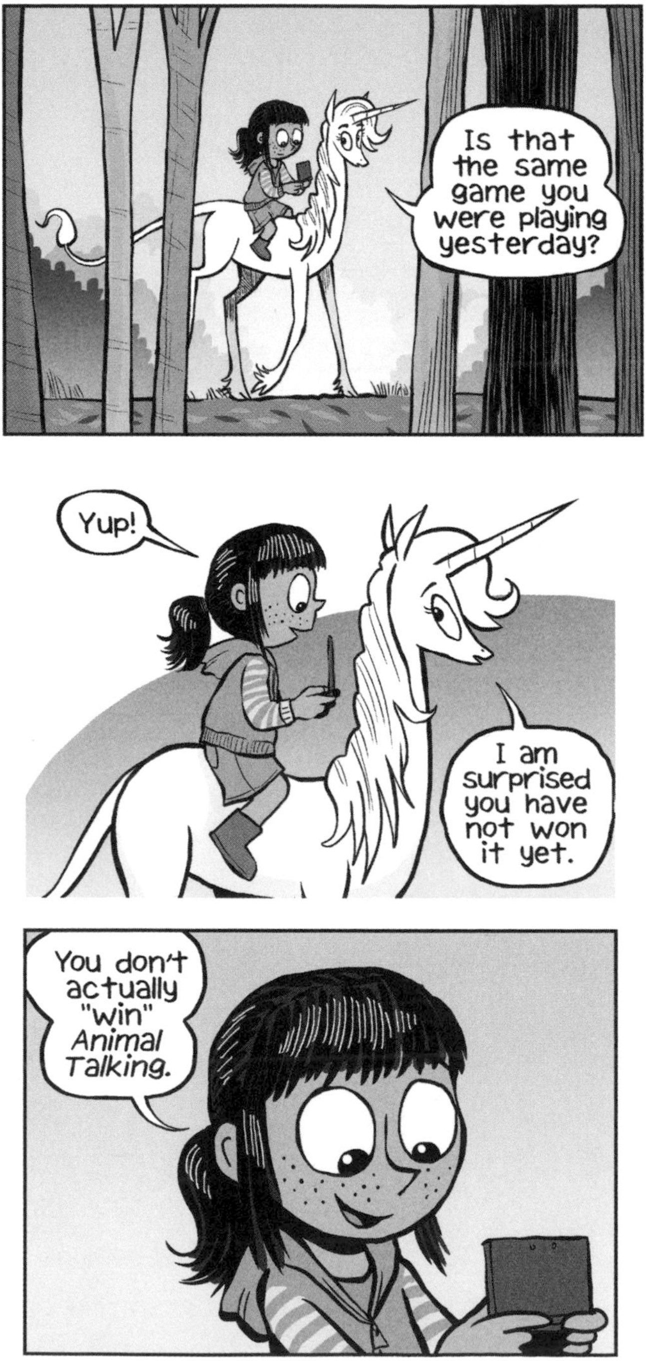
Is that the same game you were playing yesterday?
Yup!
I am surprised you have not won it yet.
You don't actually "win" Animal Talking.

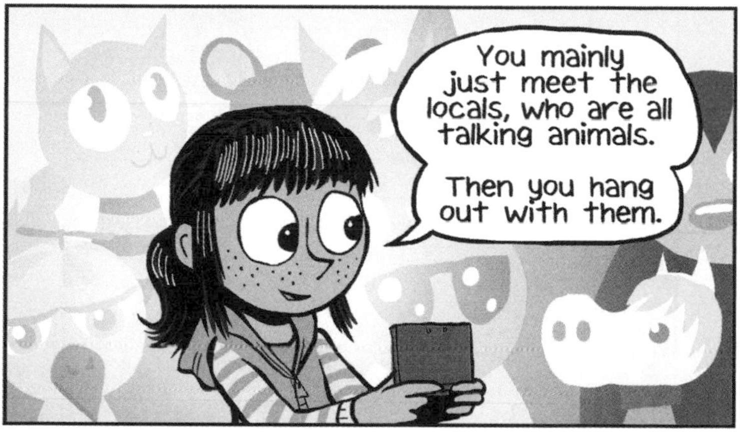
You mainly just meet the locals, who are all talking animals.
Then you hang out with them.

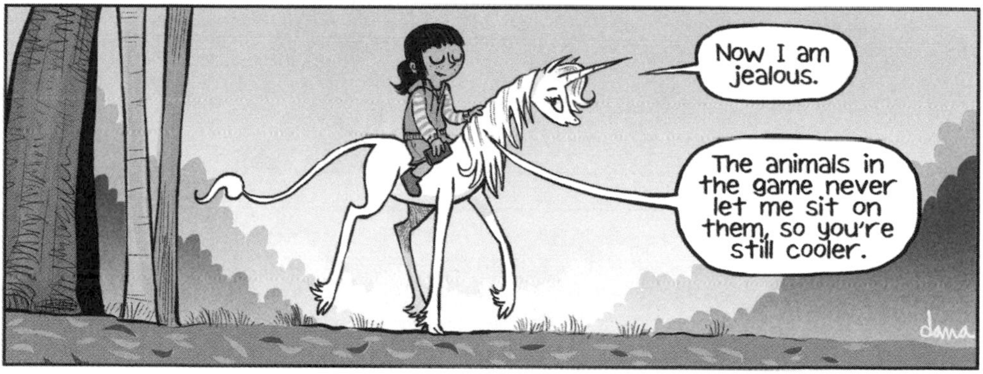
Now I am jealous.
The animals in the game never let me sit on them, so you're still cooler.
dana

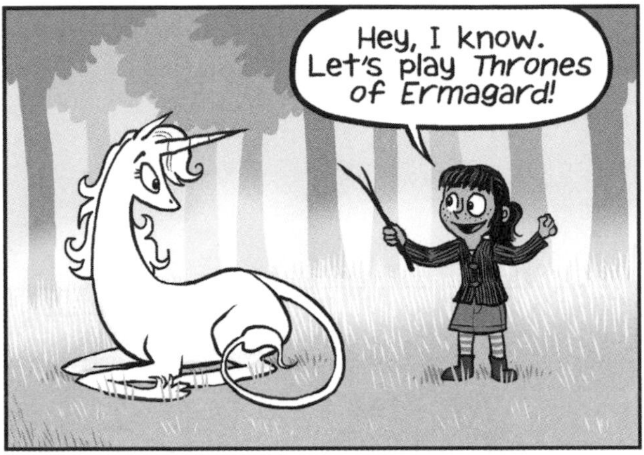
Hey, I know. Let's play Thrones of Ermagard!

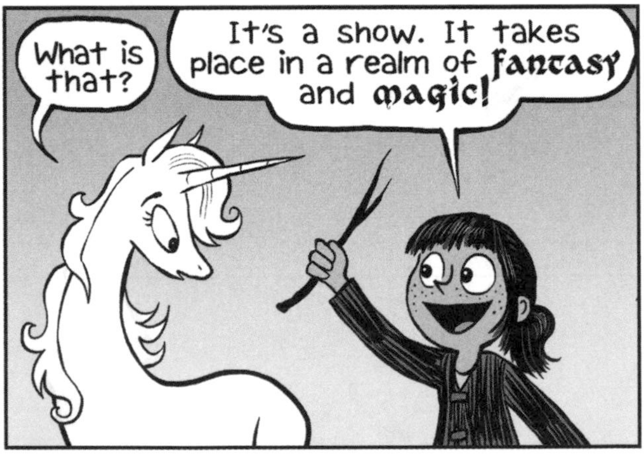
What is that?
It's a show. It takes place in a realm of fantasy and magic!

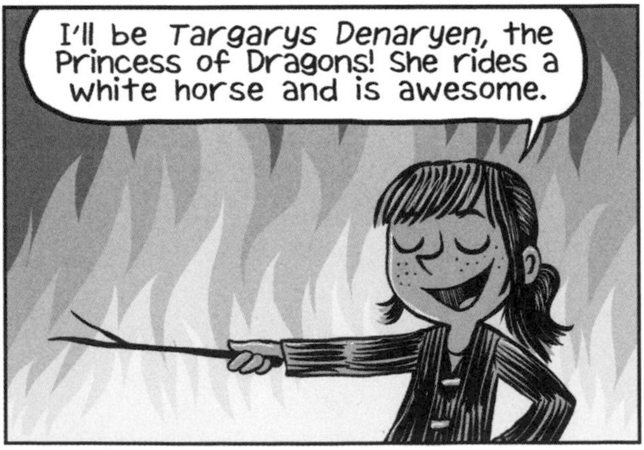
I'll be Targarys Denaryen, the Princess of Dragons! She rides a white horse and is awesome.

And you can be my horse!
I am tired of always having to be the horse.
I want to play a game in which I am a majestic unicorn, and you are a little girl I know.
That sounds like reality.
I enjoy reality.
dana

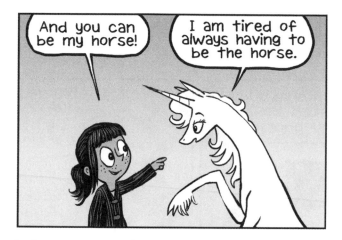

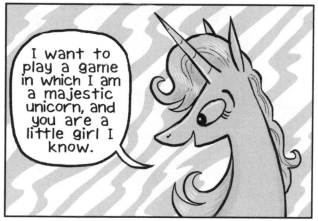

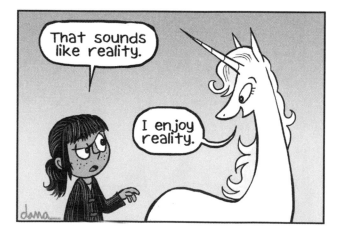

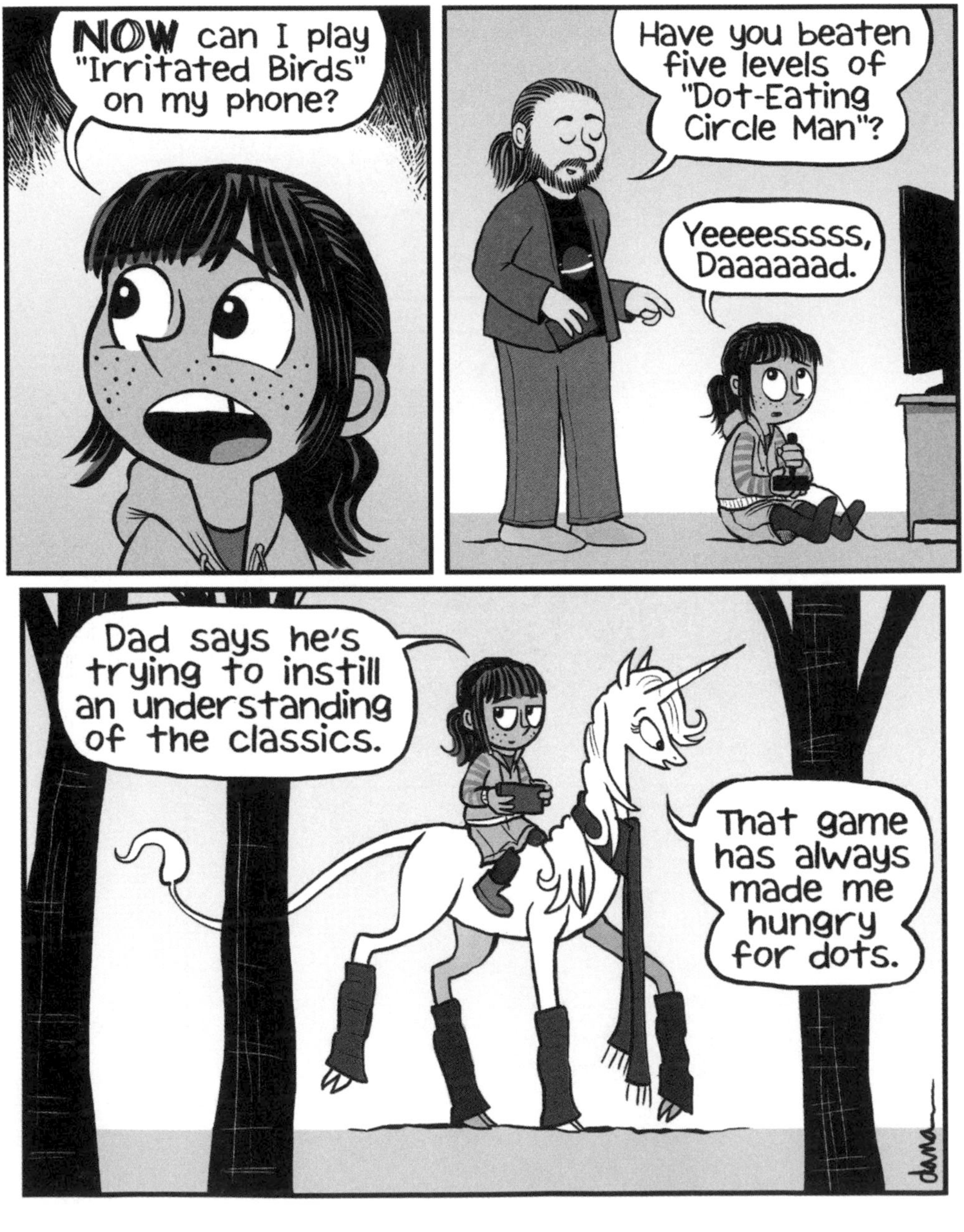
NOW can I play "Irritated Birds" on my phone?
Have you beaten five levels of "Dot-Eating Circle Man"?
Yeeeesssss, Daaaaaad.
Dad says he's trying to instill an understanding of the classics.
That game has always made me hungry for dots.
dana

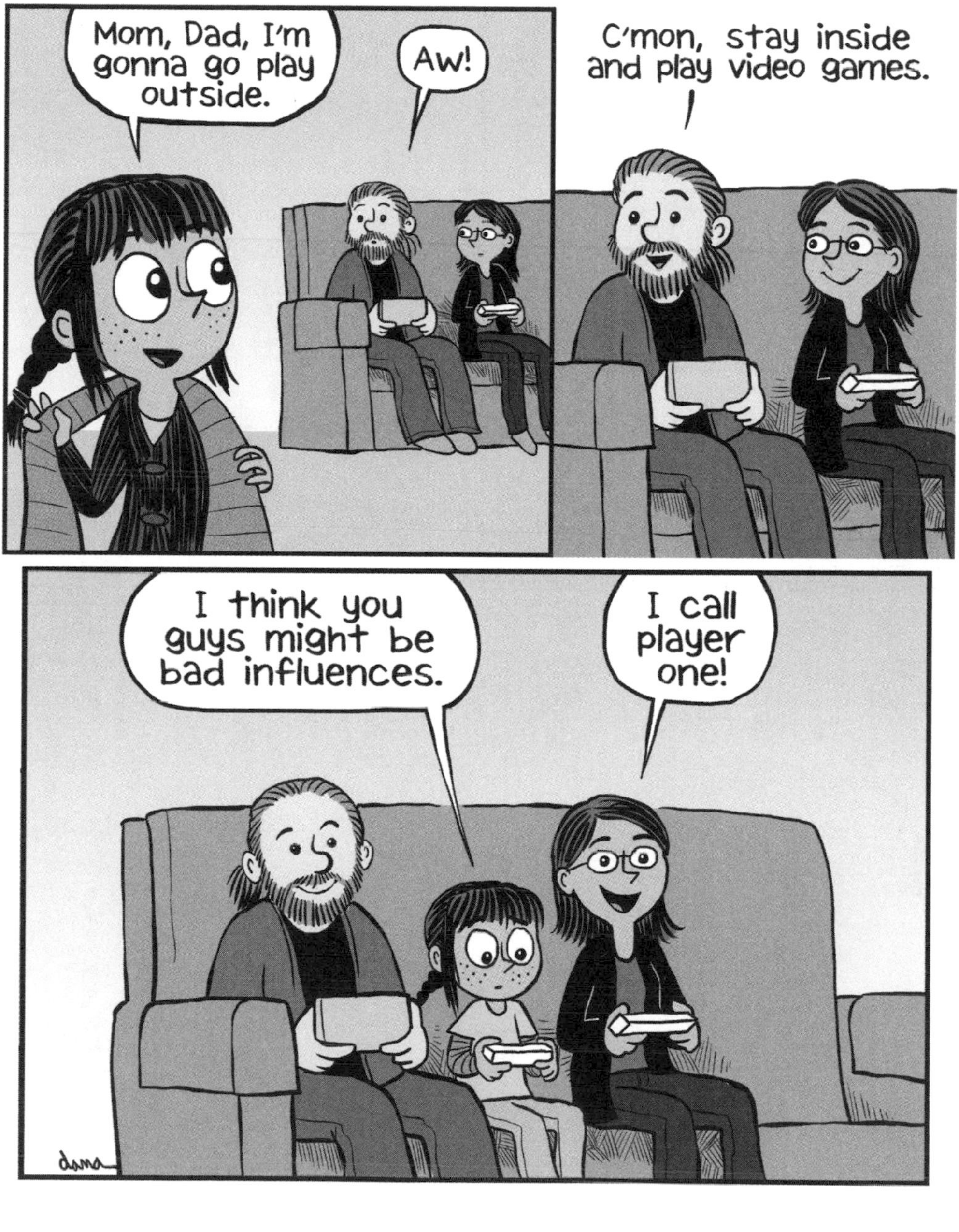
Mom, Dad, I'm gonna go play outside.
Aw!
C'mon, stay inside and play video games.
I think you guys might be bad influences.
I call player one!
dana

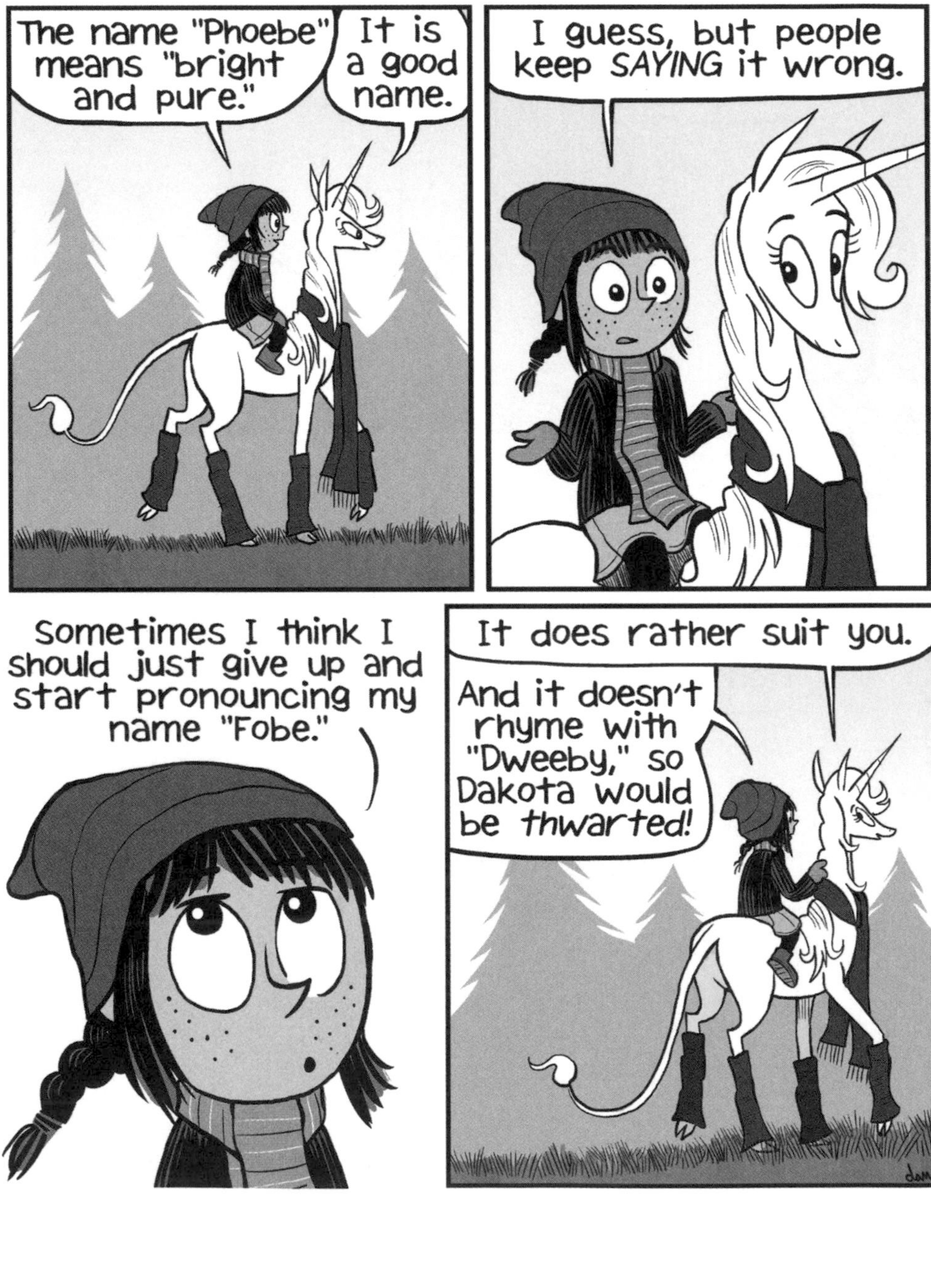
The name "Phoebe" means "bright and pure."
It is a good name.
I guess, but people keep *SAYING* it wrong.
Sometimes I think I should just give up and start pronouncing my name "Fobe."
It does rather suit you.
And it doesn't rhyme with "Dweeby," so Dakota would be *thwarted!*
dana

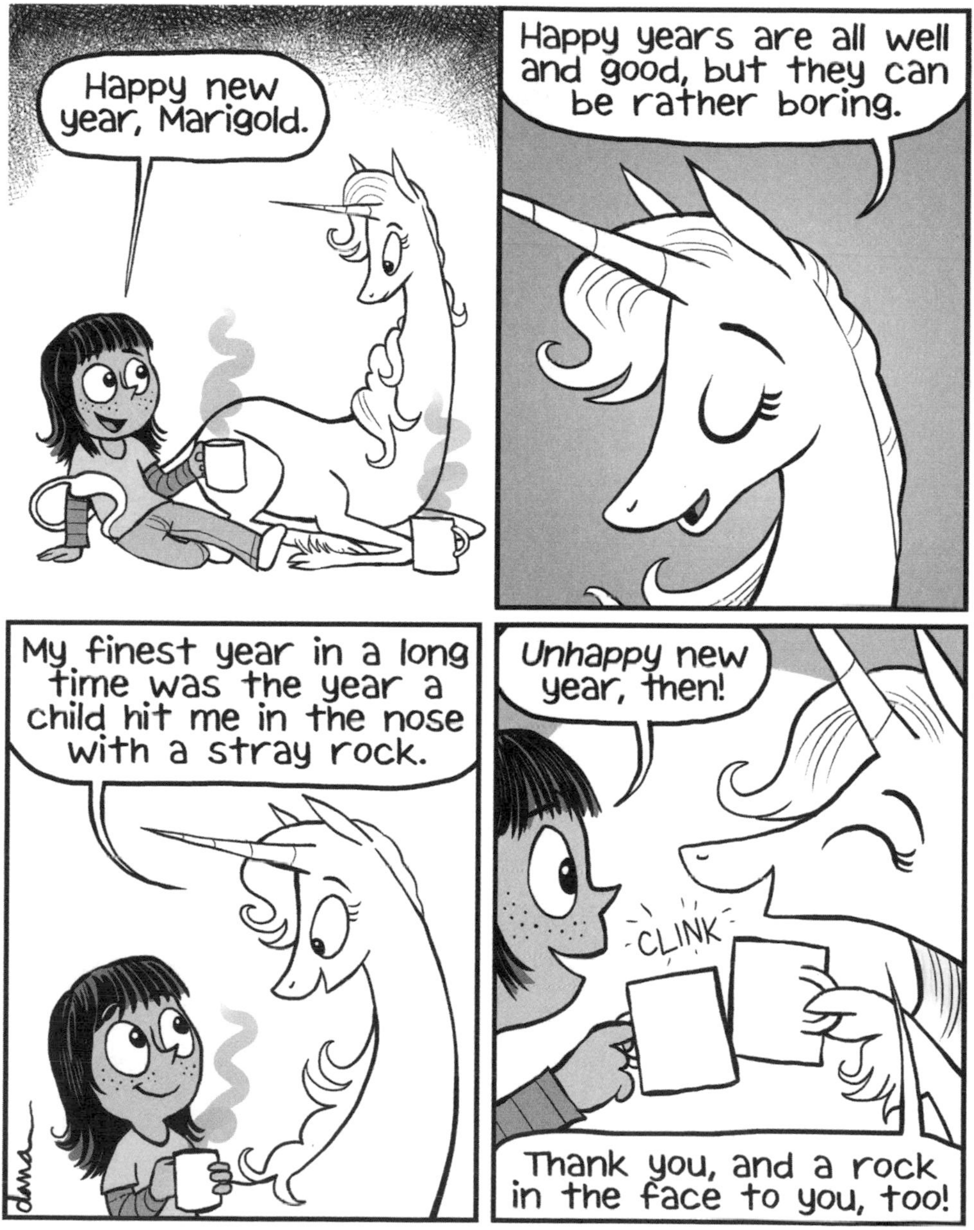
Happy new year, Marigold.
Happy years are all well and good, but they can be rather boring.
My finest year in a long time was the year a child hit me in the nose with a stray rock.
dana
Unhappy new year, then!
CLINK
Thank you, and a rock in the face to you, too!

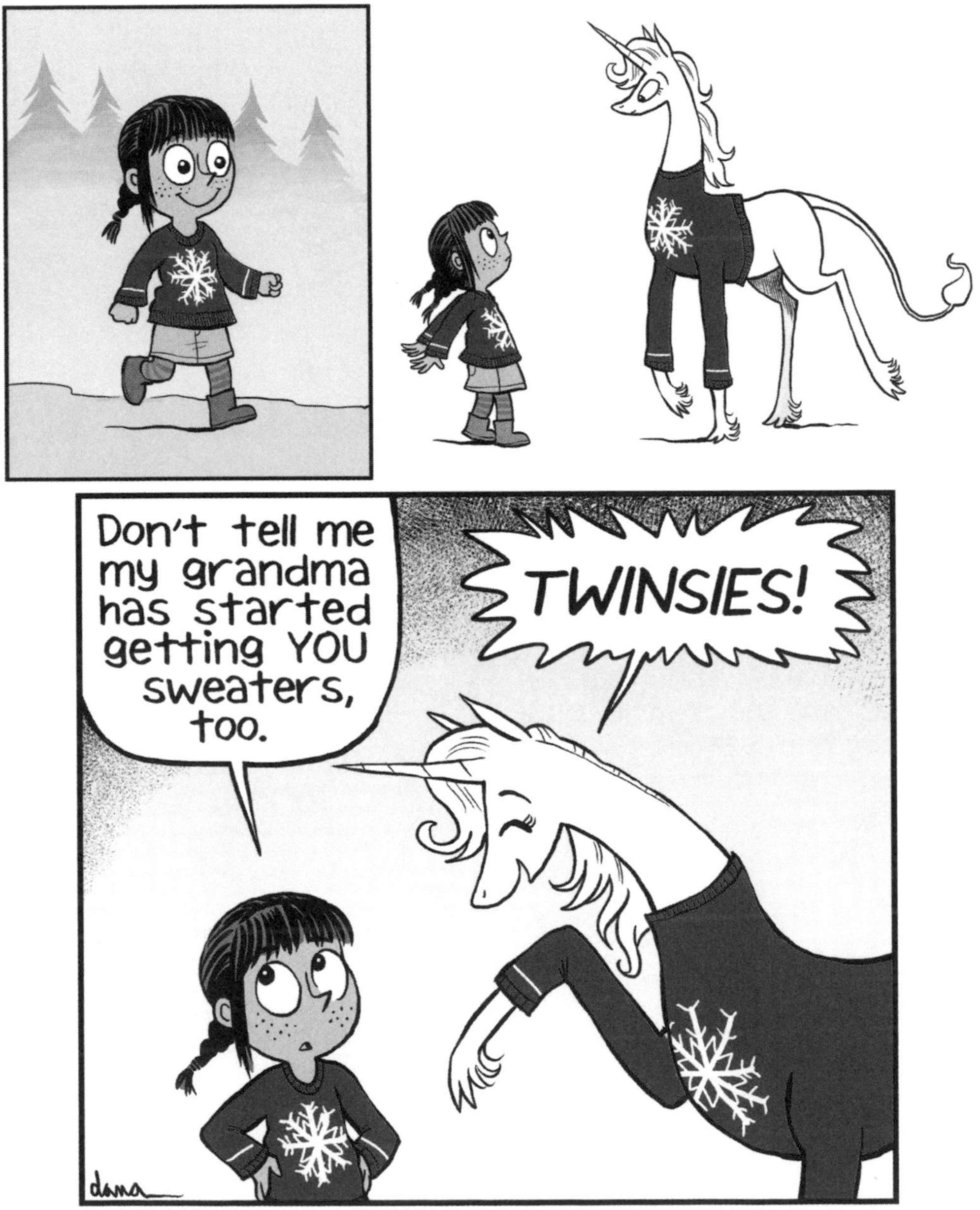
Don't tell me my grandma has started getting YOU sweaters, too.
TWINSIES!
dana

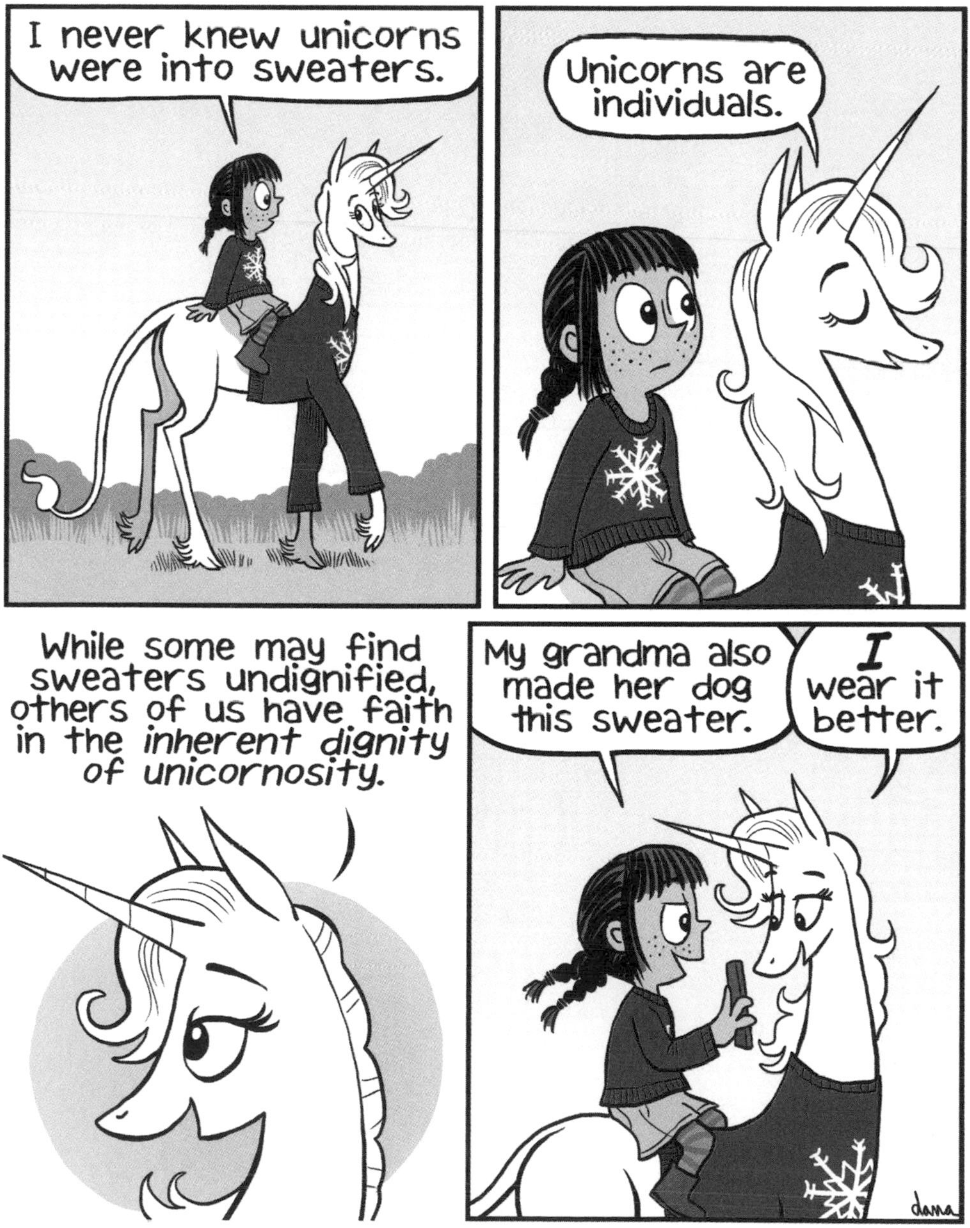
I never knew unicorns were into sweaters.
Unicorns are individuals.
While some may find sweaters undignified, others of us have faith in the *inherent dignity* of *unicornosity.*
My grandma also made her dog this sweater.
I wear it better.
dana

How come you don't fight crime?
What?
You basically have *SUPERPOWERS*. In movies and comics and stuff, that means you're supposed to fight crime.
I do not see any crime here.
Well, not *RIGHT* here, no.

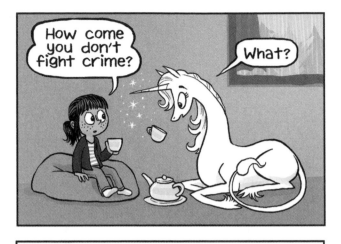

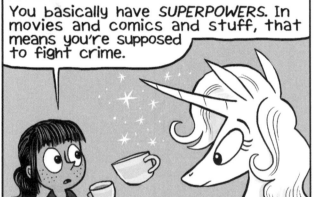

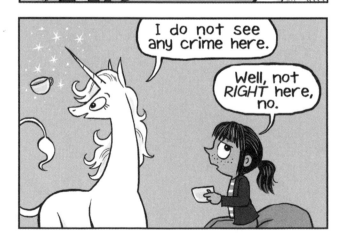

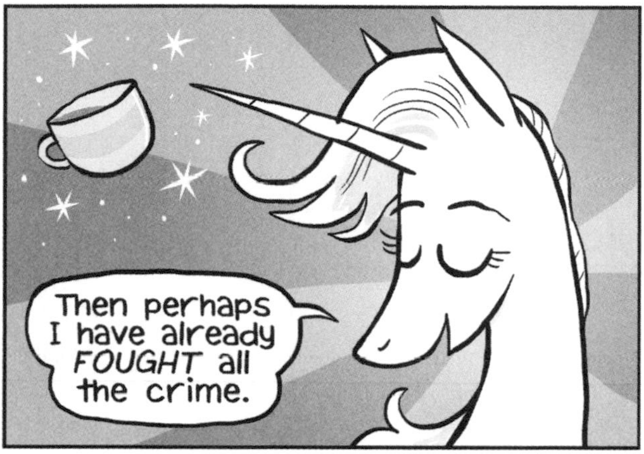
Then perhaps I have already *FOUGHT* all the crime.

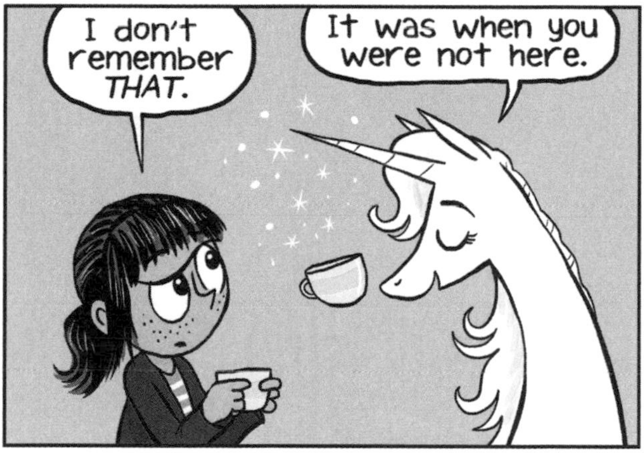
I don't remember *THAT*.
It was when you were not here.

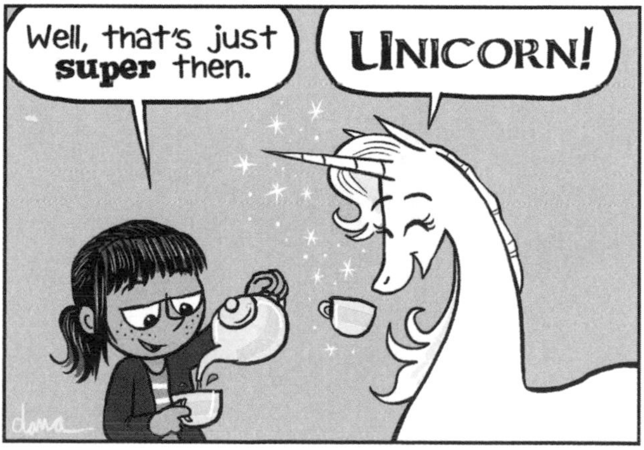
Well, that's just **super** then.
UNICORN!

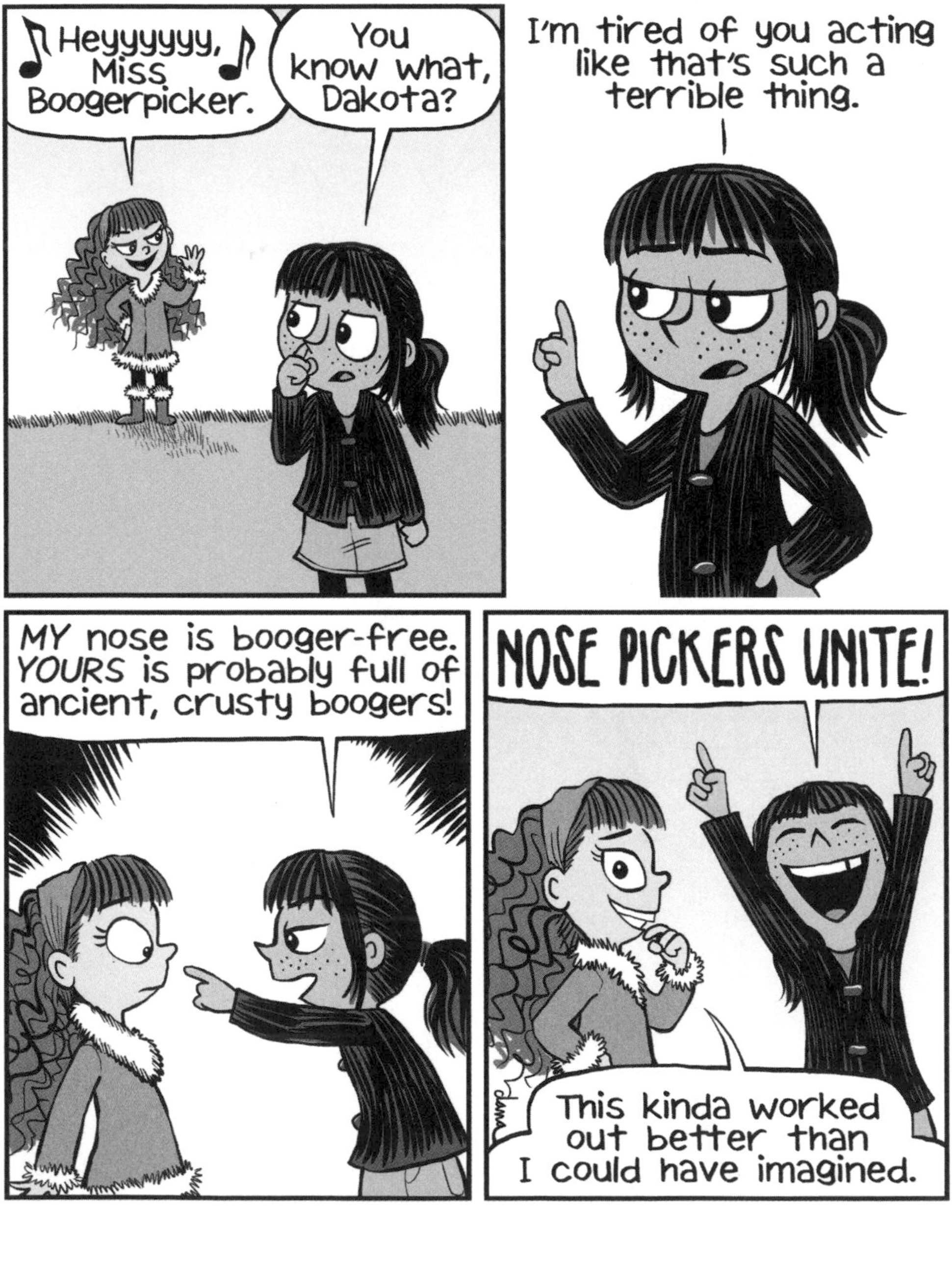
Heyyyyyy, Miss Boogerpicker.
You know what, Dakota?
I'm tired of you acting like that's such a terrible thing.
MY nose is booger-free. *YOURS* is probably full of ancient, crusty boogers!
NOSE PICKERS UNITE!
This kinda worked out better than I could have imagined.

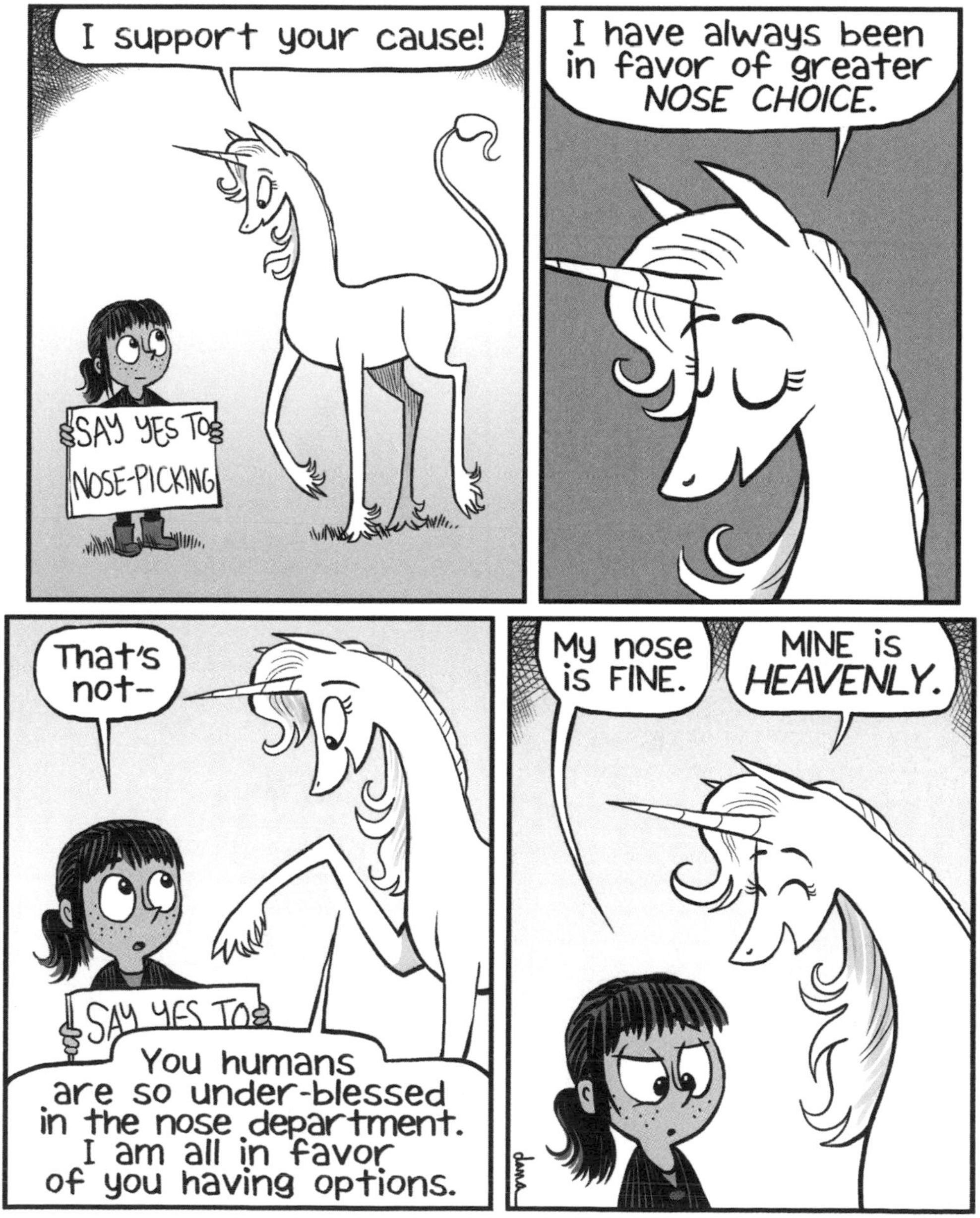
I support your cause!
SAY YES TO NOSE-PICKING
I have always been in favor of greater NOSE CHOICE.
That's not-
SAY YES TO
You humans are so under-blessed in the nose department. I am all in favor of you having options.
My nose is FINE.
MINE is HEAVENLY.

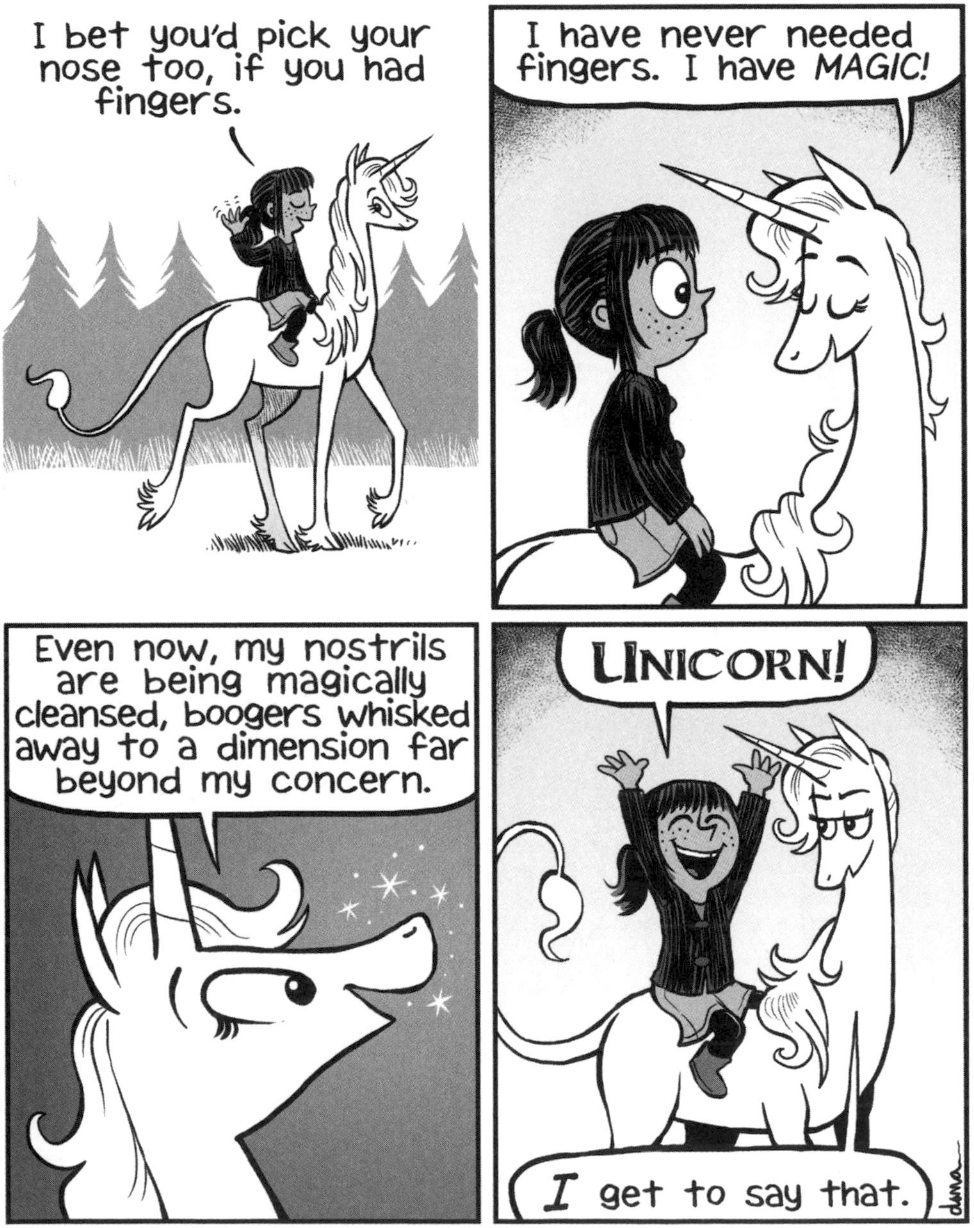
I bet you'd pick your nose too, if you had fingers.
I have never needed fingers. I have *MAGIC!*
Even now, my nostrils are being magically cleansed, boogers whisked away to a dimension far beyond my concern.
UNICORN!
I get to say that.
dana

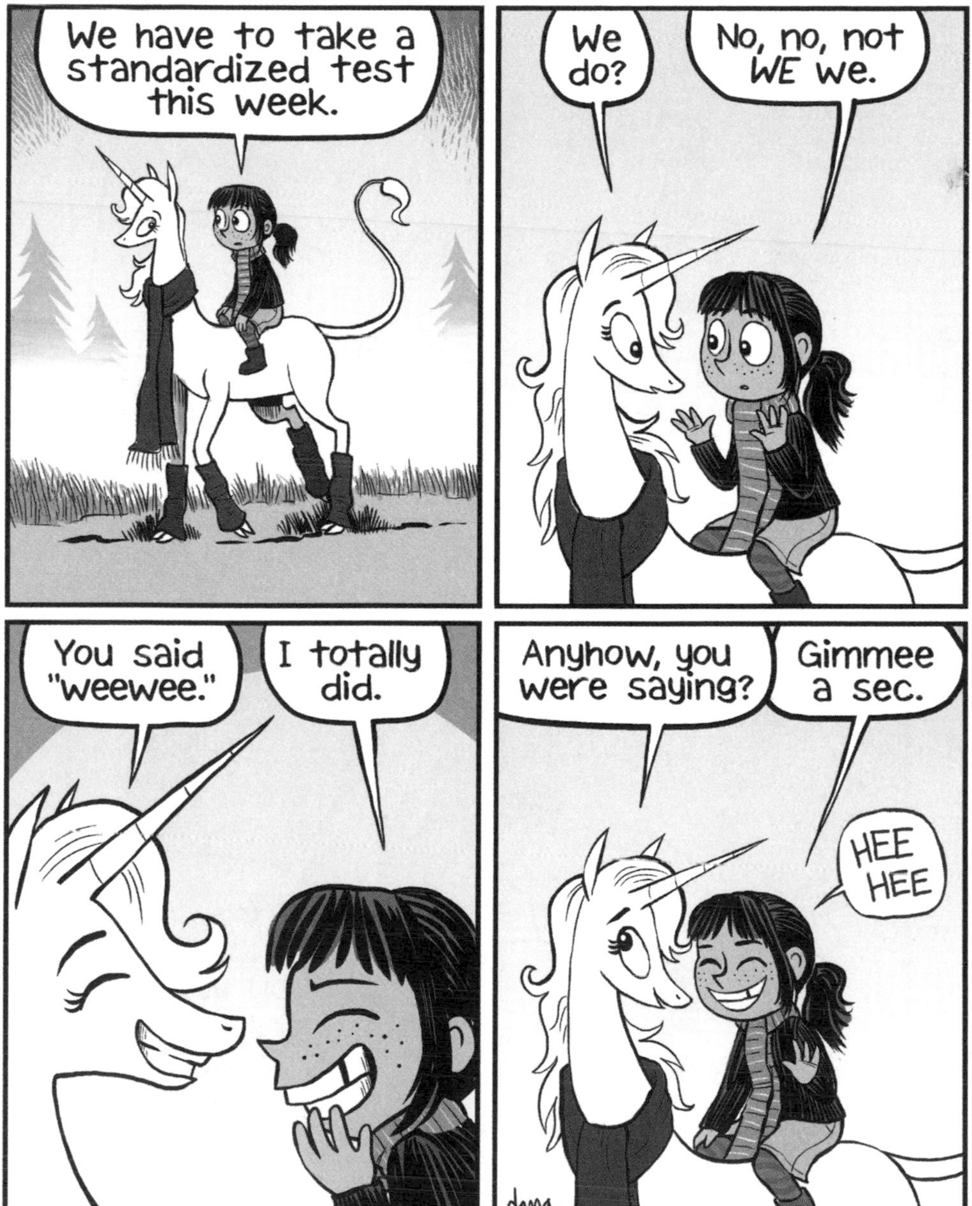
We have to take a standardized test this week.
We do?
No, no, not WE we.
You said "weewee."
I totally did.
Anyhow, you were saying?
Gimmee a sec.
HEE HEE
dana

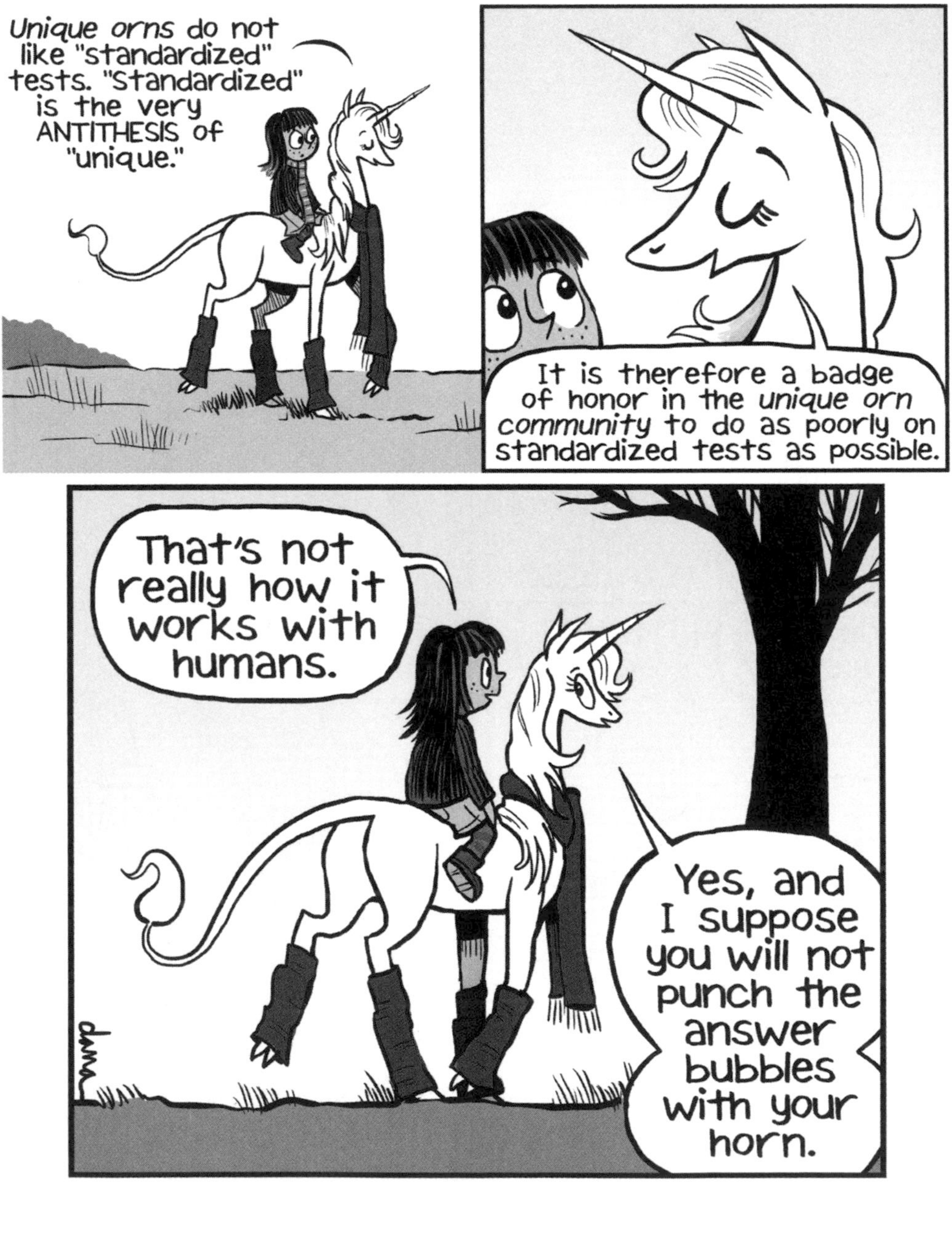
Unique orns do not like "standardized" tests. "Standardized" is the very ANTITHESIS of "unique."
It is therefore a badge of honor in the unique orn community to do as poorly on standardized tests as possible.
That's not really how it works with humans.
Yes, and I suppose you will not punch the answer bubbles with your horn.

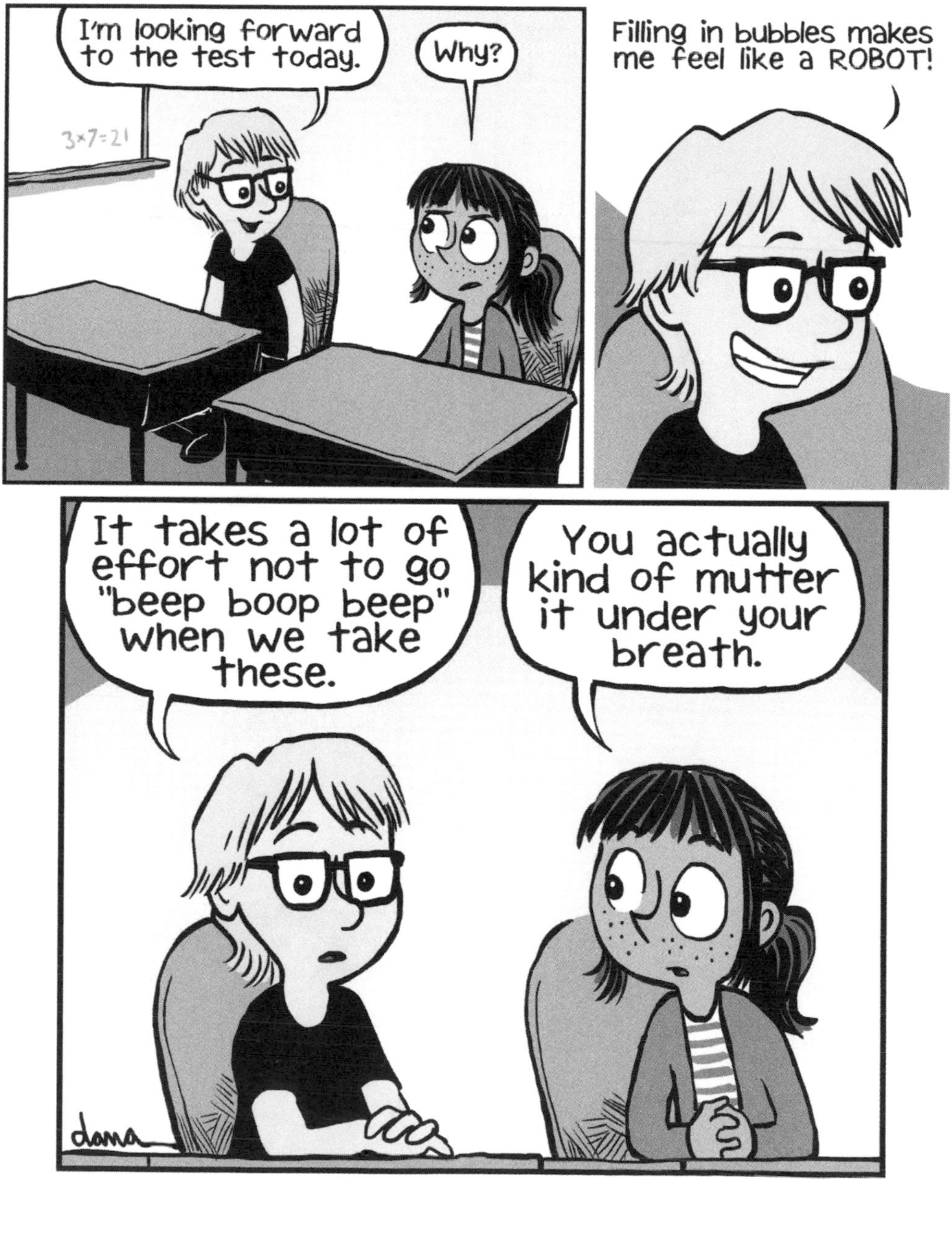
I'm looking forward to the test today.
Why?
Filling in bubbles makes me feel like a ROBOT!
It takes a lot of effort not to go "beep boop beep" when we take these.
You actually kind of mutter it under your breath.
dana

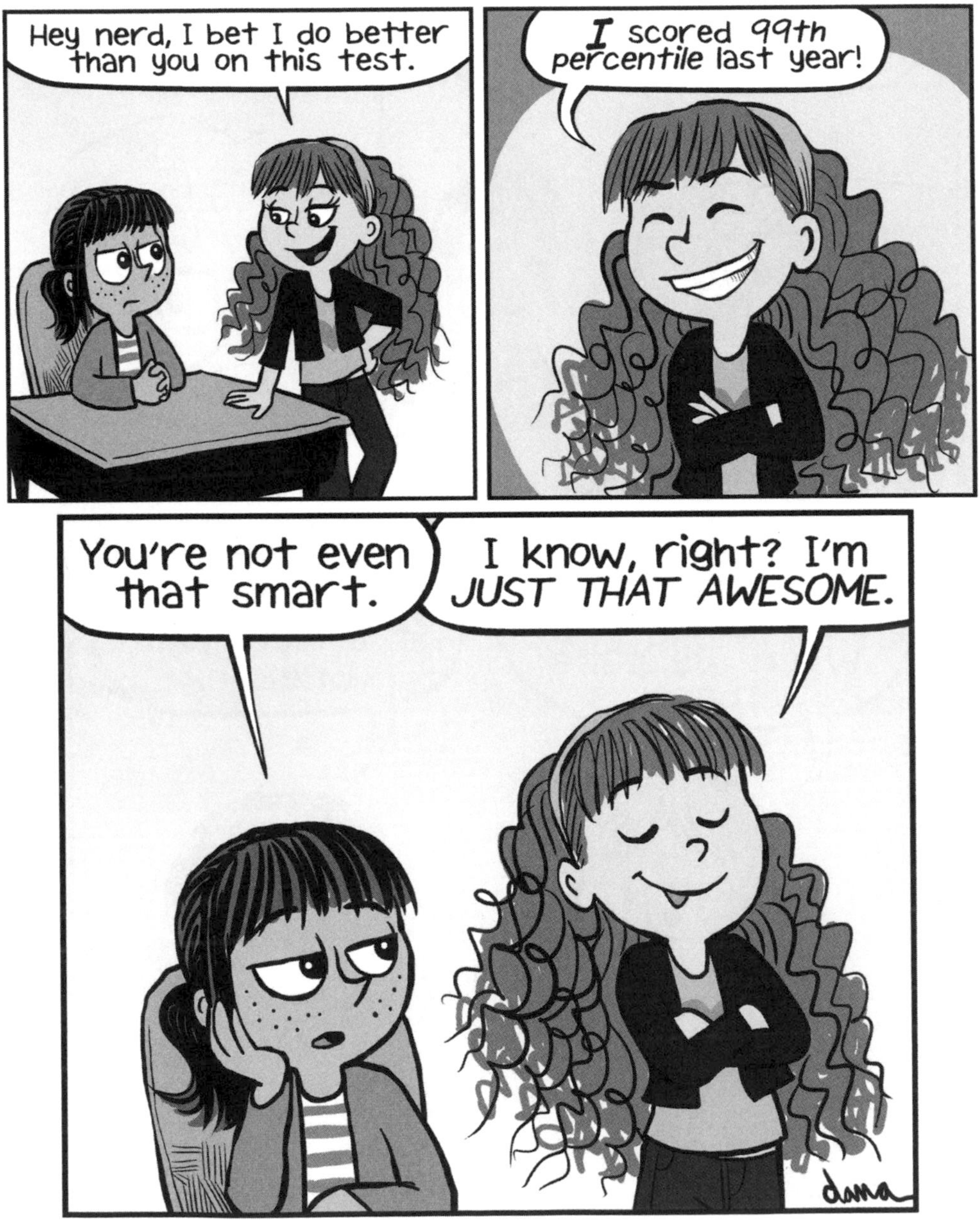
Hey nerd, I bet I do better than you on this test.
I scored 99th *percentile* last year!
You're not even that smart.
I know, right? I'm *JUST THAT AWESOME.*
dana

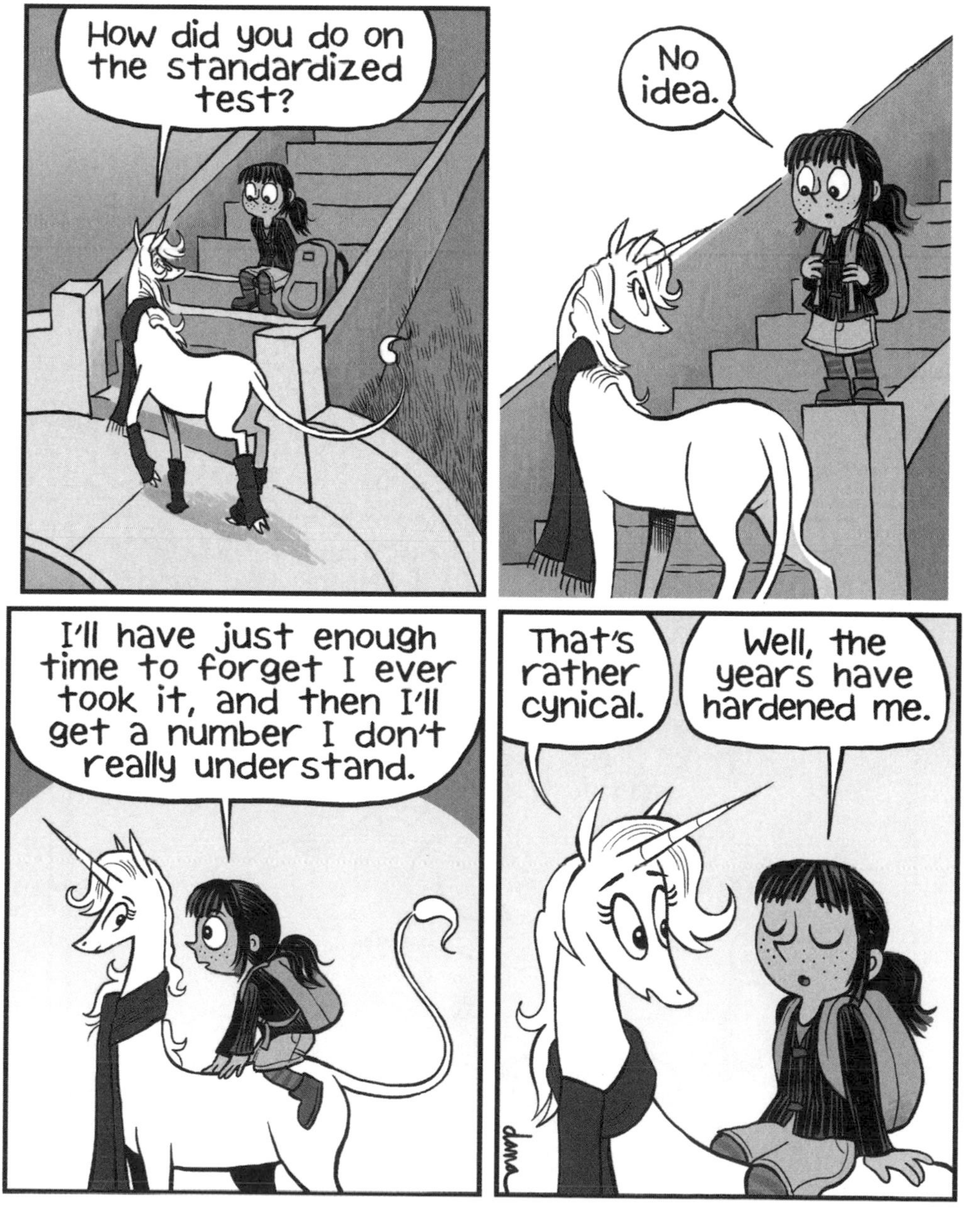
How did you do on the standardized test?
No idea.
I'll have just enough time to forget I ever took it, and then I'll get a number I don't really understand.
That's rather cynical.
Well, the years have hardened me.
dana

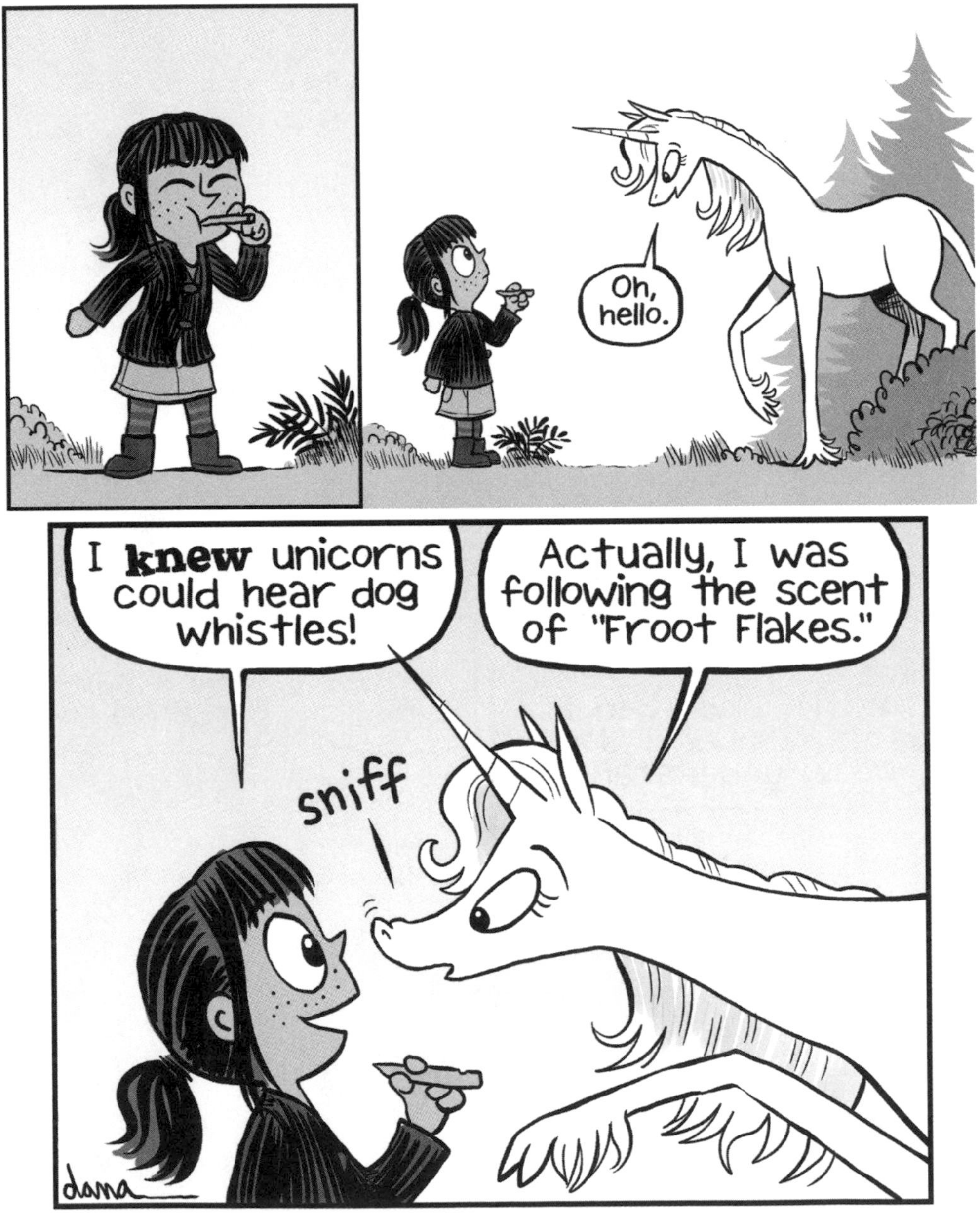
Oh, hello.
I knew unicorns could hear dog whistles!
Actually, I was following the scent of "Froot Flakes."
sniff
dana

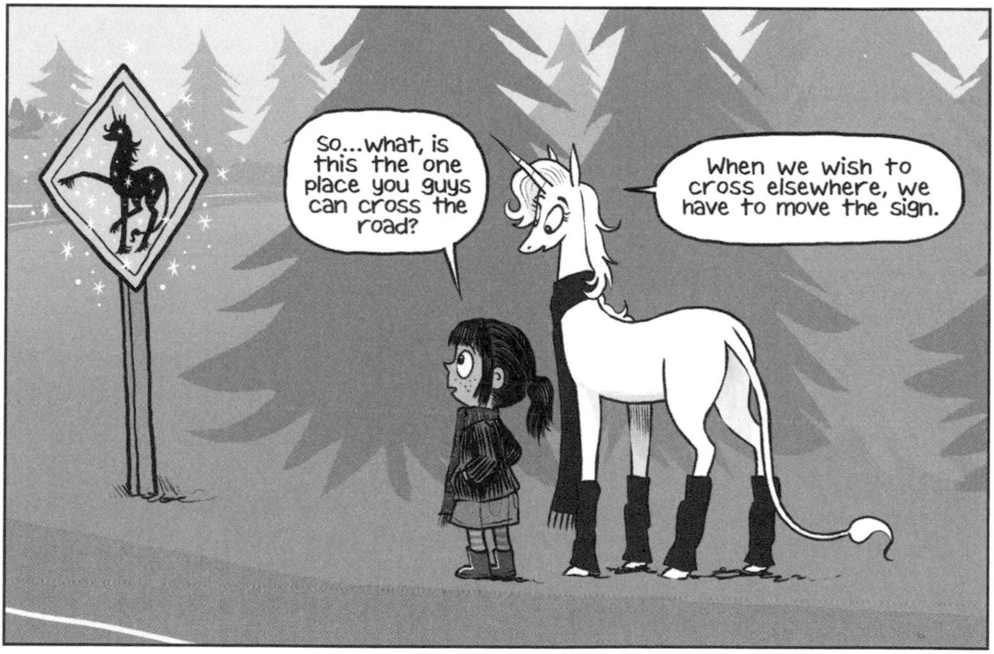
So...what, is this the one place you guys can cross the road?
When we wish to cross elsewhere, we have to move the sign.

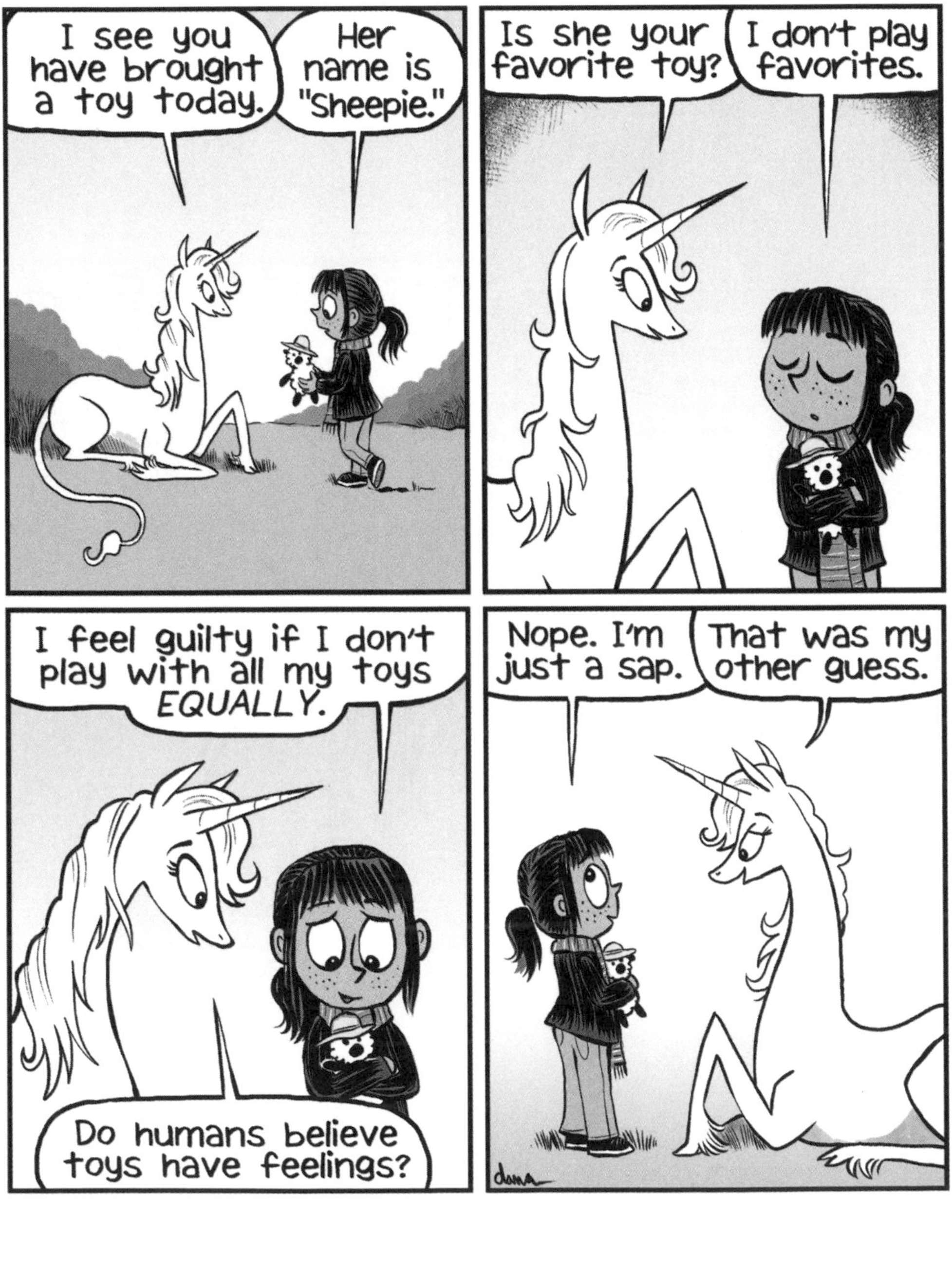
I see you have brought a toy today.
Her name is "Sheepie."
Is she your favorite toy?
I don't play favorites.
I feel guilty if I don't play with all my toys *EQUALLY*.
Do humans believe toys have feelings?
Nope. I'm just a sap.
That was my other guess.
dana

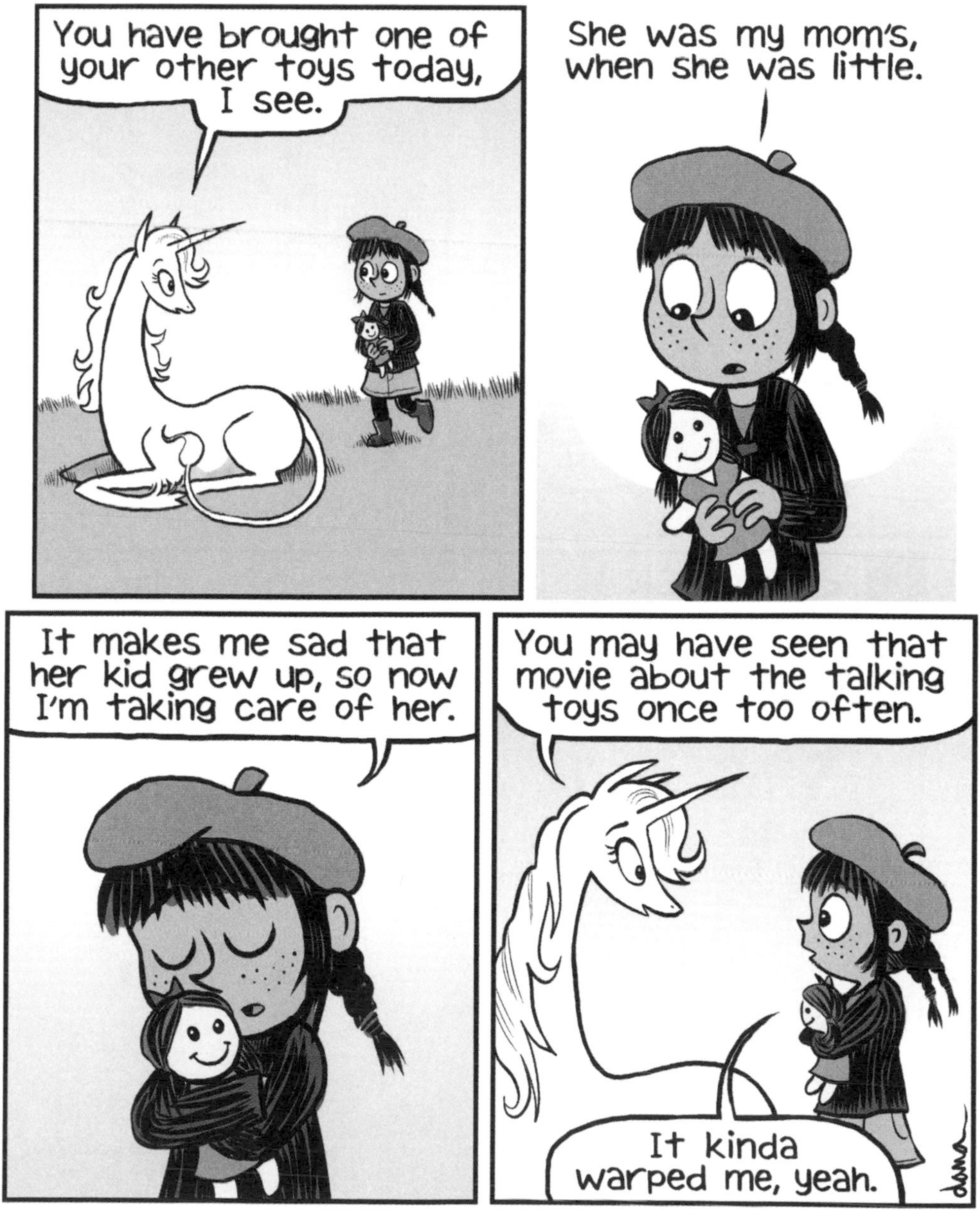
You have brought one of your other toys today, I see.
She was my mom's, when she was little.
It makes me sad that her kid grew up, so now I'm taking care of her.
You may have seen that movie about the talking toys once too often.
It kinda warped me, yeah.
dana

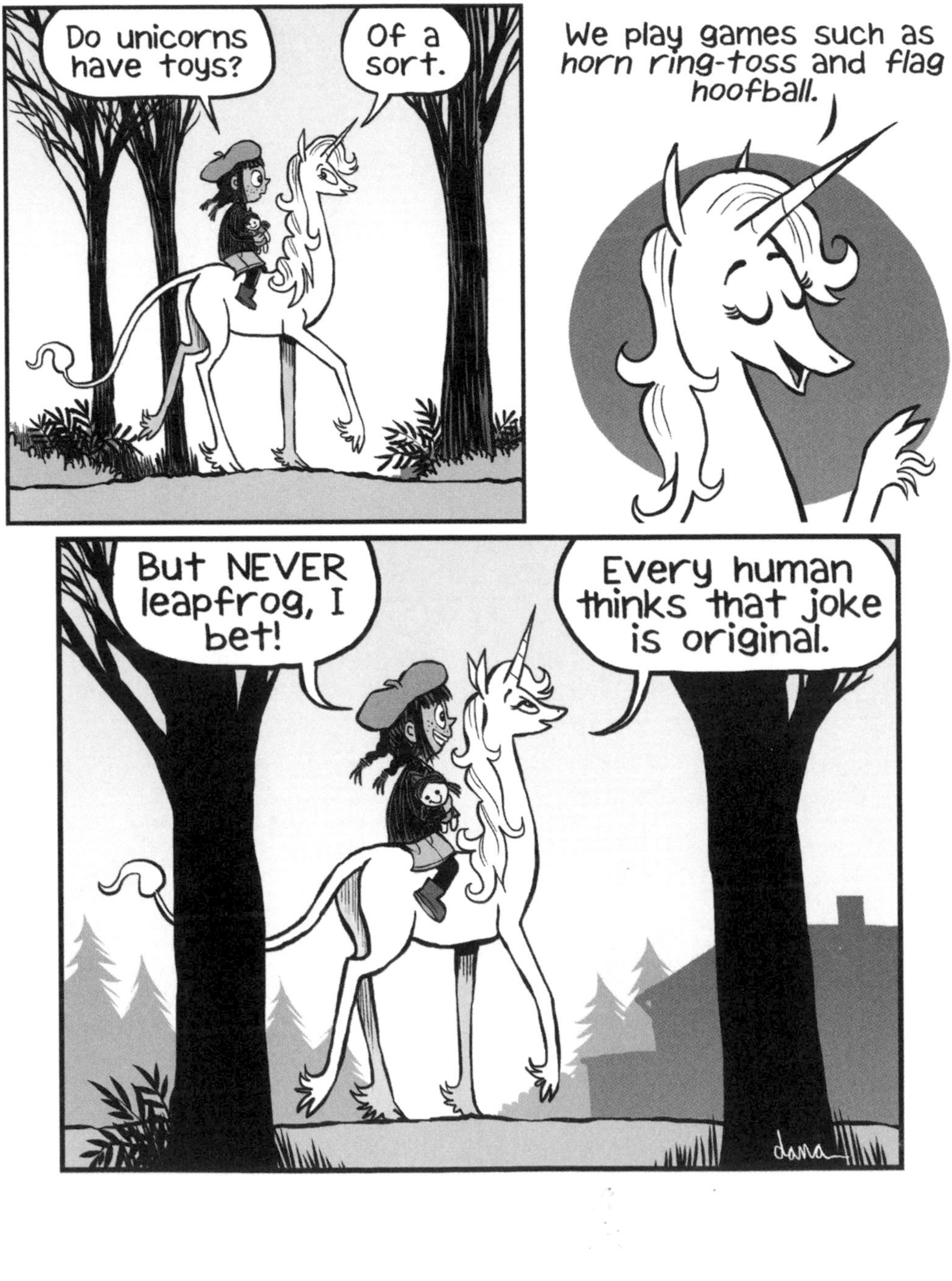
Do unicorns have toys?
Of a sort.
We play games such as *horn ring-toss* and *flag hoofball.*
But NEVER leapfrog, I bet!
Every human thinks that joke is original.
dana

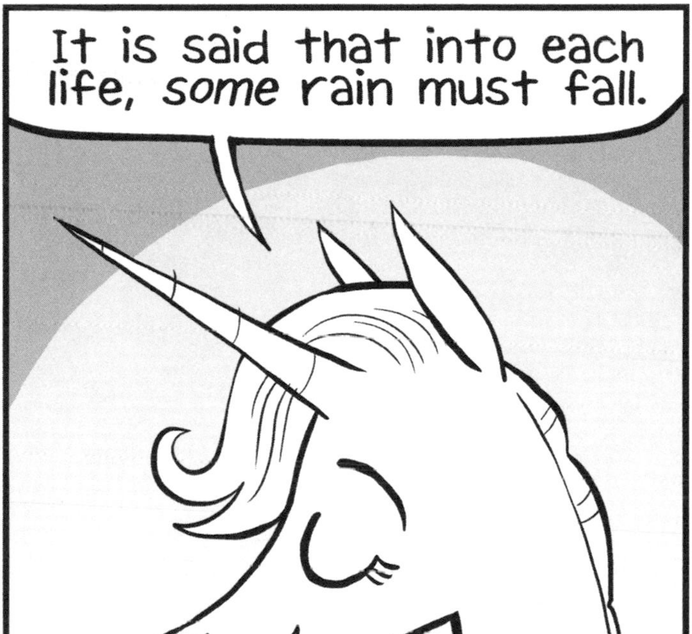
It is said that into each life, *some* rain must fall.

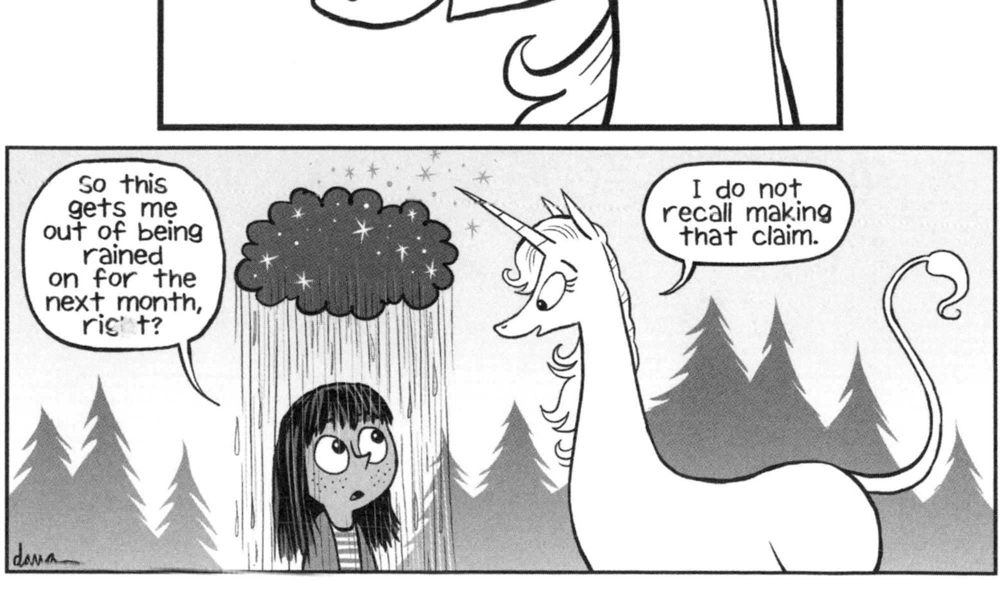
So this gets me out of being rained on for the next month, right?
I do not recall making that claim.
dana

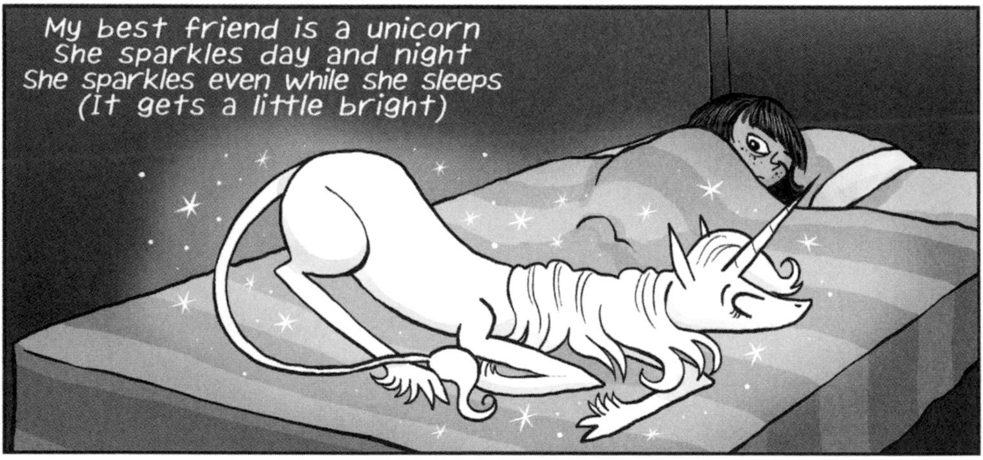
My best friend is a unicorn
She sparkles day and night
She sparkles even while she sleeps
(It gets a little bright)

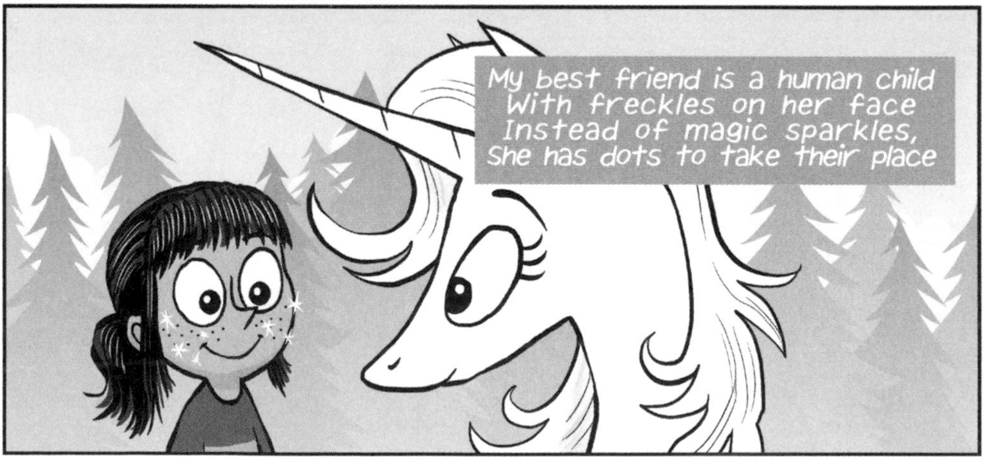
My best friend is a human child
With freckles on her face
Instead of magic sparkles,
She has dots to take their place

"Enough with all the sparkling,"
I sometimes want to say,
But in the end, as my best friend,
She sparkles up my day.

She may not be a unicorn
But freckles are a start
For when I see her freckled face
It sparkles up my heart.

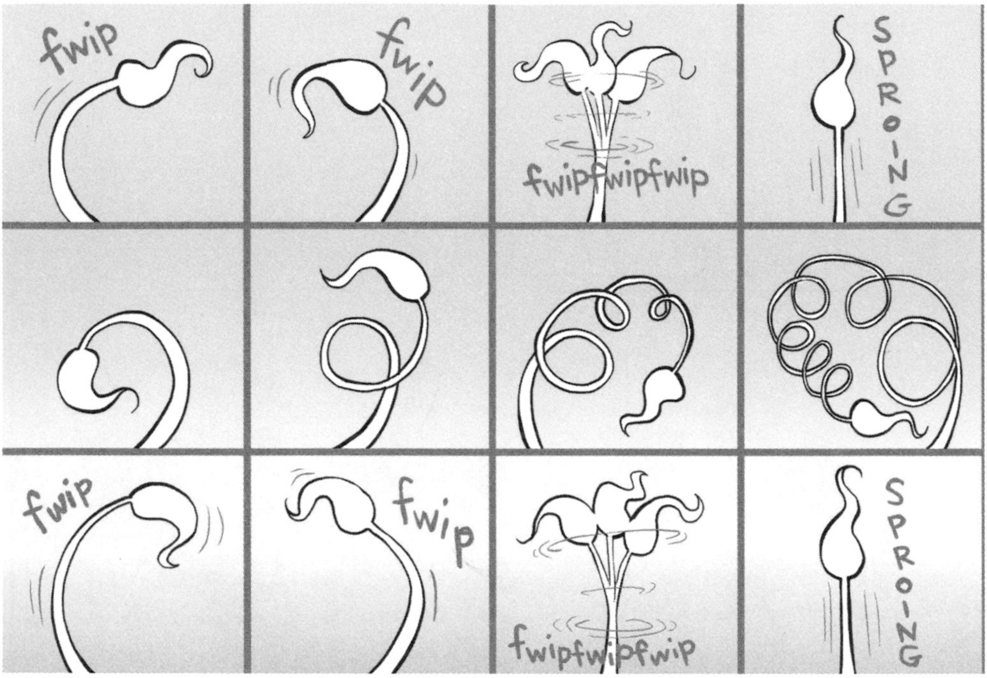
fwip
fwip
fwipfwipfwip
SPROING
fwip
fwip
fwipfwipfwip
SPROING

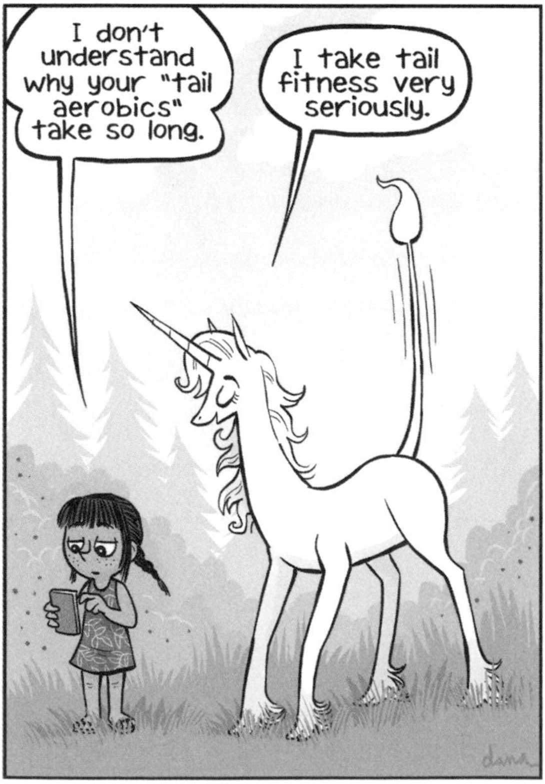
I don't understand why your "tail aerobics" take so long.
I take tail fitness very seriously.
dana

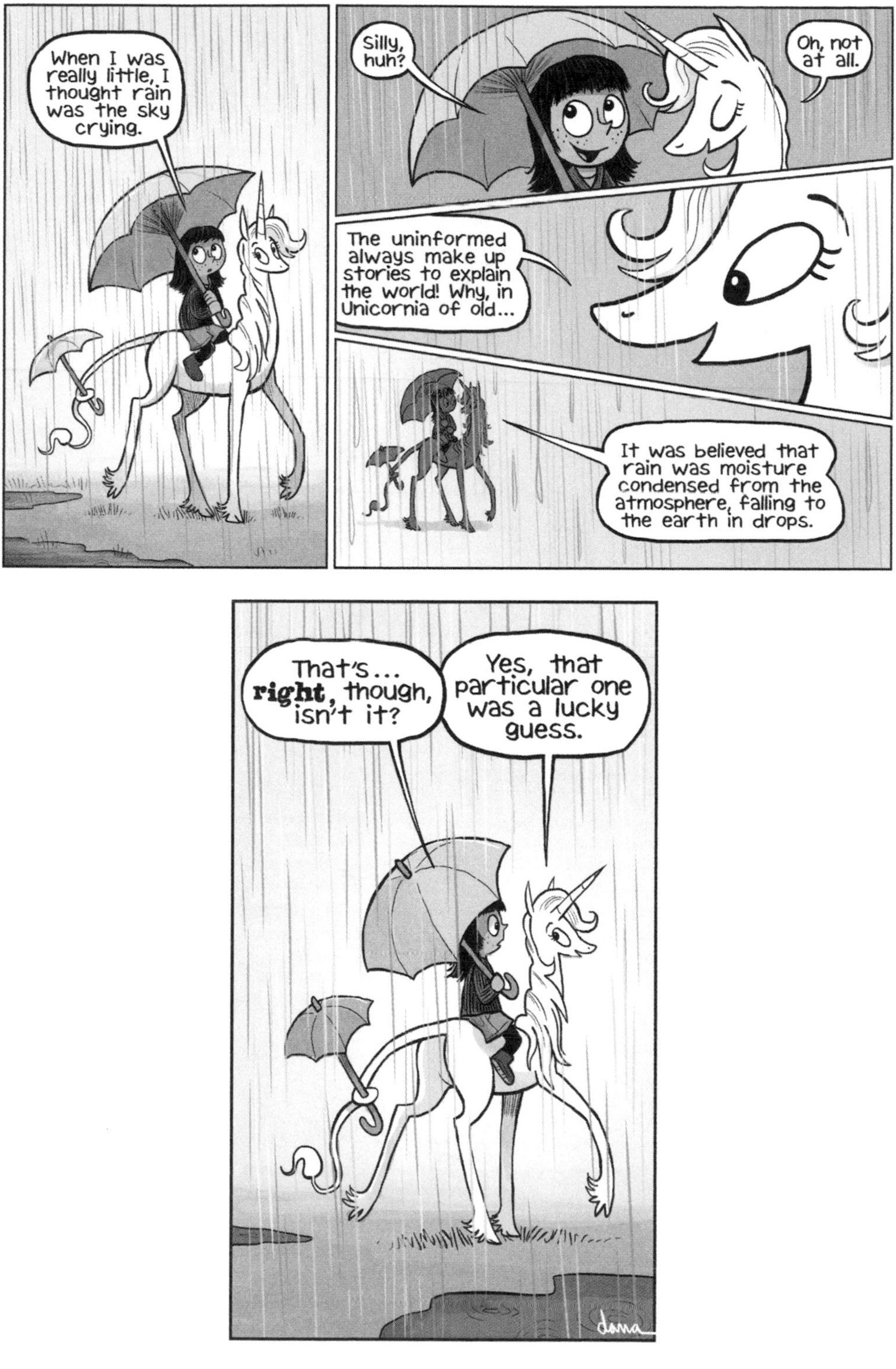

When I was really little, I thought rain was the sky crying.
Silly, huh?
Oh, not at all.
The uninformed always make up stories to explain the world! Why, in Unicornia of old...
It was believed that rain was moisture condensed from the atmosphere, falling to the earth in drops.
That's... **right**, though, isn't it?
Yes, that particular one was a lucky guess.
dana

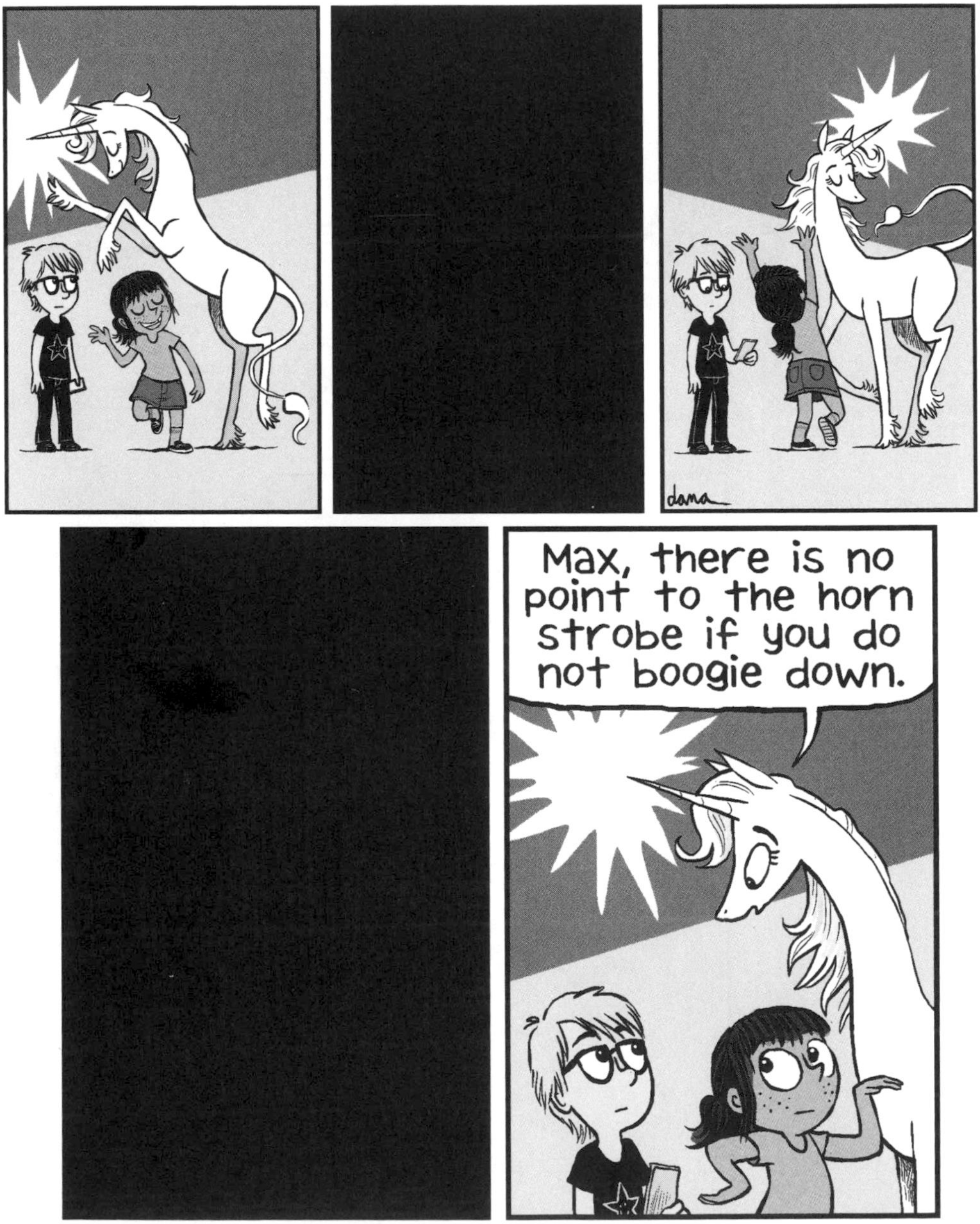
dana
Max, there is no point to the horn strobe if you do not boogie down.

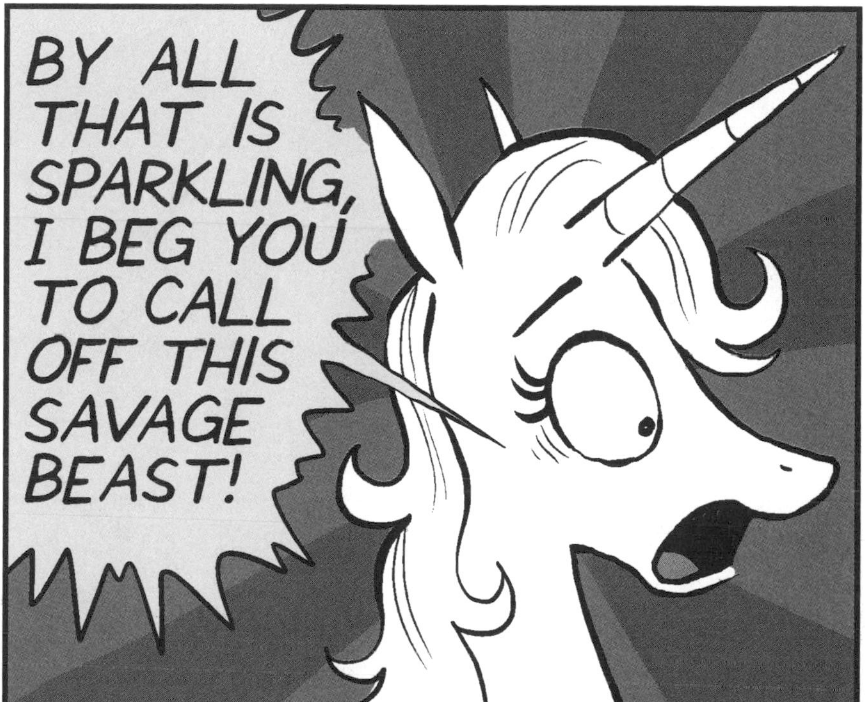
BY ALL THAT IS SPARKLING, I BEG YOU TO CALL OFF THIS SAVAGE BEAST!

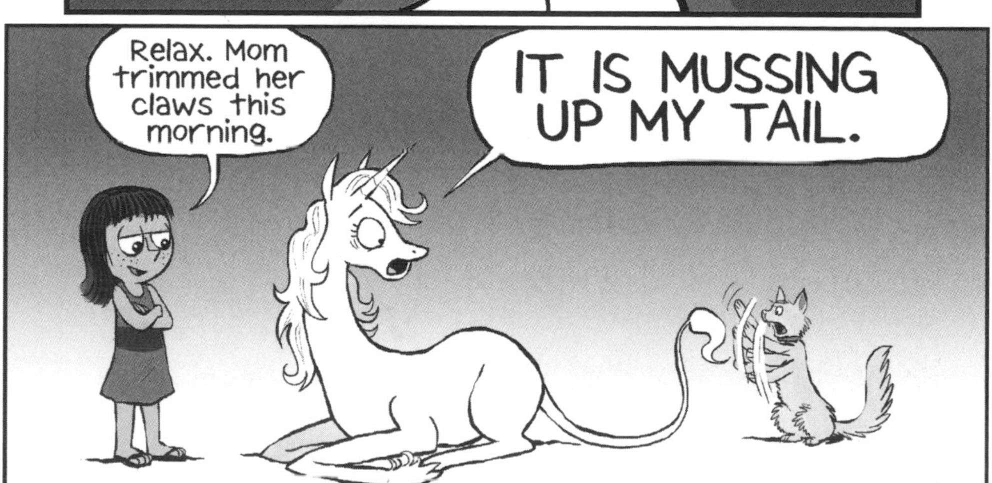
Relax. Mom trimmed her claws this morning.
IT IS MUSSING UP MY TAIL.
dana

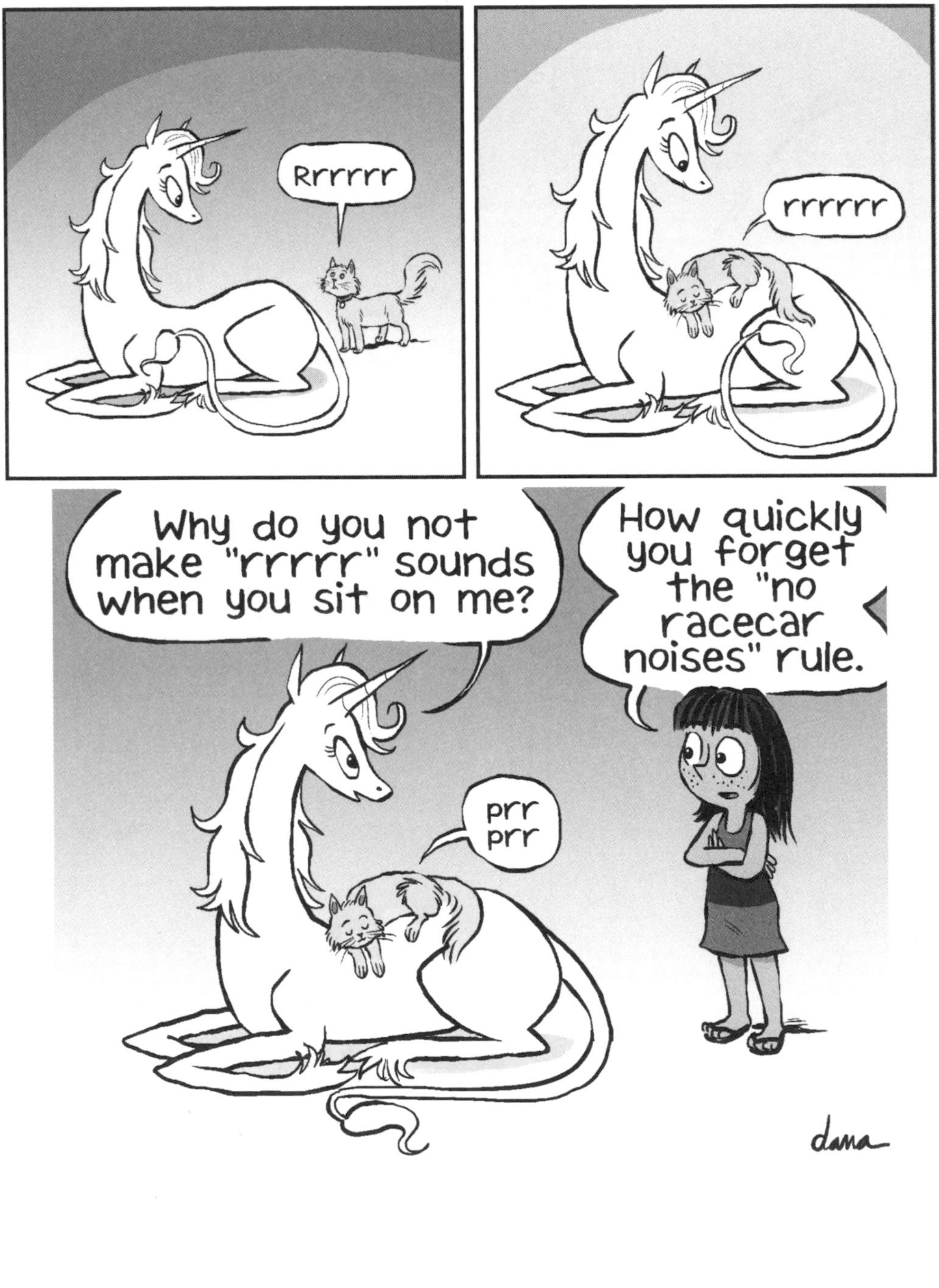
Rrrrrr
rrrrrr
Why do you not make "rrrrr" sounds when you sit on me?
How quickly you forget the "no racecar noises" rule.
prr prr
dana

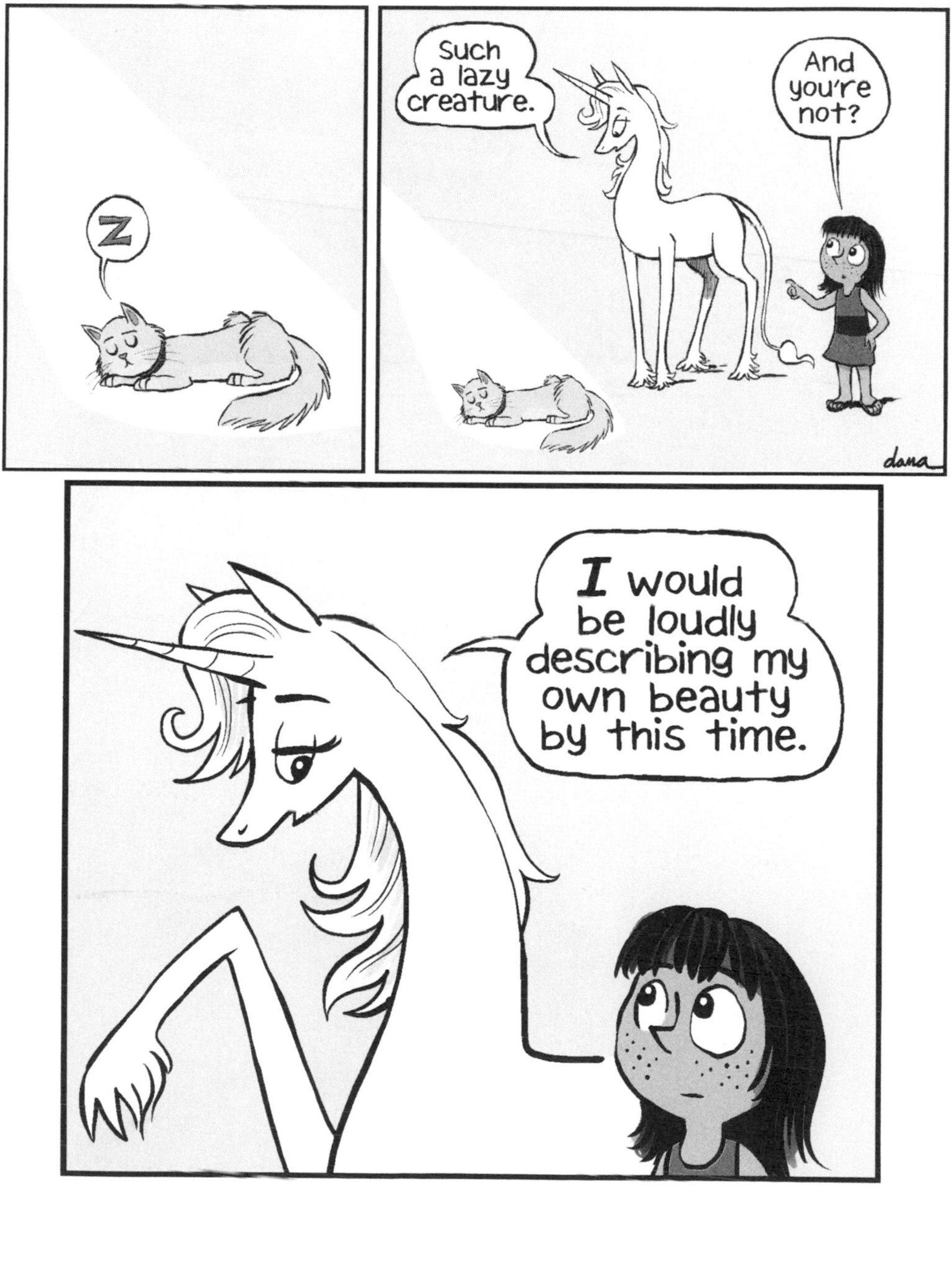
Z
Such a lazy creature.
And you're not?
dana
I would be loudly describing my own beauty by this time.

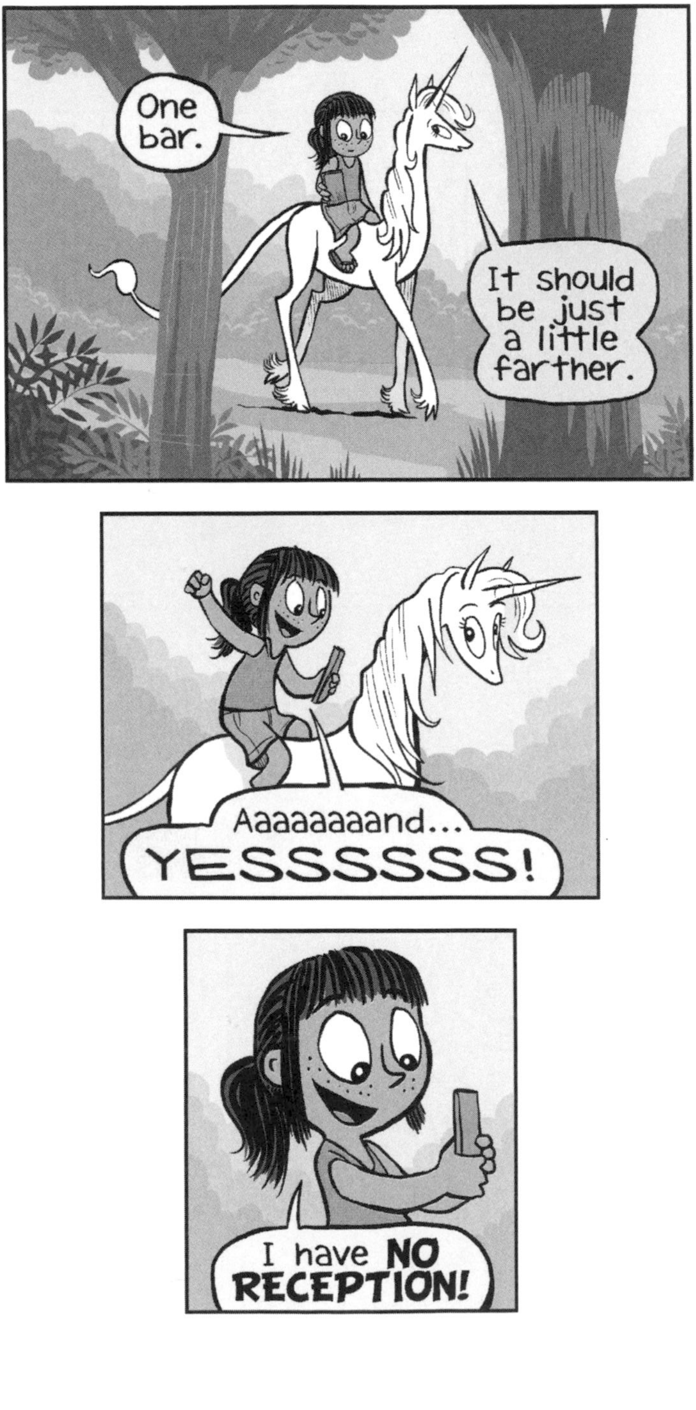
One bar.
It should be just a little farther.
Aaaaaaaand...
YESSSSSS!
I have **NO RECEPTION!**

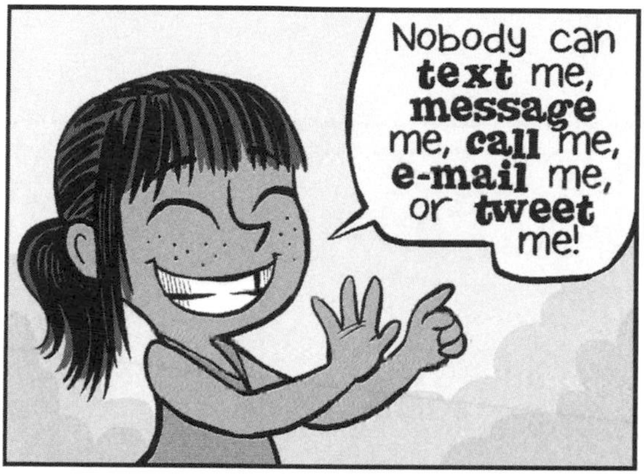
Nobody can **text** me, **message** me, **call** me, **e-mail** me, or **tweet** me!

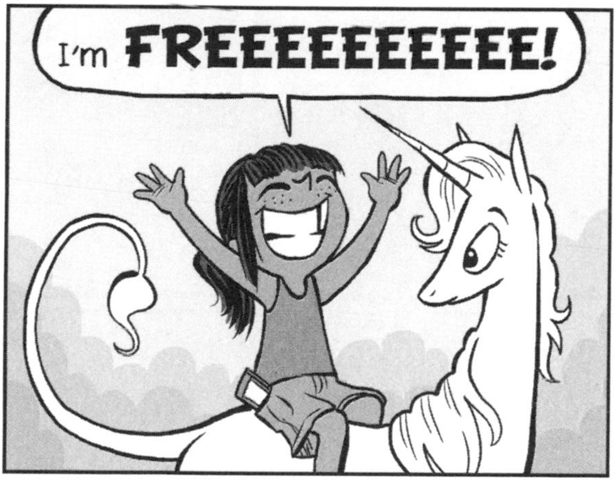
I'm **FREEEEEEEEEEE!**

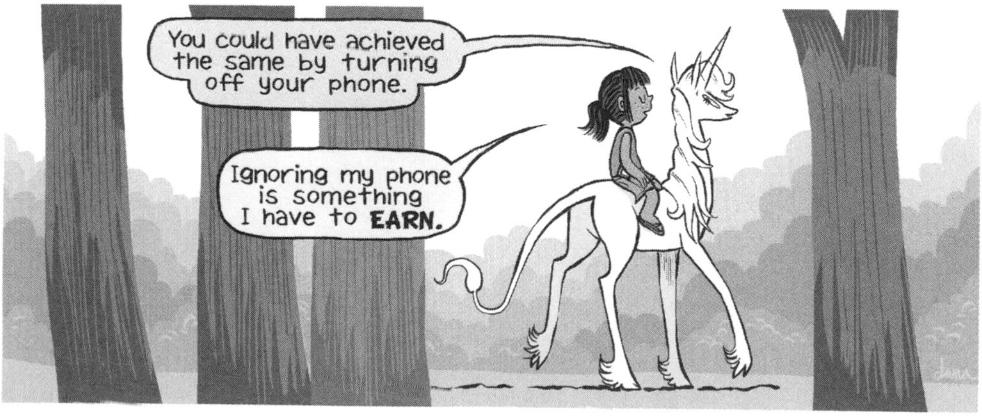
You could have achieved the same by turning off your phone.
Ignoring my phone is something I have to **EARN.**

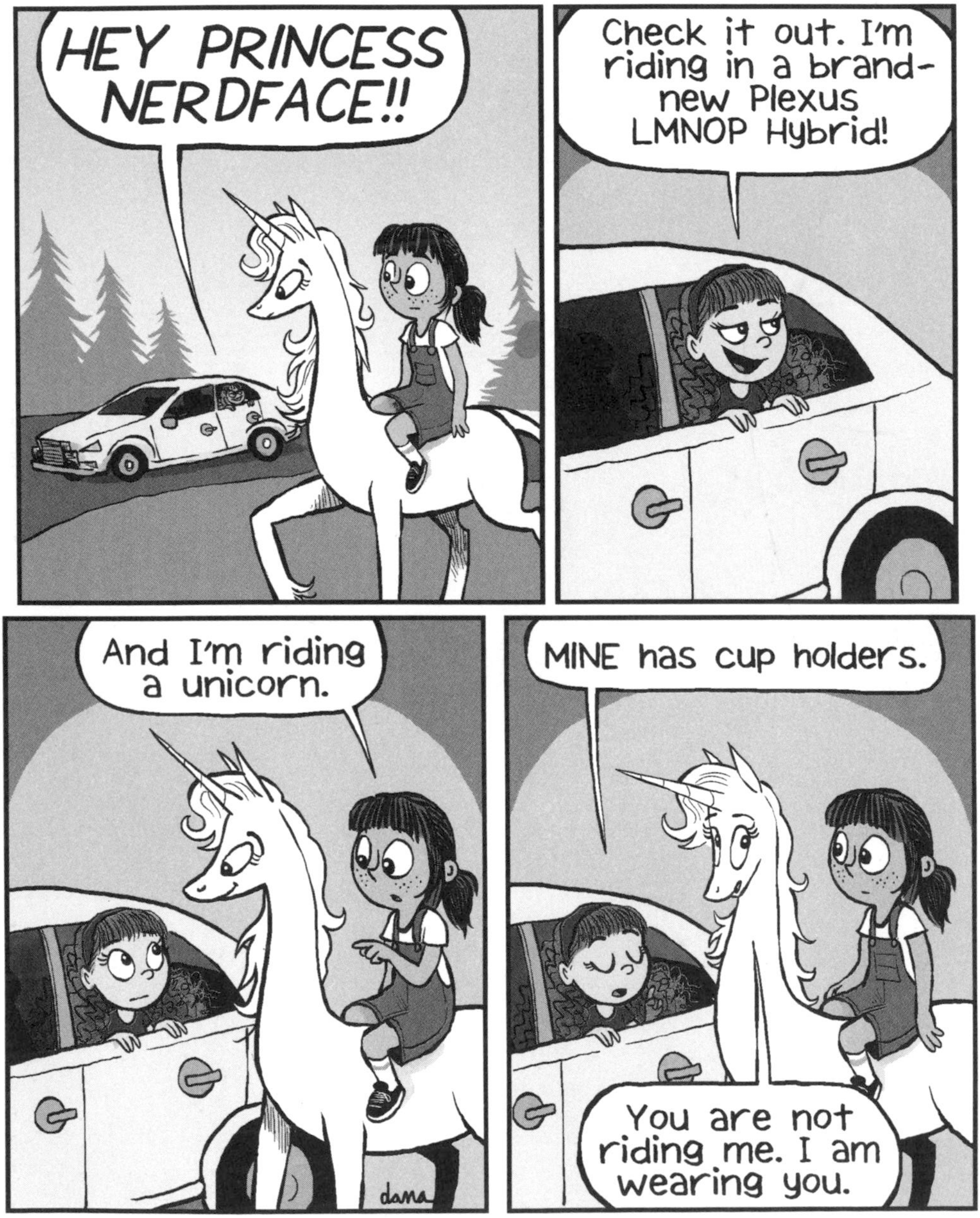
HEY PRINCESS NERDFACE!!
Check it out. I'm riding in a brand-new Plexus LMNOP Hybrid!
And I'm riding a unicorn.
MINE has cup holders.
You are not riding me. I am wearing you.
dana

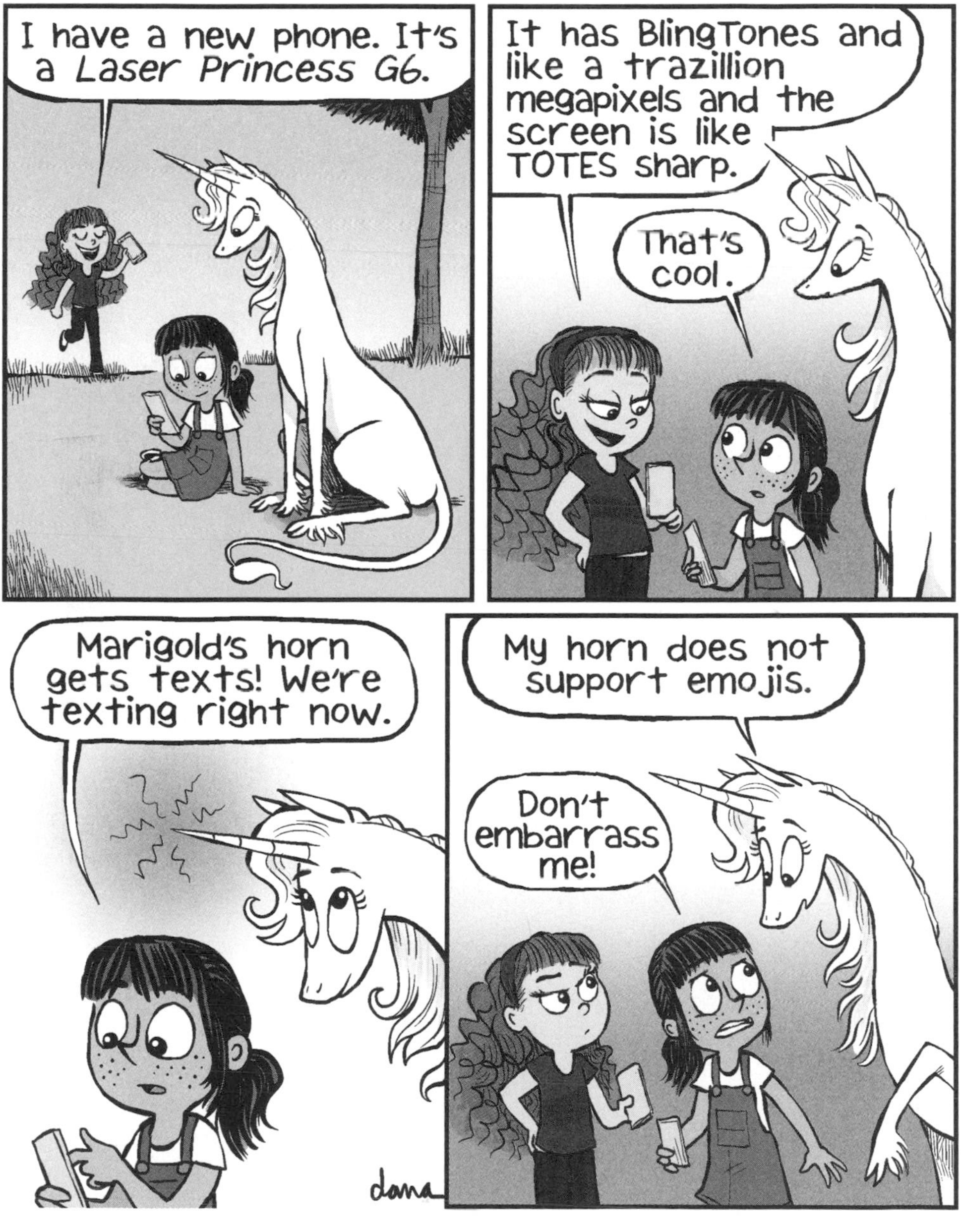

I have a new phone. It's a *Laser Princess G6.*
It has BlingTones and like a trazillion megapixels and the screen is like TOTES sharp.
That's cool.
Marigold's horn gets texts! We're texting right now.
My horn does not support emojis.
Don't embarrass me!
dana

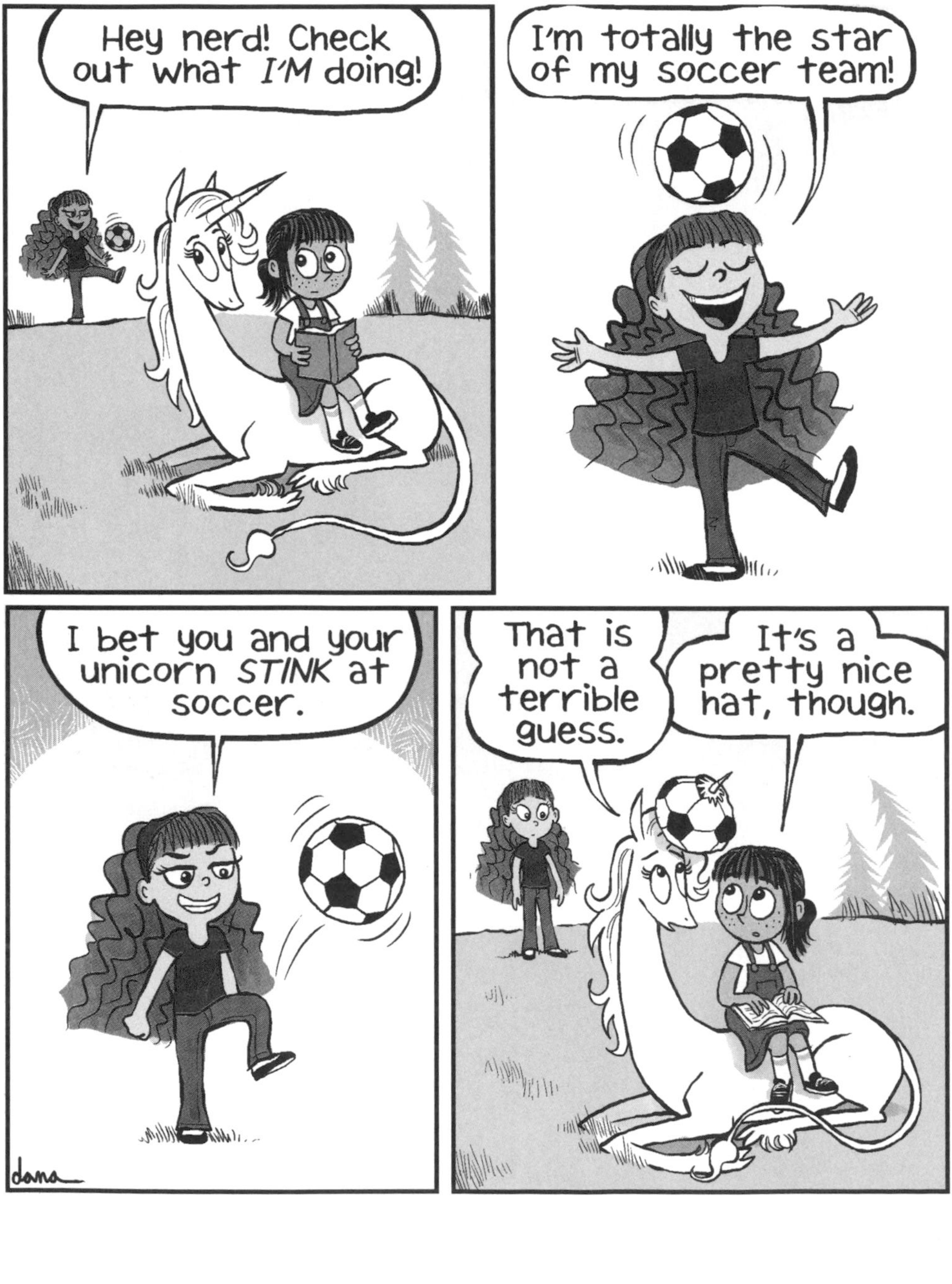
Hey nerd! Check out what *I'M* doing!
I'm totally the star of my soccer team!
I bet you and your unicorn *STINK* at soccer.
dana
That is not a terrible guess.
It's a pretty nice hat, though.

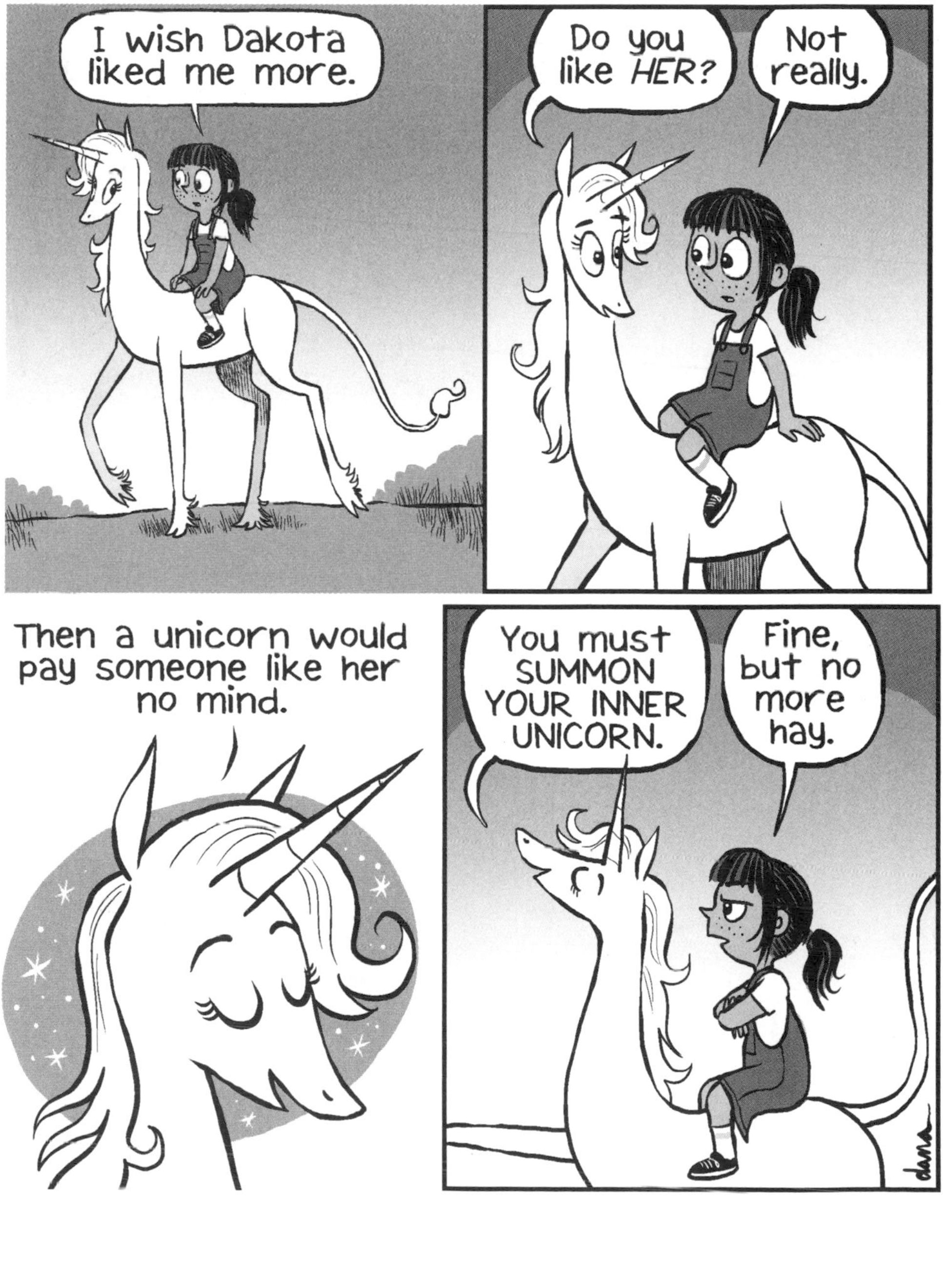
I wish Dakota liked me more.
Do you like HER?
Not really.
Then a unicorn would pay someone like her no mind.
You must SUMMON YOUR INNER UNICORN.
Fine, but no more hay.
dana

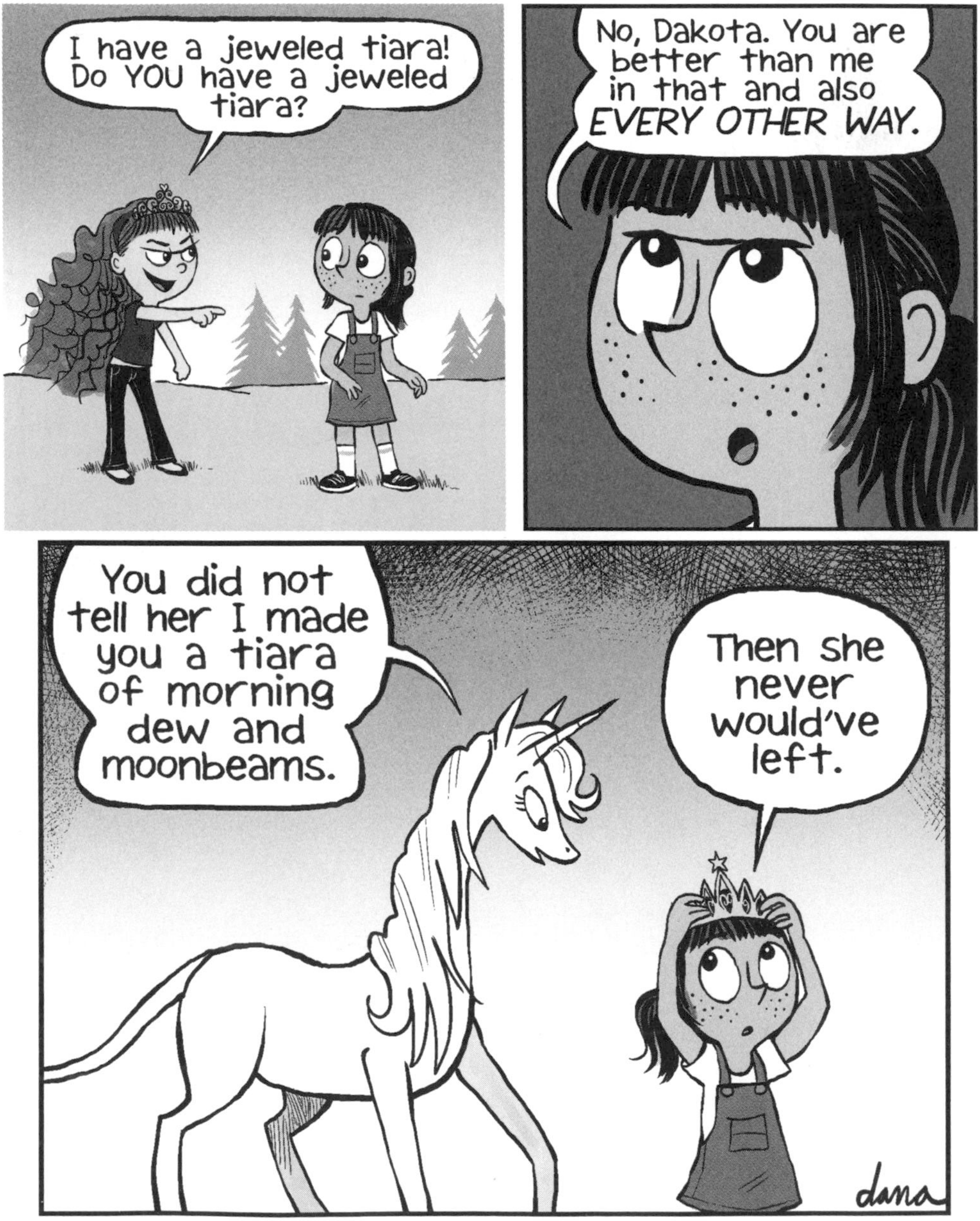
I have a jeweled tiara! Do YOU have a jeweled tiara?
No, Dakota. You are better than me in that and also EVERY OTHER WAY.
You did not tell her I made you a tiara of morning dew and moonbeams.
Then she never would've left.
dana

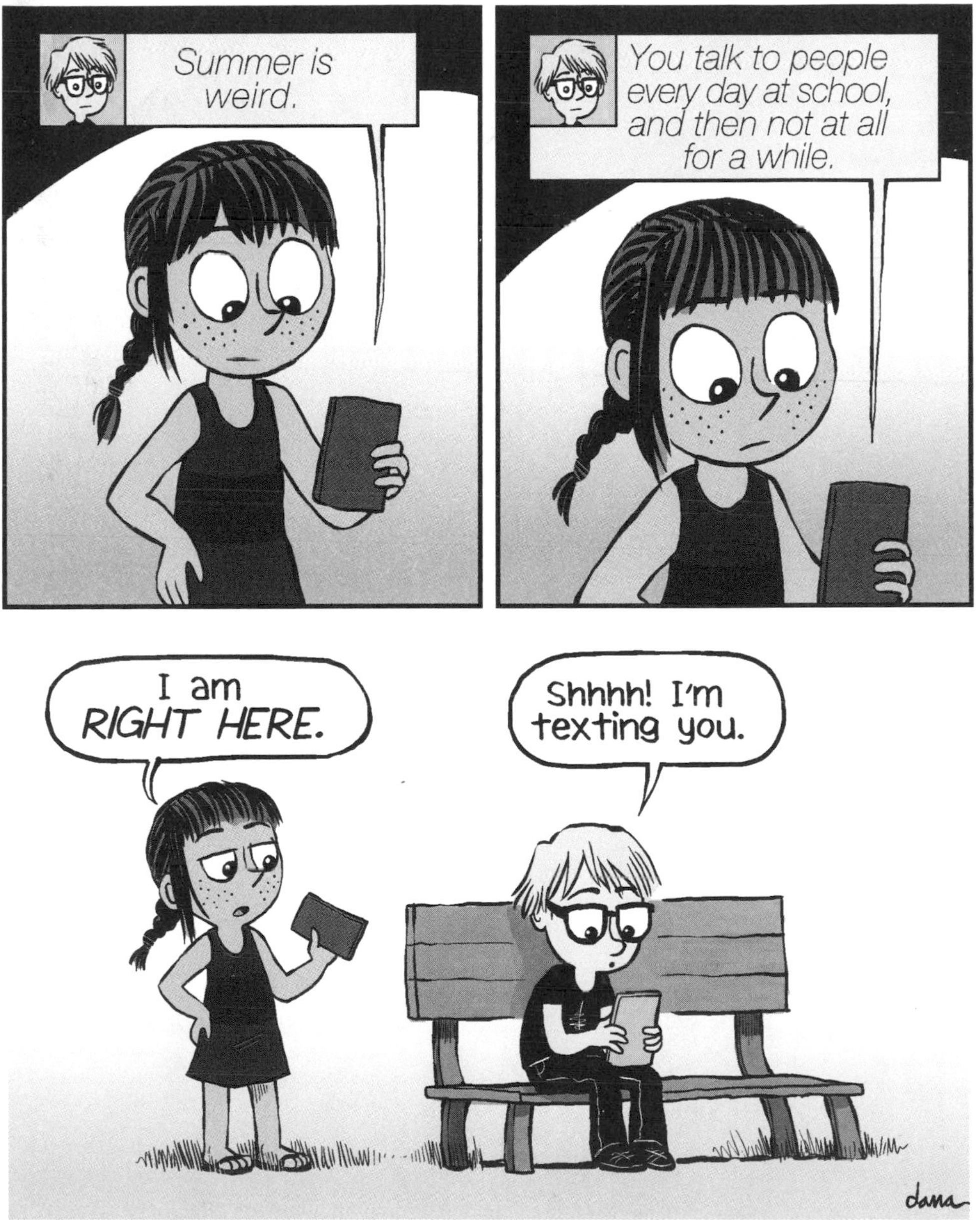
Summer is weird.
You talk to people every day at school, and then not at all for a while.
I am RIGHT HERE.
Shhhh! I'm texting you.
dana

Those are such **DAD SHORTS**.
You say that whenever I wear them.
Well, they aren't very cool.
I'm cool.
Nobody cool wears shorts like that.

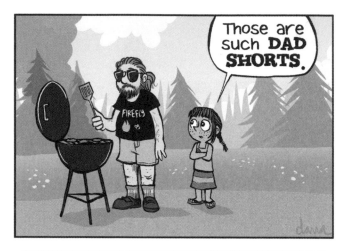

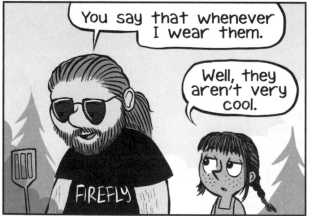

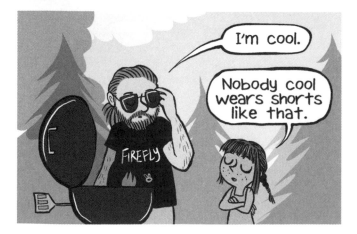

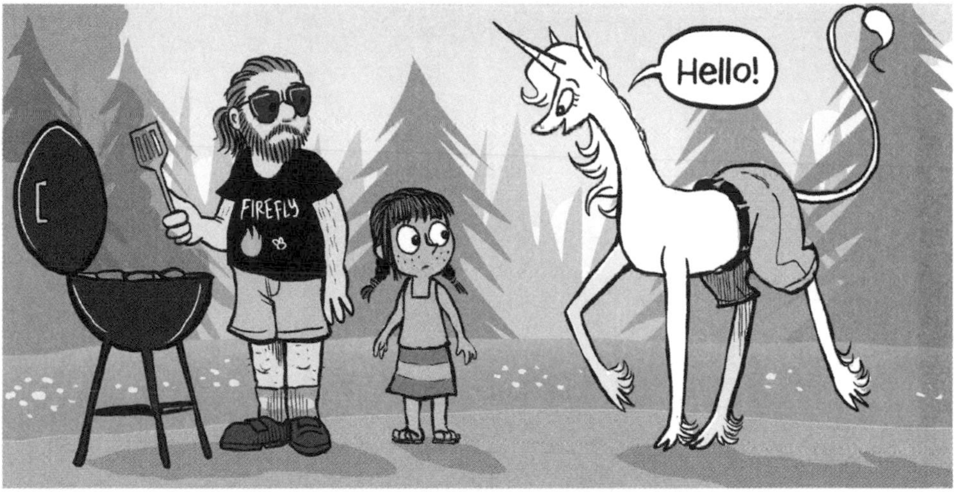
Hello!
FIREFLY

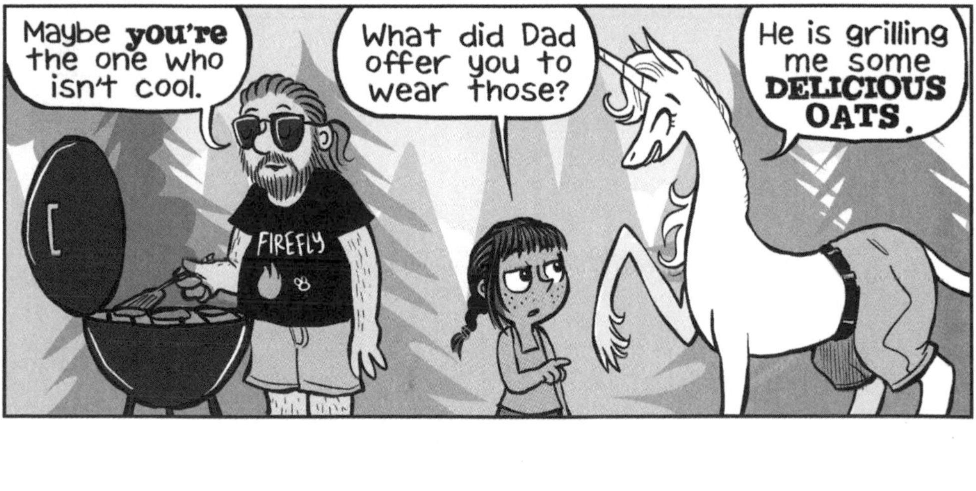
Maybe **you're** the one who isn't cool.
What did Dad offer you to wear those?
He is grilling me some **DELICIOUS OATS**.
FIREFLY

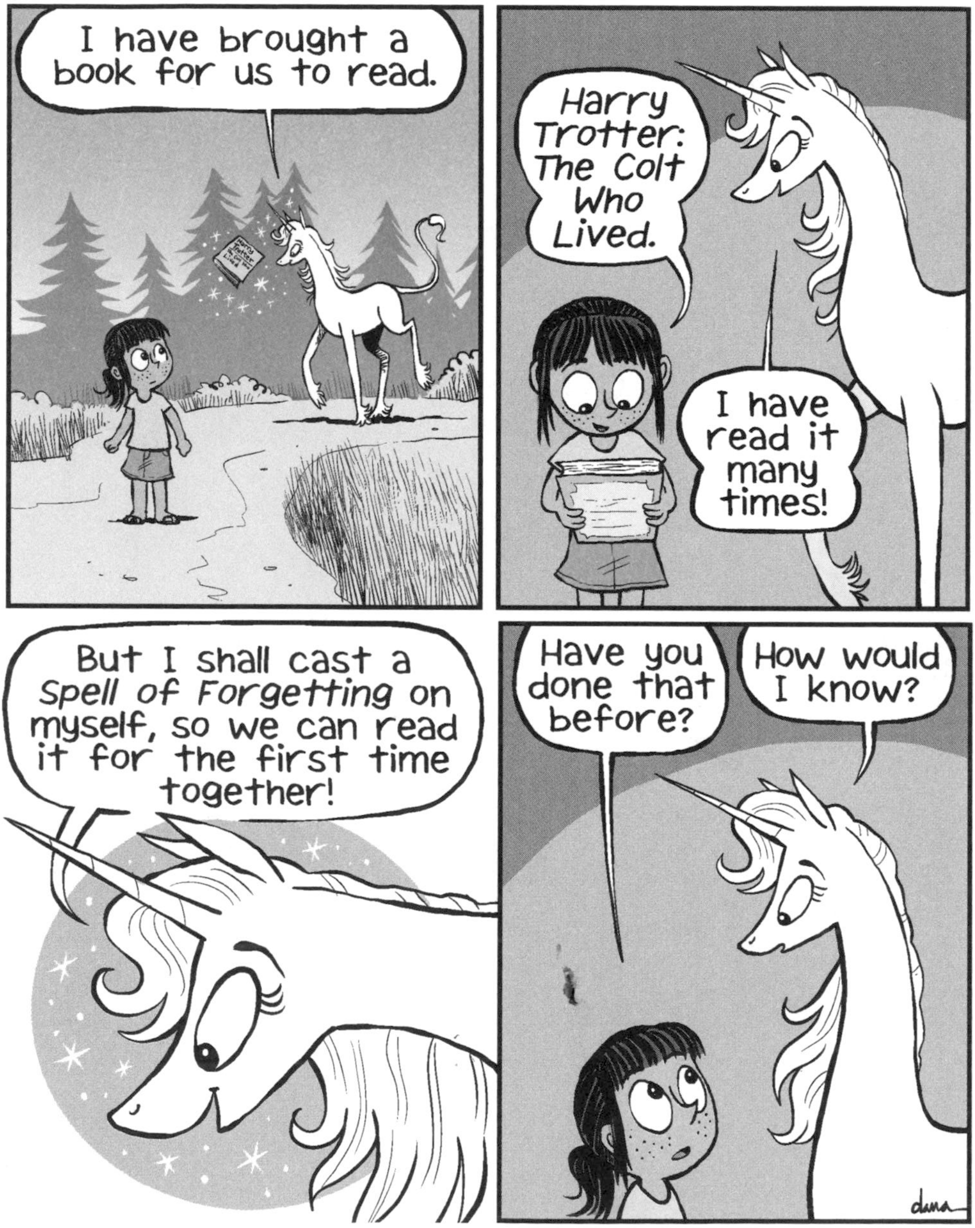
I have brought a book for us to read.
Harry Trotter: The Colt Who Lived.
I have read it many times!
But I shall cast a *Spell of Forgetting* on myself, so we can read it for the first time together!
Have you done that before?
How would I know?
dana

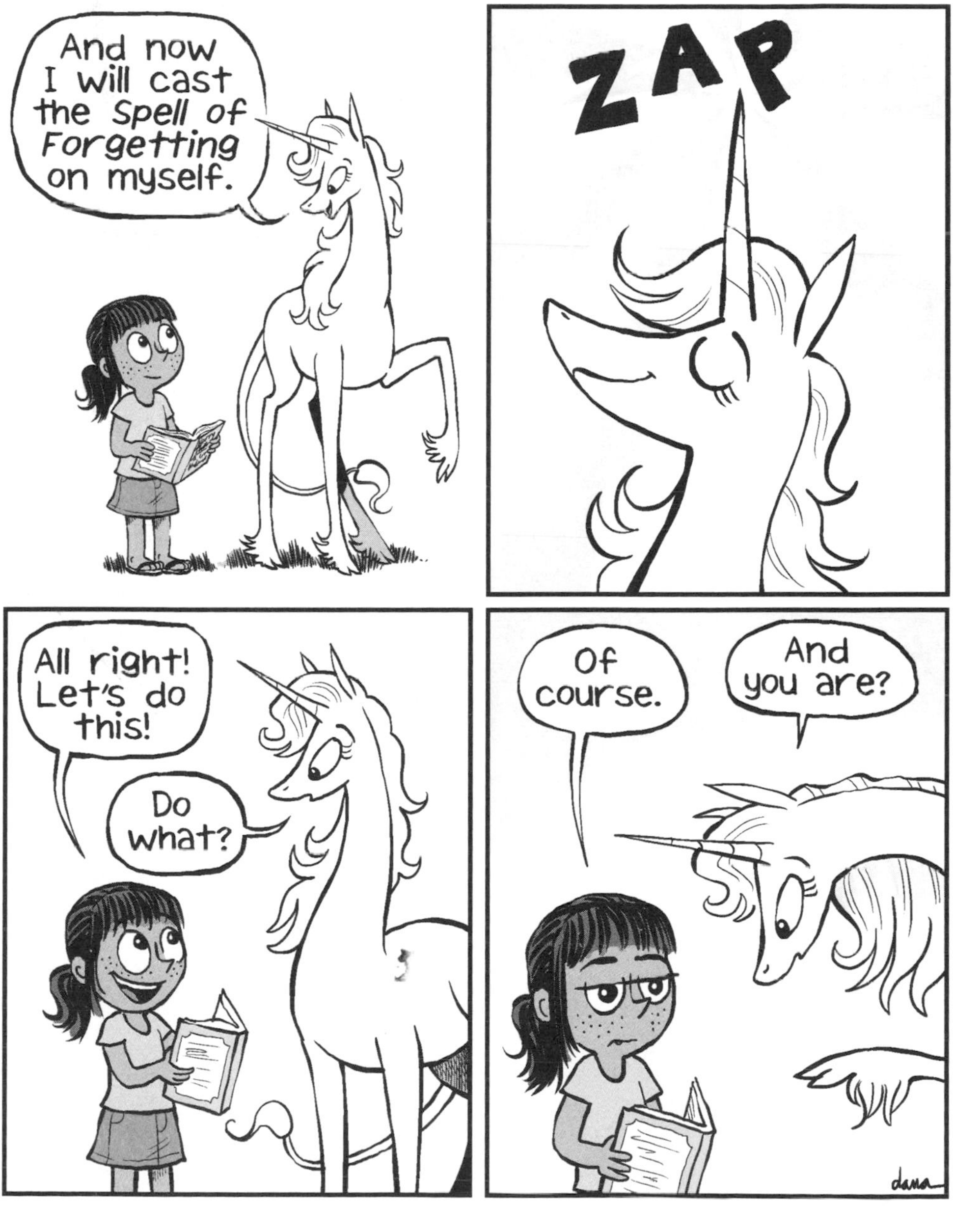
And now I will cast the *Spell of Forgetting* on myself.
ZAP
All right! Let's do this!
Do what?
Of course.
And you are?

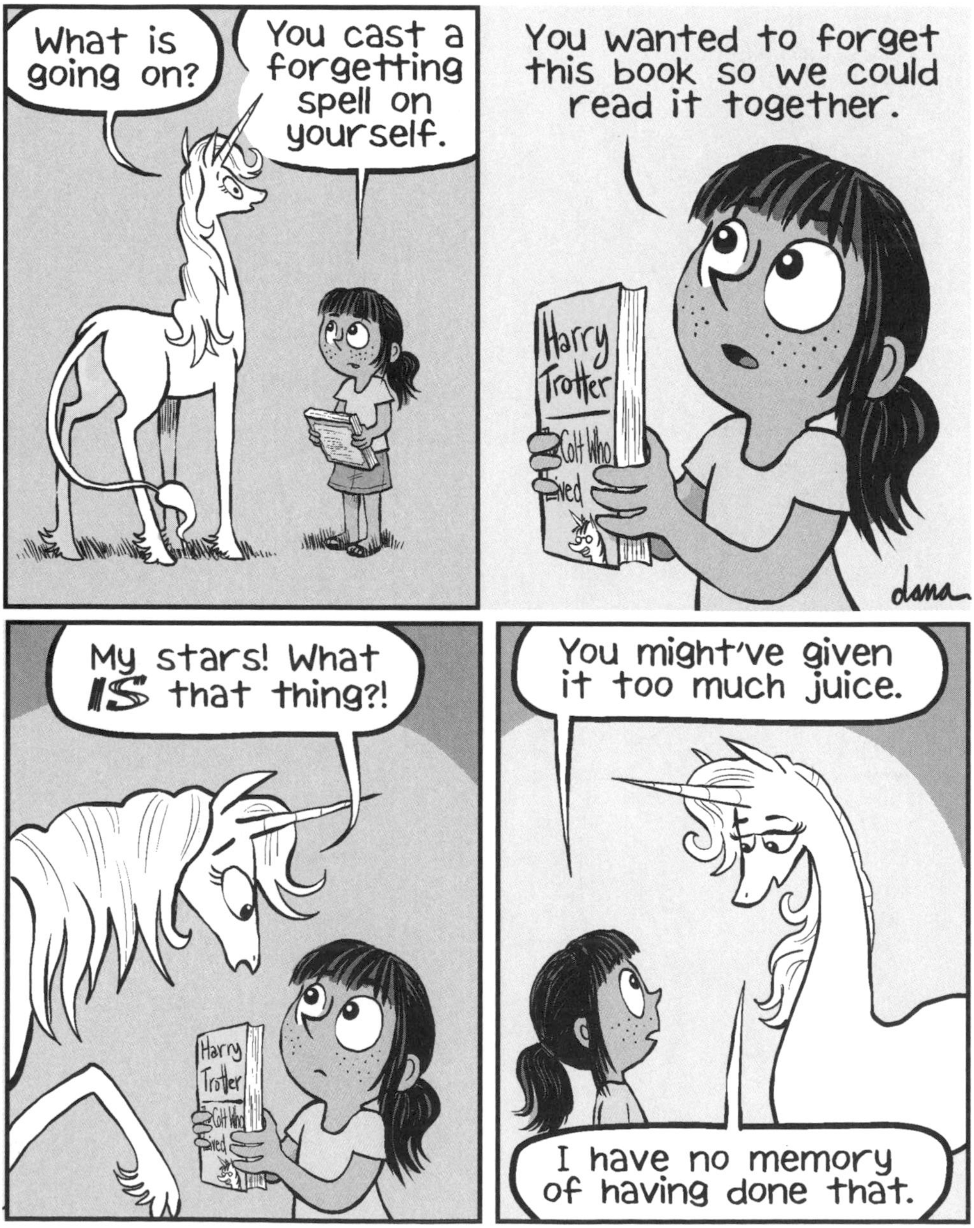
What is going on?
You cast a forgetting spell on yourself.
You wanted to forget this book so we could read it together.
Harry Trotter
Colt Who Lived
dana
My stars! What IS that thing?!
You might've given it too much juice.
I have no memory of having done that.

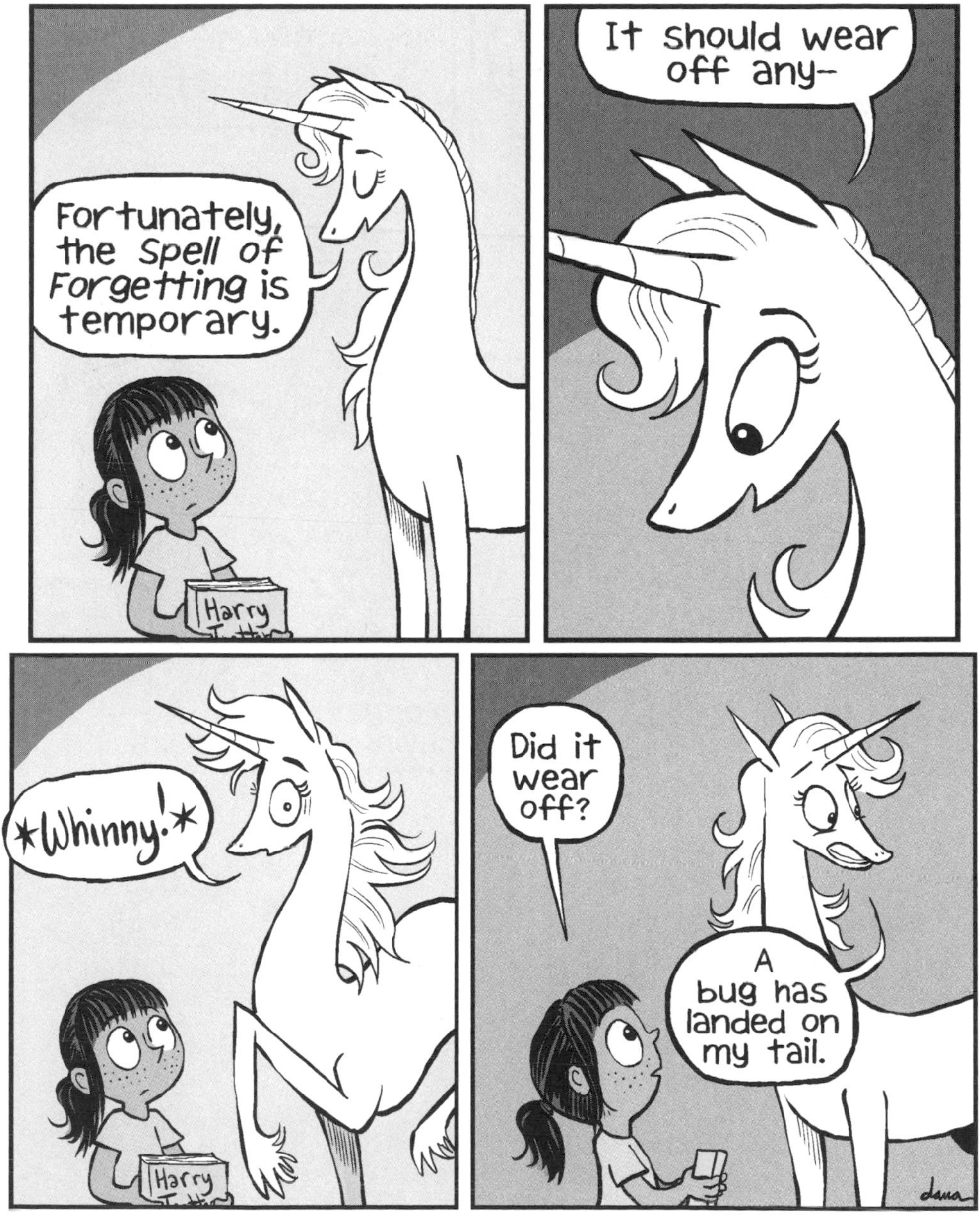
Fortunately, the *Spell of Forgetting* is temporary.
Harry
It should wear off any-
Whinny!
Harry
Did it wear off?
A bug has landed on my tail.
dana

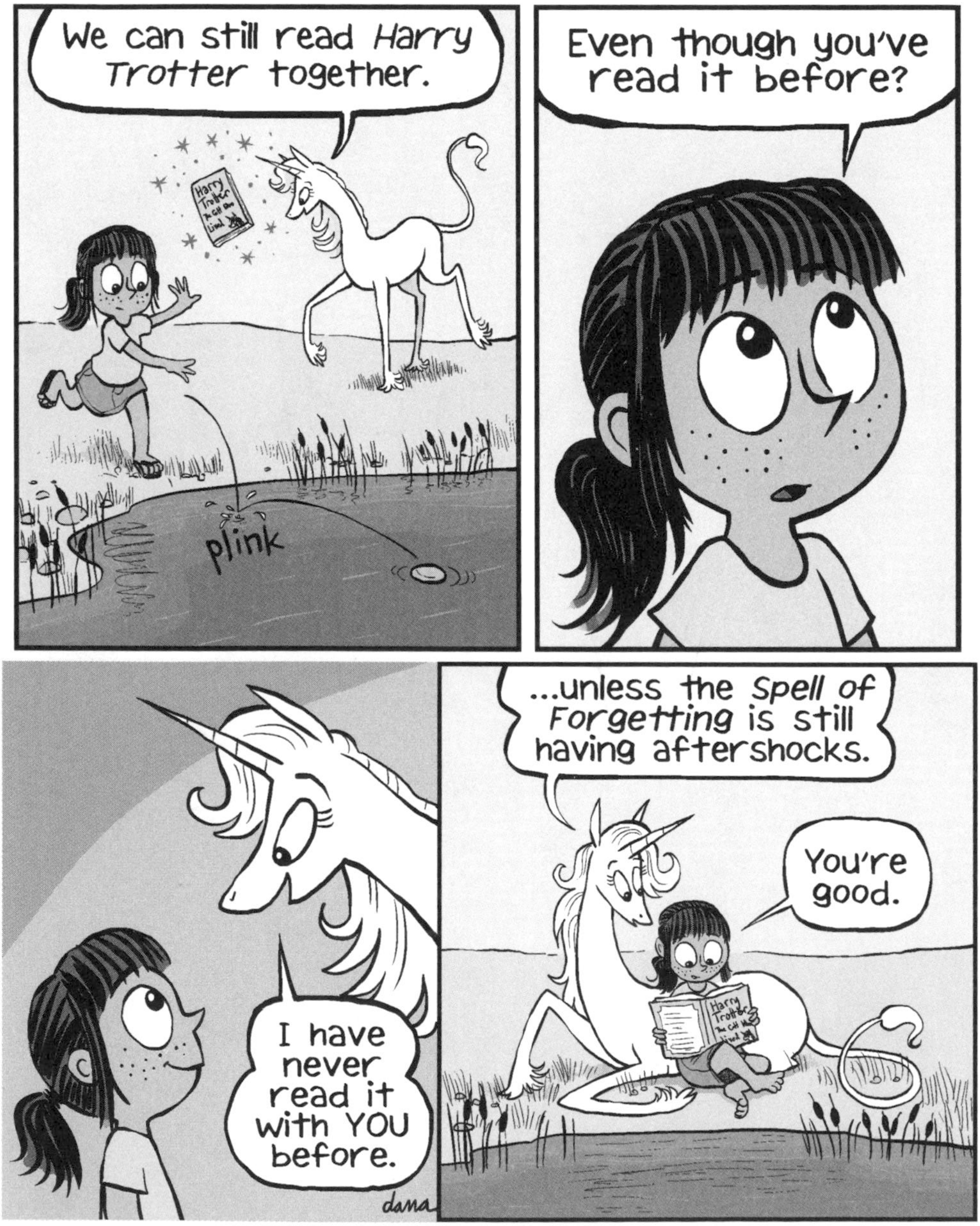
We can still read *Harry Trotter* together.
plink
Even though you've read it before?
I have never read it with YOU before.
dana
...unless the *Spell of Forgetting* is still having aftershocks.
You're good.

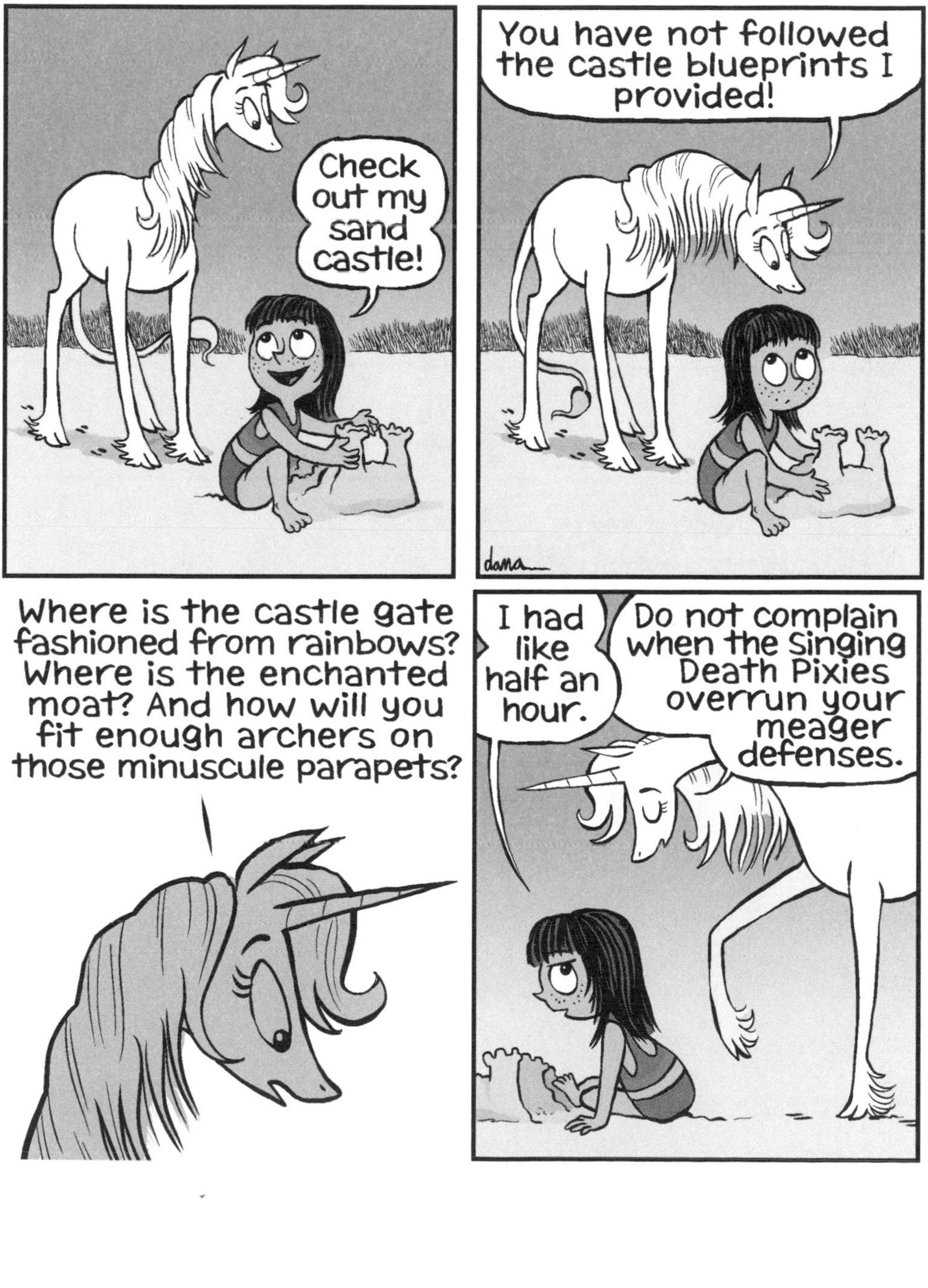
Check out my sand castle!
You have not followed the castle blueprints I provided!
dana
Where is the castle gate fashioned from rainbows? Where is the enchanted moat? And how will you fit enough archers on those minuscule parapets?
I had like half an hour.
Do not complain when the Singing Death Pixies overrun your meager defenses.

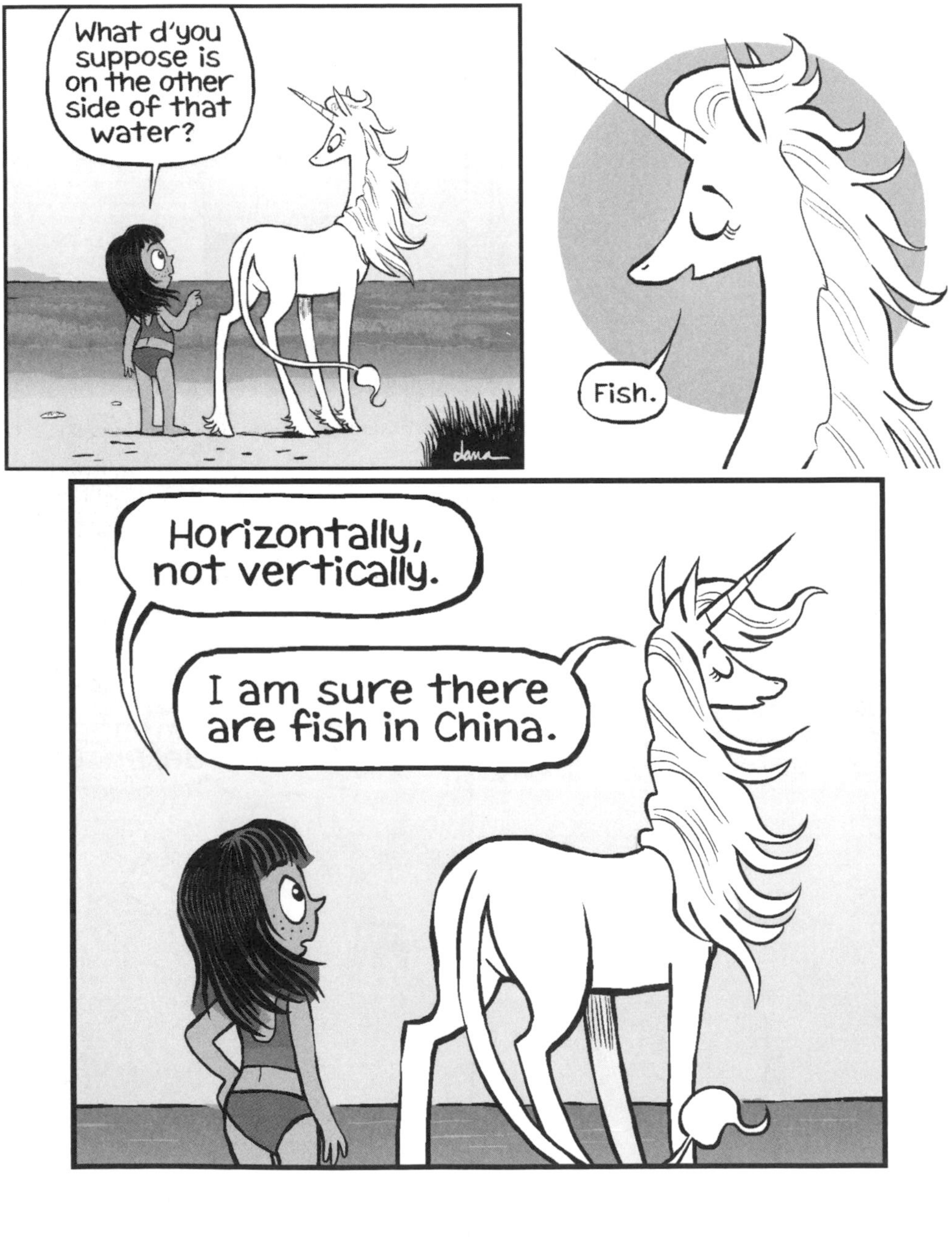
What d'you suppose is on the other side of that water?
dana
Fish.
Horizontally, not vertically.
I am sure there are fish in China.

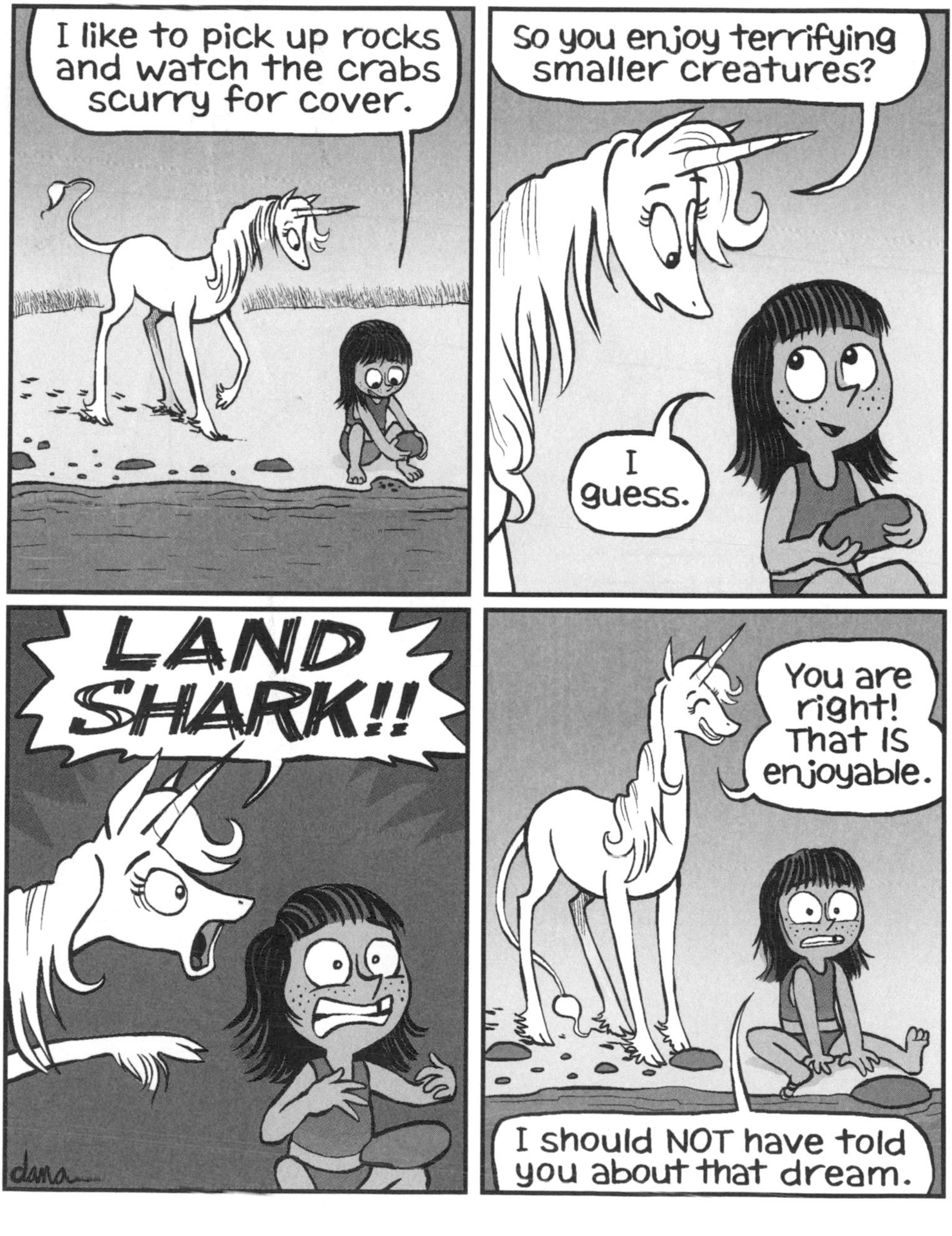
I like to pick up rocks and watch the crabs scurry for cover.
So you enjoy terrifying smaller creatures?
I guess.
LAND SHARK!!
You are right! That IS enjoyable.
I should NOT have told you about that dream.
dana

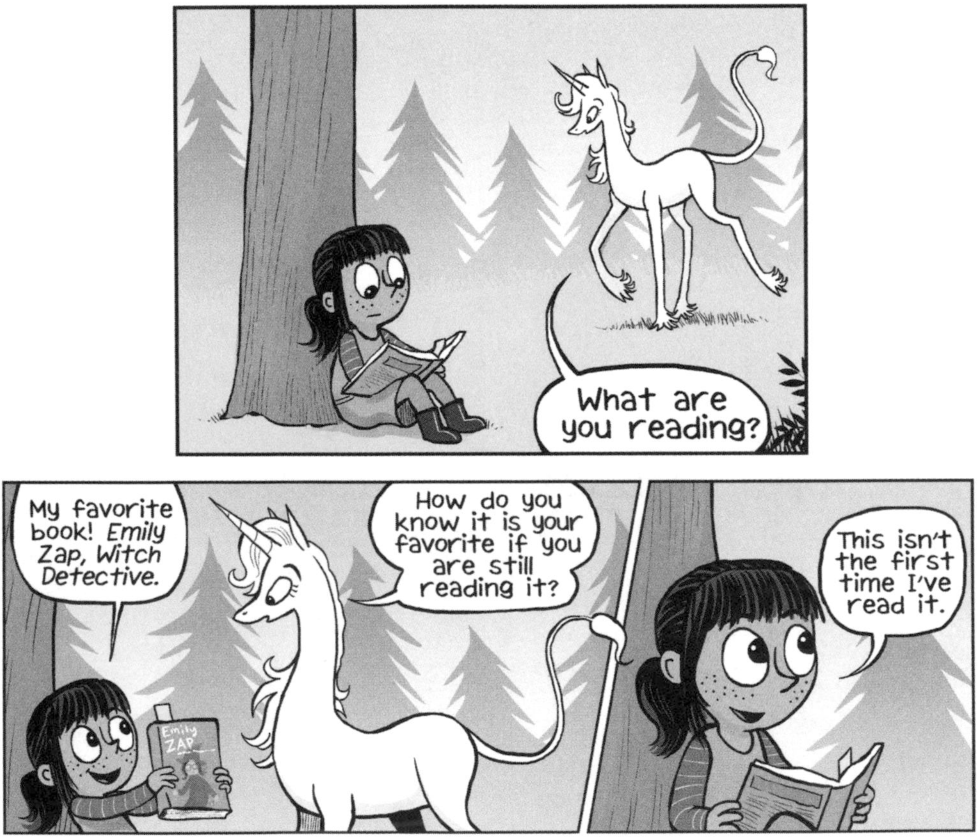
What are you reading?
My favorite book! *Emily Zap, Witch Detective.*
How do you know it is your favorite if you are still reading it?
This isn't the first time I've read it.

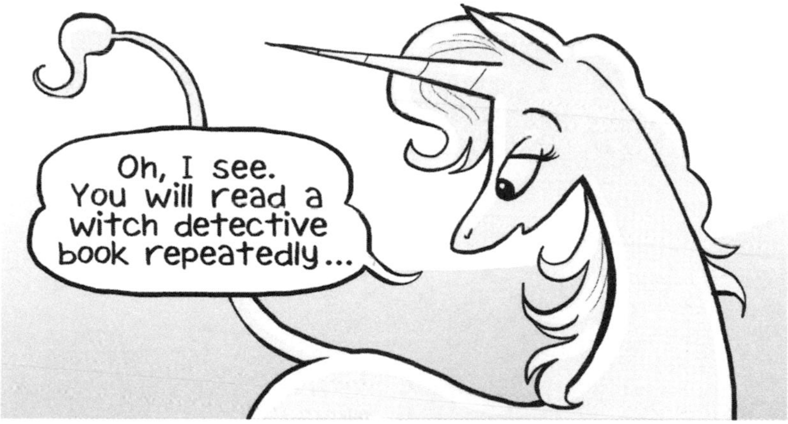
Oh, I see. You will read a witch detective book repeatedly...

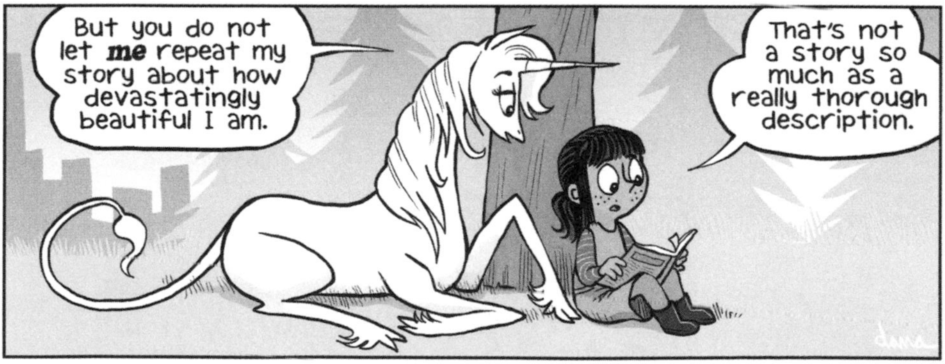
But you do not let **me** repeat my story about how devastatingly beautiful I am.
That's not a story so much as a really thorough description.

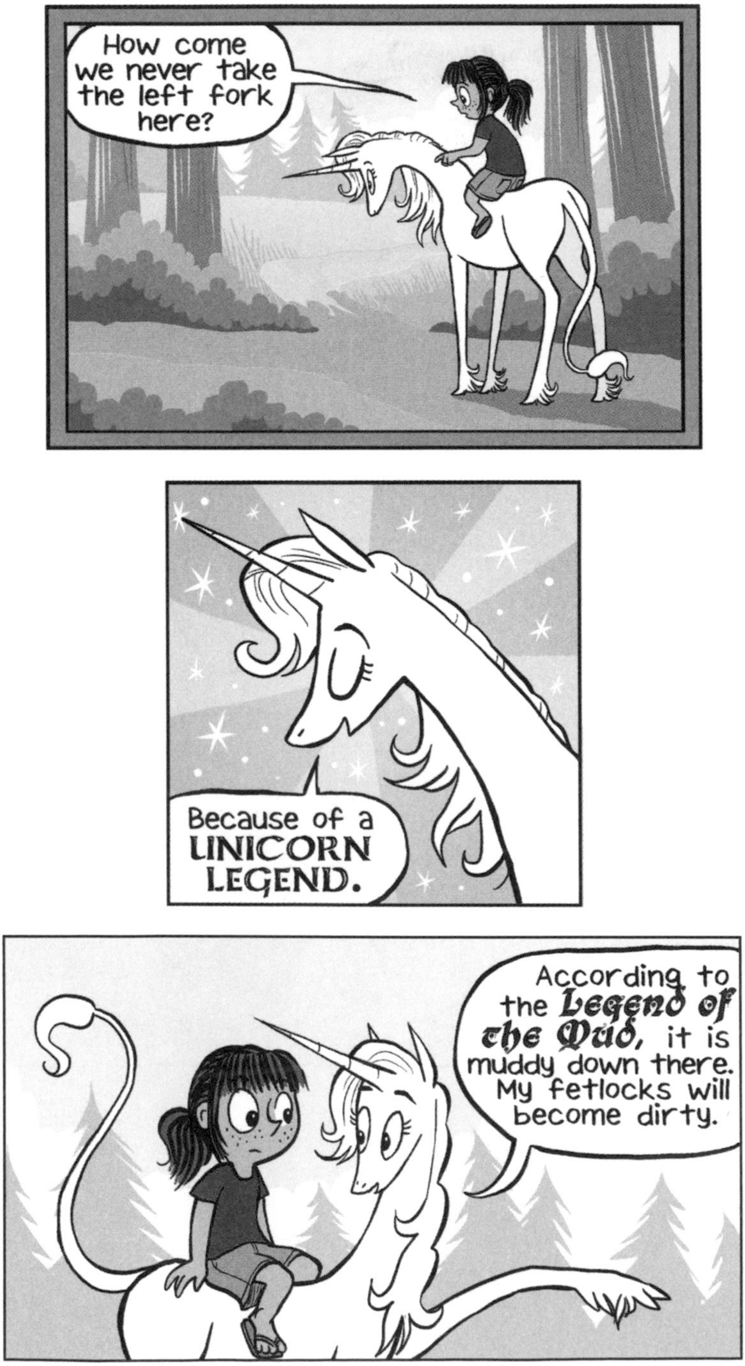
How come we never take the left fork here?
Because of a UNICORN LEGEND.
According to the Legend of the Mud, it is muddy down there. My fetlocks will become dirty.

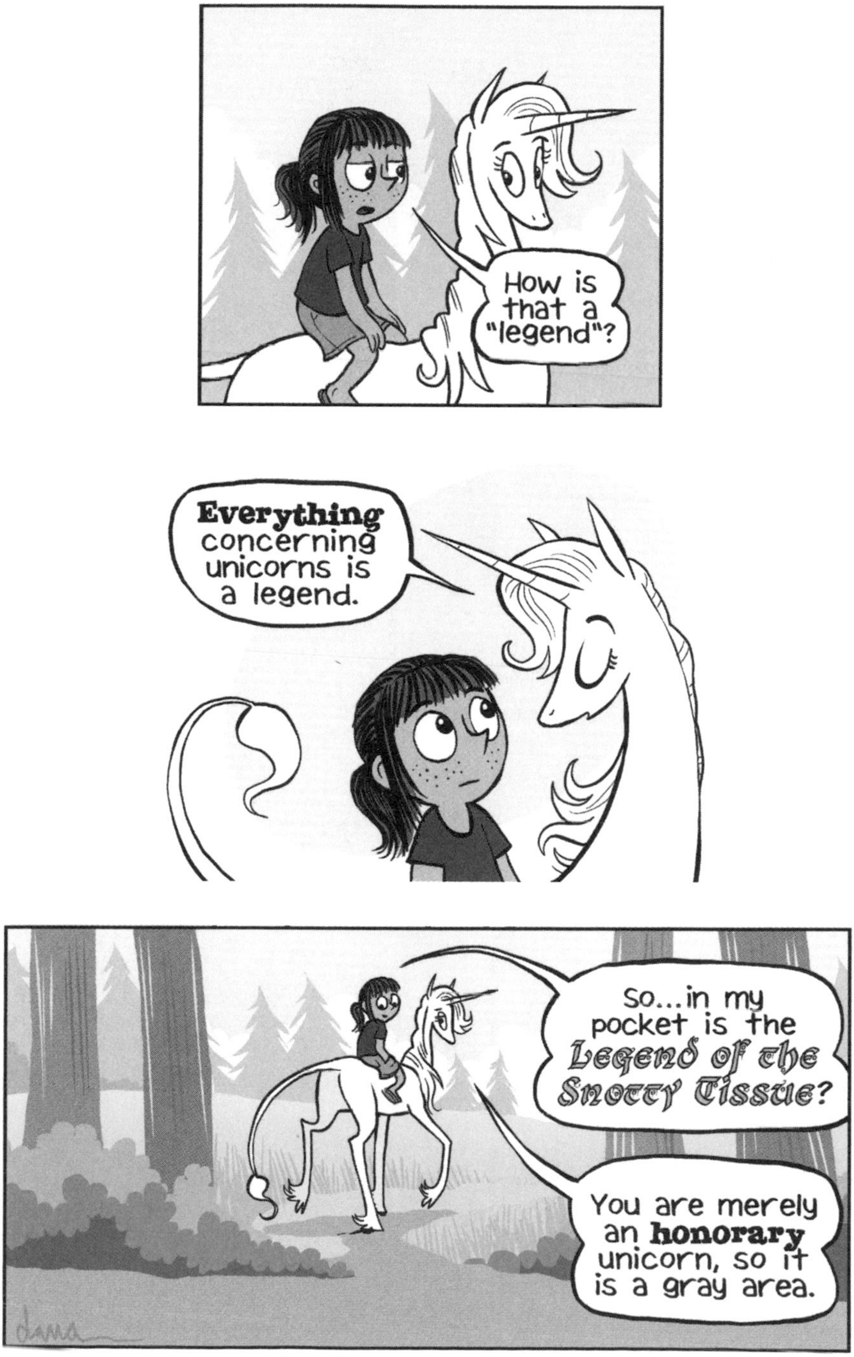
How is that a "legend"?
Everything concerning unicorns is a legend.
So...in my pocket is the *Legend of the Snotty Tissue?*
You are merely an **honorary** unicorn, so it is a gray area.

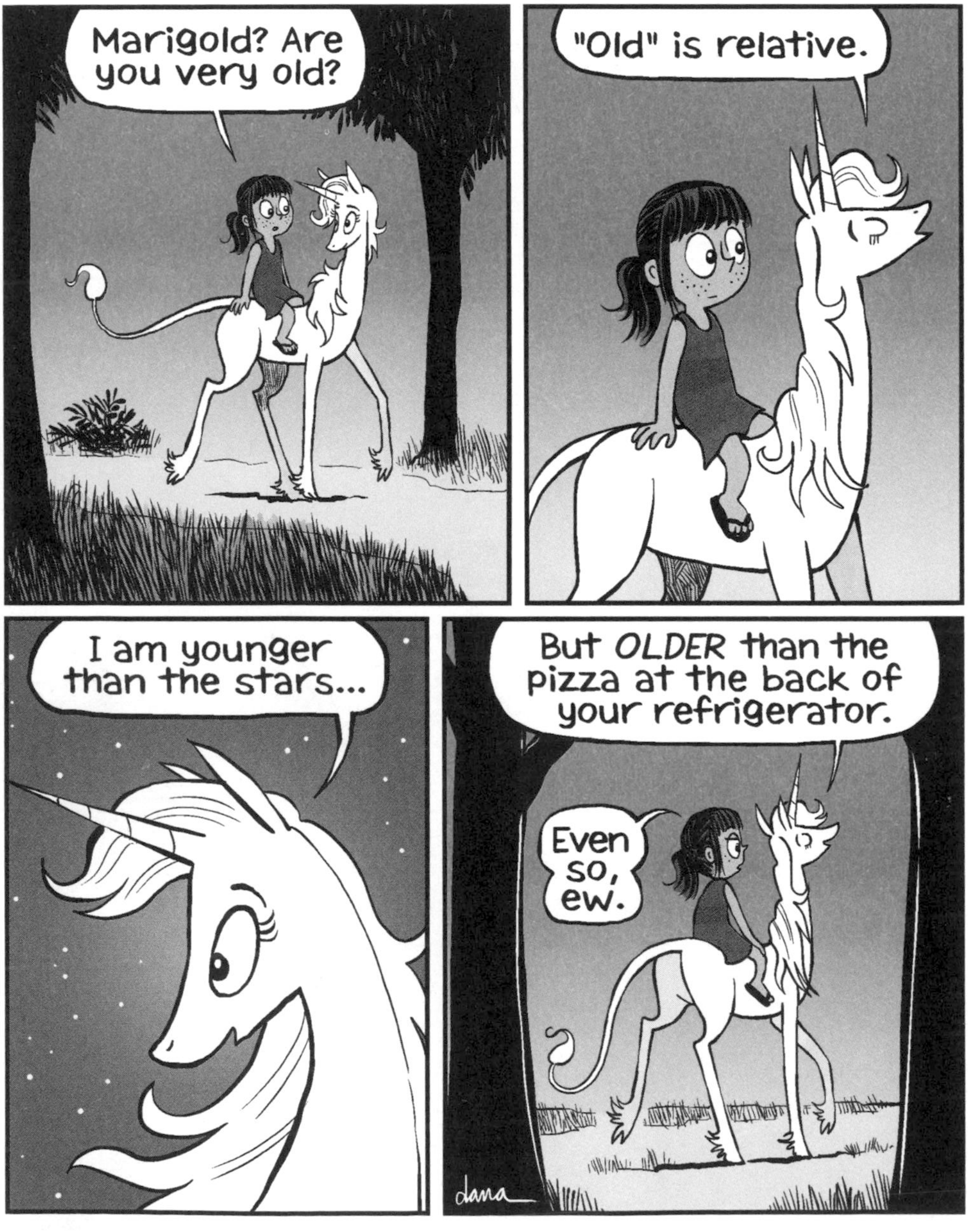
Marigold? Are you very old?
"Old" is relative.
I am younger than the stars...
But OLDER than the pizza at the back of your refrigerator.
Even so, ew.
dana

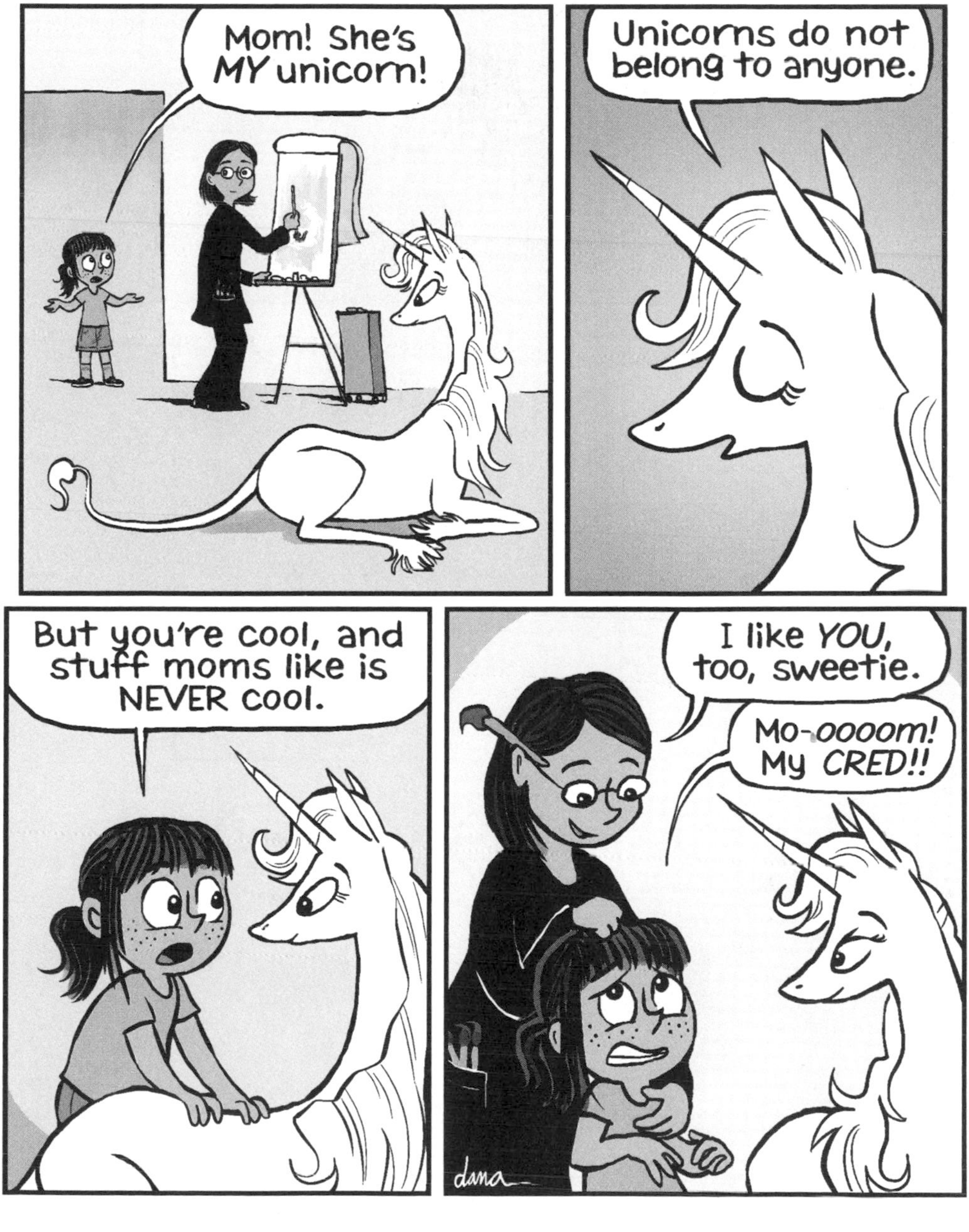
Mom! She's MY unicorn!
Unicorns do not belong to anyone.
But you're cool, and stuff moms like is NEVER cool.
I like YOU, too, sweetie.
Mo-oooom! My CRED!!
dana

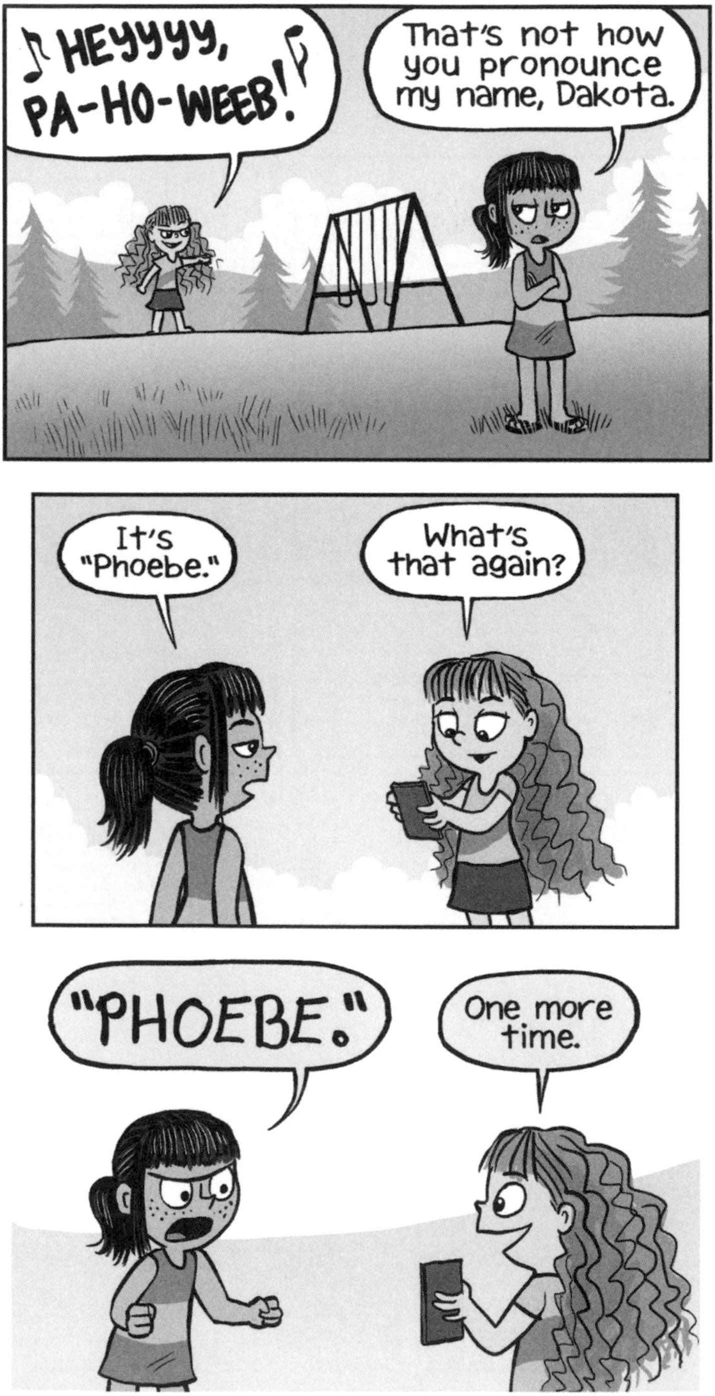
HEYYYY, PA-HO-WEEB!
That's not how you pronounce my name, Dakota.
It's "Phoebe."
What's that again?
"PHOEBE."
One more time.

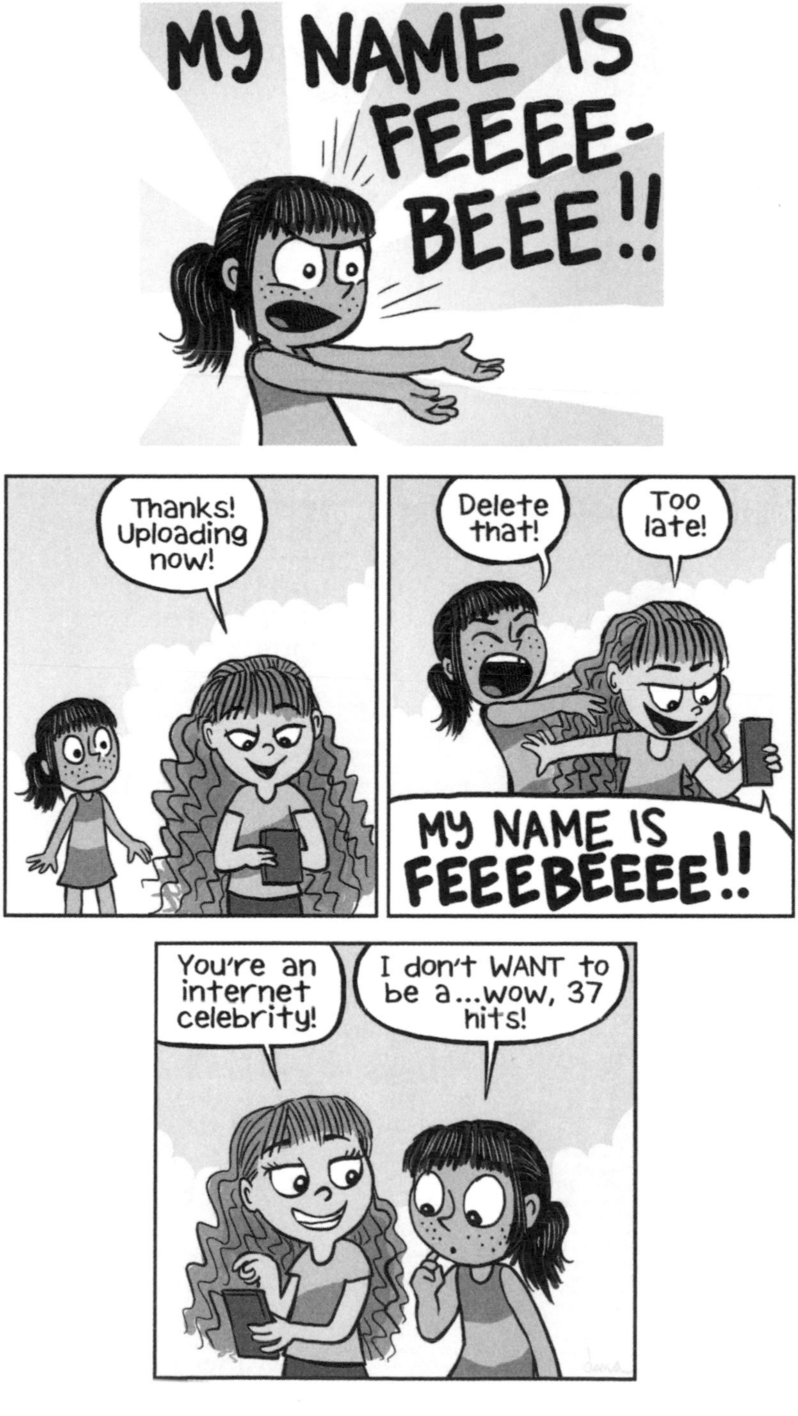
MY NAME IS FEEEE-BEEE!!
Thanks! Uploading now!
Delete that!
Too late!
MY NAME IS FEEEBEEEE!!
You're an internet celebrity!
I don't WANT to be a...wow, 37 hits!

You can see a lot more stars out here than you can at home.

Before the humans and their electric light, one could see many more.

Some unicorns believed each star was the glow at the end of the horn of a sky unicorn, who was charging directly toward us.

They were convinced we were **under siege.**

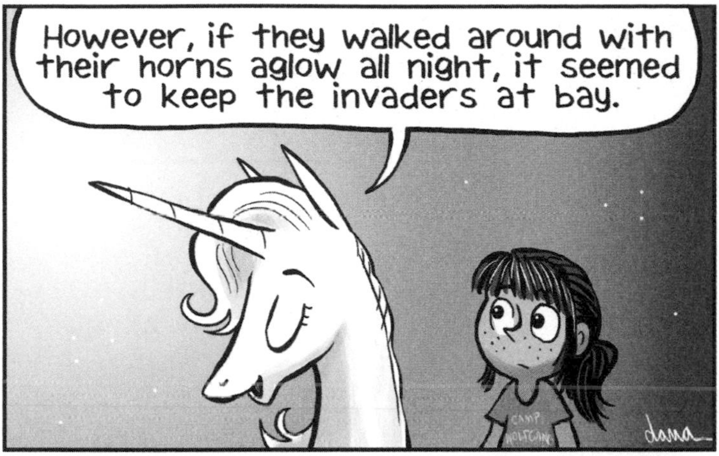
However, if they walked around with their horns aglow all night, it seemed to keep the invaders at bay.
CAMP WOLFGANG
dana

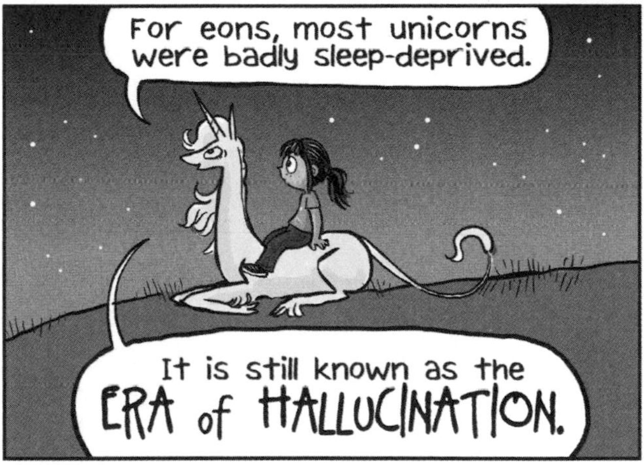
For eons, most unicorns were badly sleep-deprived.
It is still known as the ERA of HALLUCINATION.

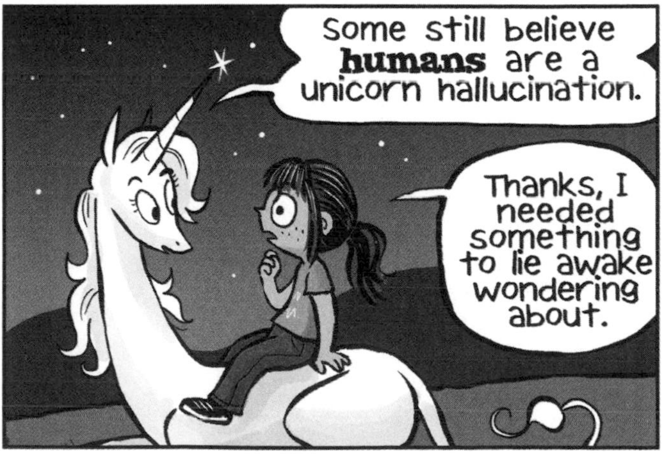
Some still believe **humans** are a unicorn hallucination.
Thanks, I needed something to lie awake wondering about.

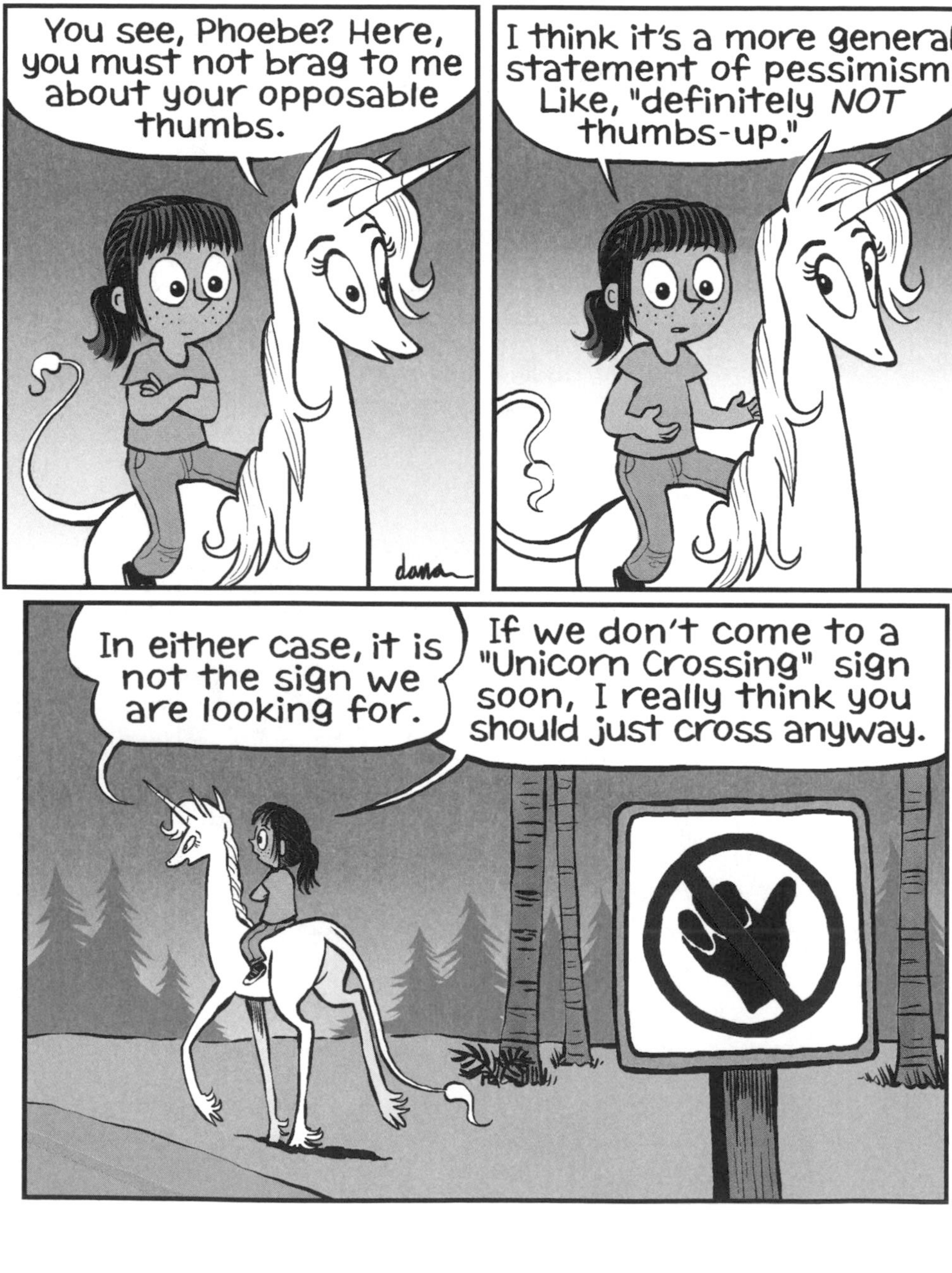
You see, Phoebe? Here, you must not brag to me about your opposable thumbs.
dana
I think it's a more general statement of pessimism. Like, "definitely *NOT* thumbs-up."
In either case, it is not the sign we are looking for.
If we don't come to a "Unicorn Crossing" sign soon, I really think you should just cross anyway.

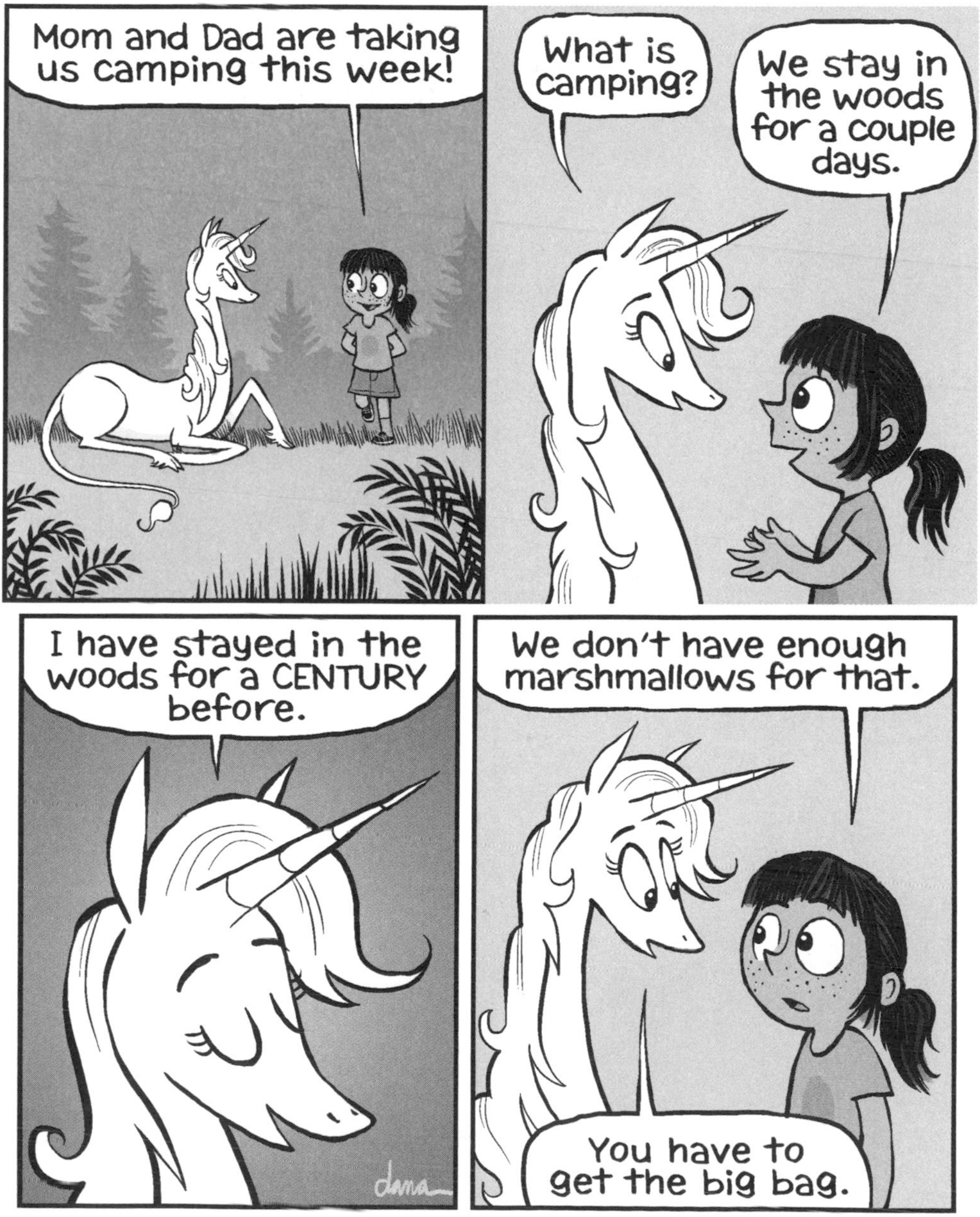
Mom and Dad are taking us camping this week!
What is camping?
We stay in the woods for a couple days.
I have stayed in the woods for a CENTURY before.
We don't have enough marshmallows for that.
You have to get the big bag.
dana

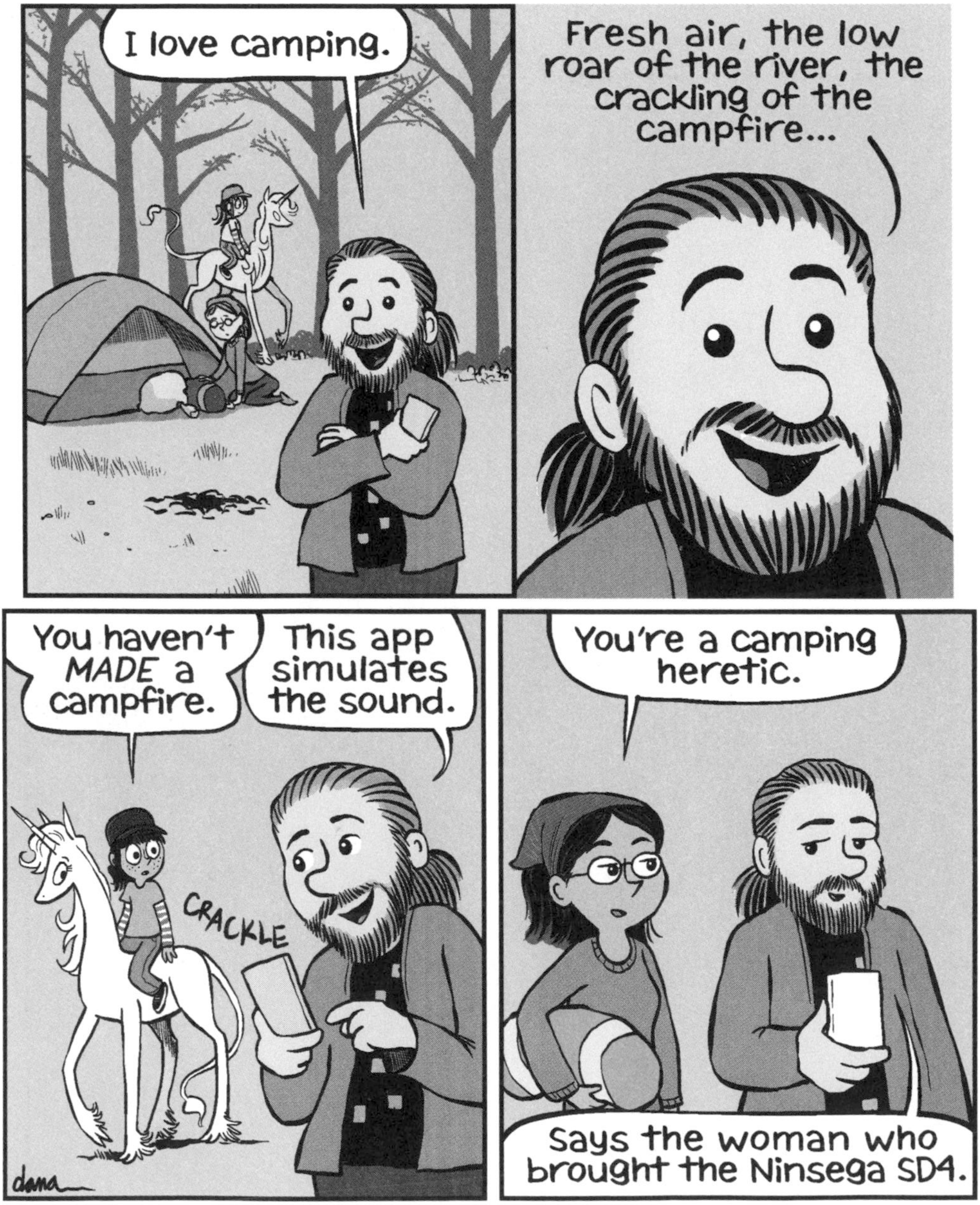
I love camping.
Fresh air, the low roar of the river, the crackling of the campfire...
You haven't *MADE* a campfire.
This app simulates the sound.
CRACKLE
dana
You're a camping heretic.
Says the woman who brought the Ninsega SD4.

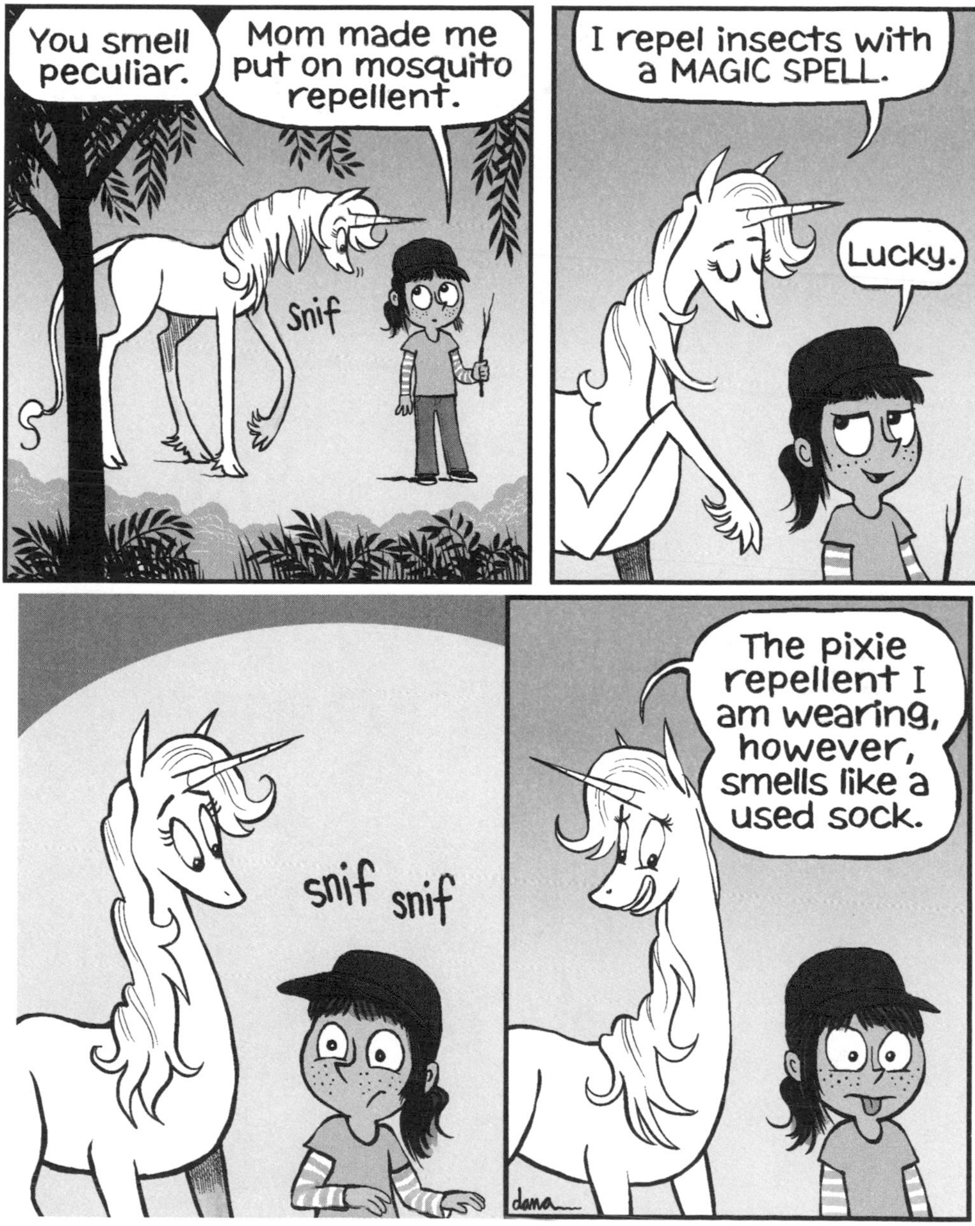

You smell peculiar.
Mom made me put on mosquito repellent.
snif
I repel insects with a MAGIC SPELL.
Lucky.
snif snif
The pixie repellent I am wearing, however, smells like a used sock.
dana

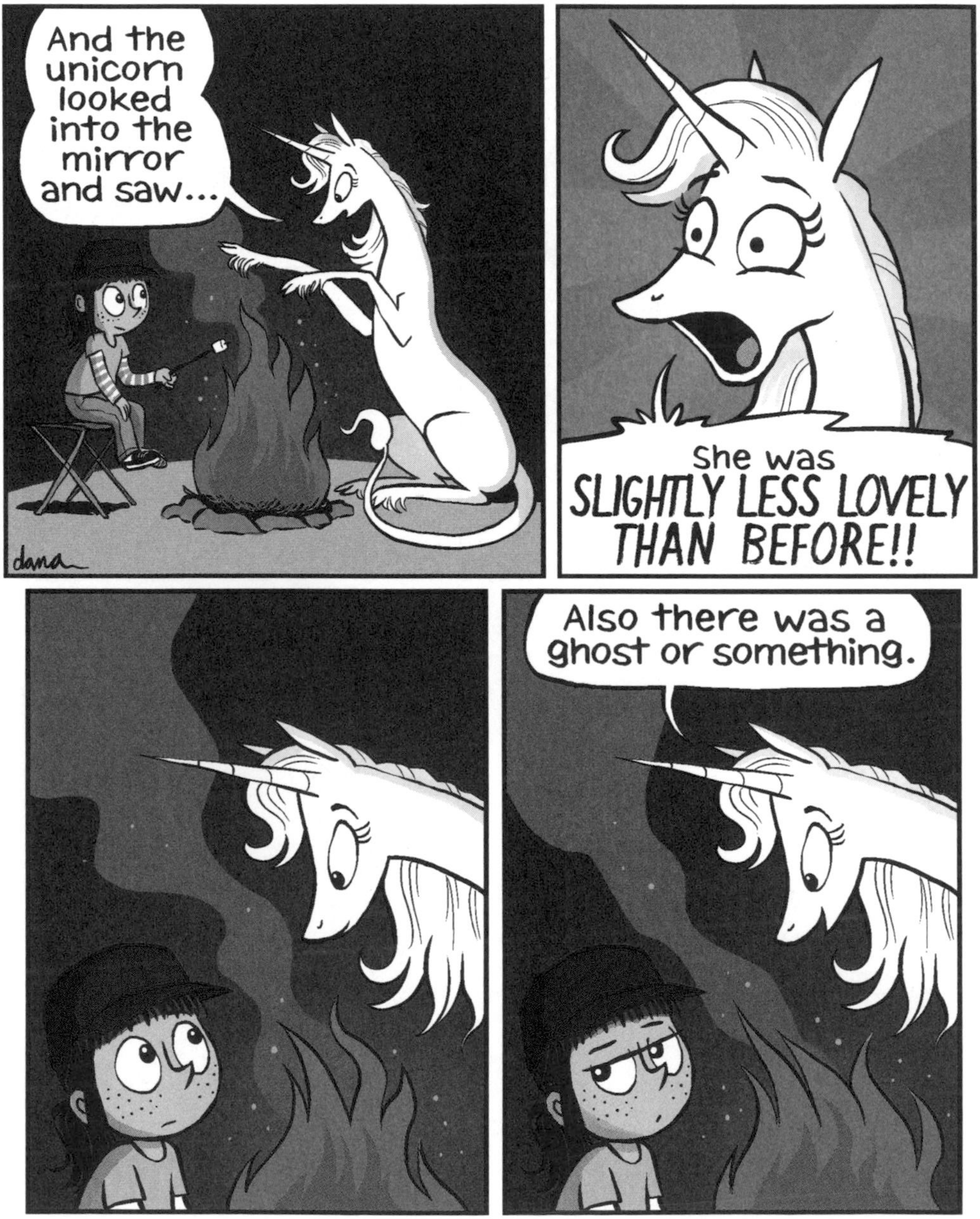
And the unicorn looked into the mirror and saw...
dana
She was SLIGHTLY LESS LOVELY THAN BEFORE!!
Also there was a ghost or something.

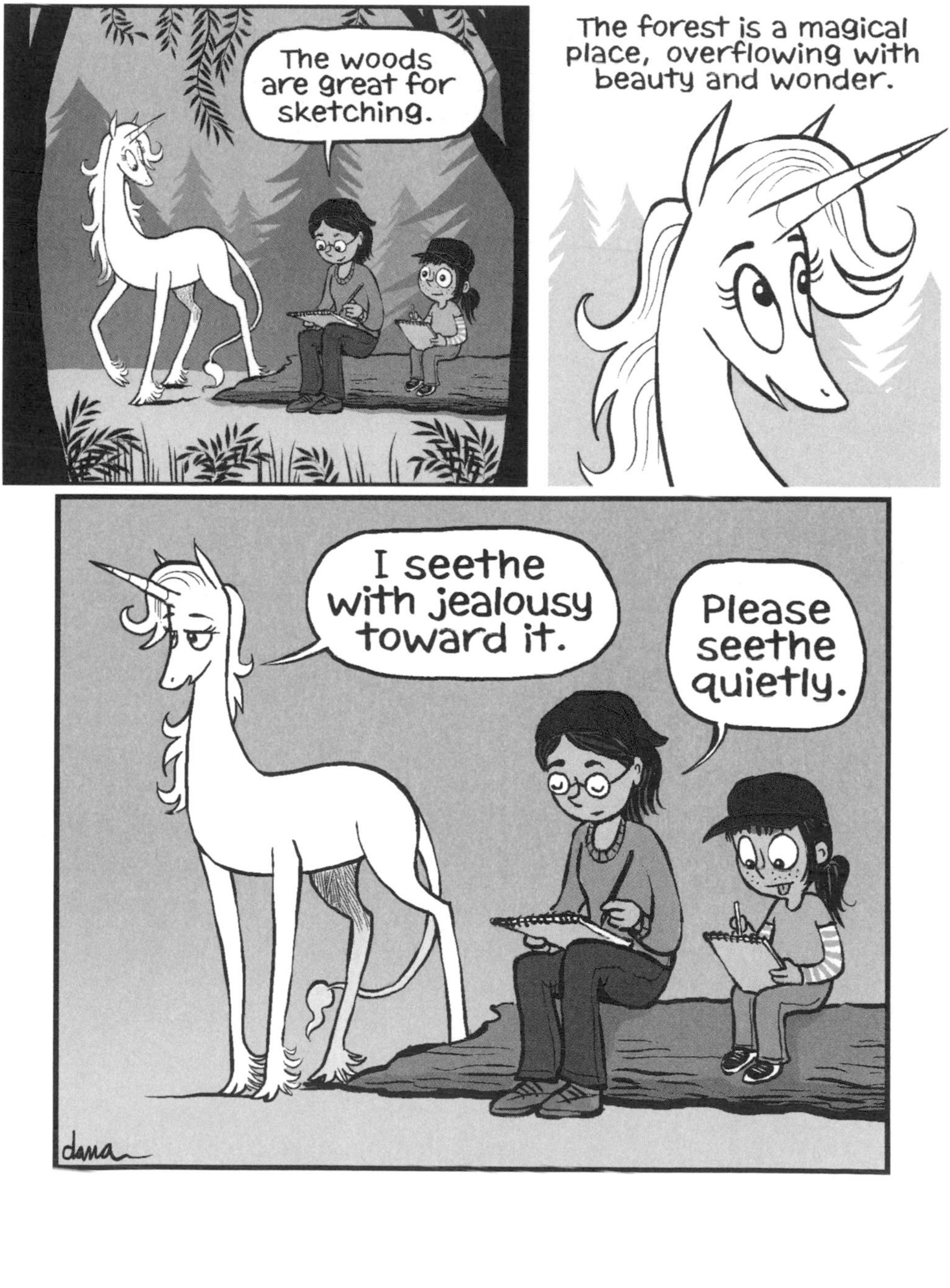
The woods are great for sketching.
The forest is a magical place, overflowing with beauty and wonder.
I seethe with jealousy toward it.
Please seethe quietly.
dana

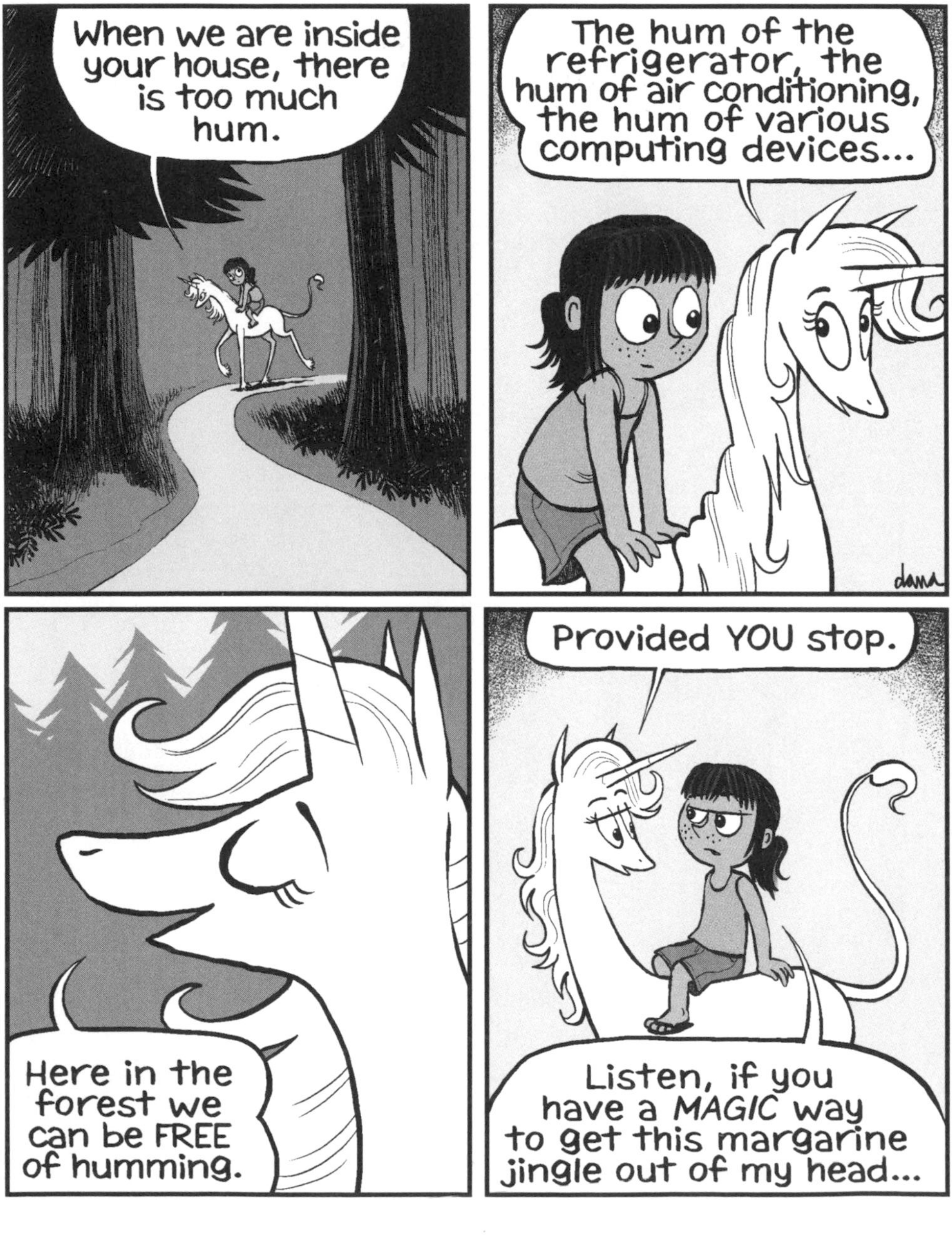
When we are inside your house, there is too much hum.
The hum of the refrigerator, the hum of air conditioning, the hum of various computing devices...
dana
Here in the forest we can be FREE of humming.
Provided YOU stop.
Listen, if you have a *MAGIC* way to get this margarine jingle out of my head...

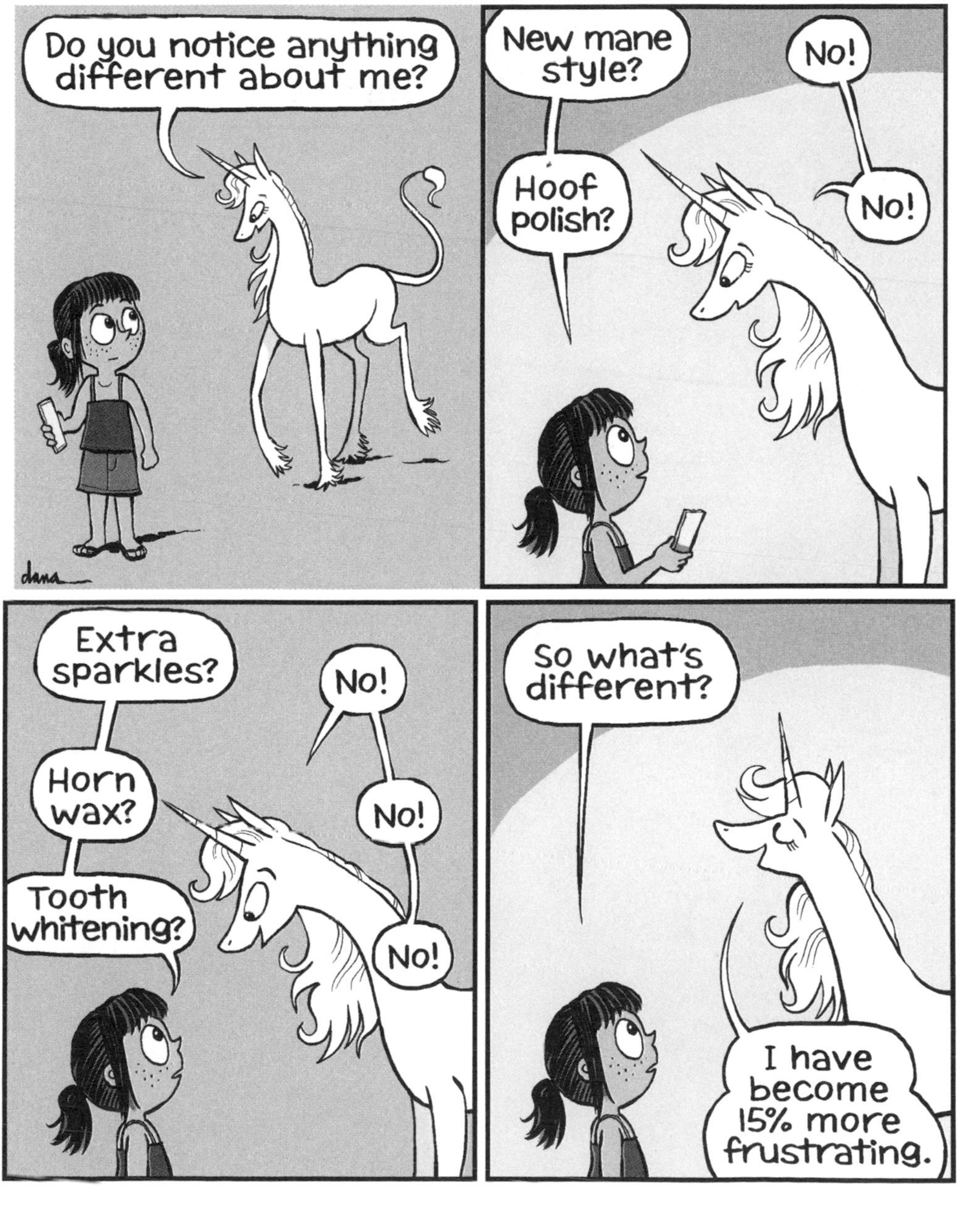
Do you notice anything different about me?
dana
New mane style?
No!
Hoof polish?
No!
Extra sparkles?
No!
Horn wax?
No!
Tooth whitening?
No!
So what's different?
I have become 15% more frustrating.

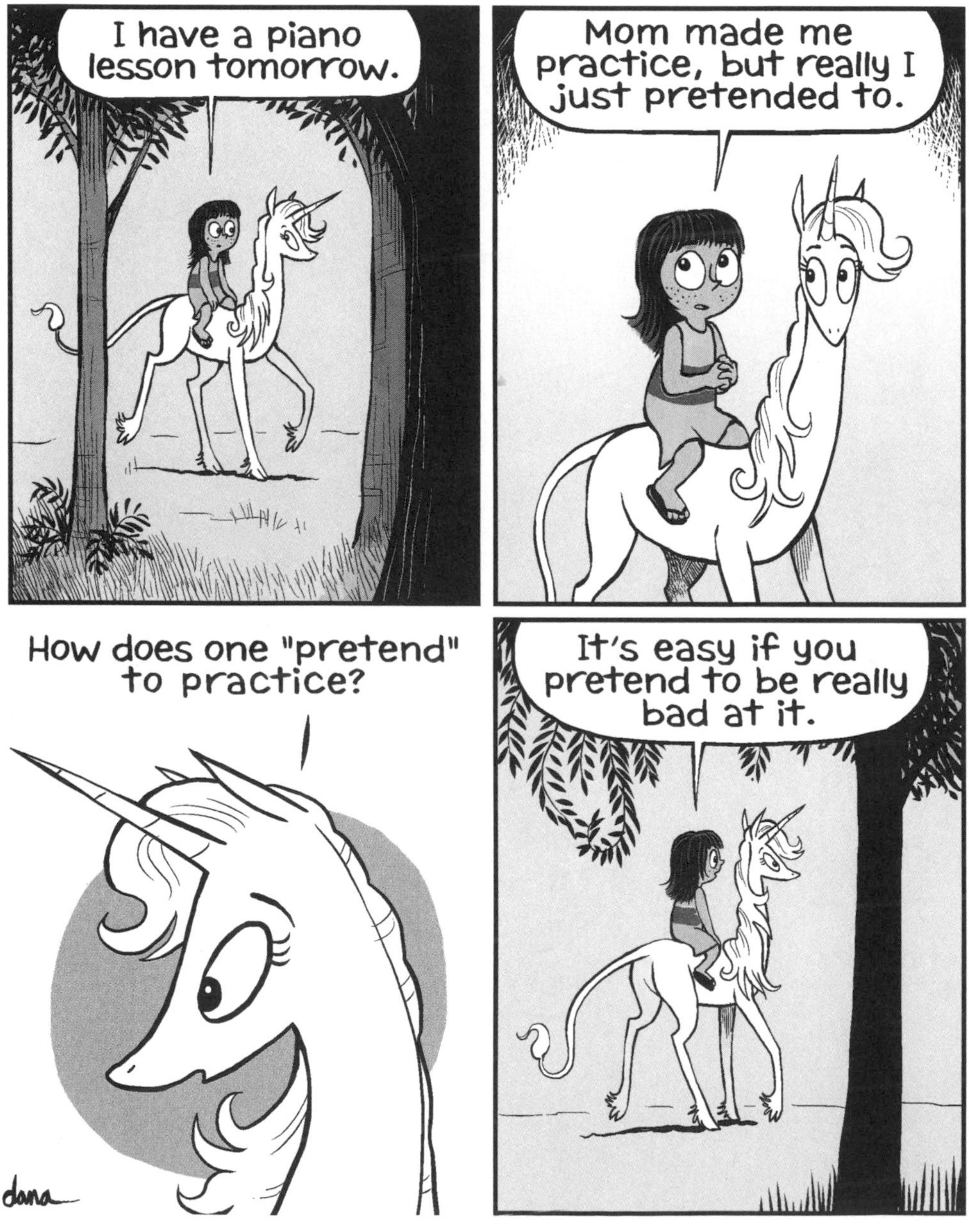
I have a piano lesson tomorrow.
Mom made me practice, but really I just pretended to.
How does one "pretend" to practice?
It's easy if you pretend to be really bad at it.
dana

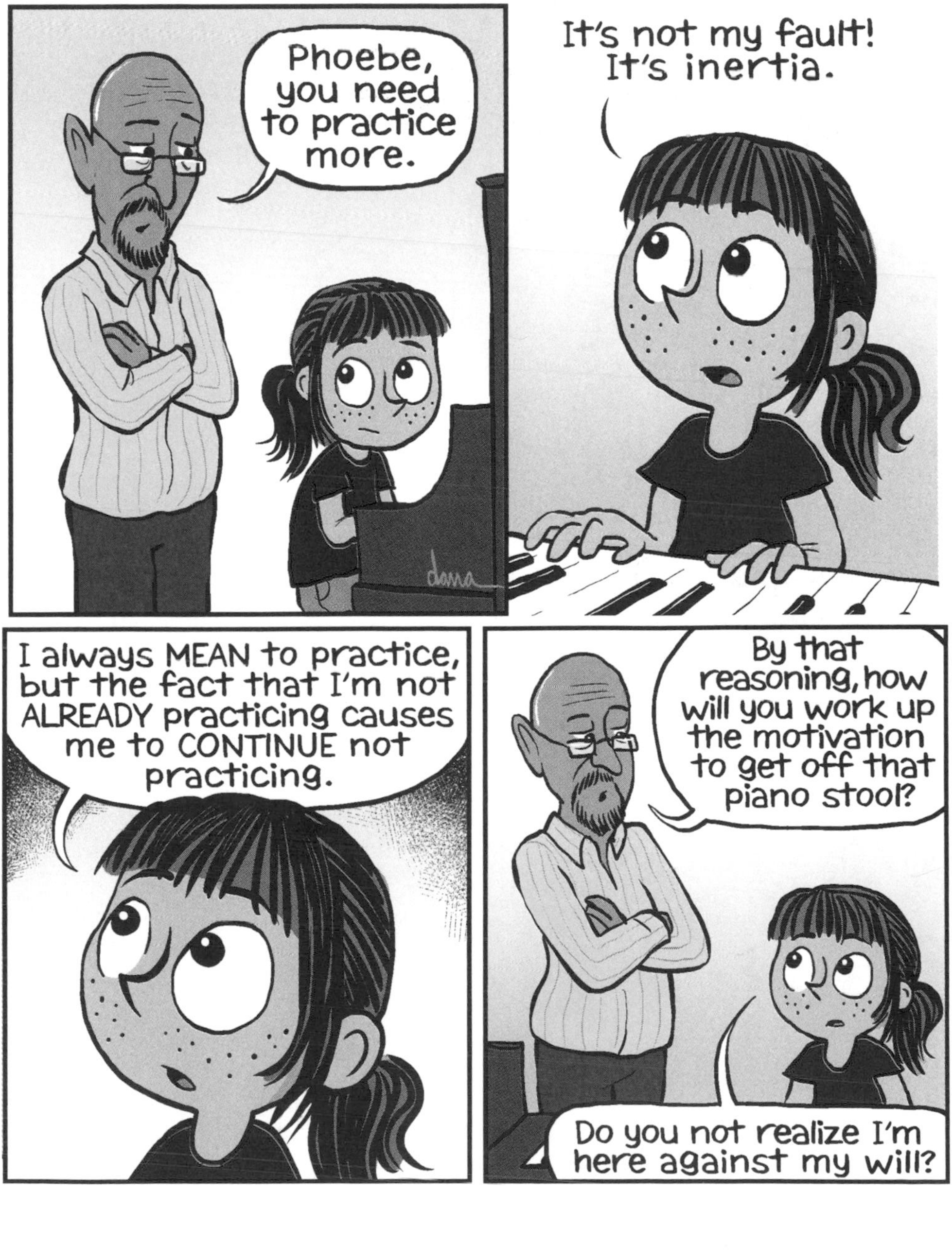
Phoebe, you need to practice more.
It's not my fault! It's inertia.
I always MEAN to practice, but the fact that I'm not ALREADY practicing causes me to CONTINUE not practicing.
By that reasoning, how will you work up the motivation to get off that piano stool?
Do you not realize I'm here against my will?

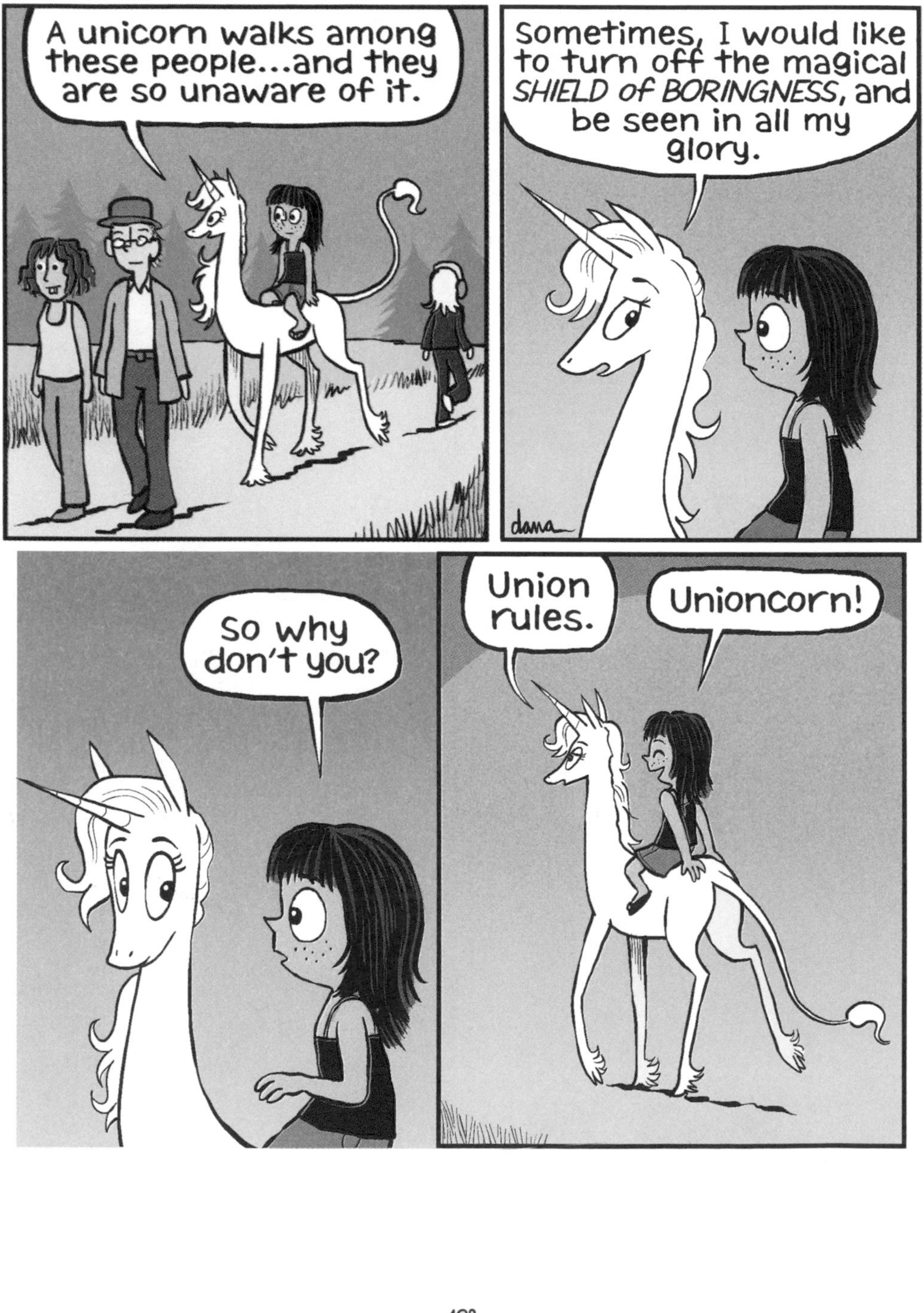
A unicorn walks among these people...and they are so unaware of it.
Sometimes, I would like to turn off the magical *SHIELD of BORINGNESS*, and be seen in all my glory.
dana
So why don't you?
Union rules.
Unioncorn!

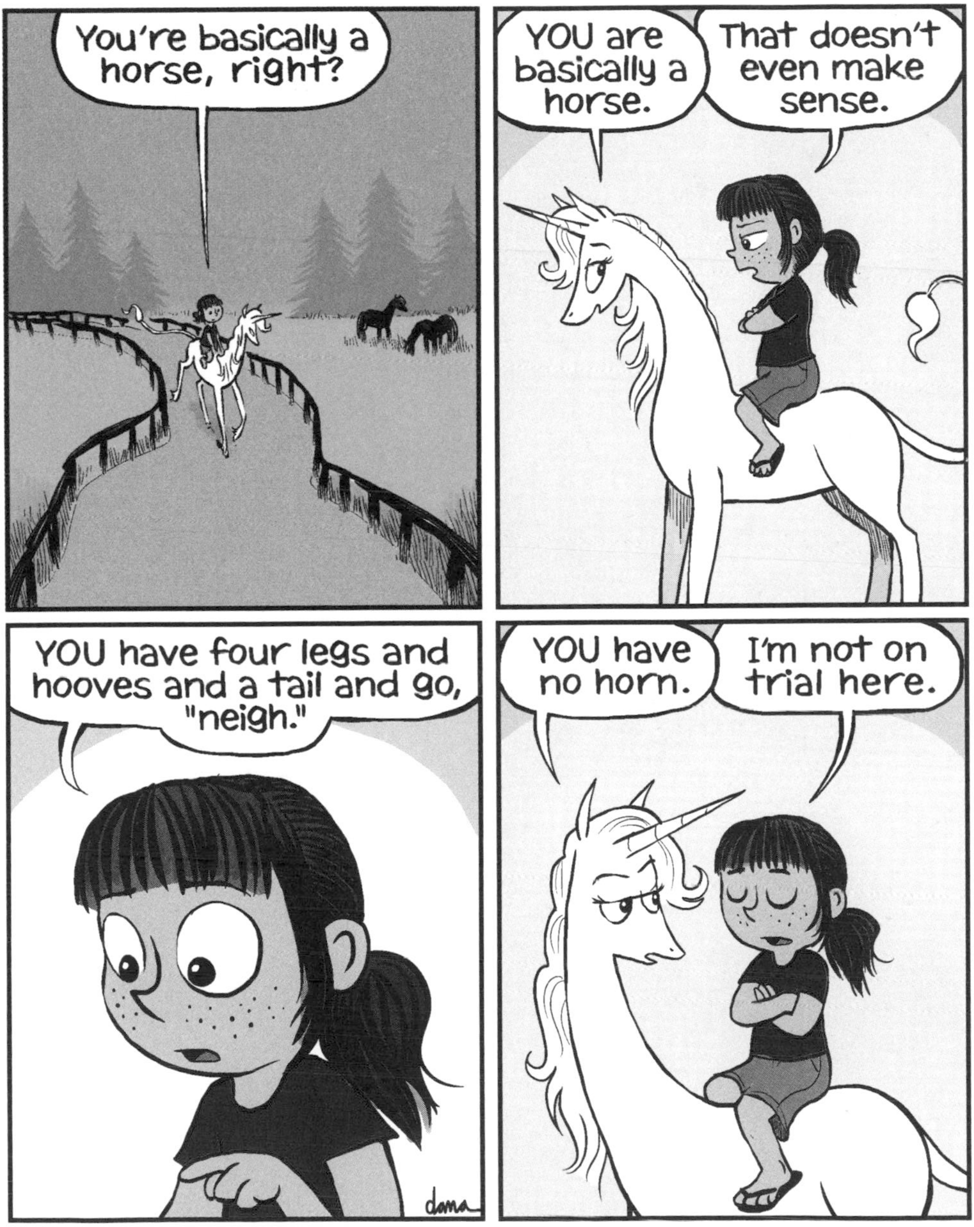
You're basically a horse, right?
YOU are basically a horse.
That doesn't even make sense.
YOU have four legs and hooves and a tail and go, "neigh."
YOU have no horn.
I'm not on trial here.
dana

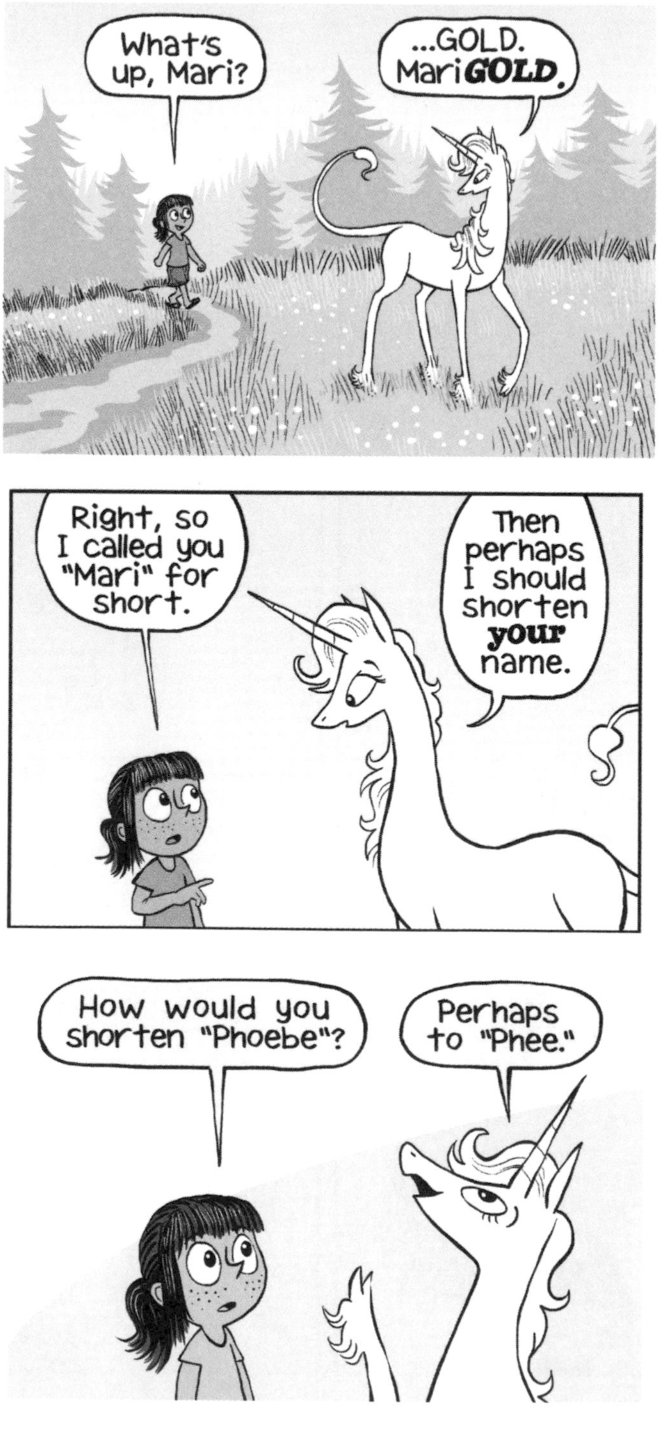
What's up, Mari?
...GOLD. MariGOLD.
Right, so I called you "Mari" for short.
Then perhaps I should shorten your name.
How would you shorten "Phoebe"?
Perhaps to "Phee."

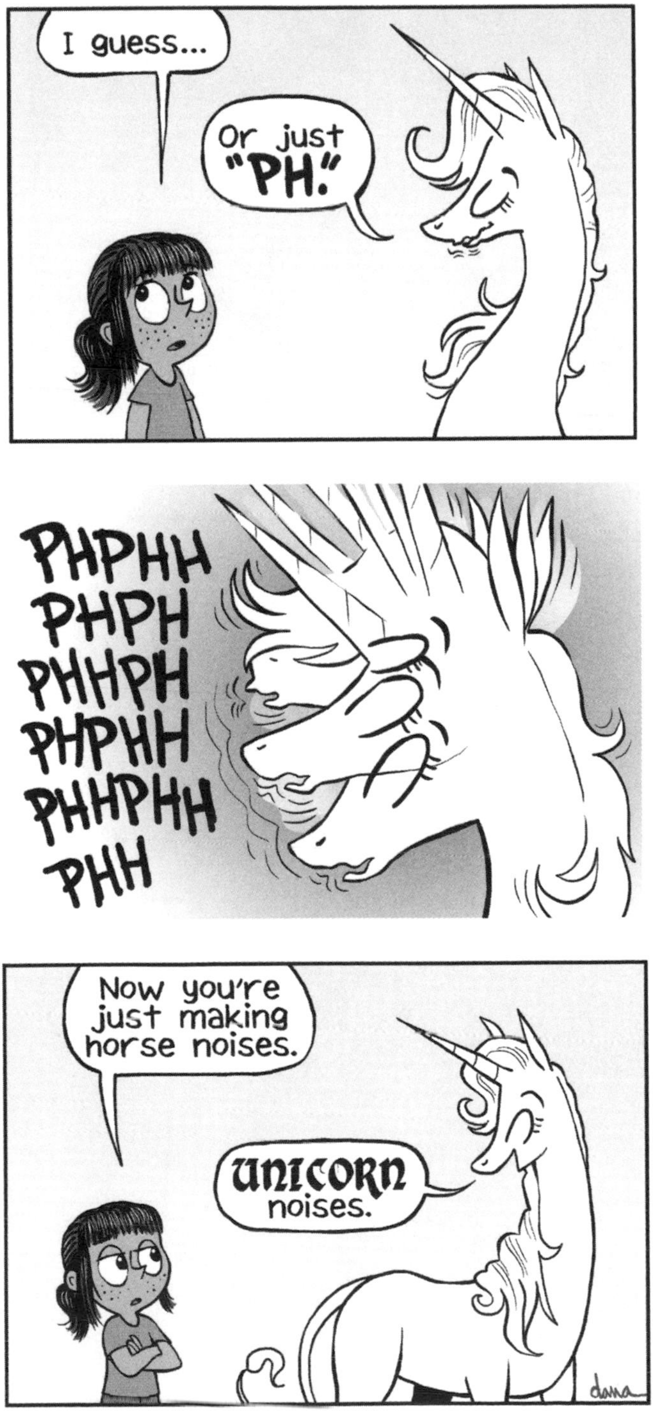
I guess...
Or just "PH."
PHPHH PHPH PHHPH PHPHH PHHPHH PHH
Now you're just making horse noises.
UNICORN noises.
dana

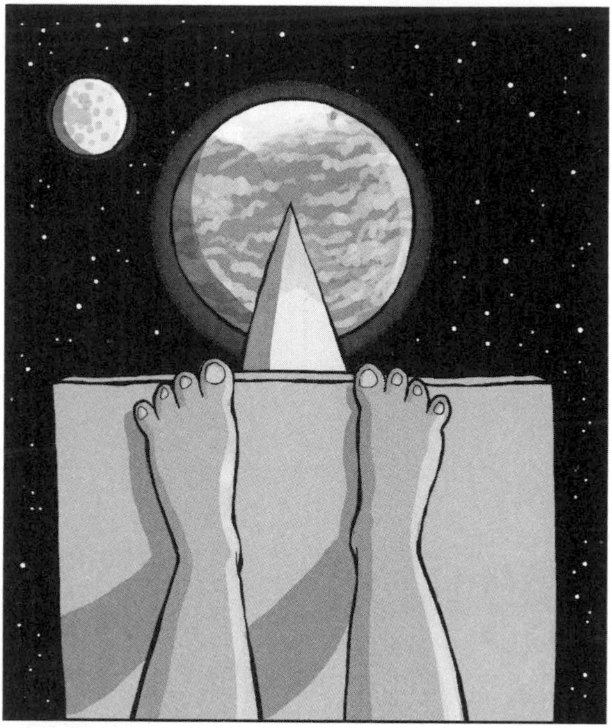

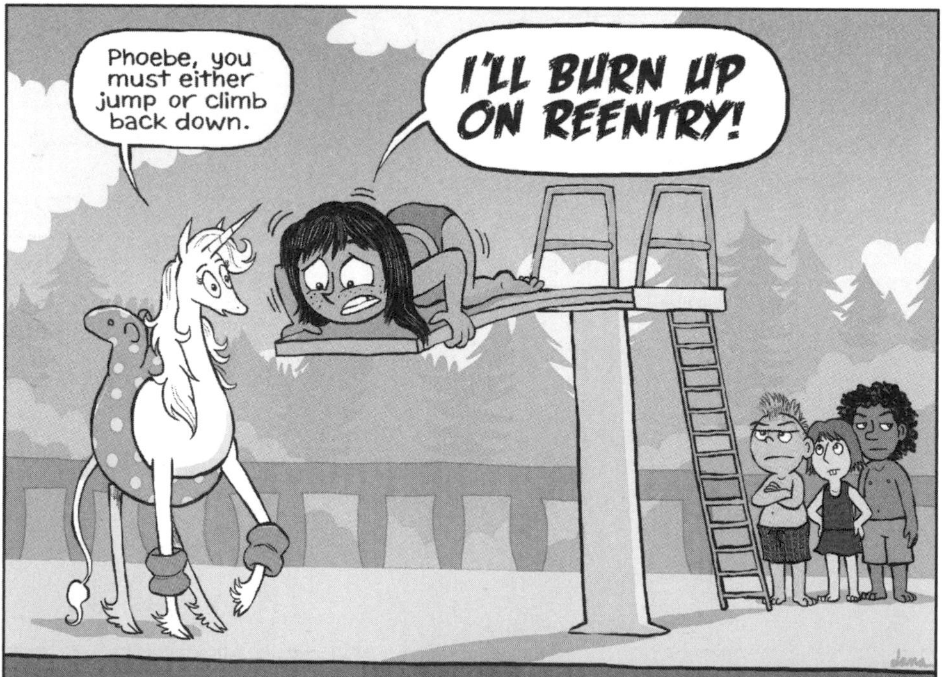
Phoebe, you must either jump or climb back down.
I'LL BURN UP ON REENTRY!
dana

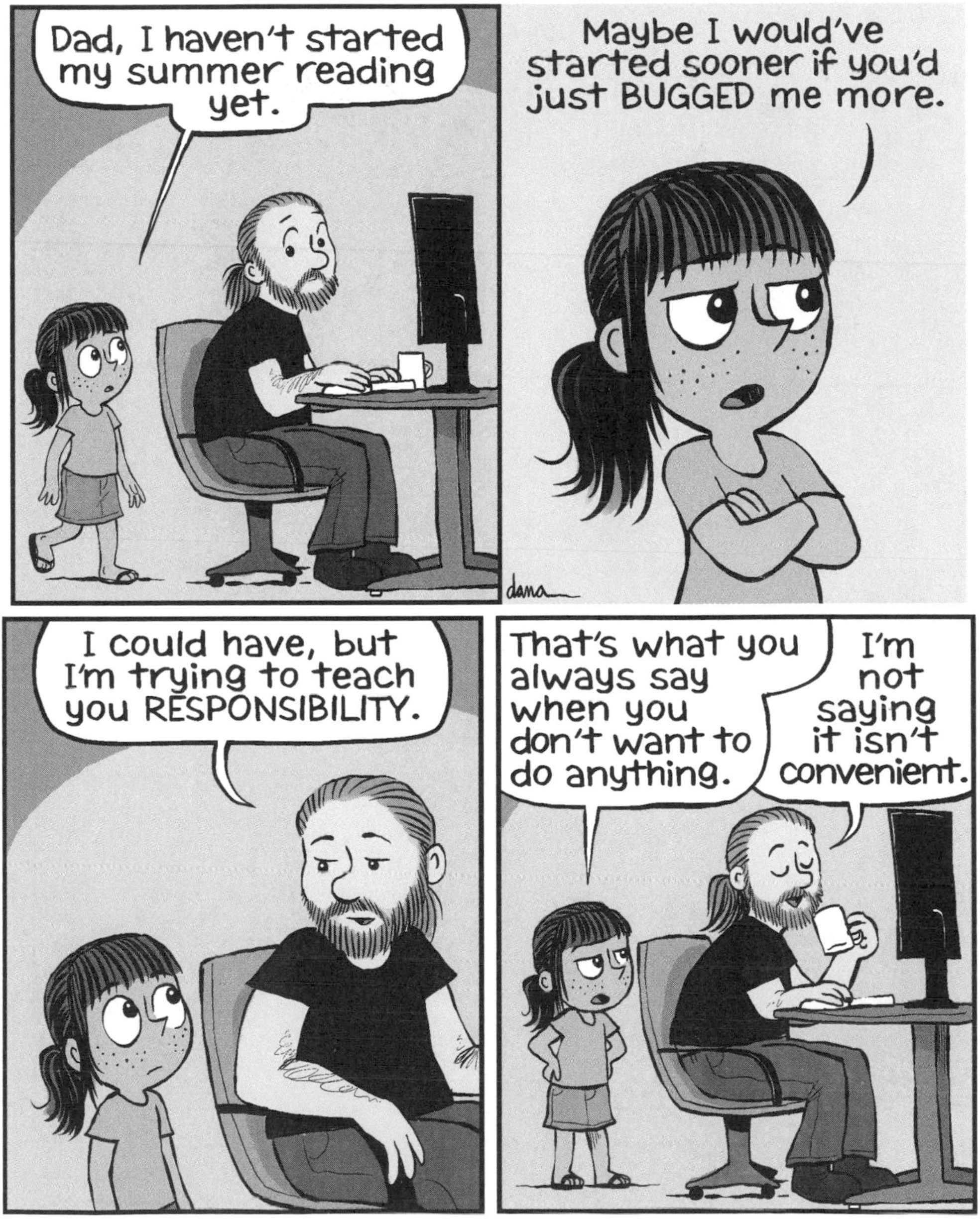
Dad, I haven't started my summer reading yet.
Maybe I would've started sooner if you'd just BUGGED me more.
dana
I could have, but I'm trying to teach you RESPONSIBILITY.
That's what you always say when you don't want to do anything.
I'm not saying it isn't convenient.

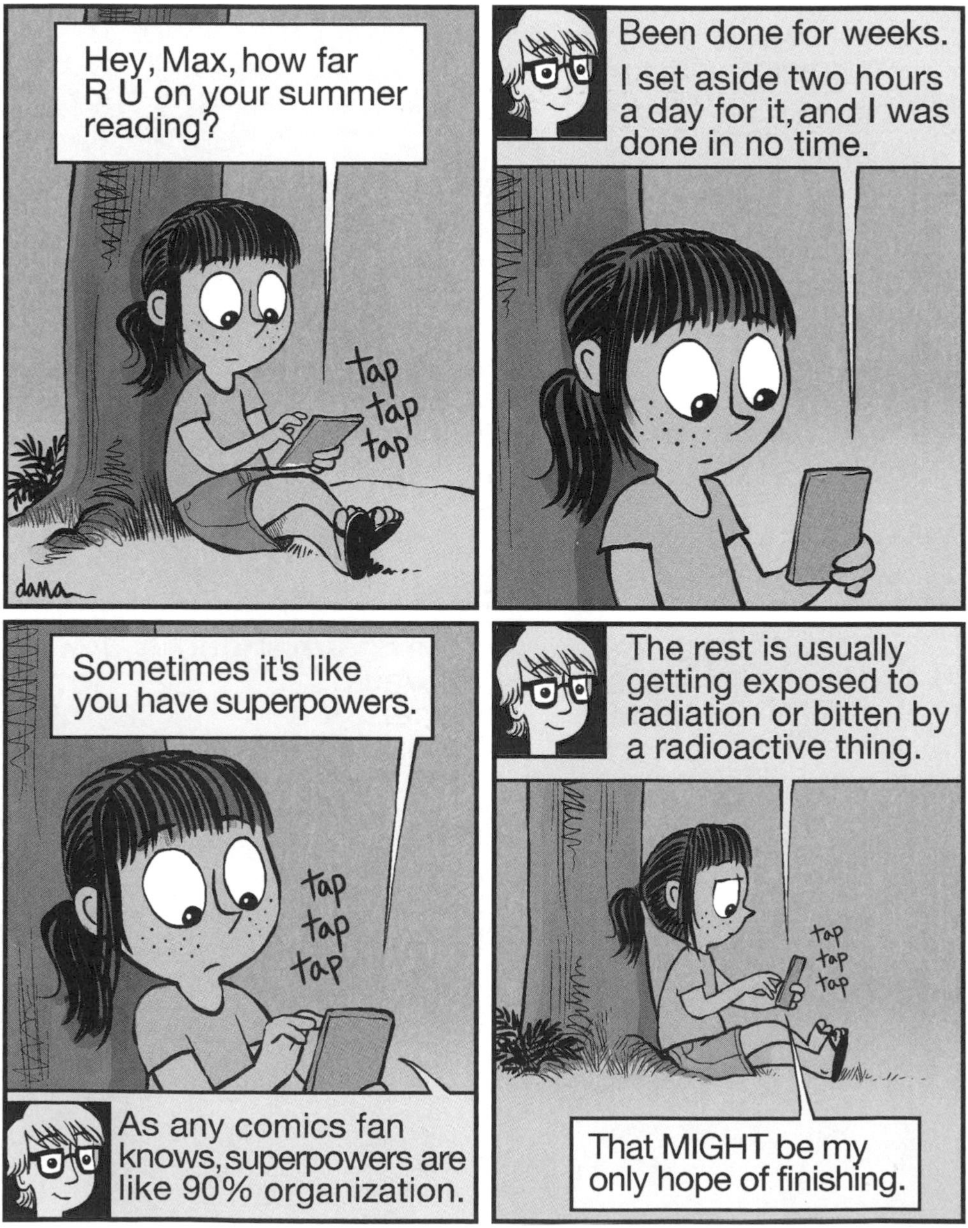
Hey, Max, how far R U on your summer reading?
tap tap tap
Been done for weeks.
I set aside two hours a day for it, and I was done in no time.
Sometimes it's like you have superpowers.
tap tap tap
As any comics fan knows, superpowers are like 90% organization.
The rest is usually getting exposed to radiation or bitten by a radioactive thing.
tap tap tap
That MIGHT be my only hope of finishing.

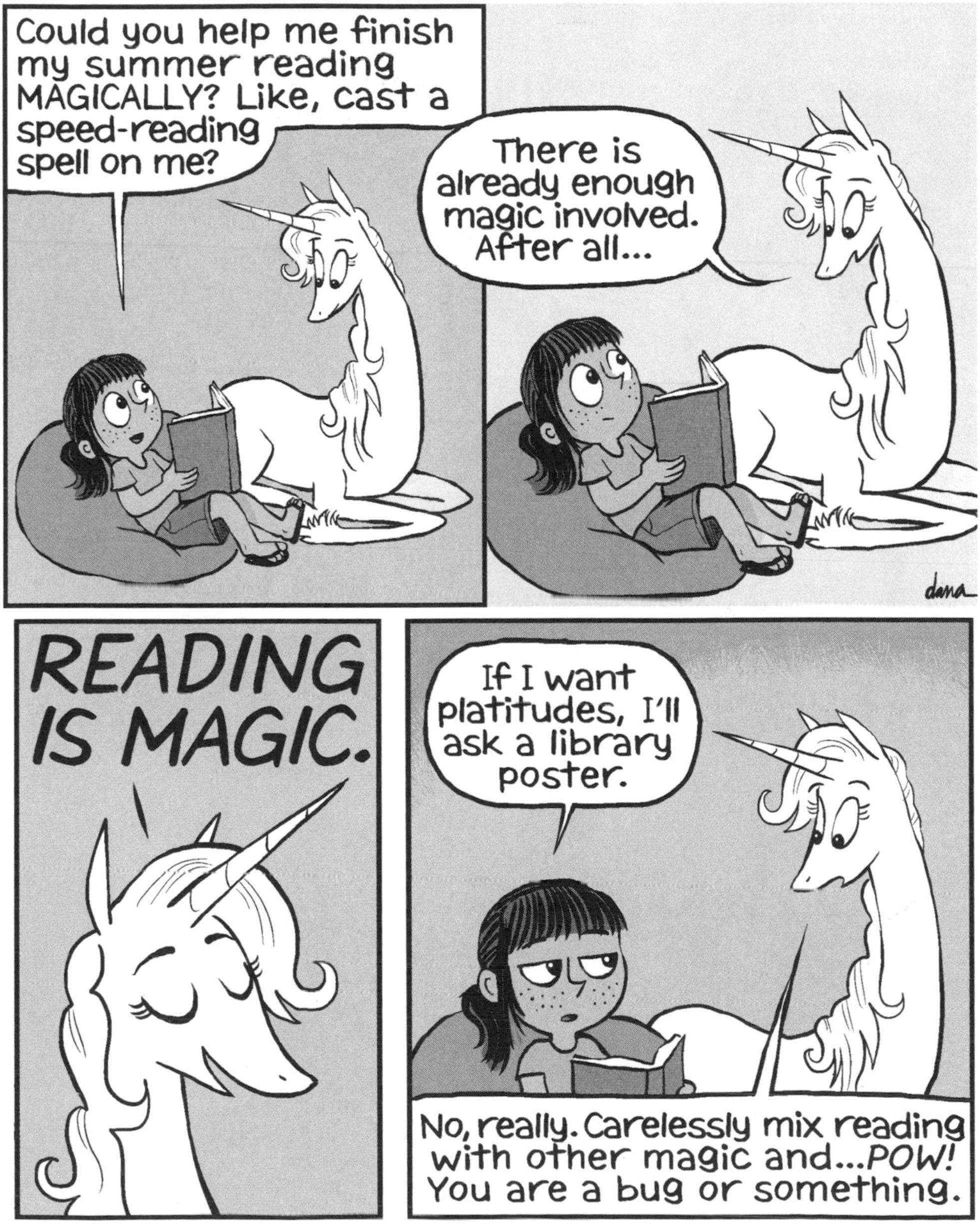
Could you help me finish my summer reading MAGICALLY? Like, cast a speed-reading spell on me?
There is already enough magic involved. After all...
dana
READING IS MAGIC.
If I want platitudes, I'll ask a library poster.
No, really. Carelessly mix reading with other magic and...POW! You are a bug or something.

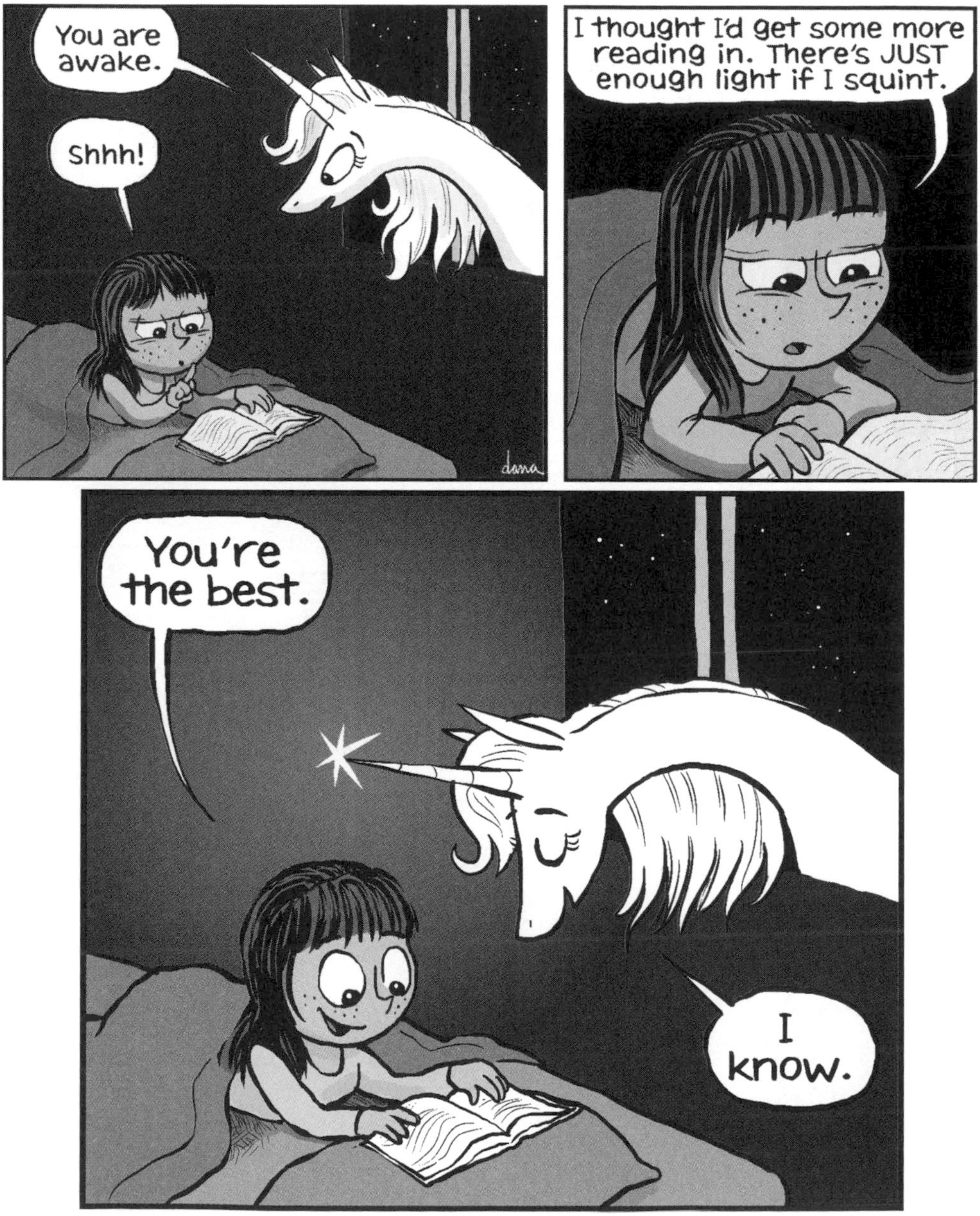
You are awake.
Shhh!
I thought I'd get some more reading in. There's JUST enough light if I squint.
You're the best.
I know.

Glossary

alfalfa (al-fal-fa): pg. 65 – noun / a type of grass grown for farm animals

amenities (a-men-it-ees): pg. 33 – noun / things that make life easier or more pleasant; comforts

antithesis (an-tith-e-sis): pg. 108 – noun / the exact opposite of something

artisanal (ar-tis-in-al): pg. 87 – adjective / traditionally made or grown with skill

asterisk (as-ter-isk): pg. 45 – noun / the symbol " * " that means something is not being said, or that there's more to an idea that's being left out

astounding (as-tound-ing): pg. 70 – adjective / surprising; amazing

benevolently (be-nev-o-lent-ly): pg. 42 – adverb / kindly; generously

brazen (bray-zen): pg. 74 – adjective / doing something shocking without any embarrassment; bold

contraption (con-trap-shun): pg. 57 – noun / machinery that is unusual or strange; gadget

cynical (sin-ick-al): pg. 111 – adjective / believing that people are typically selfish or dishonest; distrustful

deficient (de-fish-ent): pg. 79 – adjective / not having enough of something needed; lacking

denial (de-ni-al): pg. 61 – noun / a state of refusing to admit that something is sad, painful, true, or real

depression (de-pre-shun): pg. 64 – noun / a state of feeling sad, hopeless, or unimportant

discrimination (dis-crim-in-ay-shun): pg. 60 – noun / the practice of unfairly treating someone different from other people; prejudice

dodecahedron (do-dec-a-he-dron): pg. 91 – noun / a 3-D shape with twelve sides

ephemeral (ee-fem-er-al): pg. 78 – adjective / lasting a very short time; fleeting

finesse (fin-ess): pg. 30 – noun / someone's skill when dealing with a tricky situation or problem; flair (*see panache*)

hallucination (ha-loo-sin-ay-shun): pg. 153 – noun / something that seems real but doesn't really exist (like a mirage)

heretic (hair-a-tick): pg. 156 – noun / someone who believes in an idea that goes against popular or accepted beliefs; a deviant rebel

horse d'oeuvres/horse doovers are really:
hors d'oeuvres (or dervs): pg. 69 – noun / a little food served before a meal; appetizers

impending (im-pen-ding): pg. 36 – adjective / about to occur; looming

inertia (in-er-sha): pg. 163 – noun / the idea that something that's not moving will stay still, and something in motion will keep going unless stopped; inaction

inopportune (in-op-por-tune): pg. 10 – adjective / happening at the wrong time; inconvenient

newfangled (new-fan-gled): pg. 56 – adjective / newly invented

organic co-op (or-gan-ick coh-op): pg. 25 – noun / a grocery store that is owned and operated by the people who work there or the people who buy from the store; sometimes called a "food cooperative"

ostentatious (os-ten-tay-shus): pg. 74 – adjective / showing off wealth or treasure to make people envious; flashy or showy

panache (pan-ash): pg. 77 – noun / lots of energy and style; flair (*see finesse*)

parapet (pair-a-pet): pg. 141 – noun / a low wall on a castle

passé (pass-ay): pg. 41 – adjective / no longer fashionable or cool; out-of-date

platitude (pla-ta-tude): pg. 171 – noun / something said that is dull, unoriginal, or cliché

pragmatic (prag-ma-tick): pg. 83 – adjective / dealing with problems in a reasonable way; wise or practical

rejuvenation (re-joo-ven-ay-shun): pg. 68 – noun / a state of feeling young or energetic again

repository (re-pos-it-or-ee): pg. 25 – noun / a place where a large amount of something is stored (like a warehouse, library, or store)

sadistic (sa-dis-tick): pg. 21 – adjective / cruel; enjoying someone else's pain

seethe (seethe): pg. 159 – verb / to show an uncontrollable emotion, like anger; to fume

siege (see-je): pg. 152 – noun / a long and intense attack on something (like a castle)

strobe (strobe): pg. 122 – noun / a device that flashes light at high speeds, over and over

subvert (sub-vert): pg. 11 – verb / to weaken something, or to make it less effective; sabotage (*see undermine*)

thwarted (thwart-ed): pg. 98 – noun / stopped someone from doing something; foiled

undermine (un-der-mine): pg. 11 – verb / to weaken something, or to make unstable (*see subvert*)

visage (vis-ij): pg. 84 – noun / a person's face; appearance

withdrawal (with-draw-al): pg. 61 – noun / the act of ending your involvement with something

Look for these books!

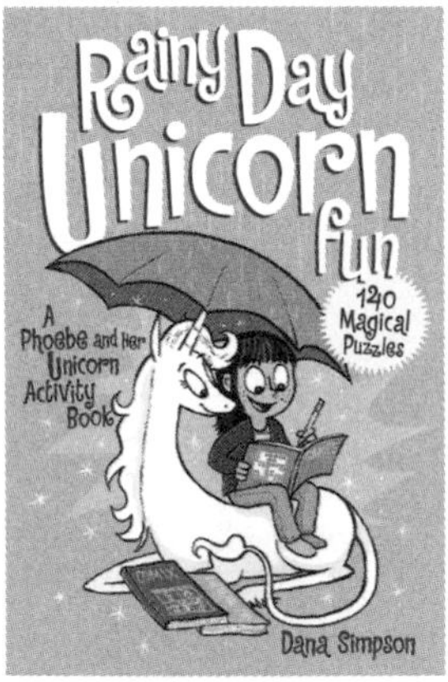
Rainy Day Unicorn Fun
140 Magical Puzzles
A Phoebe and Her Unicorn Activity Book
Dana Simpson

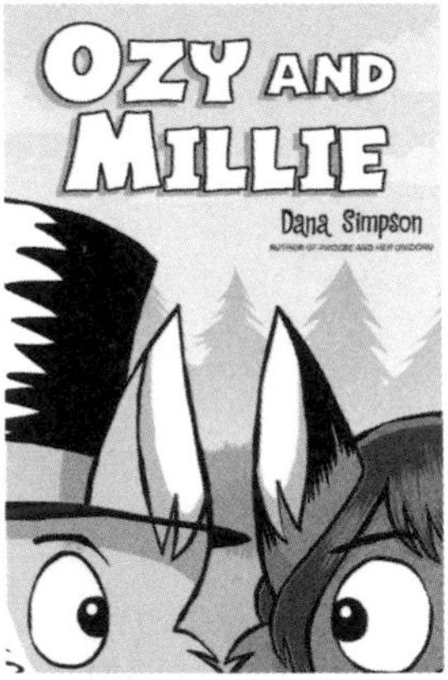
OZY AND MILLIE
Dana Simpson

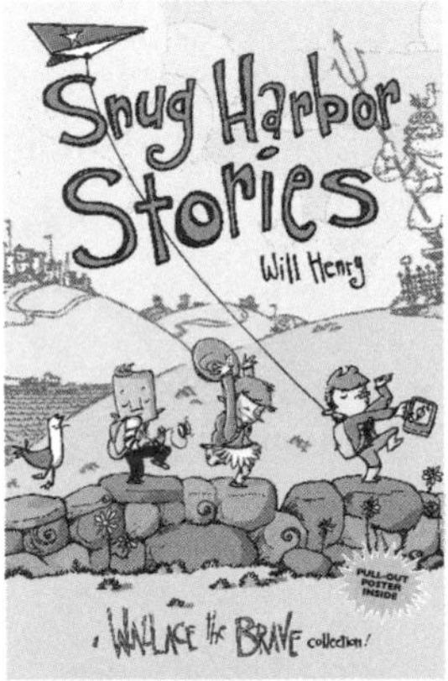
Snug Harbor Stories
Will Henry
PULL-OUT POSTER INSIDE
A WALLACE the BRAVE collection!

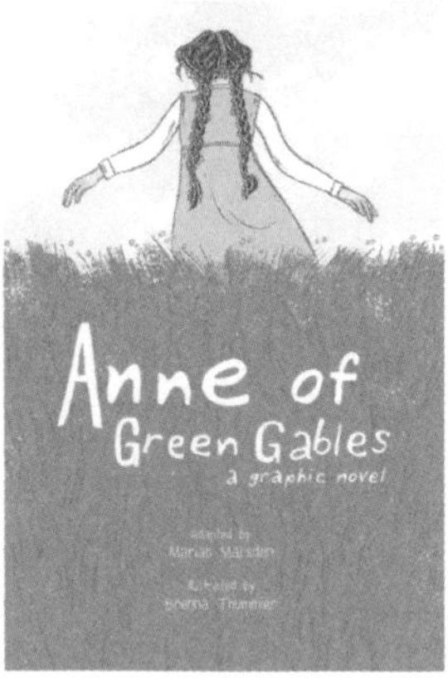
Anne of Green Gables
a graphic novel

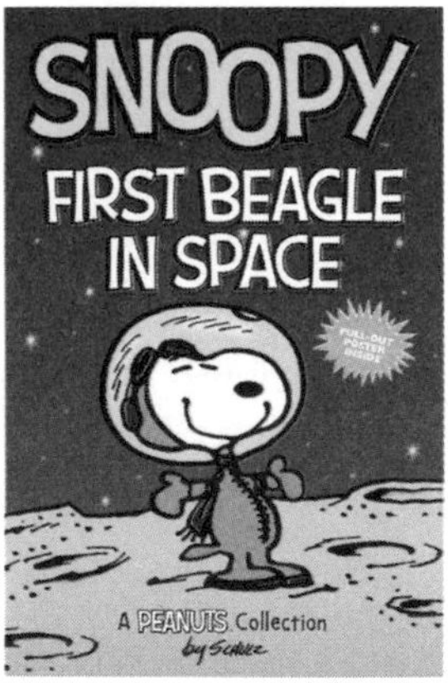
SNOOPY
FIRST BEAGLE IN SPACE
A PEANUTS Collection

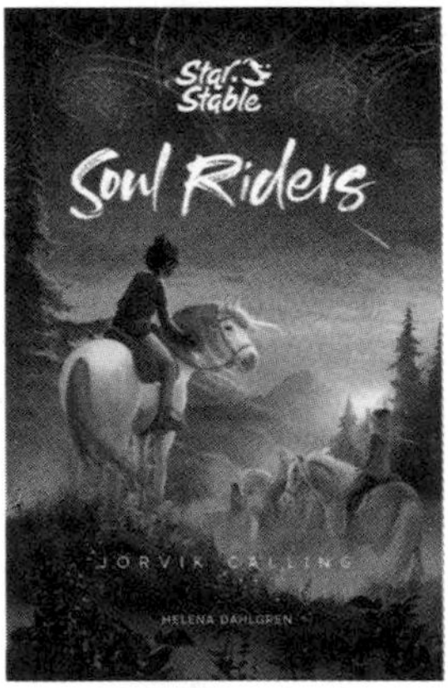
Star Stable
Soul Riders
JORVIK CALLING
HELENA DAHLGREN

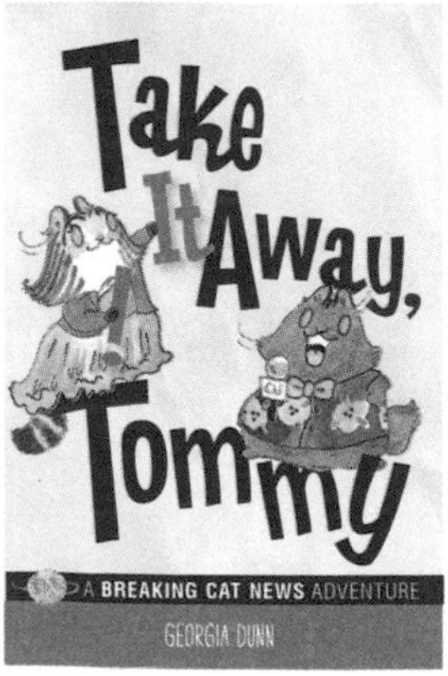
Take It Away, Tommy
A BREAKING CAT NEWS ADVENTURE
GEORGIA DUNN

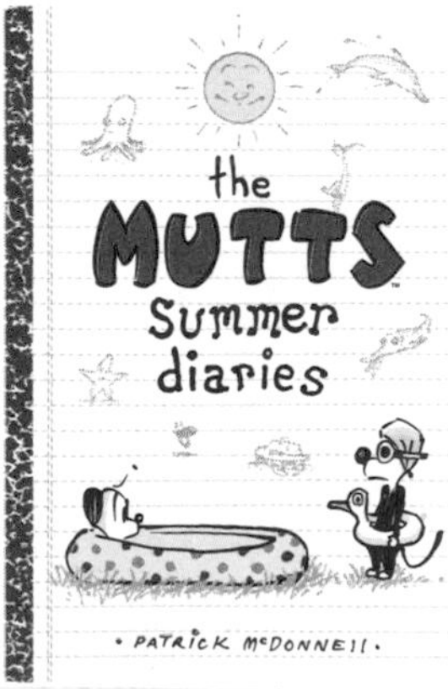
the MUTTS Summer diaries
PATRICK McDONNELL

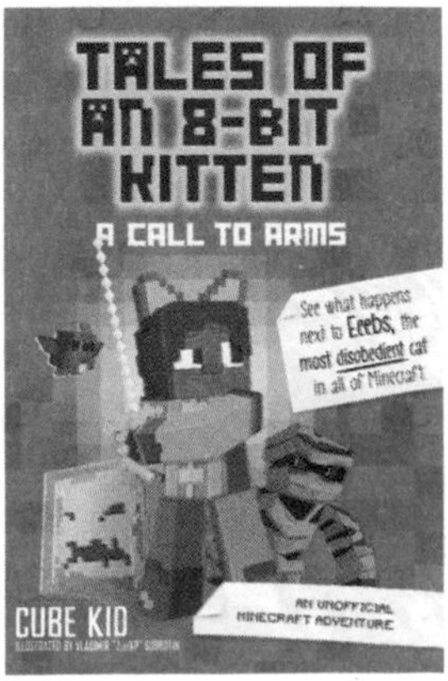
TALES OF AN 8-BIT KITTEN
A CALL TO ARMS
See what happens next to Eeebs, the most disobedient cat in all of Minecraft.
AN UNOFFICIAL MINECRAFT ADVENTURE
CUBE KID